Tim was halfway to th
he caught sight of a
verge. Hearing the en;
road and waved her s
a lift.

It was Minnie Beavers, daughter of Jim Beavers, a
good old Cockney spiv who'd brought his wife and
daughter out of Camberwell when the bombs started.
Jim had taken to country life like a duck to water. He
was a friend, his missus supplied Tim with eggs, and his
daughter Minnie was a holy terror. She was wearing a
round straw hat, a dark blue gymslip and black school
stockings of lisle. She had fair hair and blue eyes and a
figure that was hardly believable for a fifteen year old.

She pulled open the passenger door, yelped with joy,
and leapt in.

Tim shut his eyes and prayed. You had to pray when
you were an old man of twenty-two and an under-age
schoolgirl sat next to you showing the tops of her
stockings in a military vehicle prohibited to civilians.

That was just the start of Tim's troubles.

Also by Mary Jane Staples

DOWN LAMBETH WAY
OUR EMILY
KING OF CAMBERWELL
TWO FOR THREE FARTHINGS
THE LODGER

and published by Corgi Books

RISING SUMMER

Mary Jane Staples

CORGI BOOKS

To Kate

RISING SUMMER
A CORGI BOOK 0 552 13845 2

First publication in Great Britain

PRINTING HISTORY
Corgi edition published 1991
Corgi edition reprinted 1991

This book is set in 11/13pt Times by Kestrel Data, Exeter

Corgi Books are published by Transworld Publishers Ltd,
61-63 Uxbridge Road, Ealing, London W5 5SA, in Australia by
Transworld Publishers (Australia) Pty Ltd, 15–23 Helles Avenue,
Moorebank, NSW 2170, and in New Zealand by Transworld
Publishers (NZ) Ltd, Cnr Moselle and Waipareira Avenues,
Henderson, Auckland.

Printed and bound in Great Britain by
Cox & Wyman Ltd, Reading, Berks

CHAPTER ONE

On my way out of Battery Headquarters to begin my seven days leave, I called in on Bombardier Jones who was in charge of the ration stores.

'Any chance?' I asked.

'Of what?'

'Well, I've got some eggs for my week's leave.'

'Nicked 'em off some chickens, did you?' said Bombardier Jones.

'No, present from a friend. All I need now is something to go with 'em.'

'You've got a hope,' he said, but if he was in charge of the rations, I was in charge of the leave roster. 'All right, slip the conniver six rashers, Parkes.' Gunner Parkes was one of his two assistants.

'Don't be like that,' I said, 'there's me Aunt May as well. I can't go home with six rashers all to myself and none for her. She's close to wartime starvation as it is.'

'Poor old lady, ruddy hard luck,' said Bombardier Jones.

''Ere y'ar, Tim,' said Gunner Parkes, and he wrapped up a wodge of rashers in greaseproof paper and handed the packet to me. 'Enjoy yer leave, mate. When you got me down for?'

'In a fortnight.'

'Good on yer,' said Parkes.

'Who's in charge here?' asked Bombardier Jones. NCOs were always asking daft questions like that.

'You're a good old bomb,' I said, 'so long.'

I caught my train to Liverpool Street from our local station in Suffolk and had the packet of rashers tucked inside my battledress blouse when I came off the train. There were always redcaps prowling about at main stations and if they caught you in possession of what you weren't entitled to, you could look forward to a spell in the Aldershot glasshouse.

It was the second week in April, 1943. London was bright with sunshine but a bit knocked about. Evidence of the Blitz still caught the eye. So did a profusion of Yanks. GIs were everywhere. I took the tube to Waterloo and a bus from there. The clippie goggled at me.

'Well, strike me pink,' she said, 'if it ain't me one and only.' She rang the bell and the bus moved off.

'Watcher, Nellie,' I said. Nell Saunders was a Walworth neighbour, married to Bert Saunders. They were both characters. Bert was in the Navy, so Nell had taken a job as a clippie. 'How you doing, lovey?'

'Oh, up an' down, in and out, 'ere an' there,' said Nell, a sturdy young woman with a hearty laugh. 'Clip yer a tuppeny one for luck?'

'All right, give us a ticket,' I said, 'and a kiss as well.'

Nell gave me a smacker. Passengers inside the bus let go a cheer.

'Got one for me, love?' asked an old bloke.

'I'll kiss yer goodbye when you get off, Grandpa,'

said Nell and clipped me a ticket. 'Got some leave, Tim?'

'Seven days.'

'That's the stuff,' she said. 'See yer down the pub one evenin'. Give me love to yer Aunt May.'

'Bless you too,' I said and took a seat.

Aunt May was priceless, a mother to me, having fostered me since my infant days. My parents had been killed in a train crash when I was three years old. My dad's sister, Aunt May, a single woman, took me over, brought me up and gave me so much motherly affection that I never missed my natural mum. She'd been born in New Cross where her parents had a newsagents shop. We lived over the shop with her parents. She lost her mother when she was twenty-eight and I was nine. Her dad carried on with the shop and then he died seven years later, just after I'd left school at sixteen. Aunt May sold the shop and moved to Walworth, where living was cheaper: furthermore, its cockneys were her favourite kind of people. Investing the money from the sale of the shop, she had an income of about a pound a week and I contributed from what I earned in my job with an insurance company. So we managed fairly well, the rent of the house being only twelve shillings a week.

My parents were buried in Lewisham Cemetery and Aunt May and I always went once a year and took flowers. She told me that my mum and dad had been a lovely couple and were worth remembering. If I grew up to be like my dad, she said once, the world wouldn't complain about me.

The bus trundled down the Walworth Road. In the

April sunshine the old place looked quite bright and cheerful. South London had taken its share of German bombs in 1940 and 1941, but it had been tidied up a bit and there were Saturday morning shoppers out and about. The war had taken a turn for the better when Montgomery knocked Rommel for six in the Western Desert, and Walworth, accordingly, had a perky look.

I alighted at the East Street market stop. Nell saw me off the bus with a smile and a wink. There were always more winks in Walworth than anywhere else. I entered the market. It was crowded. There were wartime shortages and market stalls no longer had a fully laden look, but people were always hoping that what they couldn't get in shops they could get in markets.

I knew East Street market as well as I knew my own home. I also knew Charlie Chipper who ran a fish stall and sold kippers among other things. Edging my way into the crowds I heard a greengrocery stallholder call.

'Watcher, Tim, see you got yer khaki duds on, matey. Smart, ain't we?'

'Not as smart as you and your scales, Fred.'

The pots and pans stallholder spotted me next. Not a bit shy about all the people around, he sang his greeting in a voice full of Walworth gravel:

''Ere comes a treat, walkin' down the street,
'Obnail boots on 'is plates o' meat,
What d'yer think of that, then, Tim's gorn barmy,
Look at what he's done now, he's in the bleedin'
　Army.'

'Same to you, Eddie,' I called. Shoppers were laughing. I went on, making for the fish stall, hoping.

'Hello, Charlie,' I said as I reached it.

'Well, well, and 'ow's yerself, cocky?' said Charlie Chipper. He wore a striped apron and a straw boater.

'On leave,' I said and waited until he'd finished serving a customer or two. Then I asked him if he'd got any kippers. Aunt May had a partiality for kippers. Not for breakfast, for tea. And I liked them myself. Walworth people were notable kipper-eaters and knew exactly how to separate the juicy flesh from the many bones. But fish was as short as other foods. The country's fishermen forever had U-boats on their tails.

'Well, me young cockalorum, I tell yer no lie, I ain't got none,' said Charlie, whose stall no longer swam with all kinds of fish and conger eels. His offerings were sparse, although there was a crate half-full of mussels. 'I mean, I asks yer, kippers! Yes, lady?'

'I'll take me 'addock,' said the new customer, a lovely plump old dear.

''Addock, what 'addock?' asked Charlie.

'What you promised me yesterday an' you'd better 'ave it or me old man'll come an' do things to yer cockles.'

''Ere, yesterday's been an' gorn, yer know, missus.'

'Well, course it 'as, yer silly man, it's today now and I'd like me promised 'addock.'

'I don't see no 'addock,' said Charlie.

'No smoked 'addock?' said the old dear.

'Ah, now, well now,' said Charlie, 'yer didn't say smoked, did yer? There's smoked an' fresh, yer know.

9

'Ere, was it you wearin' a brown 'at with feathers that come and asked me yesterday?'

'Don't come the old acid with me, Charlie Chipper, yer know it was and I'm wearing the 'at now, ain't I?'

'I like it,' said Charlie, 'that's what I call a cheerful titfer and I got yer 'addock, Queenie. Smoked.' He produced it, already wrapped, from a hiding-place under his stall. This was the age of under-the-counter stuff. 'One an' tuppence.'

'Gawd 'elp us, you'll 'ave the camisole off me back if you keep chargin' prices like that,' said the old dear, but dug into her purse and paid up.

'It's the war, yer know,' said Charlie.

'Course I know,' she said, 'I been bombed out twice.'

'All right, me old darling,' said Charlie, 'see yer up the park on Sunday. Wear yer best frillies.'

'I'll give you frillies, yer saucy bugger,' said the old dear and went on her way with her smoked haddock and a twinkle in her eye.

'Now, about the kippers,' I said.

'Now, Tim, me young mate, I got me reg'lars to think about.'

'My Aunt May's a regular.'

'So she is and yer been a soldier for a couple of years or so, Tim.'

'So how about a couple of kippers before I die for my country and your smoked haddock?'

'Fancy some mackerel?' suggested Charlie.

'Fancy getting your stall blown up?' I countered. Kippers were like gold dust, of course, but there was always a way of getting a favour out of Charlie and that

10

was to carry on a palaver with him. And I had a feeling some kippers were hiding themselves under the stall. I was after treating Aunt May.

'Yer twistin' me arm,' said Charlie. 'Still, if yer'd like to say a few kind words about me to yer Aunt May, I might be able to oblige yer.'

'Yes, I'll tell her to be up the park on Sunday wearing her best frillies,' I said.

'Now yer talkin',' said Charlie and he gave in with a grin. He ducked under his stall with a sheet of newspaper in his hand and came up a moment later with the newspaper wrapped round something just as three more customers arrived, all hard-working Walworth women.

'There y'ar, soldier, pound of fresh Cornish pilchards,' he said, in case the new customers got ideas. 'One an' four.'

'Ruddy robbery,' I said, paying up. 'Still, ta, Charlie love.'

'Give 'im a cuddle as well, soldier,' said one woman. ''E'd like that, wouldn't yer, Charlie? And I'll 'ave some of them pilchards.'

I left Charlie to explain he'd just run out of pilchards and walked down King and Queen Street. It was no surprise to me to see a GI arm in arm with a girl. They stopped at the door of one of the flat-fronted houses. The girl opened the door by pulling on a latchcord and took her GI in. It was a fact, GIs were everywhere, they'd even found King and Queen Street in the heart of Walworth.

I crossed Browning Street and turned into Walcorde Avenue, where the small terraced houses were fronted

11

by iron railings. Walcorde Avenue was considered fairly posh. Well, there weren't too many streets called avenues in Walworth. This one led directly to St John's Church by a little paved pathway. It was a cul-de-sac as far as traffic was concerned and it always looked neat and respectable. Aunt May, like most women, was in favour of respectability, although she wasn't fanatical about it, being broad-minded.

These days there were very few street urchins or ragamuffins. Nobody was very rich but most families were a little better off than in pre-war years. The war had created full employment and kids went about in fairly decent clothes and without a hungry look. Actually, there was a bit of a dearth of kids. Thousands of them had been evacuated. There were a few in the village of Sheldham, the Suffolk village a mile from Battery Headquarters. So far, they'd only managed to burn down one barn. Accidentally, of course.

I let myself in, and went through to the kitchen.

'Here we are, old girl,' I called, putting my small travelling valise down on a chair. The valise was one that had fallen off the back of an army lorry.

'Who's that, as if I don't know,' said Aunt May, coming in from the scullery. 'Well, bless us, look at you. Lanky lamp-posts and all.' She smiled. She was a nice-looking woman of forty-one, invariably bright and unflappable. She had a good figure, brown hair and brown eyes. She was wearing a pretty patterned apron with pockets and there was always a hankie in each pocket, as if she still needed to be ready to wipe my

12

nose. My nose, when I was a kid, went runny if I had a cold.

'How's things, old darling?' I asked.

'All the better for seeing you,' she said and gave me a kiss and a cuddle. She was given to handing out kisses and cuddles. I asked her once if the milkman ever got any, he being a sad-looking bloke who seemed in need of some. Aunt May said what a question, you saucy devil, what would the neighbours say if they saw me kissing and cuddling the milkman on my own doorstep? When I said she could treat the bloke on someone else's doorstep or behind the parlour curtain, Aunt May fell about laughing. She was given to laughing as much as to kisses and cuddles. I'd never known her to have moody moments, although all through my school years there'd been times when she'd been strict and corrective. She didn't mind boisterousness or natural larkiness, but she did care about the right kind of behaviour. She said the right kind of behaviour mattered, never mind whether you were poor or rich. There were Walworth people who sang outside the pubs on Saturday nights and did the knees-up until bobbies on the beat arrived and told them to go home. And mostly they went home. That was the right kind of behaviour to Aunt May. It was civilized, she said, to go home when told to.

She was a bit superior for Walworth on the whole, but never acted as if she regarded herself so. When both her parents had gone she simply decided to get out of the flat she'd lived in all her life. She wanted elbow room, she said, she wanted a house with an affordable rent. She'd been here six years, she knew everybody in

13

the immediate vicinity and got on so well with them that anyone would have thought she was Walworth born and bred. She liked the fact that cockneys were a resilient lot and probably the most cheerful people in England. Right from the start she'd sallied forth into the heart of things, with a smile and a hullo for everybody. She was charitable towards all, even towards Alf Cook who, when the worse for drink, chased his kids up and down Browning Street, roaring at them and brandishing his leather belt. But since Aunt May's tolerance couldn't last for ever and since she could be very forthright, she'd stopped him once, when we were on our way to the Walworth Road. She'd planted herself in front of him and he'd had to stop. He'd have trampled her to death otherwise, being a burly council navvy.

'Gidoudavit, yer dozy female!' he bawled.

'Now, Mr Cook, behave yourself,' said Aunt May. 'All this shouting and hollering on a nice Saturday afternoon won't do the neighbourhood much good, nor you, either. I knew a man like you in New Cross once—'

'Oh, yer did, did yer?' said Alf. 'Well, sod off back to 'im.'

'Really, Mr Cook, shame on you,' she said. 'I wish you'd listen, I'm trying to tell you that this man, just like you, went about bawling and bellowing whenever he was one over the eight. And what happened to him, yes, what? He went and fractured his larynx.'

'Well, bleedin' 'ard luck!' bawled Alf, red in the face. ''E shouldn't 'ave 'ad a larinch! I ain't got one.'

'Of course you have,' said Aunt May, 'we all have, it's where our voices come from. This man fractured his

14

with too much hollering and he can't even talk now, let alone holler.'

'Gawd blimey O'Reilly, what do I care?' roared Alf. 'You goin' to stop standin' in me way or ain't yer?' He brandished his belt threateningly, but I didn't think Aunt May was going to need any protection, I was sure she could handle him.

She said, 'Mr Cook, your trousers are coming down.'

'Eh?'

'Your trousers are coming down,' I said.

'Yes,' she said, 'so you'd better stop waving that belt about and put it on. Just look at your trousers. Whatever would Mrs Cook say if she came to know they'd come down in front of everyone in Browning Street? You don't want to be a disgrace to your own wife, do you?'

Alf Cook, in his shirt sleeves, looked down at his navvy's corduroys. They were sagging dangerously. 'Oh, dearie me, fancy that, beg yer pardon, I'm sure,' he said in growling sarcasm and he hiked his trousers up.

'That's better,' said Aunt May, who obviously thought some straightforward talk was desirable. 'According to your wife, you're a nice reasonable man when you're not one over the eight. It's not a bit reasonable to go roaring about after your children and walloping the little loves, is it?'

'Little loves? Gawd give me strength,' bellowed Alf. 'D'yer know what the young perishers went an' done while I was at work this mornin'? Pinched me Sunday watch an' chain an' bleedin' pawned it for pocket money.'

'Oh, dear,' said Aunt May wryly. Then, brightening up, she said, 'Never mind, Mr Cook, it could have been worse, they could have dropped it down a drain. What a blessing they only pawned it.'

'Bloody 'ell—'

'Now, Mr Cook, not in front of young Tim, if you don't mind,' said Aunt May.

'Young Tim?' bawled Alf. 'That there young Tim's a bleedin' rip. Didn't 'e stand on me Billy's foot last week, didn't 'e near tread Billy's foot to bleedin' death? I asks yer, didn't 'e?'

'Did you do that, Tim?' asked Aunt May.

'Best thing at the time, Aunt May,' I said, 'he was trying to turn Lily Burns upside-down.'

'Oh, poor little Lily,' said Aunt May, 'I just hope that'll be a lesson to Billy. And you, Mr Cook.'

'You done, May Hardy, 'ave yer?' said Alf.

'Yes, that's all, Mr Cook,' said Aunt May.

Muttering, Alf went back home, looking as if he'd lost a painful argument.

Aunt May wasn't very pleased when the country had gone to war against Hitler in 1939. On the other hand, if there was one person who could really get her goat it was Germany's raving Führer. Late in 1940, with a slightly sad look, she saw me off to a Royal Artillery training camp.

It was a relief to her that so far I hadn't been blown up. The battery had had a busy time during the night-bombing raids in 1941, but nothing fell on us. We were in Essex then, close enough to London to see its sky

16

lurid with the glare of flames and to worry about what was happening to families. Walworth caught it, along with other inner London boroughs and Aunt May spent lots of nights in public air raid shelters, where she was no doubt a cheerful help to the nervous.

I was very fond of Aunt May and it was nice to be home with her again.

'I hoped you'd be in time for lunch,' she said, 'I'm going to do liver, with fried tomatoes and mashed potatoes. The butcher let me have the liver when I said you were coming home.'

'There's a good old girl,' I said, and handed out a cuddle myself.

'I'll give you old,' she said and went out to the gas cooker in the scullery to start the lunch. I followed, with two packets.

'Here you are,' I said, 'bacon for our breakfast and kippers for our tea this evening. And I've got a dozen eggs in my valise.'

'Bacon?' said Aunt May, looking happy.

'A dozen rashers at least.'

'Where did you get all that many?' she asked, putting the liver on.

'Back of a lorry?'

'Now, Tim, you know I wasn't born yesterday.'

'They're perks, Aunt May.'

'Oh, I see.' Aunt May understood about perks. She thought all servicemen were entitled to perks. 'And the eggs are from your village friends?'

'Yes, the Beavers. I've told you about them.'

'My, they've done well for a family not used to life

17

in the country,' said Aunt May. 'And did you say kippers as well?'

'Look.' I unwrapped the kippers. They were fat, golden-brown and shiny. I put them on a plate in the larder.

'Kippers,' said Aunt May, 'well, you're doing me proud, Tim.'

'Mind you, I had to hit Charlie Chipper a couple of times before he coughed up from under his stall. And I told him that as a reward, you'd meet him up the park on Sunday in your best hat and frillies.'

'I can hardly wait,' said Aunt May. 'Here, just a moment, what d'you mean, my best hat and frillies? You saucy devil. I'll have a little more respect from you, if you don't mind.' She took a look at potatoes that were on the boil. She was smiling.

'We'll have an early kipper tea before we go out,' I said.

'Go out?' Aunt May turned the potatoes out in a colander over the sink, then put them back in the saucepan to mash them. 'Go out, Tim?'

'Yes, time I treated you. Let's go to the first evening performance of the Crazy Gang show.' Seeing as it was wartime and London was full of people looking for a dose of escapism, the Crazy Gang were giving two performances every evening.

'You don't want to take me,' said Aunt May, giving the potatoes a drubbing and watching the frying liver.

'Why don't I? You're pretty—'

'Don't go mad,' said Aunt May, laughing. I took over the mashing of potatoes and she pushed the

18

liver pieces about and turned them.

'Then there's all the cuddles and apple pie I've had from you,' I said. 'You're overdue for a treat.'

'That's all very well,' said Aunt May, 'but why don't you take some nice girl? There's Meg Fowler just round the corner in Turquand Street and just home on leave herself from the Waafs. She looks really nice in her uniform and I'm sure she's got a soft spot for you.'

'Some soft spot. She knocked me flying only two weeks after we moved here. Fourteen she was at the time and she knocked me flying. What's she going to get up to now she's twenty and wears a uniform?'

Aunt May said, 'I'd like to know what you were getting up to yourself at the time.'

'I was shouting for help. Well, all right, Aunt May, tell you what, I'll walk round and see her this afternoon. If she's fixed up for this evening, that's it. I'll take you instead. We can get there early and find a place in the upper-circle queue.'

'All right,' smiled Aunt May. 'If it happens, I'll put my best hat on.'

We had lunch in the kitchen. The kitchen was like Aunt May herself, bright and cheerful. It looked out on to the yard. The window threw welcome light over the wallpaper, patterned with plump red roses and over the linoleum floor, except during the foggy days of winter. But then the glowing coals of the range fire offered consoling heat to chilled limbs.

I often wondered why Aunt May seemed such a contented woman. She only had me and I couldn't count myself as all that special. It was certain I wasn't going to set the world alight as an insurance clerk and heap diamonds and furs on her. She might have had a lot more than she did have. She'd been engaged after the First World War, but lost her soldier fiancé when he was killed in Russia. She'd spoken about him sometimes in her open way and I felt she'd loved him very much. She said he was a man who cared about people, which made him the best kind of man.

'Well, you're the best kind of woman, Aunt May,' I said at the time.

'Not so bad yourself, are you?' she said.

'First-class mutual admiration society, that's what we are,' I said.

'Well, we get along, Tim love, don't we?' she said.

CHAPTER TWO

'Well, look who's here,' said Aircraftswoman Meg Fowler when she saw me on her doorstep.

'Mind my braces,' I said.

'Mind your what?'

'They're the King's military braces, so are my trousers.'

'Same old Tim, same old chat,' said Meg, fair hair rolled, Waaf shirt improperly buttoned.

'It's come undone,' I said.

'I'll buy it,' said Meg, 'what has?'

'That button.'

Meg looked down at herself. 'Crikey, how did that 'appen?' she asked.

'Social manoeuvres, I suppose,' I said. 'Make a change from military manoeuvres. Do yerself up before your mum spots it.'

Meg did the button up. 'Still a comic, aren't yer?' she said.

'Wish I was, I might make a bit of money with the Crazy Gang. Listen, old darling, fancy going up to see their show this evening? Early performance?'

'Oh, yer stinker,' said Meg, 'why didn't yer ask before now? I bet you left it too late on purpose, you've spent years bein' a disappointment to me. I've promised to let Bob Micklewright take me to the flicks.'

'Dear Jesus,' I said, 'is he still alive?' We were in her mum's parlour now.

'Well, he's still walkin' and talkin',' said Meg.

'He was doing all that years ago, Meg. What is he, seventy now?'

'I'll bleedin' hit you,' said Meg.

'You would too.'

'You bet I would. What d'you mean by it, comin' round to ask me out at this short notice and catchin' me already fixed up with Bob Micklewright? And what d'you mean, seventy, you daft cuckoo? He's just a bit mature, that's all and 'ave you seen what the war's left in Walworth these days? Not a decent upstandin' bloke in sight. I'm surprised you didn't get jumped on by all the local tarts on your way round here, you're a sight for sore eyes, you are.'

'You're growing up pretty good yerself, Meg, I like the look of your shirt.'

'Watch it,' said Meg. 'Still, tell me more, give me legs a mention.'

'Nice you've got two,' I said. 'Well, pity you're fixed up this evening. Never mind, can't be helped. Enjoy yourself.'

'Wait a minute, you ratbag,' said Meg, 'there's tomorrow, yer know, and Monday and Tuesday and so on.'

'So there is,' I said. Meg was an old neighbourly mate of mine and had been a real Walworth tomboy in her younger days. 'OK, I'll take you out tomorrow morning, we'll go to morning church.'

'We'll whatter?' asked Meg.

'It'll please the vicar, I'll call for you at five to eleven.'

'Blow that for a lark,' said Meg, 'I didn't come home on leave to go on church parade, you barmy teacake.'

'I'll bring Aunt May as well.'

Wallop. Meg thumped me in the chest, then did her best to shut me up by trying to stuff a chair cushion into my mouth. It sat me down. The cushion began to swing, narrowly missing family ornaments on the mantelpiece as she swiped my head with it. I wondered what the war was doing to women, I didn't think it was improving them. If they weren't going after GIs, they were getting rid of all the virtues I held dear in them. Aunt May, of course, was an exception.

'What's going on in here?' I asked.

'Bleedin' murder,' said Meg.

'What's going on in my parlour?' called her mum from somewhere.

'Ruddy murder,' called Meg.

'Oh, all right,' called her mum, who knew her boisterous daughter, 'only be a bit more quiet about it, can you, love?'

Meg gave me a final swipe.

'Tell you what,' I said, 'let's go out tomorrow afternoon, let's take a bus ride to Hyde Park, like we used to when we first met.'

Meg let a little grin show. 'You looked at my knickers when I was growing up,' she said.

'Couldn't help it, could I, when you were always standing on your head,' I said. 'But all right, I won't look tomorrow, not in Hyde Park, nor on the bus.'

'Oh, that's a promise, is it?' she said. 'It sounds like you're goin' to be a disappointment to me again.' Meg said things like that. They were all bluff. Meg was going to keep herself to herself until she met a bloke who she recognized as just her type. Someone like a hammer-thrower. And as far as I was concerned, I didn't go in for mucking about with young ladies. Aunt May was strictly against that kind of thing and she'd brought me up to behave myself. A girl once asked me if I'd always behaved as if I was in Sunday School. I said not half, it stopped girls' dads coming after me with a meat axe.

'OK, Meg,' I said, 'pick you up at two-thirty.'

'Well, Tim?' smiled Aunt May when I got back.

'I bring good news,' I said.

'Not before time,' said Aunt May. 'You should have suitable company when you're on leave. Meg's a lively girl, you'll enjoy a nice evening out with her and it doesn't have to be serious.' That meant Meg was suitable company, but not to be considered as a serious prospect.

'No, Meg's not coming,' I said, 'she's going to the flicks tonight with Bob Micklewright. I'm taking you.'

'You said good news.' Aunt May was rolling dough on the kitchen table. 'That's not good news.'

'It's good enough for me,' I said, 'so you can get your best hat ready.'

Aunt May shook her head and laughed. 'You're a funny one, Tim,' she said, 'but you'll have to get down to being serious sometime.'

'There's a war on, old girl, that's serious enough at the moment. Let's get that over with first.'

'Yes, but I can't help thinking about your future,' said Aunt May, 'I'm not going to have you turning into a stuffy bachelor.'

'Listen, I'm only twenty-two.'

'All the same,' she said. I think she'd spent the last twenty years with my future in mind. But what about herself? What would her future be like if I got married? I honestly didn't like the thought of Aunt May being alone.

'What're you making?' I asked.

'A plum pie for tomorrow's dinner with some bottled plums.'

'You lovely old darling,' I said.

'Watch your tongue, young man,' said Aunt May, 'you'll be putting wrinkles on me next.'

'Not you,' I said. She didn't have a single wrinkle, she looked nowhere near her age. The man who'd have married her if he hadn't lost his life in revolutionary Russia, had missed years of lovely living with Aunt May.

We had an early tea. The fat kippers were first-class. When we left the house Aunt May looked a treat in a spring coat and her nicest hat. She knew how to wear clothes. We took a bus up West and got on the tail of the queue for the upper circle of the theatre. The West End had a colourful atmosphere because of the sunshine, the girls and the many different uniforms.

The country was suffering strict rationing at home and perils abroad. In 1940 and 1941 it had suffered bombs at home. London houses and buildings had been flattened and this made the old place look ruined in parts.

But fat old Goering's *Luftwaffe* hadn't flattened spirits and the people themselves didn't look ruined. The West End swarmed with pleasure-seekers, particularly Americans, who knew how to enjoy themselves. Nor did they waste time asking if there were any rules. They picked up cockney girls and suburban girls with no effort at all. They had no inhibitions when it came to making the necessary approach.

Aunt May's spring coat, bright hat and young-looking appearance put her in the firing line. I wasn't in the least surprised when a veteran GI, a sergeant who looked as if he might have served as a rookie doughboy in 1918, advanced on the queue with his eyes on Aunt May.

'Pardon me, bud,' he said, 'you doing anything special with your sister?'

'No, nothing specially special, just queueing,' I said. 'And how did you know she was my sister?'

'Family likeness, I guess,' he said. He was having me on, of course, and paying Aunt May a compliment. 'I'm a loner right now. My date took one look at my best friend and pranced off with him. I guess my maturity put her off. How about asking your sister if I could borrow her for the evening? I've a coupla stalls' tickets for the Strand Theatre and we could catch some eats at Romano's joint afterwards. I'll see her home, bud, give you my word.'

'Well, there you are, sis,' I said to Aunt May, who had a laugh in her eyes, of course. 'D'you fancy the Strand Theatre with this American gent?'

'Ask the gentleman if he's married,' said Aunt May as the queue began to move forward.

'Are you married?' I asked the mature Yank.

'Sure am. To Alma McKinley of Chicago. Only she's over there and I'm over here. You can see my problem.'

'Yes, ruddy hard luck, mate,' I said, 'but my sister doesn't go out with married men. And she's shy, anyway, aren't you, sis?'

'I'm overcome,' said Aunt May.

'Hell, ain't that a shame?' said the sergeant. 'All the same, nice talking to the both of you. Enjoy the show. I've seen it myself, it's a hoot. So long, guys.'

'Good luck,' I said and off he went to search for other talent.

Aunt May was having hysterics. 'You'll be my death one day, Tim,' she said, 'all that funny talk of yours.'

The show was a riot. Bud Flanagan, Chesney Allen, Nervo and Knox and the rest of the Crazy Gang cracked their wartime jokes, took off army generals and ATS commandants, bashed each other, tore about the stage and chucked things at the audience. The whole theatre kept erupting. Aunt May laughed until her tears ran.

When we got home we put together a pot of tea and some fried bacon sandwiches, a Walworth speciality. We listened to the Saturday night wireless programme and to the news. The news was all about how the Allies were doing. They were doing fine, apparently. Someone ought to be telling that to the Japs and Germans. It might make them give in.

When it was time for bed, Aunt May said, 'It was a lovely evening, Tim.'

'Can't be bad, can it, an evening with the Crazy Gang?'

'But take a nice girl out next time,' she said.

'Well, I'm making an effort with Meg tomorrow,' I said. 'We're going to wander around Hyde Park. Simple and healthy stuff.'

'Meg's good company,' said Aunt May.

'So are you. Aunt May, don't you get lonely sometimes?'

'Now, how can anyone get lonely in Walworth?' she said. 'Walworth is full of neighbours and doorsteps.'

'I wonder sometimes if you couldn't have had a lot more than you have had,' I said.

'Now, how can you say that after we've had twenty years together?' she asked.

'Yes, but—'

'They've all been worthwhile, love, every one.'

Meg enjoyed Hyde Park. She wasn't a girl to get bored if she wasn't riding the moon. Hyde Park was a green playground and the afternoon was bright. She looked swingy in her uniform and ready for fun, as long as it wasn't the kind of fun where she had to fight her way out of it. She helped boys to sail their toy boats on the Serpentine, much to their delight. There was a regiment of smart-looking Yanks about and several arrived to give Meg and the boys some American advice on the sailing of boats. A broad-shouldered wallop of a GI began to take Meg over. He thought that as a Waaf she was cute. Meg was responsive. She liked extrovert males. This one said he was Steve Schuster from New Jersey. He and Meg seemed like kindred spirits. They exchanged stories of their lives and both seemed to have enjoyed tearaway years.

Steve invited both of us to a party. Some joint in Bloomsbury, he said. He'd got the address and an invitation. The party was to begin at six in the evening. How about it? Meg was all for it. I went along in case she needed help.

The party was based on gin and tonic and instant fraternization. The GIs brought the gin and bottles of tonic kept appearing like magic. I lost count of how many GIs were there. They heavily outnumbered the girls. Meg stood up to encircling tactics like a real Walworth trouper.

'Hands off, mate, I'm in uniform,' she said.

'Sure fancy you out of it, honey,' said one hopeful GI.

'You'll be lucky,' said Meg.

Girls yelled and rushed about, upstairs and downstairs. Whose house it was, nobody seemed to know, or if there were actually a host and hostess. The GIs kept asking where the ice was.

'It's not where you're looking right now,' said a young lady from Penge, smacking the hand of an investigative bloke from Virginia.

A charming lady in maroon silk with no shoulders to the dress floated around with a cigarette holder between her teeth, asking if anyone had brought cheroots. A GI said sure, he'd brought cheroots. Thank you, darling, said the charming lady. This way, he said. Which way? Follow me, lady, he said. She floated out in his wake. I think her addiction to cheroots cost her dear, because she never reappeared.

29

Meg sorted me out at nine o'clock. 'Where've you been, you carrot?' she asked.

'Just standing here and talking. I've been invited to Oklahoma after the war.'

'Bloody marvellous, I don't think,' said Meg. 'I've just escaped a fate worse than a messy death while you've been standin' and talkin'. What kind of a soldier friend are you?'

'Good question, that, Meg, ask me another.'

'I'll break your leg in a minute,' said Meg. The party was getting chaotic. 'Let's go home. Whose bottle of gin is that on that chair?'

'No idea,' I said.

'Pinch it,' said Meg. 'Me mum an' dad can have it.'

'Where's Steve, your new friend?'

'Upstairs. He can't come down, not yet, I've just done the bugger an injury.' Meg liked a lark, even a wrestle, but in common with most Walworth girls she wasn't prepared to be on the losing end of any wrestle.

We took the bottle of gin as perks for her mum and dad and had a talkative bus ride home. Meg came in to share a pot of tea and some slices of Sunday cake with Aunt May and myself. She described what the party had been like and what Steve Schuster from New Jersey had been like. Aunt May smiled a bit and gave me a look or two.

'Didn't you look after Meg?' she asked.

'I played gooseberry,' I said.

'Oh, I didn't need Tim,' said Meg, 'I took care of my uniform all by meself, I just 'anded out a few wallops.'

'Some kinds of behaviour leave a lot to be desired in

30

wartime,' said Aunt May, 'and I don't know if there are any winners. But I do know the losers are always women.'

'Not this time,' said Meg. 'This time Steve from New Jersey was a loser. He'll 'urt from 'ere to Christmas.'

'Oh, dear, poor man,' said Aunt May, but she looked quite cheerful about it.

I had a restful leave on the whole. I went to the pub a few times and met friends and acquaintances there, including Nell Saunders, the bus clippie. I took Meg with me a couple of times. She liked a shandy and the kind of boisterous company that was always prevalent in Walworth pubs. I also took her to the pictures. We were mates, no doubt about it.

'D'you feel you'd like me as a brother?' I asked her.

'Try me,' she said. So I kissed her.

'How was that?' I asked.

'Champion,' said Meg. 'No, I don't want you as a brother.'

'Bosom chum?' I suggested.

'Sounds a lot better,' said Meg, 'but don't go mad, it might knock a ruddy great 'ole in our chummy friendship.'

Meg was a joker. I left it at that. It suited me.

'I'm off, Aunt May,' I said. My leave was up and I had a train to catch.

'Well, it's been lovely having you home,' she said.

'Twice over for me,' I said. 'God bless yer, old girl, ta for everything. Look after yourself. Keep your head down, put the milk bottles out at night, don't let Mrs Marsh's cats in, they wee on the passage floor, and order your coal early for the winter. Oh, I've oiled your sewing-machine by the way.'

'Anything else?' smiled Aunt May.

'Yes, you're my best girl,' I said.

She laughed and sent me off with a warm kiss and a warm cuddle.

CHAPTER THREE

Back at Battery Headquarters I was having an ordinary day in my life as an ack-ack gunner, temporarily desk-bound. I'd been transferred from a gun site ten months ago to fill a gap in the orderly room. The site commander, Lieutenant Rogers, told me BHQ wanted a clerk and that I would do.

'Here, give over, sir, I'm not—'

'All right, we know you're not a genius, but you can read and write, can't you? Yes, of course you can. Get your kit and push off. The ration lorry's here. You can go in that. Enjoy yourself.'

That was typical of how life was organized for you in the Army.

BHQ wasn't as comfortable as site. There were guard duties, fire picquet duties and other things that mucked you about. However, it was better than Burma, where the jungles and the Japs made life a bit sickening.

Sergeant Johnson, in charge of the orderly room, clumped in. 'That you under your haircut, Hardy?' he said. I failed to answer. I was busy. I had a pile of pay books on my desk, his included. I also had railway leave warrants to fill in. 'Listen, grab the Austin utility and flog off to the station. There's an American sergeant and two privates to pick up off the next train. Don't keep 'em waiting, we don't want Eisenhower sending a written complaint. Get going.'

He'd have gone himself normally so that he could find time to call on the village newsagent's married daughter, whose merchant navy husband had last been seen on a raft in the Atlantic. I knew why he was sending me on this occasion. It was nearly time for midday dinner.

'Pardon me,' I said, 'but I'm busy. It's pay parade this afternoon. In addition I don't want to be last in our dinner queue. I know you don't want to be last in the sergeants' mess queue and I feel the same way.'

'Shove off,' said Sergeant Johnson.

'It's a mistake, anyway,' I said, 'we've already got two American officers and a top sergeant here. There's been a duplicated cock-up.'

'Sounds possible,' murmured ATS Corporal Deirdre Allsop.

Battery Headquarters, a mile outside Sheldham, consisted of a requisitioned mansion and a collection of Nissen huts, the latter plonked down in what had once been a large and handsome garden. The mansion held administration offices, officers' quarters, officers' mess, sergeants' mess and RT room. There was a vehicle park and a workshop across the road. We had three Americans seconded to us. They were keen and active. They buzzed around the gun sites, picking up information that was as useless to them as it was to us, even if it was supposed to relate to the defence of the American Air Force bases in East Anglia.

'Don't muck about,' said Sergeant Johnson, 'just flog off while we're still friends.'

'Can't we draw straws?' I asked, but Bombardier Wilkins, Gunner Frisby, Corporal Deirdre Allsop and Corporal Deborah Watts all kept their heads down. No-one minded if I missed my dinner as long as they all got theirs. 'What happened to comradeship?' I asked as I came to my feet.

'Good question,' said Frisby, whom I'd known since training camp days and who was supposed to be my mate.

Some mate, I thought. I belted over to transport, signed for the Austin utility, burst from the vehicle park in second and banged down the road to the village in lunatic top. If I could get to the station and back in twenty-five minutes, I might just make the last of the fried meat loaf. Cookhouse staff never saved anything for latecomers. Any overs were fed to Major Moffat's great slavering Dalmatian. Major Moffat was our OC.

Halfway to the village I caught sight of a figure swinging along the grass verge. Hearing the engine, she turned. She stepped into the road and waved with her school satchel. She plainly wanted a lift. I couldn't run her over, I wasn't as bitter as that, so I stopped. I recognized her. It was Minnie Beavers, daughter of Jim Beavers, a good old cockney spiv who'd brought his wife and daughter out of Camberwell when the war began in 1939. He said he'd excavated them in case of bombs. He meant evacuated. His wife's aunt lived just outside the village, she'd married a Suffolk man. Jim had taken to country life like a duck to water and in just

35

over three years had acquired a wide range of options on how to survive the war without actually having anything to do with it. He was a friend of mine. His missus supplied me with eggs.

His daughter Minnie was fifteen, pert and pretty and a holy terror. She was wearing a round straw hat, a dark blue gymslip and black school stockings of lisle. She had fair hair and blue eyes. She also had a bosom that was hardly believable.

Pulling the passenger door open, she gave a yelp of joy. 'Oh, you Tim!' she cried.

'OK, me Tim, you heap little laughing devil. Get in, laughing devil.'

She hitched her gymslip, unnecessarily, and leapt in. She plumped into the seat beside me. I shut my eyes and prayed. You had to pray when you were an old twenty-two and an under-age schoolgirl sat next to you showing the saucy tops of her black school stockings in a military vehicle prohibited to civilians.

'That's it, get me shot at dawn,' I said. 'If you don't adjust your dress you can either buzz off or get chucked off.'

'Crikey, what a fuss and when no-one's lookin' too,' said Minnie. But she put her gymslip back into place and I resumed my rapid journey. The hedgerows, green with April growth, rushed by.

'Why aren't you in school?' I asked sternly.

'Half-day,' said Minnie. 'Tim, ain't you ever goin' to kiss an' cuddle with me?'

'Never. Never, d'you hear? I'll fight it all the way. I'll fight it on the beaches, I'll fight it in the streets and

I'll fight it in your parlour. It'll probably kill me, but what's the alternative? I suppose you know blokes get hanged for doing things to schoolgirls.'

'Oh, you soppy date, course they don't,' she said. 'Be rapture, it would, you an' me.' That was a little bit of Suffolk. Like her parents, she'd picked some up. 'I could eat you, I could.' She'd been like this almost from the day I met her, ten months ago. Daft as a turnip.

'I'll chuck you off for sure if you don't behave,' I said.

'But I'm pretty,' she protested. She was too. 'Why don't we 'ave kisses an' cuddles, Tim?'

'Because I like your mum and dad, because you're too young and because it's illegal.'

Minnie laughed. The sound was like honey gurgling out of a warm stone jar. She was incredible for fifteen: she was five-feet-seven and her legs were terrifying, long and slender they were, and her bosom didn't bear thinking about. Her complexion was a rich country peach and she was urgent to be sixteen, the age of consent. She'd hook an American GI then with no trouble at all. She'd have probably hooked one already if it hadn't been for her dad's gimlet eye. Minnie might possibly be the only village virgin left in the UK. The GIs were laying waste to the lambs. The thought depressed me. I had old-fashioned ideas about brides going virginal to the altar. Aunt May had let it be known that she had the same ideas.

Belting into the village, I pulled up outside the Beavers' cottage.

'Ta, Tim,' said Minnie.

'All right, push off, infant, I'm in a hurry.'

'Kiss first?' she suggested.

'With all these people about?' There were two women in the high street, about the only street of any consequence in Sheldham and two women were as good as a crowd in a village like this. 'Just buzz off, there's a good girl.'

Minnie made a face, but got out. Impudently, she waved to the crowd, then blew me a compromising kiss. Little she-devil Minnie Beavers was.

'Oi! Tim!' It was her dad. He put his green-hatted head through the open window. He'd acquired the hat with the cottage when he moved into it late in 1939. The hat had originally been brown. It was now green and mossy and probably as old as he was. In 1918, at the age of eighteen, he'd been conscripted to serve in Flanders. He took a blighty one in the leg and by the time he'd recovered the First World War was all over. He was thankful, of course, that he was too old for this one. 'Watcher, Tim lad, missus says eggs is on. Fancy 'em?'

'Missus is a love,' I said, 'I'll pick 'em up on my way back from the station. Have 'em ready for me, I'm in a hurry.'

'Ain't costin' yer, Tim,' said Jim, whose brown face, pointed nose and bright beady eyes gave him the look of an inquisitive fox. 'Missus says yer a good 'un. Ah – er – any porridge goin' spare?'

Grateful for the offer of eggs I said, 'In the back, but don't take all day and return the can when you hand over the eggs.'

38

He whisked round to the back of the van, found the spare can of petrol and as I belted away again I glimpsed him with his jacket hiding the can. Minnie was with him. When I got to the station it was empty and hollow. I knocked on the wood of the ticket office. The wood opened and old Shuttlebury, with his moustache and his peaked cap, showed his face.

'Where's the gorblimey train, gaffer?' I asked.

'Which train?'

'The twelve-thirty-five.'

'Late,' he said.

'Ruddy marvellous. Now I'll miss the afters as well.'

'Ain't my doin',' said the station gaffer.

'Well, how late's late?'

'Fifteen minutes, I reckon.'

'I'll wait,' I said. I had to.

'Seat on the platform,' he said.

'How kind.'

'Penny,' he said.

'What for?'

'Platform ticket.'

'You saucy old darling,' I said. There was a shocked rattle to the wood as he closed it. I kicked moodily around. Our regiment of three batteries had been stuck in East Anglia for two years and everything had been relatively quiet for a whole year. But it all meant there was no promotion. On the other hand, the quickest way to wartime promotion was over the dead bodies of your comrades.

I was certain to miss dinner. It was served at twelve-thirty and the train didn't arrive until one, when Mrs

Amelia Jessup got off. She was a chubby Sheldham woman. Gaffer Shuttlebury appeared, peaked cap straight and collected her ticket. She treated him to a dig in the ribs. She treated me to a smile.

'Are you the lot, Amelia?' I asked.

'Good lot too,' she said and walked out laughing.

Where were the Yanks?

'Hi, soldier.'

There they were. And they were all females. One, a sergeant, briskly unfolded a railway warrant. She pushed it under the gaffer's nose. The gaffer nuzzled it. The two other Wacs were privates, a blonde and a brunette in smart olive-green. The blonde, fair hair rolled, offered a friendly wink. The brunette, taking the war more seriously, looked in suspicion at me.

'You our wheels?' asked the blonde, shoulder bag rakishly slung.

'Come in,' I said. It was the best I could manage under the strain of having missed my eats.

'Come in where, buster?' asked the blonde.

'What a surprise,' I said, 'I thought you were going to be three more hairy cowboys.'

She laughed. 'Get you,' she said.

The brunette retreated a step.

'I'm Tim Hardy,' I said.

'Maureen Cassidy,' said the blonde, 'and this is Cecily. Cecily Peterson.'

'My pleasure,' I said. I was resigned now. 'Good trip?'

'Lousy,' said Cassidy. 'I guess you'll grab our bags?' On the platform were three bulging Wac valises.

'Pardon?' I said.

Their sergeant came up. 'Hi, there,' she said cheerfully, 'where's it all happening?'

She was dark, her hair raven where it showed beneath her cap. She had blue eyes, thick black lashes, a wide American mouth and brilliant American teeth. That Wac sergeants could look like this was news to me.

'I'm Tim Hardy,' I said, 'I'm your transport.'

'I'm Kit Masters. We're honoured. Let's go, shall we?'

'Who's moving our packs?' asked Private Peterson grimly.

I gave a hand. When they saw the Austin they looked as if they were facing up to the unbelievable.

'What is it?' asked Sergeant Masters.

'Your transport,' I said and chucked in the valises. My empty stomach was churning in search of what wasn't there.

'Does it go?' asked Cassidy.

'Never fails. OK, mount up, comrades and we'll mosey along to the old Suffolk homestead.'

'Come again?' said Cassidy.

'Just trying to make you feel at home. Climb aboard.'

'Where?' asked Private Peterson.

'Sergeant up front, privates in the back.'

Cassidy, already a friend, said, 'You're kidding, Tim old boy, it's a mousetrap.'

'Well, try it for size,' I said, 'and if you find any cheese, save some for me.' I parted the rear canvas. 'Hop in.'

'OK, I'll play,' said Cassidy. She hitched her skirt and swung a leg up. It looked good enough to eat and probably would have been if she'd spent eighty days in

41

a lifeboat and had drawn the wrong straw. I helped her aboard as decently as I could. Private Peterson was a different kettle of fish. Having watched her sister soldier's leg show with visible disgust, she was dead against being helped.

'Get lost,' she said and unwisely tried to hurl herself aboard at a reckless speed. She made a terrible mess of it. In the little van her legs suffered seconds of exposure before she was able to right herself. I closed the canvas on her yell of mortification. Poor girl. Insecurity, that's what it was. There was a lot of it about among some girls, mostly due to the way roving GIs addressed the problem of being far from home.

Sergeant Masters sat next to me as I tanked my way back to the village. I asked her what she thought of life in the American Army. She said it was a temporary condition that couldn't be helped and she was trying to learn to love it.

'I don't know if you'll learn to love Suffolk,' I said, 'it's pretty rural.'

'I'm looking forward to it,' she said, taking a keen interest in what she could see of it right now. She'd just been railroaded from Chelmsford she said, in a funny old toy train. She had a very self-confident air. I had a gloomy feeling she was faultlessly efficient. I wasn't too keen on that kind of woman. I didn't mind Aunt May's motherly efficiency, it had been a blessing to me, but I had fixed ideas about women and top of the list was the conviction they were designed by nature to be kind, loving and a bit incompetent, except in a kitchen. Sergeant Masters said she hadn't been long in the UK but liked what she'd seen of it so far. Entering the village, she saw a medley of thatched roofs and said they were really cute, part of old England.

'They harbour livestock,' I said, 'but they're pretty, I suppose.'

'Pretty?'

'All right, cute,' I said and pulled up outside Jim's cottage. He was at his gate, the petrol can wrapped in sacking under his arm and a cardboard box in his hand. Up to my window he came and handed in the cardboard box.

'Six eggs,' he said.

'Ta, old love,' I said, thinking of what they could do for my empty stomach. 'Big 'uns, are they?'

'Ain't pullets' marbles,' said Jim. ''Ello, 'ello, who's yer lady friend, lad?' He gave Sergeant Masters an interested look. She had an attractive curve to her jacket. 'Found a good 'un there, Tim, 'ave yer?'

'American,' I said, thinking of fried egg sandwiches if I could get some bread from our sergeant-cook.

'Ain't 'er fault,' said Jim, 'people can't 'elp where they're born.'

'What's he saying?' asked Sergeant Masters, obviously foxed by cockney twang laced with a little Suffolk burr.

'That you're rare,' I said.

'Watch it, Hardy,' she said.

'She's a sergeant,' I said to Jim. I was no longer in a hurry.

'That ain't 'er fault, neither,' said Jim, 'it's the gawd-help-us war that's done it. Unnatural, though.' Jim

43

considered females were for cuddling, not soldiering. Nor saluting. 'It's the war done it all right, Tim. I'll put the porridge tin back.' He disappeared.

'What's a porridge tin?' asked Sergeant Masters, who'd at least heard that correctly.

'Oh, nothing very—' A shriek interrupted me.

'You dirty old ratbag, I'll get you run in!' It was Private Peterson. I'd carelessly overlooked her presence.

'What's with Cecily?' asked Sergeant Masters and she climbed out. I followed. The village was quiet, the couple of shops shut for lunch and the *Suffolk Punch* pub was only a sleepy murmur. Jim's hat was over one ear and there was a look of confusion on his face. Private Peterson was halfway out of the canvas curtains and swinging punches.

'He groped me!' she yelled.

'Not old Jim,' I said, 'he goes to church at Christmas.'

'He's a randy old goat!' Cecily was livid.

Jim tried to explain about replacing a porridge tin. Cecily wasn't having any.

'No harm done,' I said.

'He's lousy with hormones,' she yelled, 'and so are you. One look at a girl in uniform and you're all like Attila the Hun.'

Cassidy was laughing. Sergeant Masters was frowning at Cecily.

'I ain't partial to them kind of goings-on,' protested Jim. He was very attached to his missus, she being comely. He was also attached to his chickens, his smallholding and his fiddles. 'See yer, Tim,' he said, and escaped.

44

'I'll report that kook,' said Cecily.

'Don't be like that, lovey,' I said, thinking the porridge might get a mention. 'We're all mates together, you and us. I know there's Hitler, and your generals and our generals, but the rest of us ought to be bosom chums, or what've we got that's worth dying for?'

'Am I hearing things?' asked Sergeant Masters.

'Bosom chums?' said Cassidy, a kind of glee in her eyes.

'He's at it again,' cried the upset Cecily. 'Isn't there any guy who can think of candy and blueberry pie instead of how a girl is put together?'

'Wrap it up, Cecily,' said Sergeant Masters.

'Being molested, that's got to be wrapped up?' asked Cecily, who was better-looking than she deserved to be.

'I don't believe it was meant,' said Sergeant Masters.

'He looked a cute old guy to me,' said Cassidy.

I took a peek inside the van. The petrol can was there, the sacking having fallen away. Couldn't be helped.

When we were on our way again, Sergeant Masters said, 'It's none of my business, of course, but I thought porridge over here came in cartons.'

'It's the war,' I said, 'we're short of cartons.'

'I think I've got you,' she said.

'Where now?' she asked when we reached BHQ. I indicated the orderly room. All three of them marched smartly into the mansion, leaving me lumbered with their kit. So I dumped the valises in the hall outside the orderly room in the kind of untidy heap that would make Battery Sergeant-Major Baldwin think about court-

45

martial charges. In the orderly room, only Bombardier Wilkins was on duty. He had a well-fed portly look. He'd eaten, of course. I was growling with want. Having seen what the three Wacs looked like, Wilkins suggested I could keep an eye on the orderly room while he showed them to the ATS quarters and where to catch some eats.

'I'll show 'em,' I said, 'I'll fall in half if I don't catch some eats of my own.'

'Excuses, excuses,' said Bombardier Wilkins. 'OK,' he said to the Wacs, 'Gunner Hardy will take you, but you'll have to report back here afterwards.'

'Will do,' said Sergeant Masters crisply, 'I believe I'm to meet up with a Top Sergeant Dawson.'

'You don't need him,' said Wilkins, 'you've met me.'

'We're touched,' said Sergeant Masters, 'but I've got orders.'

Wilkins was on a hiding to nothing, anyway. Top Sergeant Dawson, six feet of Kansas beef, wasn't likely to let a ravishing Wac sergeant be sucked into turmoil by a short, lumpy British bombardier.

I took the three of them round to the Nissen hut quarters of the ATS.

'Where do we get the eats?' asked Cassidy.

'Go through that door straight ahead,' I said, 'and ask for Mavis. If no-one answers or nothing happens, pop over to our cookhouse and I'll fry you an egg each on a slice of toast.'

Sergeant Masters, surveying things, asked, 'Is it kind of primitive here?'

'I'd be a liar if I said it wasn't. Cold water ablutions,

PT at six in the morning, including winter, and no candy. I hope you've all brought woolly knicks.'

'Woolly what?' asked Cassidy.

'Don't ask for details,' said Cecily, 'he's a nutter. Hey, hold it, what's happened to our bags?'

'Oh, they'll be walking about somewhere,' I said and left at the double.

In the cookhouse, which was out of bounds, I asked the sergeant-cook if there was any dinner left. 'A bone'll do, sarge, as long as there's some gravy with it.'

'Listen, d'you know what the time is?'

'Yes, dinnertime. All over the country.'

'Not here, you dozy tentpole,' he said. 'Here you nosh at twelve-thirty. So there's nothing left. What there was went gluey. I don't allow gluey leftovers to idle around in my kitchen. Nor you. Pee off.'

The leftovers had obviously been fed to the OCs ravenous Dalmatian. So I gave the sergeant a fresh egg all to himself and he let me make some fried egg sandwiches with the rest. The yolks were golden. I'd have to thank Jim's missus next time I saw her.

CHAPTER FOUR

A little brown-paper packet arrived from Aunt May, containing knitted grey socks and a letter. She was always doing things like that, sending me soldiers' comforts. In her letter she recounted local happenings that had taken place since my return to BHQ. The vicar, she said, had preached a sermon of rebuke last Sunday. It was aimed at people who thought the war gave them an excuse to be irresponsible, uncaring and even faithless. Aunt May thought the sermon came about because everyone knew Edie Hawkins was going to have a baby. It was uncomfortable news because Edie's husband was in the Middle East and had been for nearly two years. Aunt May sounded sad about it, she didn't like that sort of thing. Moreover, Edie's mother had told her that it was all because Edie had lost her head on Wimbledon Common one night last September with a married Canadian soldier. Then there was Alf Cook. He was going to be charged with assault and battery outside a pub. Aunt May said Mr Cook was a terrible headache to poor Mrs Cook, which was such a pity because he'd been heroic during the Blitz.

I replied, thanking Aunt May for the welcome socks and telling her I was sorry to learn about Edie Hawkins and her embarrassing predicament. Edie would have been better off, I said, if she'd stuck to playing tennis on Wimbledon Common. There was a lot of the other stuff about, I said, and not only on Wimbledon Common. I also told Aunt May I'd met a very good-looking American sergeant. I had to add a 'PS' after I'd finished the letter. Lady sergeant, I wrote.

I didn't want lovely old Aunt May to think I'd gone peculiar.

BHQ gave Sergeant Kit Masters and her two assistants an office on the first floor of the mansion. There, in the best traditions of American efficiency, documents were typed in quadruplicate and filed. In the orderly room, our ATS corporals never got beyond triplicate and the filing system was guesswork, due to Corporal Deborah Watts being in charge of it. Not having joined the Army to do filing, Deborah simply took no interest in it.

'I'm not a square peg in a round hole yet,' she said.

'Other way about, I'd say,' said Gunner Frisby.

'Mind your eye,' said Deborah.

'Only mentioning the obvious,' said Frisby.

'Watch it,' said Deborah.

'I am,' said Frisby.

There were mounds of reports daily for the American girls, emanating from the two American officers who came and went like anonymous shadows, in company with their driver, Top Sergeant Dawson. But nothing was secret in rural Suffolk and everyone knew they mixed military business with social pleasures. However, they did come up with a profusion of reports which Sergeant Masters said, were written in illiterate Egyptian. But

49

orders were orders, even in the American Army and so it was all translated into English by the Wacs, then typed and filed.

In keeping with a War Office belief that female Allied service personnel needed protection from male British soldiery, Sergeant Masters and her assistants were declared out of bounds to other ranks as far as their office was concerned. However, off-duty hours were another matter. Even the War Office hadn't yet thought of a way to cage other ranks off duty. Several BHQ gunners were very taken with Cassidy, the friendly blonde. Gunner Dunwoodie thought her sheer magic. But he lacked self-confidence. He was also fairly brainless. It all came to nothing, however, for Top Sergeant Dawson put in a claim that made Cassidy exclusive to him.

The news grieved Dunwoodie. 'Done it on me,' he said.

Everyone said jolly hard luck, mate.

I occasionally saw Sergeant Masters in passing. She would smile and wave, then pass briskly on. She tidied up as she went. She would correct the position of a fire extinguisher standing in the tiled hall of the mansion, adjust a displaced whitewashed lump of the stone that bordered the paths of the complex around the Nissen huts, or pick up a piece of paper that had managed to escape the eye of the sergeant-major. She would hand the scrap to the first gunner she met and say crisply, 'I guess that's yours, soldier.' She did it to me one day when we came face to face outside the ration stores.

'I guess that's yours, Tim old boy, old boy.'

I studied the scrap. It was kind of nondescript. 'No, I don't think so,' I said and handed it back.

'Wrong move,' she said and stuffed it up my battle-dress blouse. 'Listen, you're not the friendliest guy in the world, are you? You keep passing me by.'

'I thought that was you, I thought you were a born passer-by. I like a bit of stopping and talking meself. I suppose it's more difficult for sergeants, they've got a responsibility to be efficient, they can't stand about waiting for someone to come up and chat.'

'That's talking?' said Kit. 'All that eyewash? You've got room for improvement, old buddy. I'll do what I can to help. Let's see, where do you go during the evenings in this wildly exciting place?'

'Village pub, mostly.'

'You're an alcoholic?'

'Not yet.'

'Is it recommended?'

'Too much drink?'

'No, you muttonhead, the village pub.'

'Well, I like it,' I said. She brushed an eyebrow with the tip of her finger. She had a clean look. She smelled clean. And she was very American with her wide mouth and white teeth. 'It's cosy and fuggy.'

'Excuse me?'

'Fuggy.'

'Is that a word?' she asked.

'Yes, adjective of fug,' I said, showing off my secondary school education. 'Fug's smoky fog.'

'Is this a conversation?'

'Just talk.'

'It's beating my brains out,' said Kit. 'All the same, see you in the pub one evening, then?'

'Can't wait, lovey.'

'Excuse me?' said Kit again.

'Pardon?'

'What's with lovey?'

'Me,' I said, 'you get me as well as the fug.'

'I think I need time to work that one out,' said Kit.

'Help yourself. By the way, are you a bit incompetent at some things?'

'Is that a question?' she asked.

'Just thought I'd ask.'

'Why?'

'Well, I want you to know it wouldn't worry me if you were.'

'I might have been incompetent at fixing some things when I was five,' she said, 'but that's all ironed out now.'

'I was afraid of that.'

'Come again?'

'Hope the weather holds,' I said. 'See you in the pub one evening, then.'

'Don't break your back,' said Kit.

It was quiet on the whole. At least, it was in the UK. It wasn't in the Pacific or Russia, or Burma or Tunisia. And it might not have been on Wimbledon Common, either, now that the weather had turned warm. BHQ was very quiet, much to the liking of everyone except Major Moffat, our battery commander. He preferred happenings. Accordingly, when he was alerted to the possible misappropriation of WD petrol, he was only too happy to conduct an enquiry, even though he must have known it might result in two unwelcome findings. One, the misappropriation could have taken place under his nose. Two, someone in his battery could turn out to be a fiddling shower.

The first I heard about it was a week after I'd brought Sergeant Masters and her two girls to BHQ. The information arrived with Jim Beavers' daughter, the precocious Minnie. As I came off duty one afternoon, Frisby advised me she was waiting to talk to me. She was loitering outside the open double gates in the high brick wall fronting the forecourt of the mansion. In her straw boater and gymslip she looked like a peachy-faced angel, but I knew the holy terror was lurking.

'Dad sent me,' she said.

'What for?'

'To tell you.'

'Tell me what?'

'Not 'ere,' said Minnie, 'someone might be listening.'

'And looking as well,' I said, quite sure that across the road the workshop personnel were interesting themselves in what I was doing to a village schoolgirl.

Minnie got moving and I moved with her. She had a lively walk, typical of a healthy country girl. She was a south London cockney who'd turned herself into a country girl with no trouble at all. Bursting with health, Minnie was.

'Well, let's hear it, then,' I said, 'but if it's anything saucy I'll wallop you.'

She gurgled. 'Ain't you comical, Tim? You make a

girl laugh, you do.' She stopped, and from under her boater her blue eyes cast their cheekiness.

'Come on, why did your dad send you?'

'He said someone's been round.'

'Who, your Aunt Flossie?' That was her mother's aunt.

'Course not Aunt Flossie. Oh, you Tim,' she said and another gurgle escaped from her Cupid's bow. 'I'm praying, I am.'

'Praying?'

'Yes,' she said, 'I'm praying I'm goin' to be your best girl soon as I'm sixteen.'

'Well, I'm praying that when you're sixteen you'll disappear in a puff of smoke,' I said. 'Now, come on, who's been round to see your dad?'

'Some soldiers, he said. From your lot. Dad said better he didn't come and tell you himself, better he kept away. You go, Min, he said, it'll only look as if you an' Tim is courtin'.'

'Don't say things like that, Min, you'll give me a headache.'

'I didn't say it, Dad did.' Minnie fluttered her lashes. 'They went an' took his drum of petrol. He said they couldn't, they said they could an' they did. He said he thought you ought to know.'

'Nothing to do with me,' I said. 'Still, tell him I'd better not have any more eggs from him for the time being, tell him to keep them tucked into the bosom of his family.'

'Whose, Mum's or mine?' asked Minnie.

'I'll tan you,' I said.

54

'Honest?' Minnie looked eager. 'Would you, though? Be bliss, it would.'

'Don't talk daft.'

'Not daft.' Her smile was terrifying. 'You're fun, you are, Tim. Best ever. But you're shy, like.'

'Shy? Of what?'

'Me. I don't mind, though. It's nice in a way. Goin' to be your best girl, I am, you see. Oh, Dad said he won't say.'

'Won't say what?'

'Don't know, do I?' she said, the April sunshine dancing on her boater. She did know, of course, but nobody was going to prise it out of her. Good little Suffolk scout she was. In a frightening way. 'All that porridge and all, Tim.'

'Never mind what your mum gives you for breakfast, just tell your dad to say the drum dropped off the tail of a Heinkel. All right, off you go, Min. Ta for coming.'

'Kiss first,' said Minnie, standing in the lee of the hedge and pursing her lips.

'Not this year, Min.'

'But I'm sixteen in June.'

'That's not now. If I'm going to be shot at dawn with your dad, I don't want to be hanged as well.'

'Oh, I never 'eard anything dafter,' said Minnie, 'you can't be hanged just because I'm still at school and look 'ow grown up I am.' I wasn't going to look. If I did she'd take a deep breath and puff herself up.

'Buzz off, Min, behave yourself.'

'Oh, come on,' said Min. A secretive little smile appeared. 'Kiss me like you did on rising summer night.'

55

Rising summer night still had hazy recollections for me. Sheldham celebrated the advent of summer not on the first of May, but on the first Saturday in April. It was something to do with the ritual of rising summer. The village hall had been packed, American GIs there in droves. Barrels of cider were tapped, cider being the only strong beverage allowed. And it was Suffolk cider, not Somerset. Whoever brewed it had squeezed every last drop of biting juice from the apples and its heady tang was of a ripe harvest, bitter-sweet. It was a great help to the GIs, it sent them in pursuit of everything in skirts and there was a bumper crop of those. Taking no notice of whatever the band was playing, the GIs turned every number into a flying jitterbug. The ancient rustics of Sheldham looked on, nodding with the wisdom of people who knew what rising summer cider was all about. Flushed housewives and rosy-cheeked maidens were whirled around. The band was a mixture of baldheads, roundheads and whiskers, all native-born, and their music reached back to some pagan mystique of long-gone ancestors. The ritual song, 'Rising Summer', kept cropping up. There were a hundred verses to it, someone said and the natives knew them all. I only managed to pick up the first line of the chorus. *'Put 'em in a barrel and roll 'em in the barn.'* Eventually, the music and the rhythm took complete hold of the senses and everything else sounded raw and wrong.

The cider did for me. It was my first encounter with Sheldham's rising summer night. Some BHQ personnel who'd attended last year said watch the cider. And Jim Beavers said the same thing. I did watch it, pouring from a barrel into my glass several times, but once it was down my throat it was out of sight. I jitterbugged in a fog with no idea who my partners were. But one of them resolved into Minnie, at which point I made a rolling exit from the over-heated hall in search of cool fresh air. I also needed a wall to lean against. The fresh air and the coolness of the April night kind of clouted me. Minnie insisted on helping me in my search for a wall. I had a vague idea that a lot of wall was occupied by GIs and village maidens, but Minnie found a welcome piece of secluded brickwork for my back.

'There, ain't that nice, Tim?' she murmured.

'Where's a bed?' I asked unthinkingly. I meant a quiet spot where I could fall quietly down without breaking a leg. I knew I'd never trust Suffolk cider on rising summer night again. Minnie drew her own inference.

'Oh, no need for a bed, Tim,' she said. 'It'll be bliss any old how with you and I won't tell Dad.' She put her mouth to mine.

Fortunately, I fell down then and Mother Earth drew me to her cool and comforting bosom. When I came to I had a racketing head and the hall was emptying. Minnie had disappeared. I didn't think anything had happened until I tasted lipstick. Then I worried a little. Then I didn't. Nothing illegal could have happened, the cider had pole-axed me.

But I wasn't too keen now on her secretive little smile. 'Hold it,' I said, 'what d'you mean, kiss you like I did on rising summer night?'

'Ain't telling, am I?' she said, trying to look coy. Coy? What a hope. 'Won't tell Dad, neither.'

'Won't tell what?'

'Not saying, am I?' She looked sunny and girlish and innocent against the green hedge. Wonderful little actress, she was.

'I hope you're not going to grow up a bit devious, Min.'

'Me? Course I won't, I couldn't, not with you,' she protested. 'Want to be your best girl, don't I?'

'But don't you fancy a GI from Hollywood, like all the girls?'

'Hollywood, that's a laugh,' she said. 'I'm not soppy, yer know. Just want you, Tim.'

'Min, that's silly,' I said.

'No, it ain't,' said Min, 'it's nice an' you don't want someone else to get me, do you?'

'If anyone gets you at your age your dad'll slice his legs off. It's not going to be my legs. I need them for walking about and marching. Now be a sensible girl and go home.'

'Tim, just one kiss, can't you?' she said.

I looked around. The narrow winding country road was quiet. I gave in. I kissed her. A peck on her mouth. But her lips parted and she started to eat me. I almost fell over. I thought of village eyes from which nothing escaped, even at this distance. I thought of a court of law and of Minnie in her gymslip giving evidence, saying I overpowered her. She would too. Self-protective young maiden, she was. She had to be in a village as small as Sheldham. I pushed her off. She looked at me, her eyes wide open, her breath escaping.

'Minnie—'

'Oh, you Tim,' she said faintly and actually dropped her head.

'Not my fault you didn't like it.'

'That's all you know.' Her boater came up and her face wore a little smile. 'Wasn't it lovely, rising summer night?'

'I don't know, was it? I was knocked out myself.'

The little smile was secretive again. 'I'll tell Dad,' she said.

'Tell him what?' I asked, feeling alarmed.

'That you give us a good 'un.'

'Good what?'

'Kiss,' she said. 'Soon as I'm sixteen, can I tell 'im an' Mum we're walkin' out?'

'If you carry on like this, you terror, by the time you're sixteen you'll be lethal and I'll be dead.'

She laughed. She looked creamy and larky. 'You're fun, you are, Tim. Never goin' to want anyone but you. I'll tell Dad I told you about the porridge.' She went then, jauntily and with a little swish of her gymslip. What the war had done to evacuated cockney girls had to be seen to be believed. Meanwhile I had to think about the fact that Jim had been shopped, his illicit juice confiscated. It would be analysed. WD petrol contained more lead than rationed civilian stuff. The law would lay its wartime hand on Jim and in the court he'd have to take his hat off, which he never did normally.

I went back to BHQ. I tasted lipstick. I'd tasted it before. Same flavour. Going through the gates I saw Kit coming out of the house, a thick folder in her hand. She liked work. She liked it enough to carry it about with her.

'Could I have a word?' I asked.

'I can lend an ear to you, Tim, old boy. Is it going to be for real this time? Only you've got a lean and hungry look.'

'Better than Top Sergeant Dawson's fat look.'

'Correction, soldier,' said Kit, 'Sergeant Dawson's a fine manly guy.'

'Yes, fine, big and fat.'

'I'll give him your message,' said Kit, her smile crisp. 'By the way, can you tell me why this cosy place is full of men called gunners and bombardiers and not a gun in sight?'

'We're admin,' I said, 'like your Washington admirals.'

'*Touché*,' said the lady sergeant, 'I'll pass on Washington admirals.'

'You're very kind. Listen, remember Jim Beavers?'

'Should I?'

'You met him in the village the day I bused you here.'

'Oh, sure.' Her response was friendly but a little cautious, I thought. 'That was Jim Beavers, Private Peterson's private nightmare?'

'I think Major Moffat dropped in on him,' I said.

She frowned. 'Well, I guess that had to happen,' she said. 'Is he going to drop in on you, too?'

'I hope not. I mean, I hope you and I are on the same side.'

60

Kit looked me straight in the eye. 'What does that mean?' she asked.

'Well, someone put the finger on Jim,' I said.

'Old buddy,' she said bitingly, 'you're an amateur.'

'Amateur what?'

'Comic,' she said and went briskly on her way.

Sergeant Johnson passed by. He gave me a hatchet look. I had a feeling I was going to fail the inquiry.

CHAPTER FIVE

The *Suffolk Punch* was packed out, mainly with GIs. There was an American Air Force base a few miles away. The GIs thought the pub was cute, but that its name was a crazy one for a horse. Both bars, the saloon and the public, provided them with welcome opportunities to fraternize with the local talent. Gunner Frisby conceded the village maidens were on to a good thing. Not only were the GIs relatively rich, but they all lived in Hollywood. Or near it. Frisby said he'd decided not to compete, that he'd wait until the war was over and all the Yanks had gone home. Then he might be able to take his pick of some of the maidens who'd been left behind.

I didn't think that was too brilliant. Suppose there were no maidens left, suppose the GIs took the lot?

'But there's millions of maidens,' said Frisby.

'There's millions of GIs too,' I said. 'There's nearly a million in this pub.'

I was in favour of a nice, well-behaved maiden myself. So was Aunt May. She was devoted to the idea of my ending up with a sweet and respectable girl.

Frisby, formerly a young and ambitious clerk in a town hall surveyor's department, favoured post-war bliss with a little woman who'd be a help to him and didn't put curlers in her hair at night. He fancied working up from a semi-detached and a mortgage to a manor house by the time he was fifty, with his offspring riding about on horseback. Currently, that idea was taking a hiding, for he hadn't met any potential little woman who didn't prefer a Californian manor house next door to Gary Cooper.

'Makes you feel resigned to waiting till the war's over,' he said. We'd managed to take possession of a table in the corner of the public. At the bar, GIs were jammed six deep and in the jam were several local females. 'By the way,' said Frisby, 'I hear there's a stink on about flogged juice.'

'Just a rumour,' I said hopefully, sipping my old and mild.

'The major's mounting an inquiry,' said Frisby. 'I heard he sent troops to storm someone's chicken shed. Foxy old Jim's shed, was it?'

'Old Jim? Backbone of England,' I said. Someone had shopped him. I hoped I hadn't been mentioned. Major Moffat had no understanding of perks.

Sergeant Masters came in then with Cassidy and Cecily. Cecily looked as if she'd rather be somewhere else. She twitched at the horrendous number of men present. Cassidy blinked in the fug. The scrum of GIs broke apart and invited the Wacs into their midst. Cecily retreated as far as she could. Her skirted bottom nudged our table. She hissed, jumped and turned. Frisby, fascinated by her behaviour, rose to his feet.

'D'you need help?' he asked.

Cecily looked at him with dark suspicion. Frisby offered a helpful smile.

'Drop dead,' she breathed. A GI approached, touched her elbow and asked her if she'd like a drink. She sprang back. Frisby insistently saw her into the safety of the corner chair. She subsided, quivering, poor girl.

'Like a cider?' offered Frisby.

'Go away.'

'Nowhere to go,' he said 'All right, you just sit there, I'll see that nobody gets to you. Don't mind if Tim and me play draughts, do you?' He opened up a draughts board and we played amid the din. Frisby was a suspect opponent. He had a shocking habit of reversing a move after he'd taken his hand away.

'Hi, Brits.' Cassidy had arrived, so had Kit. They both had drinks. Gin and tonics. 'OK to join you guys?' said Cassidy, 'It looks safer here than it is over there.'

'Welcome,' I said. I pulled up a couple of chairs and they sat down.

'Checkers?' said Kit, eyeing the board with interest.

'Draughts,' I said.

'Same game,' she said and took off her cap. Her hair shone blue-black in the smoky light. 'Carry on playing.'

It was my move. I put a hand on one of my kings. Kit shook her head.

'No?' I said.

'It's not your best move, is it?' she said. I took my hand away. Kit, convinced I needed help, made my move for me. Frisby, leaving Cecily strictly alone, eyed the move suspiciously.

'Any advice, Miss Peterson?' asked Frisby, hand poised over the board.

'Miss Peterson?' said Cassidy. 'Who is this guy? I thought I knew him.'

Cecily put more space between herself and Frisby. 'Get lost,' she said. She had a very limited vocabulary.

'I just thought you might have an interesting move in mind,' said Frisby.

Cecily glared at him, obviously thinking he was propositioning her. Frisby gave her a fatherly smile. Fatherly? Frisby? Cecily muttered. Frisby pushed his leading king forward, thought for a moment and then left it there. Kit gave me a triumphant smile. Frisby, noticing, moved his king back. Kit sat straight up.

'You can't do that,' she said.

'Can't do what?' asked Frisby.

'You can't alter a move once you've taken your hand off,' said Kit.

'Wasn't a definite move,' said Frisby, 'just a feint.'

'You must play to the rules or what's the point? And there are principles.' Principles? 'Look,' she said to me, 'it's up to you to discourage this guy in his sneaky cheating. If you don't you're an accessory to his delinquency.'

'So how does that grab you, Tim, old boy?' said Cassidy.

'Sounds all right,' I said.

'It beats me, all this carry-on because I like to think twice about a move,' said Frisby.

'Get on with it,' I said and we resumed the contest.

Cecily gradually came to life, though in a guarded

way and joined forces with Cassidy to make a back-up team for Frisby, while Kit interfered helpfully with my play. The game ended in a draw. I caught sight of Jim Beavers then, a briar pipe poking out from under his hat. He was playing dominoes with native cronies. I looked at him. He looked at me. We decided not to know each other. Best thing under the circs.

Kit challenged me to a game. Cecily actually set out the board. Frisby gave her another fatherly smile. It raised her hackles.

'Don't worry, you're doing fine,' he said.

Kit and I began our game, eyeball to eyeball. Her white teeth gleamed. She played with verve and confidence. She thrust forward, plunging into my ranks, but left a hole or two so that when it appeared she had me scattered, I crowned a couple of kings and annihilated her.

'Cute,' she laughed.

'How about it, Cecily, care for a game?' asked Frisby in a kind way.

'Keep off,' said Cecily.

'Sure?' said Frisby.

'Oh, OK, but don't louse me up,' said Cecily. She proved so good that Frisby, tottering on the edge of disaster, broke the rules again. He took a move back. Cecily stared at him.

'Fact is, I hadn't actually made up my mind,' he said.

'He's doing it again,' said Kit. 'He's unbelievable.'

'Look,' said Frisby, 'if Cecily thinks I'm pulling a fast one—'

'No, that's OK,' said Cecily. 'Carry on.' Well, good

old Cecily, she'd come round to saying something friendly.

Frisby's defeat, however, was only delayed. It caught up with him three moves later. 'Done me,' he said, 'what a turn-up.' He gave Cecily an admiring look. Cecily swallowed. 'Don't worry,' he said kindly, 'it hurt me the most.'

Top Sergeant Dawson thundered in like a walking tree trunk in a hurry. He cast his eyes around, looking for Cassidy.

'Here's my guy,' said Cassidy, and wrinkled her nose.

'I'm off myself,' said Frisby, 'no late pass. Like to come with me, Cecily?'

'Oh, hell,' said Cecily, but in surprising fashion she got up and went with him.

Kit said she had to get back. She also said she wanted to talk to me. We left the pub together. It was a twenty-minute hike to BHQ. The evening was cool, its freshness welcome. The cottages, their windows blacked-out, peered darkly at us. Kit walked with a brisk swing, her right hand on the strap of her shoulder bag.

'You had something to say to me?' I asked.

'Sure, I do,' she said. 'About your friend. Jim Beavers, that's his name, isn't it? You said he was in trouble. He is. He's suspected of being in unauthorized possession of army gasoline.' We were passing Jim's cottage. It was quiet. The chickens were roosting, the dogs lying in wait for foxes.

'Can't believe it of old Jim, can you?' I said.

'I can. And if it's true, he's a saboteur, a fifth columnist.'

'Never. Not old Jim. He's a Suffolk cockney, the soul of old England.'

'Don't make me hysterical, old buddy,' said Kit. 'By the way, if you're worried about yourself, I can tell you your name hasn't been mentioned.'

'Hasn't been mentioned by whom?'

'One can't answer every question. I just thought you'd like to know it's only your friend, the soul of old England, who's due for comeuppance.'

'I might not like it too much,' I said, 'I might be someone who worries about his friends. In any case, I could still be sunk myself. They'll check the spare cans of every vehicle. Every driver is logged for every journey. I mostly drive the Austin. If they find its can empty, they'll work backwards to find out who emptied it.'

'You can say you did, can't you? You don't mind lying, do you?'

'Well, we're only talking about allowable perks.'

'Allowable perks?'

'Goes back a long way. It's traditional. Take your lot in your Civil War, nicking chickens. That's perks. Look, if I said I used that spare juice, I'd have had to log it and report it to the workshop staff-sergeant.'

'Why didn't you?'

'I had some eggs to fry, I'd missed dinner.'

'Hasn't anyone driven that mousetrap since then?' she asked.

'Probably and they'll be suspect too.'

'So you'll own up?' she said.

'Pardon?'

'Well, you do have a conscience, don't you?' she said, her skirt swishing in the darkness.

'Look, love,' I said, 'everyone concerned will fall down in a fit if I own up. When they've got you in uniform for the duration, you leave your Sunday School conscience at home and concentrate on survival. Doesn't it strike you as trivial, fussing about a spare can of porridge?'

'So that's what you call army gasoline. Poor old buddy, don't you know chickens always come home to roost?'

'Not if you can get them into the oven first,' I said. We were well out of the village, walking along the quiet country road towards BHQ. It was winding, and hedged on both sides. And the night was dark and someone was behind us. I stopped and turned. I could only see shadows. Even so, I thought about someone with frustrations and the sex appeal of Sergeant Masters. She stopped herself then, some twenty yards on. One shadow moved and materialized into something dark and wiry. Under a hat.

'Hold on a moment,' I called to Kit and went to have a word with Jim. 'Stop lurking about,' I said, 'you'll frighten people.'

'I ain't lurkin', just follering,' said Jim in a hoarse whisper. 'You got yer female sergeant there. Good 'un, is she, Tim? Ain't 'er fault she's soldiering, it's the cock-eyed war, that's what it is. Only she's in the way just now, seein' I got what we need.'

'And what's that?'

'This. Some o' yourn.' He showed me a rusty can. I

could just make it out. 'Me reserve stock, like. Keep it in a potato sack.'

· 'It's WD stuff?'

'Ain't like the muck they took,' he said. 'There was a bit of WD in that there drum but not much and what there was was mixed with paraffin an' turps. I wasn't born yesterday, it don't do to be born yesterday.'

'You're right, Jim. What's this can of WD for?'

'Refill.' He grinned. 'There's an empty can, ain't there? That's 'ow they're goin' to nick you, Tim boy, on account of the empty one. Know what they done with all the cans?'

'I only know they pinched your drum.'

'That won't give 'em no joy. Listen, they got them cans cuddlin' up in your vehicle workshop, me young mate. I got to hear round about teatime today. A friend knocked on me back door. Them cans is being inspected official in the morning, to see what's full and what ain't. One's empty, you reckon?'

'The Austin's, for sure, unless any of the workshop staff checked it and had it filled up. But then, Staff-Sergeant Dix, who's in charge, would have wanted to know more about why it was empty.'

'Well, lad, you show me and if it's still empty, we'll fill it up with this canful,' said Jim. 'You don't want no army messin' you about. Missus likes you. Make sure our Tim don't get executed, she said. So you lead and I'll foller.'

I had a few more words with him first, about how to get into the workshop without being spotted, then rejoined Kit.

'I know who that old goat is,' she said as we resumed our walk.

'Yes, he's a useful old handyman,' I said. 'I'm glad you're fond of him too. Now, when we reach BHQ, you talk to the guard on the gates to keep him occupied—'

'Come again?' said Kit.

'While I pop across to the workshop. It won't take long.'

'Right first time it won't,' she said, 'I'm not doing it. Leave me out.'

'I can't do that,' I said, 'you're our anchor man and you can't hide behind those upside-down stripes all the time. You've got to stand up and be counted when a friend's having problems.'

'What friend?'

'It'll be quite simple. I'll explain.'

'Don't bother,' she said, swinging along at a brisker pace.

'It's part of the night guards' duty to keep an eye on the workshop to make sure a vehicle doesn't get nicked by some farmer short of transport for carrying cows to market. I'll take you to a Suffolk market when the war's over and you can buy a cow to take home to your family. Better than a fake brass rubbing from Birmingham. There'll only be one guard on duty. Just keep him occupied with some encouraging female talk and keep him with his back to the workshop.'

'Encouraging female talk?' said Kit. 'That's out for a start. Nothing doing, old boy. When a crook gets himself stuck in the mud, let him pull himself out. Giving him a hand would be a mistake. He'd not only think he was

71

entitled to it, but there'd be the risk of being pulled in with him. Is that loud and clear, Hardy?'

'It ruddy well is, but is it friendly? Is it even right? Not on your nelly. You can't stand aside and see a brother soldier go under.'

'Can't I?' she said. We were nearing BHQ. Jim was a silent ghost behind us. 'Listen, you crook, how long would I have to keep the guard occupied?'

'Only about ten minutes. Easy for a good-looking sergeant like you.'

'Cut the soap,' she said. 'Where's the nearest Episcopalian church?'

'Hold on, you're not going to bring Jesus in, are you? Do we want to?'

'Where is it?'

'Your kind of church? Nearest one's probably in Sudbury. That's fifteen miles away and I don't think you'll catch a service at this time of night.'

BHQ loomed up. Kit came to a halt.

'I'm crazy,' she said. The vehicle yard and workshop opposite BHQ were just visible from the gates. Occasionally, the man on guard would cross the road and patrol about the place.

Jim sidled up. 'Is she on, Tim lad?' he whispered.

'Oh, shoot,' she breathed and left us. She was on. She walked to the open gates. We waited, tucking ourselves out of sight. We heard her voice. It sounded cooing. Cooing? A cooing sergeant? That had to do the trick.

Jim and I slipped across the road, rounding a parked Bedford lorry to ghost into the workshop. Everything was locked up, of course. Jim produced a small torch with a tiny but bright beam. The staff-sergeant in charge of vehicle maintenance had an office in the workshop, with upper glass panels. The torch picked out six petrol cans in lined-up formation on the office floor. The door was locked. Jim fumbled in a pocket and brought forth a ring of many keys. He began trying them, one after the other.

'Don't muck about, Jim, it's not Christmas. Get it open.'

The lock clicked.

'Good 'un, you are,' said Jim to the lucky key and we went in. 'Where's yourn?' he whispered.

'How do I know? They're all WD cans, all the same. Just find the empty one.'

Jim, running his beam of light over the identical cans, disclosed the fact that there was a chalked number on each. I hefted them, one by one. Four were full, two were empty. Two? Someone else was in the market?

'Them two's both empty?' said Jim.

'Ruddy hell, yes.'

'Bleedin' old system's up the spout, then,' he said. 'Ain't much help to you if we fill the wrong one. Missus won't like that, she'll knock me 'ead off.'

'Fill 'em both,' I said.

'Corker you are, Tim boy,' said Jim and filled one of the empties from his rusty can. I filled the other from one of the full cans. As the juice gurgled in he asked, 'You after Minnie?'

'Am I what? You off your rocker? What sort of a question is that at a time like this?'

'Only askin',' said Jim.

73

'Listen, Minnie's too young for that kind of lark.'

'You might be, she ain't.' Jim chuckled. 'She's been sayin' you fancy her. I know she fancies you.'

'Find her a decent GI when she's sixteen.'

'That won't work, Tim. It's you Min's after.' The petrol gurgled to a stop. A minute later we were out, the door locked again, the workshop at our backs. Jim got lost before I realized he'd gone. I approached the gates and went through. I heard the crisp patter of retreating footsteps. That sounded as if Kit had just finished doing her good deed. Good old American scout she was, after all.

The guard appeared and poked his rifle at me. 'Friend or foe?' he demanded. It was Gunner Dunwoodie. If I'd known, I'd not have worried so much. On the other hand, even a fellow squaddie short on brains can sometimes rate good conduct marks more important than comradeship. We all hoped for promotion and a corresponding increase in pay.

'Don't get excited, Woodie,' I said. 'It's only me.'

'Thought it was,' he said, peering. 'She said it would be.'

'Who said?'

'The Wac sergeant. You been followin' 'er?'

'Why not? I've just won her in a raffle down at the pub.'

'Don't gimme that. Think I'm daft? She told me you'd been actin' queer, lookin' at 'er in the pub with staring eyes. That ain't good, yer know. She said you were creepy and asked me if you'd got a prison record.'

'Poor woman, what a sad case,' I said. 'Enjoyed your chat with her, did you?'

The gormless turnip smirked. 'She told me what a healthy change I was after your staring eyes. You ain't gone peculiar on 'er, have you? Tell you what, I think I fancy 'er meself, I think I wouldn't mind meetin' 'er under the ATS shower.'

'All right, lovey,' I said, 'I'll hold your rifle while you join her in the ATS ablutions. But take your towel with you or she'll think you've come for more than a shower.'

'What d'yer mean?' he asked.

'And keep your trousers on as well,' I said.

'Eh?'

'Or you'll get arrested yourself,' I said and went off to bed.

CHAPTER SIX

'Right,' said Major Moffat. Broad, rugged and vigorous, he had been a territorial officer when the war broke out and had worked his way up from first lieutenant to battery commander by sheer dedication. He expected similar dedication from everyone in uniform. He also expected military smartness. Even the ATS personnel weren't safe from his eagle eye. If he saw any girl with the slightest wrinkle in her khaki stockings he'd rap out, 'Pull 'em up, girl, pull 'em up.'

He had seven men lined up in the workshop, including me. He cast his glinting eyes over us, looking as if he was quite sure one of us was a traitor. His enormous Dalmatian hound and Staff-Sergeant Dix stood by. The dog was not without the right kind of instincts, especially where food was concerned. I think it knew one of us was to be served up for its dinner.

The spare petrol cans were to be checked in our presence. The major, on a point of principle, wished us to know the inspection wasn't going to be carried out behind our backs. All seven of us had been logged as having taken out transport on a particular day. I was sure I knew which particular day. No-one cared to advise the major that there was a certain amount of friendly casualness concerning spare petrol, that it came under the heading of perks.

The cans were brought from Staff-Sergeant Dix's office and placed in a neat line. The major surveyed them and his hound nosed them. The major smacked one gloved hand with his cane. 'Staff-Sergeant Dix,' he said, 'in the event of any of these cans being empty, I'll want to know which vehicles they belong to and which driver or drivers used that vehicle on said day. I'll want to know why it was that use of spare petrol wasn't reported, wasn't logged and wasn't even bloody well noticed.'

'Sir,' said Staff-Sergeant Dix smartly.

'A quantity of petrol has been removed from the premises of a civilian,' said the major. 'It's being analysed. I hope it doesn't prove to be WD petrol emanating from here. It could mean the gallows for some despicable fairy. Is that clear? Carry on, staff.'

Sergeant Dix produced a notebook. A gunner in denims put his hand on the can chalk-marked number one.

'Full,' he reported, as he hefted the can.

'Bedford, sir,' said Sergeant Dix, referring to his notebook.

Number two can, full. A Morris. Number three can, full. The Austin utility. Number four can, empty. The Hillman, Major Moffat's own official transport.

'What?' said the major.

'Empty, sir,' breathed the workshop gunner hoarsely and the major cast a fiendish eye at Sergeant Dix, who referred again to his notebook.

'Yes, Hillman, sir,' he said faintly and carried on dazedly. The fifth and six cans were both full. 'Sir?' said Dix in an ill voice.

'Almighty Jesus,' said the major and looked at his driver, Lance-Bombardier Burley, lined up with the rest of us. Burley closed his eyes and silently prayed. The Dalmatian rumbled impatiently. The major walked slowly around the cans. He struck the empty one with his cane. It rang hollowly. Getting his breath back he said, 'This one belongs to the Hillman, you say?'

'Yes, sir.' Numbly, Sergeant Dix explained that each can had been carefully numbered before being lifted from its vehicle and placed in his office, all under his careful supervision.

'You weren't told if a can was full or empty?' enquired the major.

'Orders, sir, were that we were only to number the cans and deposit them under lock and key.'

'The clot who lifted that can from wherever didn't mention it was empty?'

'No, sir, not to me,' said Sergeant Dix.

It was obvious what the major thought. That an empty can had been filled from the Hillman's can. His face was a study, his eyes a metallic grey. He addressed us. 'You bleeders,' he said. We stood rigidly to attention. 'It's an out-and-out fiddle, you hear me? By God, I never thought I'd live to see the day when some conscripted disciples of Fagin would frame their battery commander. You horse-tails, which of you is the big shot, eh? Who's the smart Alec who's master-minding the piracy?' He walked up and down the line, eyeing each of us in turn.

He knew he'd not only been diddled, he also knew he had no hope of discovering how. His dog seemed to share his frustration. It growled. 'Down, Jupiter,' he said, 'down, boy. You'll have to wait. But we'll get 'em. The whole festering bunch are in on it, I shouldn't wonder. But who's the ripe pineapple, who's the po-faced ring-leader?' He looked piercingly at me. 'Is it you, Hardy?' I kept quiet. 'You've got all the chat and the crust and he's a friend of yours, isn't he?'

'Who, sir?'

'The village black marketeer, Jim Beavers.'

'I wouldn't call him that, sir.'

'I'll get the bleeder,' said Major Moffat, 'and anyone else who's his partner in crime. This is a deferred hanging party. All right, dismiss them, staff.'

Dismissed, we filed out. The Dalmatian rumbled. I made my way to the orderly room. Heads lifted as I entered. Corporal Deborah Watts, standing beside Sergeant Johnson's desk, showed a slight wrinkle in one stocking.

'Pull 'em up, Deb,' I said.

'Beg your pardon?'

'Yes, message from Major Moffat. Pull 'em up.'

Knowing what that meant, Corporal Watts took a look at her stockings. 'Some people,' she said and retired behind her desk to sit down and do what was necessary.

'Well, Hardy,' said Sergeant Johnson, 'been remanded pending a court-martial, have you?'

'Tim, was it really you?' asked Corporal Deirdre Allsop, currently the ambition of a GI from Baltimore

79

and accordingly looking most of the time as if the war was a bit of an irrelevance.

'Was it me what?' I asked, sitting down.

'Were you the juice flogger, that's what,' said Bombardier Wilkins.

'It fell down dead,' I said.

'What did?' asked Frisby, in line to become Cecily's friendly psychoanalyst.

'The inquiry. It fell down dead. False alarm.'

'Sounds like the triumph of iniquity to me,' said Sergeant Johnson.

'No, survival of the innocent,' I said. 'Jesus was with us.'

Later, I ran into Sergeant Masters. In the hall. 'I was coming to see you,' she said. 'What happened?'

'Not guilty.'

'You got away with it?' she asked disbelievingly.

'It all went up in smoke,' I said. 'You're a good old sergeant, thanks for your help and I'm overlooking what you told Gunner Dunwoodie about me.'

'I'm touched,' she said, 'but why I let you turn me into a half-wit I'll never know.'

'Hand of friendship, that was,' I said. 'Look, we could have a few dates, if you feel keen enough.'

'I think we've already got a date,' she said.

'Have we? I didn't know.'

'I'm working on it,' she said and whisked away up the stairs to her out-of-bounds sanctum. Her stocking seams were arrow-straight.

I called on Jim that evening. In the twilight. Halfway

down the village street, I met Minnie. What a walking advertisement she was for all that the rural life of Suffolk could do for a cockney girl. Not only had she acquired a healthy country look, but her fair hair was the colour of ripe corn. But was it Suffolk or Camberwell that had made a minx of her?

In a blue dress, she danced up to me. 'Oh, you Tim,' she said in her usual scatty way.

'All right, you Min, take it easy, I've had a long day.'

'Blessed old war,' said Min, 'but bliss meetin' you. I'll put it down in me diary tonight, like I always do. I'll put down I met Tim and 'e give us a good 'un.'

'What good 'un?'

'Kiss,' said Minnie.

'Not likely, I'm fighting that.'

'Won't do you no good, Tim,' she said, her smile stunning. 'Glad you got off, Mum said if you didn't she'd knock Dad's block off.'

'How'd you know I got off?'

'Little dicky bird flew in, didn't it?' she said and laughed. Then she gave me an accusing look. 'Dad said you're gettin' to know that American girl sergeant. You'd better not.'

'Better not what?'

'Break 'er legs, I will, both of 'em,' said young Miss Beavers.

'Listen, you daft infant—'

'Ain't an infant,' she said, 'nearly a woman, I am. You Tim, don't you go takin' American girls out or I'll fall down dead. You wait for me, I'll be old enough soon.'

81

'I'll fall down dead myself in a minute. Why aren't you indoors doing your homework?'

'Done it, now I'm going to see Aunt Flossie.'

'You ever going back to London to live?' I asked.

'Don't know, do I?' she said. 'Except I like it here. D'you like it here?'

'Well, it's got to be better than Burma.'

'I know one thing,' said Min and laughed and went on her way. She turned. 'Goin' to be your best girl, that's what I know.' And she laughed again.

I went to Jim's cottage and knocked on the front door. His missus appeared. I was fond of his missus. She was thirty-seven and as handsome as a squire's wife. Suffolk had laid its rich rural mark on her too. She was brimful of female health. Her brown hair was thick, her brown eyes full of milk chocolate. She was generous and warm-hearted. Her smile showed it. And she looked a picture of Suffolk ripeness in a white sweater and a pleated brown skirt. The sweater was her own knit. She was what Aunt May would have been if life had been kinder to her, a complete wife and mum.

'Why, Tim ducky.' Her smile became even warmer. 'Come in, do, there's a love.'

We were friends, me and Missus. I'd done one or two odd jobs for her, like re-hanging a door and fixing a couple of disjointed banister rails. Jim only did outside jobs. He couldn't stand messing about in the house. There was no profit in it.

'Jim in?' I asked, stepping through the front door into a little hall and accompanying Missus into the parlour which was full of good old-fashioned furniture.

'Jim's down the pub,' said Missus, 'he's had an 'ard day. Sit yourself down, Tim, you been up against it yourself lately. Still, it's all come right, we heard.'

'Yes, I heard you heard. How did you hear?'

'Dicky birds, love. One come by and flew in.' Missus sat me down on the sofa and plumped cushions up for me, her bosom softly brushing my shoulder. 'All that fuss over a bit of petrol with a war on and all. You're a nice young chap, Tim, like Jim was when I met him in Camberwell years ago. I'll make us a cup of tea while you wait for him, he'll only be a couple of hours.'

'How long?'

'Don't you worry now, you and me can have a talk. And would you like a ham sandwich? I'll make one.'

'I don't know I ought to be here two hours, Missus, with Jim at the pub and Minnie at your Aunt Flossie's.'

'Oh, you met her on the way did you?' smiled Missus. 'Growin' up, that girl is. I sent her to Aunt Flossie's so Aunt Flossie could give her a talkin'-to about growin' up. Best if girls get talked to by their aunts and not their mums. Now you sit there, I won't be a minute.'

She wasn't long. A pot of tea and a ham sandwich appeared in no time at all. Like Aunt May, she was a marvel in a kitchen. In a kitchen, women do wondrous works. Women are born to make men fit to face life. We all ought to have one. It hardly matters that some of them are a bit barmy.

I didn't ask where the ham came from. It was off the bone. Jim and Missus both had ways and means. She shared the pot of tea and the sofa with me.

'Minnie says she likes Suffolk, Missus.'

'Likes you better, Tim, a bit gone on you, that she is.'

'Can't you find her a growing Boy Scout?'

'Our Min? That girl's gone past Boy Scouts, love. Got her eyes on you.' Missus frowned. 'We can't let her get you, though, not at her age, can we? Mind, she's comin' up for sixteen soon and fancying her chances. Jim and me can't have that, sixteen's still too young. Not that she won't make a nice bride when she's eighteen.'

'I'll be old enough to be her dad by then.'

'Course you won't, Tim, what a daft thing to say and she's got a dad anyway. She's got female curiosity too, you know how it is with growin' girls.'

'Don't know a thing,' I said, 'I've never been a growing girl. I've been a growing boy, but that's all in the past now.'

'Ah, you're a manly young chap,' said Missus in Suffolk fashion and smiled softly. 'You got nice ways too, but you're a bit shy, like. Haven't you never had a girl, Tim?'

'I'm saving myself for when it's legal, Missus.'

'Legal wedlock I expect you mean, ducky. Best we talk about these things. You don't want to hold back, not when you could be a pleasure to a woman.'

'Eh?'

'Mrs Ford across the street now, she said you're the nicest soldier she ever met. Look at the way you mended her shed when you had a Sunday off.'

'I didn't mend it, Missus, I stood it up and rebuilt it. Somehow her evacuee, young Wally Ricketts, had managed to push it over.'

'Yes, all the trouble you took over it,' said Missus warmly. 'She was that grateful, what with her hubby bein' away at the war and all. She said you didn't want payin', not a farthing, not anything.'

'Just a small good turn, Missus. Who wants paying for that?'

'Still,' said Missus.

'And she did give me several cups of tea and some cake.'

A laugh escaped Missus. Rich and creamy, it was, like Minnie's. Thoughts of my future at that point took in a picture of a healthy country girl.

'Pity you never had a girl, Tim, you wouldn't go backin' off if you had.'

'Well, I don't feel desperate,' I said. 'Mind, I do feel nice girls are getting less. I think it's these GIs, they're all over the place. Still, I'll take a chance on finding one eventually, one who'll make a nice wife.'

'Yes, legal wedlock's best, Tim.' Missus smiled again. It was like melting honey. 'But it's best you know how to be a pleasure to your bride, best you know what she'd like you to know.'

'Yes, I suppose so. Pardon?'

'A bridegroom ought to know what he's doin', lovey, and the bride won't ask questions, she'll just be grateful like.'

These were deep waters to me. 'How's the chickens, Missus? Still laying all right, are they?'

'There you go, Tim, backin' off and bein' shy.' Missus shook her head at me. 'You ought to learn a bit of lovin' before you get married, it won't be no good bein' a shy bridegroom. It's brides that's shy, it's natural with brides.'

'Virgin brides, you mean?' I asked.

Missus looked shocked. 'Now don't you go marryin' no girl who isn't,' she said. 'Jim and me wouldn't like some tarty girl gettin' hold of you. I'll help you, love.'

'Kind of you, Missus, but if I can't manage to find the right kind of girl myself—'

'I don't mean that, lovey, I mean I'll help to learn you how to be a pleasure to her.'

'Eh?'

'It's what nice married women are for, bein' helpful to nice young chaps.'

'Now watch what you're saying, Missus, I don't fancy—'

'Don't lay down no law, Tim. Married women like to be helpful, so don't go discouragin' them. I'd be terrible pleased to be a lovin' help to you.'

'Holy cows,' I said, 'I'll faint in a minute. Are you saying—'

'Yes, course I am, love.' Missus cooed. 'I could start learnin' you now.'

'Over my dead body,' I said. 'And over Jim's,' I added for good measure.

'Ah, Jim, now he got help from my Aunt Flossie,' beamed Missus. 'She liked him when he was a shy young chap like you and learned him very lovin'. On our weddin' night—'

'No, save it, Missus, I can't listen to any more.'

'Yes, you can, love, it's educatin'.' Missus seemed determined to paralyse me. 'I was a terrible bundle of nerves on our weddin' night, even though Aunt Flossie told me not to worry. She was right, Jim performed magical.'

'Well, I'm pleased for you, Missus, but I'm not sure we're in the same room together. And suppose Jim was listening, he'd have kittens.'

'Course he wouldn't, love.' Missus smiled re-assuringly. 'He knows I'm set on helpin' you. I told him I'd give you some learnin' and he said I was born kind and helpful. Best you let me learn you, love, you don't want some tarty girl doin' it, you never know where they've been. Tim, is that you blushin'?'

'Well, I tell you, Missus, I'm hot all over and that's a fact. It's not on and Jim ought to be executed for agreeing to it. Look, a bit of porridge in exchange for some eggs now and again, I can live with that, but I can't go in for this sort of stuff. It's ruddy social anarchy.'

'Bless us,' said Missus, 'don't you talk lovely, Tim? Now we've got plenty of time for learnin'—'

'Not tonight, Missus,' I said, 'I think a sergeant friend of mine is waiting for me in the pub.'

'Ah, that female American sergeant,' said Missus knowingly. In this village they knew about everything before it happened. 'Best you be careful with her, our Min can get terrible jealous.'

'Nothing to do with Min.'

'I told you, she's a bit gone on you, love. Now, let's—'

'Nothing doing,' I said and escaped before she had a chance to paralyse me.

She followed me to the front door. 'There, you're still shy, Tim, I can see that,' she said. 'We'll wait till next time, say tomorrow or the evenin' after. Get Jim to treat you to a Guinness. Give you iron that will and turn you into a real manly young chap. There.' She kissed me, her lips warm and luscious. What a saucy woman.

I left feeling life in the country wasn't simple any more. Out of the dusk, a boy appeared.

'Watcher, Tim.' It was Wally Ricketts, ten years old and an evacuee from the East End who was living with Mrs Lottie Ford. If Minnie was a holy terror, so was young Wally. Small village girls ran all ways whenever Wally was about and even some of the bigger ones were arming themselves. ''Ere, I got news for you, Tim.'

'If you've pushed Mrs Ford's shed over again, I'll break your leg.'

'Me? Course I ain't. 'Ere, would yer like a couple of rabbits?'

I knew who would. Aunt May. She liked baked rabbit and rabbit pie. 'Fresh?' I said, thinking. Gunner Simpson was going on leave tomorrow. He lived in Kennington.

'Course they're fresh, they was alive up to an hour ago,' said Wally, capable of undermining the existence of anything that moved. 'Would yer like 'em for a bob the pair, Tim?'

'Hand 'em over,' I said.

'Be a tick,' he said, and disappeared. Back he came, with a pair of large dead rabbits in a paper carrier bag. ''Ere y'ar, Tim, done 'em in special for you, I did.'

'I bet.' The carcases still felt warm. I gave him a bob, which melted his wayward heart and went on to the pub. Jim was in the public bar, at the far end of the mahogany counter. I swam through the crowd in a light-headed way. Cecily and Frisby were at a corner table with Cassidy and Top Sergeant Dawson. Cecily didn't seem quite so much a hunted and haunted doe. She was even drinking, she was even talking to Frisby.

I wasn't quite sure how to look at Jim. But I had to. I had to do something about my head. He moved and we met on the outside of the crowd.

'You old bugger,' I said.

He eyed me from under his hat and over his pipe. He was a tall wiry bloke, with slightly stooping shoulders. 'Been with Missus, 'ave yer, lad?' he asked.

'Yes, I did knock and she did invite me in.'

'Ah,' said Jim cryptically.

'Ah what?'

'Thought you might knock tonight. Treated you nice did she, Tim?' Jim couldn't have been more himself.

'I'm having trouble talking,' I said.

'Missus done you a mite of good, did she?'

'No, she didn't, she turned me into a nervous wreck. I'll have a Guinness.'

'I'll have old and mild,' said Jim, 'it bein' your turn, Tim boy, and also seein' yer didn't get crimed this mornin'. Got to be your treat.'

I got the drinks. The scrum at the bar swayed and heaved, much to the happy confusion of hemmed-in village maidens.

'All right, get that down you,' I said, 'but you don't deserve it, conniving with Missus to make a goggle-eyed man of me. You bleeder.'

'Now, Tim lad, it's just that Missus is an obligin' woman. Takes after 'er Aunt Flossie.'

89

'Blow Aunt Flossie,' I said, 'she's the cause of Missus going off her chump.'

A squeezed maiden squealed. Jim frowned. It was his opinion that Hollywood GIs weren't the best thing that had happened to the eligible females of Sheldham. What a character. He didn't mind his Missus learning me but he did mind the learning Sheldham girls were getting from the GIs.

'Now you oughtn't to talk like that about Aunt Flossie, Tim,' he said.

'Well, I'll admit, I don't know her and I've never seen her. But I've just heard about her. Ought to be burned at the stake. So ought you, for conniving with Missus.'

'Do yer good, Tim. Bring you on a fair treat. You got the makings of a man, lad. Just need a bit of 'elp, that's all. Missus is willin' to give that 'elp. She's a lovin' woman, yer know. She won't spoil you, just make you good at it.'

'Good at what?'

'Pleasurin'. You don't want to be 'eavy- 'anded, Tim, like some of these Yanks. A lady customer of mine, a young widder woman, told me she accidental give in to a Yank once, said it was like a 'aystack fallin' on 'er. Missus wouldn't like you to be like that, yer know.'

'I don't want to hear about your lady customers. You're unbelievable. And so are they, probably. As for Missus, what about my respect for her? I happen to think you should respect women.'

''Ere, I respect Missus too, Tim lad,' he said, swallowing some of his old and mild. I sank some Guinness. It seemed all right, dark as night it was and thick with richness. 'I told yer, Missus is a lovin' and 'elpful woman, like 'er Aunt Flossie. I ain't complainin' about that, so you shouldn't. Not when it's all in the fam'ly, like.'

'You unprincipled old goat, I'm not in the family.'

'Good as. Besides, you're Walworth an' we're Camberwell an' now we're all Suffolk as well.' Jim took a long draught of his ale, then a suck at his pipe. 'Missus is fond of yer, means to turn you into a pleasurin' young bloke, not an 'aystack. Tim lad, there's more to life than fixin' doors an' just talkin'. I grant yer, yer a good talker, but you ought to get some learnin' into yer before you get sent to France with them there guns o' yourn. It's got to come, this 'ere invasion of France. Missus won't want you goin' off without a fair bit of learnin' inside yer. She might not get to see yer again, she'll worry about you not bein' able to do yer bride proud when you're churched. Missus don't believe in disappointed brides.'

'Well, good old Missus, ta very much for that bit of news, but she's already banged my ears with it. And I dare say she is loving and helpful. Unfortunately, she frightens me to death.'

'There you go, just talkin' again,' said Jim, shaking his head.

'Ruddy hell, what—'

'Don't get excited, Tim. We don't want people 'earing, nor foreigners.' Jim wagged his pipe at me. The public bar was bursting with noise but Jim always liked private talking to be carried on in undertones, even if there were no ears around. 'Keep it in the fam'ly, lad.

Missus is a busy woman but she'll find time to give yer some reg'lar learnin'.'

'Is that a fact? But it's not compulsory, is it? I don't have to turn up, do I?'

'Best yer do, Tim, be good for yer, like I already said.'

'You fiddling old ratbag, d'you realize you're talking about your own Missus committing adultery?'

'Not adultery, Tim, not when it's just doin' yer a good turn. You talk long words sometimes, but that ain't enough. You got to realize there's a fine young woman out there waitin' for yer, not just Lottie Ford's shed or this 'ere cantankerous war. Missus'll feel hurt if you back off. I can't rightly think of anyone she's more fond of than you. Well now, I got it back this afternoon.'

'Got what back?' I asked vaguely.

'Me porridge drum,' he said. 'Brought it back, your lot did. Said it wasn't no kind of petrol. Said it 'ud blow up a ten-ton lorry if it was put in that.'

'So you're as clean as a whistle now, are you?'

'No scratches on you, neither,' he said with a grin. ''Eard yer major ended up bein' stood on 'is 'ead.'

'I could still be suspect,' I said, 'but I owe you for bringing that can along.'

'That wasn't nothing, Tim, an' nor don't you need feel you got to owe Missus for all 'er good works. Them's for free, yer know.'

'Just the job, I don't think,' I said. I'd always thought rural life was rustic and simple, but there were un-dreamed-of depths. What Missus had in mind for me would blow her thatched roof off and next door's as well, probably. It wasn't for me. And Aunt May wouldn't stand for it. She'd tie me to the kitchen table first and say, 'Now you just stay there, Tim, while I go and talk to Mrs Beavers.'

'What yer got in that bag?' asked Jim.

'Pair of bunnies.'

Jim had a look. 'Well, yer don't say,' he said. 'Funny thing, old Josh come in 'ere not 'alf an hour ago, sayin' some durned bugger lifted a couple right off 'is kitchen table when 'is old lady's back was turned. Dunno what this 'ere war is doin' to some people. Some people ain't honest any more. Glad you ain't like that, Tim lad. Them rabbits there is come by honest, I'll lay to that. Ain't they?'

'Well, a bob for the pair is honest enough,' I said. 'You sure it doesn't give you a pain, talking about honesty?'

'I got principles, yer know,' said Jim, 'an' you got a nice pair of rabbits.' He winked and rubbed his nose.

Young Wally. Wait till I next ran into him, I thought.

As it was, I gave the rabbits to Gunner Simpson when I got back to BHQ and told him to deliver them to my Aunt May on his way home to Kennington.

'Wait a minute,' he said, 'it's not on me way.'

'Near enough,' I said, 'and I want her to have them while they're still fresh. Catching the first train, are you, Simmo?'

'I've got that in mind, yes.'

'Good. I'll try and have your railway warrant ready.'

'You've done it, ain't you?'

'Been busy today. I'll get down to it first thing in the morning. I'll do my best.'

'All right, you peanut, I'll drop the rabbits in on me way.'

'You're a good old mate, Simmo.'

'All the same,' said Simpson, 'don't ask me to marry you.'

CHAPTER SEVEN

The month of May was well in and I was avoiding
Missus and her eggs, going past her cottage in double-
quick marching time whenever I went down to the pub
in the evenings. Minnie was at the gate sometimes,
looking as if she was watching out for me and calling
and cooing as I went by like a man defective of
sight and hearing. I had to stop on some occasions. I
don't know why I did, for I only got daft questions from
her.

'Can't yer come and cuddle with me in the parlour,
Tim?' 'When you goin' to take me to the flicks in
Sudbury?' 'Don't yer know I'll be sixteen soon?' 'Tim,
when can I be your best girl?'

I couldn't make her see sense, not even when she
made scatty allusions to how loving I was to her on the
night of rising summer.

'I'll give you rising summer,' I said. 'I'll paddle the
seat of your knickers, you Turk.'

'Oh, bliss,' she breathed. 'Could yer do it now, Tim,
round the back of me dad's shed?'

'Lucky for you I'm all talk and no do,' I said and
went blindly away.

Jim kept telling me I wasn't doing myself any good
dodging Missus. She'd catch up with me, he said. Not

while I'm still wearing trousers, I said, and she's still in skirts.

Sergeant Masters was busy. She was even working overtime in the evenings, something that made most of us feel she was letting the side down. But at least she did have a smile and some brisk chummy words for me whenever we ran into each other.

Aunt May wrote, thanking me for two lovely plump rabbits, which a very nice man, Mr Clayton, had delivered to her. Mr Clayton, she said, was the uncle of one of my battery friends, Tosh Simpson. She'd invited him in for a cup of tea. He had a limp because of a wound in the First World War, she said, but was in the ARP all the same, which she thought very public-spirited of him. Then she said that poor Edie Hawkins had had to write to her soldier husband overseas, confessing she'd lost her head with a Canadian soldier and was going to have a baby. Her mother confided it all to Aunt May, telling her that Edie's hubby, Ron, had written back by Forces Air Mail to inform Edie he was going to chop the Canadian up into little bits and give her a good hiding as soon as he had Blighty leave. He also informed her he was going to chuck the baby off the top of Tower Bridge. He didn't actually say baby, wrote Aunt May, but of course he was naturally upset, so you had to forgive him for what he did say. He gave Edie a lecture for being too accommodating, he said no wife should be as accommodating as that and besides it was against the law. He could divorce her for it. As it was, he'd make do with giving her a good hiding. Her mother said Edie was ever so relieved, she didn't mind a good

96

hiding and she was sure Ron wouldn't chuck the baby off the top of Tower Bridge, he'd never done anything like that in his life.

Well, it's taught her a lesson, wrote Aunt May, and it's taught others a lesson too about how to behave. The vicar had preached a very good sermon about how mistakes can teach one to be a better Christian and that there was great virtue in faithfulness and forgiveness, so Edie's mother had probably confided in him too.

I copped hold of young Wally Ricketts one evening, dragging him through the gate of Mrs Ford's cottage by the seat of his pants just when he thought he'd escaped.

'Ere, what yer 'olding me for, Tim?' he asked, all freckles and hurt innocent eyes.

'Nothing much,' I said, 'just a walloping. Where'd you want it?'

'I don't want it nowhere, I ain't done nuffink.'

'You sold me a couple of nicked rabbits,' I said.

'Me? Me?'

'You heard.'

'Honest, Tim, they was just lyin' about not doin' nuffink. 'Sides, I already been walloped once today. Mr Berry done it, just 'cos I accidental got 'is Emma a bit wet, just 'cos she fell over me.'

'Fell over you and then what?'

'She went in the pond. Still, I got 'er out. I dunno why I got walloped for gettin' 'er out. It ain't 'arf an 'ard life round 'ere sometimes, Tim. You ain't goin' to wallop me as well, are yer?'

'Hoppit,' I said and he scooted down the path.

'I'll nick yer – I'll get yer some more rabbits one day, Tim,' he called and disappeared.

Someone swooped on me from behind. 'Gotcher!' exclaimed Minnie happily.

'Leave go my arm, it's not dark yet.'

'Oh, you Tim, ain't you comical?'

'You're not,' I said. She wasn't. She was wearing a thin Betty Grable sweater and was highly dangerous.

'Mum's been sayin' what's come over you lately, you 'aven't been near us, nor come and looked at our chickens. Tim, you can take me to the Sudbury flicks one evenin', honest. I asked me mum an' dad if you could, an' they said all right, they'd trust you, they said. They don't mind.'

'Your dad would. He'd skin me.'

'Course 'e wouldn't.' Minnie laughed and looked joyously tickled in the twilight.

Lights were coming on in cottage parlours and black-out curtains were being drawn. A jeep pulled up outside the *Suffolk Punch* and disgorged GIs and Wacs.

'You're me dad's best friend, he likes you ever so. He keeps saying why don't our Tim take you to the pictures sometimes, Min, that's what he keeps saying.'

'No, he doesn't, you're making that up,' I said. 'I know you, you perisher. I suppose you've got the back seat of the cinema in mind, have you?'

'Oh, crikey,' breathed Min, 'you and me in the back seat, Tim. Be bliss, that would. I can't 'ardly wait, can you?'

'I'm not listening, Min, I'm unconscious.'

'Wasn't risin' summer night good, Tim?' she said.

98

'How do I know? All that cider knocked me out.'

'Lovely, you are, Tim.'

Missus showed herself at the cottage door. 'Is that Tim, love? Tell him to come in, then you can take a message to Aunt Flossie for me.'

I ran. I was in uniform, but it made no difference. I ran like a born coward.

It was a Sunday morning when Sergeant Johnson sent for me. That was a bit of a liberty, for a state of non-belligerency existed between NCOs and gunners on holy days, apart from all the shouting that went on when they were lining us up for church parade. If you weren't on fire picquet duty or some other duty, Sundays could be civilized. Officers sometimes made nuisances of themselves, but most officers were insensitive to the customs of other ranks.

Sergeant Johnson was duty sergeant for the day. That mucked up his Sunday, so I had to watch that he didn't muck up mine. He was doing some one-finger typing in the orderly room. He greeted my arrival with a morose look.

'Where's the fire, sarge?' I asked.

He inspected me. Something made him smile then, as if good news had arrived after a bitter dose of bad. 'Got you, Hardy. You're improperly dressed. Buttons undone.'

'It's Sunday,' I said, 'and I only came because we're friends. I hope it's not for nothing.'

'Nothing's for nothing,' he said. 'Listen, you're excused church parade. You're taking the Austin to

Sudbury. Report at the gate at ten-fifteen pronto. And tart yourself up.'

It was a try-on. They were going to put temptation in my way. I'd probably find two spare cans, both full, in the utility. It was so obvious I nearly felt sorry for him.

'What am I delivering and where?' I asked.

'You'll find out. Just go and tart up.'

I didn't mind missing church parade. I was at the gates in good order at ten-ten. The Austin utility stood outside. Giving it a thoughtful look was Sergeant Masters, in her best olive-green. The weather was cloudy with a threat of rain, but Sergeant Masters looked a bright picture of American military womanhood. And she was so smart I felt like saluting her.

'Morning, Sergeant Masters.'

'Hi, Tim old boy, old boy.'

'Going walking?' I asked.

'No. I'm going to church. You're driving me there.'

'Me?'

'It's our date. One of our officers arranged it with your obliging transport officer.'

'But you've got your own transport,' I said.

'Our transport, one jeep, is hogged by our officers,' said Kit. 'Do you mind that I asked for you as driver?'

'Not a bit. But you're taking a chance, aren't you? I suppose you realize it's got around, through Gunner Dunwoodie, that I've got staring eyes and heavy breathing?'

'Oh, that,' said Kit. 'Well, you asked me to keep him riveted and that was the best I could do for you. I hope you're not complaining. The cause, after all, wasn't a worthy one and I'm not sure I go along with the result. You fluked it. It placed your major on a bed of nails.'

'Bad luck if he bleeds. His dog will eat him if it smells blood. Shall we go?'

'Can we wait a few more moments? Cecily asked last night if she could come.'

Cecily arrived at that point. She too was in her best uniform.

'Morning, Cecily,' I said.

'Oh, hi,' she said in a fairly friendly way, but for one of her odd reasons failed to look me in the eye. 'Look, d'you mind if I don't come?' she said to Kit. 'Only the guys here are on church parade and I can go along with them. It's Protestant, so I guess that's OK.'

'It's OK with me,' said Kit.

'Well, Claud's going,' said Cecily, 'and he said there'll be room in the pew for me.' Good old Frisby. He was doing a good job on Cecily and Cecily was looking as if the prickles were being taken out of her shirt.

'Enjoy the hymns, Cecily,' I said.

'Oh, I'll make out, I guess,' she said.

Kit and I climbed aboard the Austin and off we went. It was a rustic drive to Sudbury, the narrow roads winding around farms and doddling through hamlets. The rain began, showery at first, then depressingly sheeting. It wasn't like blithe May at all. The hedges looked like glistening watersheds and in the distance the heavy sky dropped thick curtains of grey wet mist over Suffolk. The countryside turned into sodden blankets of greens and mustards. The hamlets, clustering around

101

their churches, sprouted brooding belfries and glowering spires.

'Mournful,' I said.

'The rain? Oh, that's nothing,' said Kit, 'and it's not as if we're on our way to a picnic or a clambake. Besides, the weather can't alter the fact that everything's very peaceful and that the war's not happening here. Are we grateful, old boy?'

'Over the moon.'

'Good.' She seemed happy to talk. She had a companionable American warmth this morning. 'What side of the road are you driving on?'

'The middle,' I said. 'The road's full of bends and there's not much of a camber. If I landed you in a ditch, I'd have to write a long report and fill in a form.'

'If you land me in any ditch, Hardy, I'll write my own report,' she said. 'What's that?' She pointed.

'A cow?' I suggested, keeping my eyes on the road.

'If that's a cow I'm George Washington.'

I took a look. We were passing a concrete drive leading to a tarry-roofed Nissen-hut complex in what had once been a Suffolk meadow. Not a soul was in sight but within a large concrete and sandbag emplacement three Bofors ack-acks were snouting under their tarpaulin covers.

'That's one of our battery's gun sites,' I said, driving on. 'We'd better not call or the gunners will want you to stay for dinner and keep you till Christmas. Even in our army, troops get a treat at Christmas. Like a bird or two.'

'Like a Christmas goose?' asked Kit.

'Turkey's favourite. But they'd make do with an American girl sergeant.'

'Now I get you,' said Kit, 'a bird is a broad is a girl, right?'

'Right,' I said, motoring on through the rain.

'Your battery's been in action?'

'Since the Blitz. It's quieter now.'

'Have you brought any planes down?' she asked.

'Two,' I said, 'both ours.'

'You shot down your own planes?' Kit turned astonished eyes on me. 'You shot down Spitfires?'

'Might have been Hurricanes. We were too ashamed to go and look.'

'Listen, you comic, isn't there any chance of having a serious conversation with you?' she asked. 'How long have you been an enlisted soldier?'

'Two and a half years.' We splashed past a farm entrance, which threw liquid mud at us.

'Good grief,' said Kit, 'in all that time you haven't won promotion?'

'Major Moffat has. As for the rest of us, nobody's died or fallen in action. We're up to establishment. One major, one adjutant, one messing officer and so on, site commanders and so on, the allowed number of NCOs and so on and no battle casualties. I've been at BHQ for nearly a year now, I was on site before.'

'I still think you should have made sergeant by now, Tim, old boy. I made it in six months.'

'Well, you've got good legs, of course, and good looks,' I said.

'I'm happy you've noticed, of course,' she said, 'but

103

they're nothing to do with promotion in the Wacs. Why can't you apply for a commission and make lieutenant as a beginning?' She pronounced it 'lootenant'. 'I'll speak to Major Moffat about you. You must have some potential.'

I rounded a bend at startled speed. The utility keeled and Kit bounced against me.

'Sorry,' I said.

'Watch it,' said Kit.

'Did you say you'd speak to the major?'

'He walked me out with his dog last night.'

'Lucky you weren't wolfed.'

'Wolfed?'

'Eaten up by Jupiter, the major's hungry hound.'

'Now you mention it, it did have a go at my skirt once or twice.' Kit smiled. 'Your major's very civilized, he fits my image of a typical British officer.'

'It's not allowed, of course, officers taking female sergeants out for a walk.'

'He gave it a go,' said Kit. 'He's kind of charming.'

'All right, try marrying him and see what happens when you come down to breakfast with a button undone. You'll get seven days potato-peeling.'

'Someone should take you in hand, old boy. It's crazy you're still a private after all this time.'

'Gunner,' I said and drove into Sudbury.

It was a nice little town, although today it was wet with summer rain. People were walking to their churches in macs and brollies were up. I found a Methodist establishment and pulled up.

'I think this is your kind of church,' I said.

104

'Thanks for the buggy ride,' said Kit and alighted. I declined an invitation to join her. I was strict Church of England and didn't want to get confused. I promised to pick her up at noon and drove to the only shop open, a newsagents. I bought a Sunday paper, found a public bus shelter and sat down to pass the time while it rained. The war news seemed better. Tripoli had been taken, Hitler wasn't having it all his own way in Russia and nor were the Japs in the Pacific.

When I picked Kit up at noon, the weather had improved. As we drove through the town the clouds were breaking, the rain had stopped and the roofs, wet and shining, looked sun-washed. We took to the winding road again. Kit, having said she'd enjoyed the church service, asked why there weren't any straight highways in England. I said I supposed they'd all been laid down by drunken road gangs. She wasn't impressed, but she was when the sun came right out and the countryside glistened, sparkled and ran with colour. A cottage perched on a little Suffolk slope looked as if it was hanging out to dry. We swished through long puddles and clipped drying fronds of new honeysuckle reaching out from hedges.

'Perfect,' she said, her gesture embracing Suffolk, lush from rain and sun. 'Don't you feel you'd like to get out and wander?'

'Can't stop now, Kit, I'll miss my dinner.'

'No, I guess not,' she said.

'It's no guess, it's every man for himself,' I said. 'Why'd you want to wander?'

'I'd like to explore some of the country while I'm

105

here,' she said. 'I'd like to climb gates and talk to horses, or knock on doors and talk to people.'

'Well, you can borrow a bike, there are several available. Then you can cycle at leisure and wander at will.'

'Is that a fact, could I borrow one?' she asked keenly.

'Why not? We're all mates. They're WD property, but you're attached to the unit and you only need a chit. I'll make one out for you. It looks as if it'll be a nice afternoon.'

'Do I have to go by myself?' she asked.

'I could make out a chit for Cassidy too, or Cecily. Which one d'you fancy?'

'Wake up,' said Kit.

'D'you mean you'd fancy me?'

'I don't have to fancy you, do I?'

'It's not compulsory. We could just be cycle mates for the afternoon.'

'Your English is very peculiar at times, Tim, old boy. Can't we just say we'll ride out together?'

'Sounds OK,' I said.

As soon as we got back I made out chits, took two bikes out of store and hid them. There was always a demand for them on Sunday afternoons. I had a cold wash after dinner to acquire a fresh clean look. Frisby caught me in the ablutions and confided news of Cecily, who had joined the ATS girls and the gunners on church parade.

'Poor young bird,' he said, 'she's got mother trouble.'

'I didn't know she'd brought her mother over with her.'

106

'Can the cackle and listen,' said Frisby.

Cecily, it seemed, was the only child of parents who had a small farm in Illinois. The marriage had turned sour and Cecily's father had walked out ten years ago. Her mother never forgave him. Living in a cheap apartment in Chicago, the farm sold, she revenged herself on her husband and all other men by regaling her daughter with mind-boggling details of what they were capable of. At the same time she lavished on the girl the selfish and possessive love that was designed to never let her go. Evenings were often traumatic, the cataloguing of the sins of men sparing Cecily nothing. Cecily developed a horror and fear of ever letting a man near her. By the time she was twenty, that fear had become an aggressive rejection of men. Then the Japs bombed Pearl Harbour. The store at which Cecily worked closed down for the day. Arriving home well before she was expected, she found her mother in bed with a man. She walked out on her, as her father had done. It did not cure her of her antipathy towards men, but it did enable her to escape the maternal straitjacket. She enlisted in the Wacs a year later, wanting to serve her country within the ranks of thousands of her own sex. She was well aware there were many more thousands of men in uniform, all of whom stalked the game. She dreamt of various fates, all worse than death.

'She actually poured all this out?' I asked.

'A bit at a time,' said Frisby. 'So now what do I do? It was a lark at first. Now she needs me, she thinks I'm the only guy who's got two hands instead of six. She really needs me.'

'As a father or a doctor?' I asked, as we walked along the path, the stone borders newly whitewashed. The afternoon had become brilliant, but Frisby was frowning darkly.

'I've got problems,' he said, 'I'm beginning to fancy her, but the last thing I can do is to let it show. She'll commit suicide.'

'Be like me, try celibacy,' I said. 'Be her father confessor.'

'I've had celibacy ever since the Yanks arrived,' said Frisby, 'and I'm at the age when it hurts. I can't guarantee I won't grab Cecily. So what d'you think, mate?'

'Just be kind to her,' I said. That would have been Aunt May's advice.

CHAPTER EIGHT

I was waiting at the gates at two o'clock, keeping both bikes warm. Kit, arriving ten minutes late, apologized. She'd been detained by Major Moffat. He'd decided to make an unscheduled round of the sites and if Sergeant Masters cared to, she could accompany him.

'A round of the sites?' I said, shaken. 'On a Sunday afternoon? He'll wake everyone up.'

'I think that's his idea,' said Kit with the misguided relish of a woman sergeant who didn't understand how men fought a war. 'After all, there are still air raids. German bombers still sneak over.'

'Not in daylight any more and not on London.'

'Your false sense of Sunday afternoon security will catch up with you,' she said, 'and you'll have egg all over your face.'

'Well, don't let's worry about that today,' I said. 'Look, you keep an eye on these bikes while I pop up to the RT room and get the bloke on duty to pass a quick word to our site commanders.'

'I'm not falling for that stuff again,' said Kit. 'And you can forget your RT room. Major Moffat has already taken steps to seal it off. He said the whole of BHQ was alive with traitors who'd do just what you thought of doing. I must say he's got a fascinating accent.'

'All right, marry him then and see what happens the first time you answer him back. His accent will burn the clothes off your back and reduce your roll-on to a smoking ruin.'

'Don't keep telling me to marry him, you clown, and don't imagine I wear a roll-on,' said Kit crisply. 'Let's go, shall we? I told Major Moffat I had a prior engagement. What's that?'

'Your bike. A ladies' machine of first-class WD quality, with khaki mudguards.'

Kit viewed the museum piece. I assured her it didn't actually creak and jangle. She mounted, finding the pedals with her brown-shod feet and off we went. Her skirt rode up, her knees gleamed and her legs looked rhythmic.

'Eyes front, Hardy,' she said.

'Good 'uns, they are,' I said. I had a bit of Suffolk in me too, like Min.

'What?' Kit asked.

'This way,' I said and I led her off the village road and made for Plaxted Farm.

In the rural quietness, Kit hummed a song as she rode beside me. Early butterflies danced to it and hedgerows murmured. The day was golden now, the fields verdant, the trees brilliant with glossy leaf. We approached a man in leggings. He was carrying a bucket. It vibrated as he saw Kit and her shining summer legs.

'A tidy pair of good 'uns you got there, soldier girl,' he said, as we rode by. Kit stopped in a little while.

'Listen,' she said, 'is this low saddle your idea? That guy saw my pants.'

'You sure?'

'Sure I'm sure. His eyes fell in his bucket. I think you'd better fix this saddle.'

I fixed it with a spanner from the little tool kit. Remounting, she said it was fine now that her knees weren't coming up to hit her chin. We rode on. I stopped when we reached a gun site just beyond Plaxted Farm. Kit, seeing Nissen huts, came about.

'What's cooking?' she asked.

'This is my old site,' I said. 'Shan't be a tick.'

I went to find Sergeant Fox, deputy site commander under Lieutenant Rogers. He was having a nap. He was cross when I woke him up, but mellowed when I let him know what the major was up to. 'Can you pass the word to the other sites on your RT, sarge?'

'Me old grandmother'll be disappointed if I can't,' he said. 'All right, can do. You're a loyal piece of leavings and I hope those ponces at BHQ appreciate you.'

'Miss me, do you, sarge?'

'Not yet. 'Oppit.'

I went back to Kit. She gave me a cryptic look but said nothing. We went on, cycling leisurely through countryside and hamlets. The hamlets slumbered in the afternoon warmth and the livestock in the thatched roofs were probably waking up to the fact that summer had arrived. There was a gentle ascent to the village of Elsingham and we rode up slowly, Kit digging her feet into her pedals. At the top we dismounted to look back over the ground we had covered, over fields, dissecting hedgerows and winding lanes. Far away the colours were hazed by the sun. A small stream near the foot of the little hill flowed into a green and leafy copse.

'Lovely,' said Kit musingly, 'it's Constable country.'

'Oh, Constable,' I said. 'He paints old mills and things.'

'Painted. He's dead now. Do wake up, old buddy. Incidentally, you spilled the beans to the men on your old site back there. You took sneaky advantage of what I told you in confidence.'

'Yes, ta for the information, Kit.'

'All your sites will be alerted?'

'You bet.'

'Did I get a mention?' she asked, eyes on the copse.

'Pardon?'

'I'd have liked a mention,' she said. 'Loyal American ally helps to save British comrades from being scalped.'

'Yes, you're a good old American guy, Kit.'

'You're cute too. Where's your home town?'

'Walworth in South London.'

'Sounds great. Do you have a girlfriend back there?'

'Not yet. But I've got an aunt. I was orphaned as an infant and she's looked after me ever since. She's my Aunt May and my good old mum.'

'Well, I rate Aunt May,' said Kit. In her musing mood, her eyes still on the view, she had a softer look. She was very good-looking, with a lovely mouth.

'How about you?' I asked. 'What part of America do you come from?'

Kit said her home was in a Boston suburb, that Boston itself was OK, even if it didn't set New Yorkers alight. But New Yorkers were almost foreigners, she said. There

112

were places in New York where English wasn't spoken, or if it was, one couldn't understand it. She had been running a little store in Boston with the help of a friend until the war interfered. A store for kids. She and her friend, Effie Charmicle.

'Effie Charmicle?'

'Yes. You don't know her, do you?'

'No. She's too far away. Are there many Charmicles in Boston.'

'There's Effie's family,' said Kit. 'Czech extraction.' She mused again. I fancied a cup of tea. Just the afternoon, it was, for a cup of tea. Kit went on to say she and Effie had felt there weren't too many stores that catered all that well for young people and even those that did got crowded out by adults. So she and Effie took a lease on a downtown shop and sold only kids' stuff. Weekend shirts, casuals, sweaters, books and anything else with teenage appeal. She and Effie pooled ideas and resources, plus unlimited enthusiasm and in six months the store had caught on and was flourishing. But by then it was September 1942 and she felt guilty. So she enlisted in the WAAC and left Effie to carry the store through the war. It had the backing of Kit's father, who had supplied some capital in the first place.

'You'll go back to it when the war's over?' I asked.

'I surely will,' said Kit. 'I've a feeling that after the war it will really take off. What were you doing before you enlisted?'

'Insurance.'

'Insurance?' Kit looked disgusted.

'Claims department.'

113

'You can do better than that,' she said. 'How old are you?'

'About forty.'

'I'm twenty-two – hold on, you comic, you're not forty.'

'No, I only said about forty. It's the war, it's put years on me.'

'Old buddy, you're not even in the war.' Kit took her cap off and shook her springy hair. She looked young and lovely in the sunshine. I wondered if Missus would think her right for me. I felt Aunt May would. Kit might be just the job to come home to in the evenings, with a pretty apron on and a cake baking in the oven. On the other hand, was that the right kind of picture to draw of an efficient female sergeant who had a store in Boston?

'What's next for you?' I asked. 'Officer rank?'

'I'm working my way up,' said Kit, 'I like doing it that way.' She would, I thought. Each step up would make her efficiency feel good.

'What's your family like?' I asked.

'Both my parents are nice guys,' said Kit, 'so are my two brothers. They're in the Pacific.'

'Wish I was. All those grass skirts and coconuts. Here you can't even get a banana.'

'You're a banana, Tim,' she said, putting her cap back on. 'Banana first-class. Come on, let's go.'

We went, wheeling our bikes through Elsingham so that she could knock on doors and talk to the natives, if she wanted to. The houses had rendered walls and painted doors. Cottages looked timeless. The one shop sold groceries, papers, stamps, a small range of hardware

114

and spare parts for bicycles. The church had a look of ancient history that Kit liked. Beyond the church, three cottages nestled together. The middle one had a timber porch. On either side of the front path were flower borders surrounding small square lawns. The grass looked in need of a cut. A woman was weeding. She was a little fat, her cotton dress tight, her healthy-looking face red from bending. She was in her fifties, a little grey showing in her brown hair. She came to the gate when she saw me approaching.

'Hello, Timmy,' she called.

'Hello, love.'

'You know each other?' said Kit.

'We met last year,' I said. 'I pass this way from time to time, whenever I've made out a chit for a Sunday bike. Come and meet her yourself. She's a widow and she's nice. She might put the kettle on for us.'

'You'd take a widow's tea ration?' asked Kit, aware of our food shortages.

'Only if she insists. Come on.'

Widow Mary Coker greeted us with a good-natured smile. She was a Londoner who, with her husband, had escaped the smoke ten years ago, selling their shop in Balham to settle in Elsingham. They'd had eight happy rural years before Mr Coker quietly died, leaving Mary to live on her pension and their savings. She managed to exist in a busy and thrifty way and she practised good neighbourliness and hospitality. She reminded me sometimes of Aunt May and I liked all women of that kind.

'You haven't been by lately, Tim,' she said.

'It's been a few weeks,' I said. Often I cycled around

115

with Frisby, but I'd been on my own when I met Mary. She'd invited me in for a cup of tea and I'd seen her regularly since then and done little jobs for her. I'd let her chat to me. She liked a good chat.

'Mary, meet a new cycle mate of mine, Sergeant Kit Masters of Boston, America. I'm giving her a guided tour.'

'I'm Mary Coker,' said Mary and shook hands with Kit over the little front gate. 'I thought they might have sent Tim to Burma by now, but I see he's still here.'

'I'm happy to know you,' said Kit, 'but I don't think Tim likes the sound of Burma.'

'Still, it might win him a medal,' said Mary and chuckled.

'Give me jungle fever more like,' I said. 'And Burmese acne.'

'He's got a funny way of talking,' said Kit.

'Oh, he's just a bit cockeyed,' said Mary, 'like Fred Plummer.'

'Who's Fred Plummer?' asked Kit.

'Village idiot,' I said.

'Don't let's stand talking out here,' said Mary. 'Come in both of you and I'll put the kettle on.'

'We really can't impose on you like that,' said Kit.

'You're not imposing,' said Mary, 'you're company.'

We propped up our bikes and went in. The small porch was half-windowed on each side and the front door opened directly on to the living-room. The cottage was clean, tidy, comfortable and homely. The living-room furniture was a mixture of ancient and modern mahogany, all of it solid and durable. The floor was

116

polished and a rug lay in front of the fireplace. On the left, a door led to a square kitchen and a brick scullery, with an old-fashioned copper boiler. On the right, another door gave access to a narrow staircase leading to the bathroom and two bedrooms. A small dining-table stood in the bay window of the living-room. The window overlooked the back garden. There were herbaceous borders, rose beds, a wide lawn, vegetable beds and a wired chicken run. The chickens were strutting and pecking in the sunshine. The lawn needed a cut.

Kit inspected everything with interest, particularly Mary's brass and copper ornaments. 'Is this place period?' she asked.

'It's falling down, so Fred Plummer told me,' said Mary. 'Still, it'll last me out, I dare say. Well, it had better had. Make yourselves comfy and I'll get some tea.'

I followed her into the kitchen, fishing out two brown paper bags from inside my battle blouse. One contained tea, the other sugar. 'Compliments of King and country,' I said.

'Tim, you shouldn't,' said Mary, but looked tickled. Then she quizzed me. 'You didn't pinch it, did you?'

'Pinch it? Leave off, Mary. It's American stuff, it fell off a Flying Fortress. But don't tell my American sergeant.'

'You sweet on her?' said Mary, putting the kettle on. 'She's ever so nice-looking. Go and talk to her. You can't leave her alone. I'll bring the tray in a minute.'

Kit was at the window, looking at the garden. Her cap

was off and she seemed pensive. The chickens were clucking.

'OK?' I asked.

'I've been thinking,' she said. 'Has it occurred to you what a lousy war this is, but that it might not have happened if your little old island hadn't let Hitler get away with murder? I mean, old buddy, think about appeasement and what it's done to widows' tea rations.'

'I didn't know you were passionate about widows' tea rations,' I said.

'Stop being a comic,' said Kit and she went on about what Hitler was doing to the world. I let her have her carry-on. All women like a good carry-on. Missus was a case in point. Thoughts of Missus brought on quivers. Ruddy unbelievable, that's what Missus was.

Mary came in with the tray. 'I've just brought a pot of tea for now,' she said. 'I'll get proper tea later on.'

'A cup now will be just fine,' said Kit. 'We won't stay for anything else.'

'You must now you're here,' said Mary. 'Sunday company's a nice change for me and I happen to have done a bit of baking.'

She poured tea, hot and golden. Kit hitched her skirt and sat down. Her legs had a delectable shine. Growing boys never really knew about women having legs until after the First World War. Before that, they only knew about bosoms. And when legs really arrived with the flappers, bosoms went out in favour of flat chests. No wonder we're all a bit confused.

'Mary,' I said, 'your grass needs mowing.' I was fond of grass. There wasn't much of it about in Walworth.

'Me mower's gone wrong,' said Mary, 'and George Whittle's packed up doing repairs and gone to be a watchman in a factory in Ipswich doing war work. I've been waiting for Fred Plummer to come and have a look at it, but it's like waiting for a blessed miracle.'

'I'll look at it,' I said. With Mary and Kit already getting to know each other, I took my tea outside.

Mary's mower was in the shed. The blades were jammed. One had a vicious kink. Mary must have hit Suffolk stone. I hammered out the kink, filed the edge and sharpened the other blades too. It worked a treat then, it was a good old reliable hand-mower. I spent the next hour mowing the lawns front and back and building up a compost heap with rich grass cuttings, while Mary had a nice time gassing to Kit.

It was good in the sunshine. Mary put her head out of the kitchen window and said I was a love. To me it was a pleasant way of spending a Sunday afternoon. Intellectual people despise suburban lawn mowers, but if we all took to living under railway arches or sharing a tent with Bedouins, think of what gardens would get to look like. And who'd grow the potatoes? Some of us have got to be homely and peasant-like.

Mary called to say proper tea was ready and Kit came out to tell me I was a welcome surprise to her.

'You're actually useful,' she said.

'Oh, Tim's been useful to me in more ways than one,' said Mary from the open window. That wasn't the best way a widow could have put it. I saw a little smile creep up on Kit. 'I wish there was more like Tim,' Mary went on, 'then I might get someone to look at my drain out here. I think it's got blocked, me water's not running away properly. I've told the council, I've told them I hope it don't mean the cesspit's full up and they said they'd come and see, but no-one's been.'

'Oh, we'll get Tim to take a look at it,' said Kit generously.

'I'd be ever so grateful,' said Mary.

'First thing after tea,' said Kit and that was something to be thankful for, that she realized tea should always come before drains.

Tea was scones made from a wartime recipe with Mary's own strawberry jam, and slices of her honey cake. Kit ate with relish. It was, she said, her first genuine English country tea. She had discarded her jacket. Her shirt was impeccably buttoned, her tie pursuing a straight and orderly path between rounded turrets. Only the gentlest of motions disturbed her shirt, due no doubt to efficient bosom control.

Mary said the front door was getting a bit of a nuisance. It let in the devil and all his draughts in the winter.

'Oh, well,' I said, 'you can't keep the devil out of any house, Mary, but as my Aunt May said once, as long as you don't shake hands with him, he never takes the best chair.'

'Old Fred says it needs taking off and re-hanging,' said Mary over her teacup.

'Old Fred is all say and no do,' I said.

'We're glad you're not, aren't we, Mary?' said Kit. She popped cake into her mouth and I thought of following it with the tea cosy, because I knew what was coming next. 'You'll look at it, won't you, when you've seen to the drains? Mary will appreciate that.'

'Oh, only if you've got time, Tim,' said Mary.

Flying pancakes, they were already bosom female chums ganging up on me. I muttered something about I'd better see first how I got on down the drain, as drains could be lethal. They simply gassed on over my mutters. Best of pals they were, already.

I finished my tea and went to look at the swinish drain. I spent the next forty minutes poking it with bamboo canes. There was a messy blockage and an inescapable stink. The day didn't seem like sweet summer any more. I got sweaty and bad-tempered, my army braces dangling, my shirt sleeves rolled up and my hands and arms filthy. But just as a squadron of Flying Fortresses flew thunderously over and I was essing everything in sight, there was a mushy, squashy gurgle and then a glorious mud-sucking rush. When Mary and Kit came out to inspect progress, the drain was clear, and the stink had transferred itself to me. Mary held her nose. Kit backed off.

Mary, seeing the unblocked drain, said through her pinched nose, 'Oh, lovely, Tim.'

'Pleasure,' I said hypocritically.

'All that muck gone,' said Mary, 'there's just a bit of a pong now, that's all.'

'That's me,' I said, 'I'm pong.'

'Just a small stink,' said Kit.

'I'll go and light the geyser,' said Mary, 'and you can have a bath. Thanks ever so much, Tim, I don't hardly know how to thank you.' Off she went to light the geyser. I heaved the drain cover back into place.

Kit gave me a kind smile. 'You're surprising me,' she said again, 'you can do things.'

'I'll go and grab that bath,' I said.

'What about Mary's front door? You've still got that to look at.'

'Stop organizing me,' I said and went into the cottage after wiping my feet. 'Or I'll assault you,' I said, but only to a piece of crest china from Norwich.

I climbed the stairs. Mary was in the bathroom where the antique geyser was making threatening noises and shaking itself silly. An eruption seemed likely. 'Jesus,' I said, 'if that thing blows up while I'm in the nude, I'll—'

'It's all right,' said Mary and gave the geyser a bang with a back scrubber. It calmed down at once. She left me to my bath. I enjoyed a hot, wallowing soak. I thought about Kit. I thought about Mary. What a woman. She was a lively cockney who, like Missus, had taken on all the characteristics of a rural female. As for young Minnie, it beat me that she had a schoolgirl crush on me and not on some GI equivalent of Gary Cooper. It wouldn't last, of course. With any luck by the time her birthday arrived she'd be looking at me as an uncle.

After my bath, I looked at the front door. It seemed a fine old piece of joinery to me, of solid, weathered oak, with a heavy brass knocker that Mary always kept polished. The door had a necessary clearance, but not an abnormal one. The trouble was, it opened directly on to Mary's living-room, like so many cottage doors did and the draughts were bound to arrive around her feet, especially when her winter fire was drawing. I suggested fitting a draught-excluder.

'Oh, them things,' said Mary, which meant no thanks. I examined the porch, enclosed on both sides. It was a little less than four feet wide between the front supporting posts. With further posts butted on, a three-feet door could be hung. That would close the porch right up and turn it into a little entrance lobby that would kill the worst of the draughts. And if I still fixed a draught-excluder, that ought to button it right up. I thought I could manage the job, provided the battery didn't get posted to some battlefield. I carried the idea to Mary and Mary said what a hope that was, trying to get a door and someone to fix it. Be like waiting for another miracle, she said, but I was a lamb to think of it.

'Don't worry, Mary,' said Kit, who'd made herself really at home. 'The miracle's here. You'll fix it, Tim, won't you?'

'I was going to say I'd give it a go.'

'There's a good guy,' said Kit. 'Mary, have you ever thought about central heating?'

Flaming Amy, I thought, she's not just an American disturbance, she's an interfering earthquake.

'Oh, I don't want no foreign central heating,' said Mary.

'But for someone living on her own,' said Kit keenly, 'it's very labour-saving and much more efficient than an open fire. I'm sure Tim would—'

'Pardon me, dearie,' I said, 'but no, I wouldn't. I'm

123

not a heating engineer, I'm just a bloke who drops in sometimes.'

'Don't be self-defeatist,' said Kit. 'Be a tiger.'

'He looks nice after his bath,' said Mary in an irrelevant, motherly way.

'He smells better, I'll say that,' said Kit.

'I think I'll stick to my coal fire,' said Mary.

'Well, you do that,' said Kit. 'I guess some things shouldn't get changed and this is a sweet old English cottage. Mary, this has been just the nicest Sunday I've had since I arrived. I can't tell you how much I've enjoyed it.'

'Come again anytime,' said Mary, 'I like company.'

'I might just take you up on that,' smiled Kit.

We cycled leisurely back to BHQ. The May evening was warm and the lustre left by the morning rain was still evident. The setting sun was beginning to flush the countryside and to tint the tops of trees. I rode ahead, Kit behind me, keeping her legs to herself. The country quiet made the war seem remote.

'Tim Hardy! Come back!'

I stopped and turned my head. She was off her bike. I rode back to her. She had a flat.

'Hard luck, old girl,' I said. 'Well, stay here and guard the puncture and I'll shoot back to BHQ and see if one of your officers will motor out and pick you up.'

'Oh, no you don't,' she said, 'you're not dumping me here with a flat. You got me here and it's up to you to get me back. How about some English chivalry, how about fixing the tyre?'

'Take ages,' I said and she gave me a crisp look. I'd

124

heard that American men were brought up to do as they were told. I believed it. 'OK, I'll take a look,' I said weakly.

Out of the quietness came the deep hum of a speeding car. It came careering round a bend, but slowed as it approached us. It was a Hillman, bedecked in WD war paint. It pulled up. At the wheel was Major Moffat. In place of Lance-Bombardier Burley, his driver, was his horse-faced Dalmatian, already licking its lips at the sight of Kit's tasty legs. I saluted. The major put his head out. He didn't look as if he'd had a satisfying afternoon. He looked as if he knew some traitor had sabotaged his plans to give site personnel a shake-up. Then he recognized Kit. His ruggedly handsome face creased into a smile. He saw her flat tyre. He glanced at me.

'Trouble, Gunner Hardy?'

'Sergeant Masters has a puncture, sir.'

'Well, well.' He seemed pleased about it. 'You're outside the permitted area. D'you have a pass?'

'Yes, sir. And a chit.'

'Come here,' he said and I advanced so that he could address my ear alone. He was a military martinet, but preferred the unconventional to red tape. Kit looked on solemnly. 'I know about chits, you fiddling Himalayan yak.'

'Yes, sir.'

'What are you doing out here with an NCO of the Wac?'

'Showing her the countryside, sir.'

'I hope I've arrived in time to save her. All right, stuff

125

her bike into the boot. I'll take her back to BHQ.' He called to her.

'Major?' said Kit.

'Climb aboard, Sergeant Masters,' he said. 'Can't let you walk.'

Kit hesitated. The Dalmatian licked its lips again. The major gave me a look. I took the hint and opened the passenger door for Kit. Jupiter thrust his jaws out. The major cuffed the hopeful animal and it scrambled over on to the back seat. Kit got in. I closed the door.

'See you,' she said and gave me her warmest smile yet.

'The major made off with his treasure a few minutes later, the bike sticking out of the boot. Pity, I thought. It could have been a lingering evening, I could have begun to do some learning on my own initiative.

Acceptable learning.

I biked back. When I approached BHQ, there was a girl waiting some twenty yards from the gates. Minnie in a bright Sunday dress and with sparks in her eyes. She made me stop, by plonking herself in my way.

'Now what?' I said.

She tossed her head and her hair whipped and flew like an angry banner of August gold. 'Where is she? You been out with her, you been out on bikes with her. Oh, you Tim, you've never been out on bikes with me and I'm goin' to push 'er face in. Where is she?'

'Probably putting her feet up in the ATS quarters, or taking a shower,' I said. 'And how d'you know I've been out with her?'

'Someone said, didn't they?'

126

'Who?'

'I ain't saying, am I? I know, that's all.' Minnie was flushed and upset. 'Fancy goin' out with someone like that, I never seen anyone more ugly. Aunt Flossie says I'm easily the prettiest woman in Suffolk—'

'Now, how could she say that about a scatty school-girl?'

'Never you mind, she did say it.' Minnie kicked the front tyre of the bike. 'Why can't you take me out on Sundays instead of someone ugly and with rotten legs?'

'She's got good legs.'

'Oh!' Minnie let out a cry of fury. 'You've been lookin' at them in some field, you never look at mine and they're easy better than hers!'

'Oh, come on, Min, pack it up, you know you're just putting it on and playing games with me.'

'I ain't, I'm not, I wouldn't, I couldn't! Oh, you wait till I'm sixteen and the Yanks line up to take me out, I'll go out with hundreds of them I will and send you all dotty and grief-struck with jealousy. You'll want me for your best girl then, when you can't 'ave me.' She eyed me woefully. 'I just don't know why you can't say you love me.'

'Eh?'

'I'm grown up nice, ain't I?'

'A terror, more like,' I said.

'You didn't say that at rising summer.'

'Leave off about that, Min, there's a good girl.'

'All that lovin' and all,' she said.

'All that imagination, you mean.'

127

'I won't say anything, will I? Don't want Dad to go for you with 'is chopper, do I?'

'Holy cows,' I said, 'you're making holes in my head.'

'Just don't take that ugly old American woman out any more, that's all,' said Min. 'Just come round when I'm sixteen and take me out.'

'I'm going to have to talk to your dad about you.'

'And I'm goin' to talk to that boss-eyed, bandy-legged sergeant woman,' said Min. 'I'm goin' to tear all 'er rotten hair out.' And off she went in high dudgeon.

I walked down to the pub with Cassidy, Cecily and Frisby later. Top Sergeant Dawson seemed to have got lost in a rural backwater somewhere, so Cassidy said she'd like a nice quiet evening. Going through the high street, young Wally Ricketts called me. I went back to see what he wanted.

''Ello, Tim,' he said, 'I can get yer a pair tomorrer, say, seein' yer didn't wallop me that time.'

'You can pinch another helping of bunny rabbit, can you?'

'Dunno what yer mean,' said Wally. He was far browner than he probably ever was in the East End. His freckles were a burning gold. 'I can get 'em dead honest for you, Tim.'

'I'll let you know, Wally. I need someone who's going on leave to deliver 'em.'

'You ask anytime, Tim, you're me mate,' said Wally, 'and ain't that Minnie Beavers an eyeful? Is she stuck on yer? Cor, I wouldn't mind bein' you. Seen yer wiv 'er at risin' summer.'

'What d'you mean, you saw her with me at rising summer?'

'Kissin' and all,' said Wally, a grin on his face.

'You were in bed.'

'Well, I was for a bit, then I got up,' he said. I could imagine that. The sounds of revelry and the inclinations of an adventurous boy. He'd want to get a look at what was going on.

'How would you like to be pushed under a train?' I asked.

''Ere, I wouldn't tell on yer, Tim,' he said. 'Could yer lend me a tanner so's I can send me dad a birfday card?'

'Meet me at the pond in half an hour, when it's dark,' I said.

'Can't yer lend me the tanner now?' he asked.

'I'm not going to lend you a tanner, I'm going to drown you,' I said.

'Me? I ain't done nuffink, Tim.'

'All right, here's tuppence,' I said. The trouble was I had a blank mind about Min that night. I supposed I might have gone in for some heavy kissing while inebriated up to my eyeballs. Wally accepted the copper coins with a boyish smile.

'Yer me best mate, Tim,' he said. 'I 'opes yer flattens the 'ole German Army by yerself. I wouldn't 'arf be proud.'

'Flog off,' I said and went to join Frisby and the Wacs in the pub.

CHAPTER NINE

I was glad to get out one evening, after several days of having Major Moffat on my back. He meant to get me for something, even for having a button undone.

I walked to the village and knocked on Jim's door. Minnie answered. In her gymslip. She blossomed into smile, a forgiving one.

'Oh, you Tim, you've come to take me out?' she said.

'Well, no, not yet, Min, you're still not eighteen.'

'No, when I'm sixteen – sixteen. That's when I can start goin' out. Oh, Mum heard you were comin' round this evening.' It was almost frightening. I'd said to Frisby I was popping down to the village, did he want to come with me. He'd said he had a date to walk about with Cecily.

'Just how did your Mum get to know that?' I asked.

'Dicky bird flew in again, didn't it?' said Min. 'But we 'aven't heard you've gone out with that ugly old American sergeant again. It's best you don't, Tim, I'll get ever so cross if you do. Oh, I couldn't have come out with you this evening, anyway, I'm goin' to Aunt Flossie's again. Mum said to give 'er a bit of company.'

Missus was up to something again. Minnie was being got out of the way.

'Well, be good,' I said.

130

'Rather be good with you,' she said, 'good an' lovin'.'

'Wouldn't be good, would it, if I got run in for it.'

A gurgle of laughter issued. She looked over her shoulder. There was no-one in the little hall. 'Kiss, then,' she said and pushed herself close.

'Get off—' Too late. Her arms were around me, a warm girlish mouth clinging. I was aghast. I thought of the village eyes that were always at the ready behind curtains. Young Minnie was incriminating me on her doorstep in the light of the summer evening. And what a figure she had. One like that should be forbidden to girls of her age.

She let go. A little noisy breath escaped her. For a moment an actual blush seemed to show. 'Oh, you Tim, ain't you bliss to a girl?' she breathed.

'Min, I'll thump you. Don't do things like that at your front door, they'll be written down by old Mother Goggle opposite and used as evidence.'

'Course they won't,' said Minnie, 'everyone knows I'm goin' to be your best girl.'

'Oh, everyone's had a visit from a dicky bird, have they?'

'No, me,' she said. 'Told everyone, I 'ave.'

'Everyone? The village bobby as well?'

'He likes me. He likes you too, said you were a good 'un.'

'You little monkey, the stories you make up.'

'No, I don't,' said Minnie. She smiled, then turned and called. 'Dad, Tim's come round. Mum, you can take your apron off, Tim's 'ere.' She was away to Aunt Flossie's then. Down the street she whisked, a threat to civilization, although I'd heard from her mum that she was doing so good at school that her teachers thought she could be an asset. Yes, I thought, to the Windmill Theatre.

Jim and his old hat and pipe appeared. He drew me into the parlour. 'Min's gone off, I reckon,' he said.

'Gone off at fifteen?'

'Eh?' said Jim.

'What? Oh, see what you mean, gone off to Aunt Flossie's.'

'Well, Aunt Flossie's fond of 'er,' said Jim. ''Elping to bring 'er up.'

'Some help. Aunt Flossie sounds a dubious old haybag to me.'

'Now that ain't nice, Tim lad. You come to see Missus, to enjoy a nice talk with 'er and so on?'

'I don't mind a nice talk, I'll fight any so on.'

'Well, I tell yer, Tim, 'er mind's made up to be educational to you an' she always sees any job through to a good finish. Likes to do things proper.'

'You've got some gall, you have, using a word like proper about something that's indecent.'

'Ain't indecent, Tim,' he said. 'Nothing more natural than a good woman bein' special 'elpful to a young bloke.'

'Natural?' I said. 'Pornographic, more like. It'll take us all over.'

'Won't 'ave time to, I reckon,' said Jim. 'Your lot'll soon have to go an' start firin' yer guns again. Still, there'll be time enough for you to get some good learning in. Friend of the fam'ly, you are.'

132

'I'll talk to Missus. But before I do, can I inspect your shed?'

'Now that ain't no place for learning, lad. Cushions an' things, that's best.'

'Look,' I said, 'I just want to see what's in your shed. I'm after some wood.'

We went around to his garden shed. It was as big as his cottage. In it he stored everything he collected, lifted or otherwise acquired. It was a little bit like a run-down bargain basement.

'What kind o' wood?' asked Jim.

'Just an old three-feet door that nobody wants and some other junk not worth anything.'

'Ain't got no stuff like that,' said Jim, 'it's all got a price. I ain't Father Christmas.'

'We'll see,' I said and I searched around. He had enough old seasoned timber to build a new Ark, with lifeboats. 'This'll do.' I spotted a solid three-footer with peeling paint. 'It's for a crippled old war widow in Elsingham. It can't be worth more than a pint of old and mild. And I'll have some of that rotten stuff there as well.'

'Ain't rotten,' said Jim. 'Them's high fence posts, four by four.'

'Just right. I'd like two eight-foot lengths to use as doorposts. Nice you've got a van and can cart the stuff over.'

'She's a widder you said?' enquired Jim. 'What widder?'

'Mary Coker, Beech Cottage.'

''Ere, she ain't old nor crippled, she's a lively London

133

body and I ain't sure I can deliver to Elsingham with a war on. It ain't our parish. But if I can get to cart it over, it'll cost yer, lad. Anyway, we'll see, eh? Missus is in the kitchen.' He sloped off to the pub. I was left with the choice of standing up to Missus or running another mile. Best to do some standing up.

I did it in the kitchen. Missus was just taking her apron off.

'So there you are, Tim. Come right in, ducky.'

'It's no go, Missus. It's kind of you, I'll say that much, but it's not decent.'

Missus smiled. In a yellow button-up blouse and a brown skirt, she was a countrified knockout. 'Tim, you're shy again, love.'

'No, I'm not, I'm like iron. You're my best friends here, you and Jim. So it's not on.'

'No, course it isn't, love, not in the kitchen. Kitchen's for cookin', not cuddlin'. You go and sit yourself down on the sofa and I'll be with you directly. Oh, by the way, our Min wasn't hardly too pleased you cyclin' up Elsingham way with that lady sergeant of yours on Sunday. I told you she'd get jealous, Tim. Kicked your bike over, did she?'

'Nearly. Well, Missus, for the sake of our friendship—'

'Yes, friendship's valuable, like, ducky. You go and sit down and I'll come and be nice and valuable to you. Oh, and come to tea Sunday.'

Her mind was made up all right. So I slipped silently out of the cottage and ran a fast mile.

On Sunday morning I looked for Kit. Finding her, I asked if she'd like another afternoon bike ride. We could call on Mary again I said and let her know Jim Beavers was going to deliver a door and some timbers. Kit said shoot, I should have asked her earlier. She was otherwise engaged. I asked who with. An higher-up, she said. I suspected it was Major Moffat. I had a feeling he was after her, although not in the same way he was after me. However, Kit did say she'd keep next Sunday open. I said OK, next Sunday.

I read a book in the afternoon. Gunner Dunwoodie showed me his face at four-thirty. It was wearing an idiot's grin.

'Yer wanted, Tim,' he said.

'Who by?'

'Jim Beavers' girl.'

'Tell her I'm ill.'

'Can't, can I?' said the idiot. 'I already told 'er you're in the pink.'

'Well, tell her I've had a sudden breakdown.'

'Can't, can I, because you ain't, 'ave yer?'

What a twit. I had to go. The terror was waiting outside the gates, in her best Sunday dress of pastel blue.

'Well?' I said.

Minnie, her bike propped against the hedge, let a smile run about all over her face of honey. 'Crikey, don't yer look manly, Tim? Ain't yer grown up lovely?'

'What're you after?' I asked.

'Mum sent me. Go an' find our Tim, she said, he

135

should be here by now, 'e knows I invited 'im. See what's keepin' 'im. Oh, am I glad it's not that fat American sergeant.'

'Now, Min, she's not fat—'

'She will be,' said Min, looking triumphantly certain. 'Mum 'eard they eat more starch than elephants an' Dad said that at the Yanks' base there's some Wacs nearly as big as elephants. Six feet big 'e said an' nearly as wide. Can you get a bike out of your stores now and ride 'ome with me? Mum's goin' to do a nice tea.'

'And what's on after tea?' I asked.

'Oh, Dad and me's goin' up to the chicken farm near Sudbury in 'is van to collect some new layers. Mum says you can keep 'er company till we get back.'

'Sorry, Min,' I said, seeing the trap, 'but I'm house-bound, I'm standing by for fire picquet duty.'

'Oh, blow,' said Minnie, 'Mum's not goin' to like that. She's baked a cake special, she won't like the old war messin' you about. All fiddle-diddle the old war is.'

'I know, Min, I feel as mucked about as anybody. But I've got to stand up like a man to it.'

Minnie wrinkled her nice nose. 'Blessed old fire picquet,' she said. Then she smiled. It gave her the look of a sunripe dairymaid. What with that and what with Missus, I felt my best bet was to ask for a posting to Australia. 'Still, there won't always be a war, Tim. Best you give in when I'm sixteen.'

'Give in to what?'

'Lovin' me,' she said.

136

'I'll give in to thumping you, I'll give in to that much, you cheeky infant.'

She laughed. 'Like you best of all when you're bein' comical,' she said and swung her bike from the hedge to the road. 'Well, I'll tell Mum you can't come.' She hitched her dress and drew one leg up to put herself in the saddle. Her Sunday stockings flashed. I growled at her. 'Got good 'uns, ain't I, Tim?' She smiled, seeing me looking.

'Hoppit,' I said.

'Don't you go out no more with that American sergeant,' she said. 'Tear all 'er hair out, I will, if you do.'

She rode away, dress whisking, legs shining.

Minnie was trouble. So was her mum.

Aunt May and I wrote regularly to each other. She wanted to know more about this American sergeant I mentioned from time to time. So I told her that Kit Masters was a very efficient American soldier, but that I didn't know if she was just as efficient as a civilian woman in a kitchen. I said she looked very picturesque on a bike and that I liked her. On or off a bike.

Aunt May wrote back to say it was time I answered questions seriously, as she couldn't make head or tail of anything I'd said about this American girl. She also let me know that Mr Clayton had called again, just to ask how she was and that they'd shared another pot of tea and an interesting talk. And he'd been nice enough to ask her out. So they were going to have a walk round Hyde Park on Sunday.

I cornered Gunner Simpson in the vehicle workshop. He was a motor mechanic.

'Listen, mate,' I said, 'this uncle of yours, the one who delivered the rabbits to my aunt, what's he like?'

'Me Uncle Bill? Oh, a bit short an' fat.'

'Eh?'

'Yes, Little Tubby they used to call 'im in the last war. But he's got a kind heart and six kids. To look at him, you wouldn't think he could've managed one, let alone six. He liked yer aunt, by the way. Pretty woman, he said she was. I think she put a twinkle in 'is mince pie—'

'All right, don't go on, I've got the picture.'

I wrote a quick letter, telling Aunt May not to go walking round Hyde Park with her new short fat friend who was a married man with six kids and still had a twinkle in his eye.

Aunt May replied by return, informing me that Mr Clayton was a forty-five-year-old widower, that he had two daughters who were both married, that he wasn't short or fat, but tall and lean, with nice manners, that he was just a friend and didn't have any dishonourable intentions, if that was what I was thinking. Still, she said, she liked it that I was thoughtful about her welfare.

I went after Gunner Simpson again. He saw me coming and shut himself up in the workshop loo. Staff-Sergeant Dix came and took a look at me.

'What's going on?' he asked.

'I'm waiting for Gunner Simpson to come out,' I said.

'What for?'

'Nothing very much, staff, he's only going to lose a leg,' I said.

'Not in his working time, he's not,' said Sergeant Dix. 'Get back to your chicken shed.'

I lost out on that happening.

CHAPTER TEN

When Brigade HQ asked for site commanders and a number of NCOs and gunners to report for instruction on the new Bofors Mark V, Sergeant Johnson put my name forward. Since the personnel required were all supposed to be from sites and since they weren't doing very much at the moment, I asked why I'd been put on the list. He informed me that as I'd been a member of a gun crew and was now rusted up, I was a special case. And Major Moffat concurred. His concurrence, according to Sergeant Johnson, had been terse. 'Send the fiddling peanut.'

Not that I was upset. Courses of instruction, compared to field exercises, were a doddle. You only did a six-hour day and were excused all those duties that dated from Waterloo. A week away at Brigade HQ would give me a chance to get back to normal.

My normal was being nice to people. Missus had turned all that upside-down and Minnie hadn't helped. I felt short-tempered at times. Aunt May had written to say that in my last letter I sounded as if I was having problems, was it anything to do with the American lady sergeant I'd met and said funny things about? You're not in love, are you? That was what she asked in her letter. I expect it's something like that, she wrote. I replied to say yes, it was something like that, but that I wasn't sure of my ground, or if it would suit me to be in love with a sergeant who was nuts about efficiency and ran a store in Boston thousands of miles away.

The course at Brigade HQ was very instructional. I did it standing on my head, a Bofors gun not being unfamiliar to me and the Mark V being a beauty. My instructor, a sergeant, said if my mouth didn't hold me back I might be a passable gunner one day.

'One day soon?' I asked, thinking of the Second Front, as everybody was.

'Well, one day in the next war,' he said.

'What's all this talk I've been hearing about rockets?'

'Top secret. You shouldn't have been bleedin' listening.'

On my return to BHQ, I ran into Kit and Cassidy. Cassidy gave me a smile and a wink and left me to Kit, who was getting to look like Rita Hayworth.

'How's tricks?' I asked.

'Excuse me?' she said impartially. It made me sound as if I could be anybody. Even Gunner Dunwoodie, who was more anybody than anyone.

'Yes, how are you, lovey?' I asked, shifting my shoulder. I had a soldier's best friend with me, my rifle. Slung.

'I'm fine,' said Kit. 'Who are you, by the way?'

'That's not very friendly.'

'Oh, it's you,' she said. 'You're back.'

'Pleased, are you?'

'I wasn't aware you were away until Sunday came round and I found I'd been stood up.'

141

'Hell, what a lemon, I clean forgot. We were going to cycle to Mary's. Sorry.'

'It's OK,' she said, but she was still cool. 'Major Moffat filled in.'

'That's historical, you don't often get a battery commander standing in for a gunner.'

'He took me on a comprehensive tour of Suffolk,' said Kit, leafing through a file she held busily to her face.

'Serves me right. Did you enjoy it?'

Kit's mouth twitched. 'I'd have enjoyed it more if that crazy great dog of his hadn't been so hungry. It tried to eat half my skirt.'

'Lucky you, it could easily have been half your—'

'Skip half my whatever,' she said, 'I can read your mind, Hardy.' She looked at my best friend. 'What's that?'

'A rifle. Didn't you know?'

'Yes, but I wondered if you did. It's the first time I've seen you wearing one.' She laughed. 'Well, I guess that's all for now.'

'No, hold on a tick. Can I make up for last Sunday by making chits out for both of us tomorrow?'

'Why not?' she said. 'I think you owe me. See you around, old buddy.'

After teatime bread and cheese, Frisby took me aside and mentioned that his relationship with Cecily was a mix-up.

'Had a relapse, has she?' I asked.

'Listen, cock. I offered myself to Cecily as a father figure. Now I've got an 'orrible feeling she doesn't want

142

me as a dad, after all. What's more, she's got sex appeal she doesn't know about. Know what it's done to me? Knocked me fatherly feelings for six. I'm human, y'know.'

'I know, that's a problem for all of us.'

'Point is, mate, how can I think of doing anything unkind to a bird who wants to believe some men would make a good Christmas present?'

'With an effort, you could think about it quite easily, couldn't you?'

'Don't talk like a cup of cocoa,' said Frisby. 'I can't do things to a trusting American violet with her kind of history. But I can't make her out, she's talking about us going steady. Listen.' He recounted.

On their way back from the pub last night, he and Cecily had taken to the by-ways instead of the road. The by-ways were rural and romantic and were making Cecily twitch. Frisby assured her nothing was going to happen. But Cecily came up with a surprising invitation.

'Claud, you can kiss me, if you like.'

'No, you'll only get pent-up. Just enjoy the walk. We might get to see a fox or two.'

'But you want to kiss me, don't you?' said Cecily.

'You'll kill me,' said Frisby.

'Claud, of course I won't,' she said. 'Oh, I guess I'm no good at this, trying to get a guy to be nice to me.'

'OK,' said Frisby, 'here it comes, then, but don't drop dead.' He put his hands on her shoulders. Cecily quivered. He admitted the self-tormented Wac had unearthed a protective instinct in him, which was a surprise to him. So he kissed her nicely, that was all.

143

There was another surprise coming. Cecily gave her all in her response.

'Steady,' he said.

'Do it again,' she said.

'What?'

'Kiss me again.'

So he kissed her again and Cecily wound herself around him. He came up for air.

'Now how'd you feel?' he asked.

'Crazy,' said Cecily. 'Claud, you know you're important to me, don't you?'

'Like a father?'

'Shoot, no, I can find a nice old guy with whiskers to be my pa,' said Cecily. 'Was I OK, Claud, did you like kissing me?'

'Well, of course I did,' said Frisby.

'Isn't that great? I liked it too. I guess we're dating steady now, Claud?'

I thought that seemed an open and shut case and said so. I asked Frisby why he thought there was a problem.

'Is she forcing herself, mate, that's the problem,' said Frisby.

'More like she's after a wartime wedding. What a good job you've done on her, doctor.'

'Think so? She keeps saying she likes this tight little island, all the daisies and everything. Pretty, she keeps saying. You sure that sounds like a wartime wedding?'

'Lucky old you.'

'But should I tell her a doctor can't marry his patient?'

'Why can't you? It's legal. And you wanted a little woman for your post-war future. Now you've got one.'

144

*

I couldn't avoid Jim in the pub that evening. He wouldn't let me. He took me aside.

'Missus said come round Tuesday evenin'. Goin' bikin' again with yer nice female sergeant tomorrer, are yer, maybe? Fine legs she's got. Minnie don't think 'ighly of 'er, though. Ah, 'ere she is, just come in. Got 'er nice eyes on yer, Tim boy.'

A hand touched my elbow. I turned. Kit smiled sweetly. 'Buy me one, Tim old boy?' she said.

'A pink nightie?' I offered.

'A Suffolk cider. I'll find a table and play you checkers.'

'You're on. Can I walk you back to BHQ afterwards?'

'Sure you can,' said Kit. 'At a safe distance.' She laughed.

I had the bikes ready when she met me on the fore-court on Sunday afternoon. She inspected her machine with the cool, critical eye of a woman who knew it was second nature with men to dig pits for females. The major's myopic Dalmatian, wandering about on the loose, padded up on eager paws and made a blind try for her left leg. I tickled it with a bicycle pump and it shot off howling.

'You hit that dog, you brute,' said Kit.

'Saved your left leg, though,' I said. She bounced her bike, testing the tyres. 'I think they'll hold out,' I said.

'Yes, we don't want to run out of gas again, do we, Hardy?'

'Just bad luck last time.'

145

'Oh, sure. Let's go.'

We went riding through the gates and out into the countryside, taking the winding lanes. We rode together. Kit's skirt travelled enough to make her legs a picture. The weather was warm but breezy, the sky in the east full of little white puff-ball clouds.

Kit, riding easily, said, 'This is great, this is fresh air and sweet peace. Are you looking?'

'Not all the time.'

'Why are men stupid about stockings?'

'I think we're stupid about everything. Well, I am.'

'Never mind,' said Kit, 'you're still useful, I hope.'

In that friendly way, we enjoyed our ride to Mary's. Mary was delighted to see us again. She was a chatty old love. Kit and I meant welcome Sunday company for her. Her neighbours on either side were chummy but a bit ancient and accordingly prone to drop off during an afternoon gossip, which gave Mary's chattiness a poke in the eye. Kit's willing American ear was very welcome. The two of them were soon basking in fields of conversational clover. Lively as crickets, they were. I wandered away to do some gardening.

Mary called, 'There's a door come, Tim, I just remembered.'

'A door? It dropped in, did it?' I went back into the living-room.

'No, you silly, it was brought.'

'Oh, that door,' I said.

'With some big bits of wood.'

'Good.'

'A shifty-looking man brought them,' said Mary.

146

'Mind, he spoke friendly and was nice in a way. Mr Beavers he said his name was.'

'I've met that guy myself,' said Kit. 'I rate him suspect. Did you feel relieved, Mary, that you were still alive after he'd gone?'

'Oh, I didn't feel I was being accosted,' said Mary, 'just looked over.'

'Well,' I said, 'if a nice old bloke like Jim can't look over a well-formed widow or an American Wac without being thought shifty and suspect, I can't see any point in men and women being made differently. Mind you,' I said, making a safety move to the door, 'if we were all the same, would we face the world with bosoms or chests?'

As I disappeared, I heard Mary giggle. I heard Kit say, 'Let's face it, Mary, they're all a little screwy.'

I looked in the garden shed. The door was there, with posts and other bits of wood. Good old Jim. Disgraceful sod he may have been, conniving with his Missus, but he had his better points. The door and the posts would do. I only needed to swipe some suitable hinges off a shelf in the quartermaster's stores. And all the necessary tools were available, except a saw. That I could borrow from the stores. I only needed to write out a chit.

The open air felt good, so I did some hoeing. The chickens cocked suspicious eyes and adopted stiff one-legged attitudes in case I was there to wring a neck or two. In my shirt sleeves, I hoed in the sunshine. The sky became completely clear, the breeze dropped and the afternoon turned balmy. Kit came out and said Mary thought it would be nice to have tea in the garden, so perhaps I'd get some deckchairs from the shed. I hoed on.

'I'm speaking to you, Tim old buddy.'

'Was there something?'

'Yes. Deckchairs. Mary said—'

'All right, I'll get them out.'

I got three folding deckchairs from the shed and erected them on the lawn. Kit brought out a folding card-table. I took it from her, unfolded it and set it up.

'I could have done that,' she said.

'No, I'm the handyman,' I said.

'So what am I?' she asked, with one of her cool looks.

'You're sir.'

'That's not funny,' said Kit, 'and if you say anything like that again, I'll kick your teeth in.'

'You would too.'

'Yes, I would too.'

Mary came out and laid a white cloth over the table. Tea followed. Mary served poached eggs on toast, scones and jam. Kit tucked in, utterly enchanted by this kind of English tea. Mary talked about Fred Plummer and how he'd come to look at her mower at last and how she told him he was too late. So he said he'd look at her drains instead and she told him he was too late for that as well. She suggested perhaps he could think about getting her chimney swept before winter arrived. Fred said he'd come and look at it sometime.

'You'd never believe how many ways he's got of doing nothing,' said Mary. 'I never met a lazier ha'porth. I've got as much chance of getting him to look at my

148

chimney as I've got of getting my chickens to lay gold eggs.'

'He's not the only man in the world, Mary,' said Kit, 'so we're not licked yet. We'll find someone else.'

I could hardly credit the craftiness of women. 'Drains, yes,' I said. 'Chimneys, no.'

'You could give it a go,' said Kit.

'I'm not getting stuck up any chimney,' I said.

'You amaze me,' said Kit. 'There are thousands of brave British boys fighting it out in the Middle East and Far East and you're sitting here drinking Mary's tea and eating her cookies and you can't even bring yourself to sweep her chimney.'

'Oh, don't be unkind to him, Kit,' said Mary, 'Tim's awful obliging, really he is. And he's done a good job helping to shoot down them German bombers that blitzed us.'

'OK, Mary, I won't tell you exactly what he did help to shoot down,' said Kit.

'I'm not going up any chimney,' I said.

'You don't have to go up it,' said Kit.

'Good,' I said, 'I've got to think about fixing that door to the porch. I'll start next Sunday, Mary.'

'I just don't know anyone more helpful than you, Tim,' said Mary.

'I'll trim your hedges after tea.'

'You're a real love,' said Mary.

'Sweet,' said Kit.

When tea was over, I found the shears and started work. Kit helped Mary wash the dishes, then came to loiter and watch.

149

'There's a lot of clippings,' she said.

'Yes, I know, sir, but I'll be raking them up.'

'I'll kill you,' said Kit, 'but I'll get the rake first.'

She used the rake herself, looking trim in her shirt and skirt. She might have been hopeless with a garden rake, but she wasn't, of course. She made tidy heaps, all of which she transferred efficiently to the wheelbarrow.

'Well, that's very good, sir,' I said, when the hedges were finished and the trimmings all disposed of.

'You're losing your charm,' said Kit.

Mary said a grateful goodbye to us and we began our ride back to BHQ in the balmy light of the evening sun. Kit suggested a stop at the village pub.

'Good idea, I could sink a pint,' I said.

'My treat,' said Kit, 'you're not a bad old buddy.'

When we reached Sheldham, Missus was at the gate of her cottage. Clad in a flowery dress, she was talking to a neighbour. Seeing me, she waved. Seeing Kit, she smiled.

'Evening, Missus,' I called, cycling past.

'Another widow?' asked Kit.

'No, she's Mrs Jim. I get eggs from her occasionally.'

'Are you a womanizer?'

'Not yet.'

We left our bikes at the rear of the *Suffolk Punch* and went in. The public bar was as crowded as always. Evensong was over for the locals and they were wetting their Sunday whistles. Kit received her usual boisterous welcome from GIs and disappeared in the middle of them. As she didn't call for help, I went to say hello to Jim.

150

'Evening, Jim. Ta for delivering the wood to Mary Coker.'

'Good stuff, it was,' said Jim. 'Wasn't for free. Charged your widder woman two bob, includin' valuable cartage.'

'You old Shylock, charging any widow that much. A tanner would have been enough. Has Missus turned over a new leaf? She looked as if she had.'

'Now, Tim boy, you ain't catchin' me out with clever questions. Missus has been to Evensong in 'er Sunday best. She was put out, yer know, you not turnin' up for tea that Sunday. But she's forgiven yer, lad.'

'I'd like a pint of old ale,' I said, 'and it's your turn.'

''Ere, you sure?' said Jim.

'Sure I'm sure,' I said.

Kit was still in the middle of the scrum, talking to two American sergeants. So I let Jim buy me a pint. He said Missus still had hopes for me. 'Leave off,' I said, 'think about how you'd feel if Missus shot herself in a fit of remorse.'

'Don't talk foreign, Tim. Showin' off, that is. Anyway, Missus wouldn't know 'ow to use me shotgun. 'Ere, ain't this a damn old war, like our Min says? No room in this pub to 'ardly stand up. I ain't sayin' I don't like the Yanks, only sayin' I never knowed there was so many of 'em. Still, it looks like you been an' found that nice female one. Rides a sweet old bike, I 'eard. Got a good pair of pedallers, I 'eard.'

'Is that a fact? I'd better take a look at them, I wouldn't want to miss what you've heard. How's Min?'

'Funny, like,' said Jim, chewing his pipe. 'All broody one day, all sauce the next. Spring fever, I reckon.'

'It's summer.'

'At 'er age, lad, spring fever lasts a year. I ain't sure she don't need a tanning, I ain't sure she ought to talk about you the way she does. Blowed if she didn't say she'll chop yer bonce off if you get fancy ideas about yer lady sergeant. Best you don't get too close to 'er.'

'Look, Min can keep her virgin bosom to herself—'

''Old on, 'old on,' said Jim, 'you been at young Min's vest?'

'She wears a vest?'

'Course she wears a vest. Girl 'er age ain't decent without one. You ain't been there, 'ave you?'

'Don't be daft,' I said.

'When all's said an' done, yer know, she is me own flesh an' blood.'

'I see. After trying to chuck your Missus at me, you're now telling me your daughter's purity is precious to you?'

Jim chewed his pipe, took it out, supped beer, put his pipe back and peered at me. 'Ain't tellin' you nothing, Tim lad, except you give Min 'alf a chance an' she'll 'ave you. Eat you alive. She'll be sixteen anytime now.'

'Well, buy her a rocking-horse for her birthday.'

Kit appeared, a glass of gin and tonic in one hand and a glass of beer in the other. The beer was for me. I still had some left of what Jim had bought me, so Kit pushed her treat into my left hand.

'Well, thanks,' I said.

'You're welcome,' said Kit.

152

'Evenin', Kitty Lou,' said Jim.

'Hi, Mr Beavers.' Kit gave him a smile, overlooking what she considered was his shiftiness. 'It's Kit, not Kitty Lou.'

'Kitty Lou's pretty, though,' said Jim, his beady eyes twinkling.

'Kitty Lou is endemic to States like Louisiana,' said Kit.

'It ain't a disease, is it?'

'In a way,' said Kit. 'Play you checkers, Tim?'

'OK.'

Jim sat down with us to watch. Mostly he watched Kit, as if he meant to report on her to Missus. I had a feeling Missus was acting as proxy for Aunt May, that she wasn't going to let me take up with any woman she didn't approve of.

We played four games. Kit played with her keenness and her vitality showing, her eyes quick and alert. I was getting so fond of her that I didn't mind letting her win.

'You're fooling about,' she said.

'Me?'

'Well, that is you there, isn't it, playing like you're retarded?'

'I'm enjoying the company,' I said.

'Company's needful,' said Jim. 'As long as they got a roof over their 'eads and enough to eat, people can do without nearly everything else except each other. I wouldn't be nothing without Missus. I know I got me chickens, but I don't call 'em company.'

'I get you,' said Kit and smiled. 'What's checkers, anyway?'

153

We said good night to Jim and cycled back to BHQ. It was dark. As we passed through the village, a dog came running from across the street. Barking, it went for Kit's bike. She fell off. Someone whistled and the dog ran back. It looked like Jim's dog to me, the one that waited for foxes at night. I stopped and helped Kit to her feet.

'That crazy dog,' she said, brushing herself down.

'You OK, Kit?'

'Just a broken neck,' she said.

'Don't muck about, are you hurt?'

'Look who's talking, the number one comic in BHQ. No, I'm OK, thanks, just a little startled.'

When we reached BHQ, she actually waited while I returned the bikes to their stands outside the stores. Then she allowed me to walk her to the ATS quarters. She said she'd enjoyed the outing.

'My pleasure,' I said.

She laughed, lifted her face and kissed me. It wasn't a bad kiss, either. 'Thanks for the company, Tim,' she said.

'Good as a Christmas present, that was,' I said.

She laughed again and ghosted away.

That Minnie, the terror. She'd sent the family dog after Kit.

CHAPTER ELEVEN

Frisby was enduring a lot of self-examination. He thought Cecily ought to try marriage to save herself from a worse fate, but what would it do to her? And what would it do to him? Would what was desirable for her also be desirable for him? Would she like going to bed with a man until death did them part? Did he want to take on the worry of that? And so on.

Cecily collared me as I came off duty one evening. She was suffering some nervous twitches.

'Hi, Tim,' she said and made an effort to smile.

'Problems?' I said. 'Just hit Frisby over the head.'

'Oh, shoot, I couldn't do that, he's my nice guy,' she said.

'What's on your mind, then?' I asked.

'Kit spoke to me a couple of days ago.' Cecily swallowed. 'About that inquiry.'

'All blown over,' I said.

'Sure, but – well, I thought that lecherous old geezer was after my legs. I was mad. I was going to report you'd let him lift a can of gas from that mousetrap. Kit talked me out of mentioning you, so I told Major Moffat I'd seen the guy with a British can of gas when I was riding by in the mousetrap, that he was carrying it into his cottage. I didn't say you'd stopped outside his cottage, so I guess he thought you might have given it to him while you were parked outside the railroad station, waiting for us. He asked me questions, but I stuck to that. Cassidy and Kit refused to volunteer any information and anyway, they acted as if it was all a mystery to them. Oh, hell, I'm real sorry, Tim, honest to God I am. Kit said I ought to be fair, I ought to tell you. She was mad about the inquiry, I guess because you had an idea she spilled the beans.'

'No harm done, Cecily,' I said, 'it all turned into a powder puff.'

'You're not mad at me?'

'Not a bit. Just pleased it's all tidied up.'

'Will you do me a big favour and not say anything to Claud? He'll think I'm a lousy guy.'

'I don't think he thinks you're a guy, I think he thinks you're a girl. You're doing a great job on him.'

'I'm what?' she said.

'Keep it up,' I said.

Cecily smiled wryly. 'No, he's the dcotor,' she said.

Frisby put in an appearance at that point. Cecily flashed me a look of appeal and fled.

'What's up with my chaste patient?' asked Frisby.

'In a hurry, that's all. She brought me a message from Kit.'

'Passionate?'

'Not yet,' I said. We began the walk to our hut.

'I'm in six minds about Cecily,' said Frisby. 'Who wouldn't be with this war still going on? I could still get shot to pieces, or it might last another ten years, by which time I won't care if I'm living or dead. I mean, who can make plans? Have I got a future? I know it looks as if I've got a bird who likes my medicine and I wouldn't want her wandering the face of the earth if I disappointed her. But with things as they are, how can I make decisions? On the other hand, can I let my nervous patient wander off to rack and ruin?'

'Don't ask me,' I said, 'ask Cecily. Pop the question.'

'I might just do that,' he said. 'Someone's got to save her. She's a nice girl.'

I called on Missus one evening. Jim had dropped by and rustled six eggs into my keeping. From Missus, he said. So I had to call on her and say thanks. Missus had been a good friend until she went mad. Minnie answered the door in a jumper and skirt. The jumper shouldn't have been allowed.

'Hello, Min.'

'Oh, I won't be a tick,' she said, 'I'll get me beret.'

'What for?'

'Wearing. Where we goin' to walk to?'

'Evening classes at your school?'

'Who's goin' to evening classes?' asked Min.

'Good idea if you did,' I said. 'Better for you than buzzing round to Aunt Flossie. I don't trust Aunt Flossie.'

'What d'you mean? You've never met her.'

'I'm lucky, I suppose. Is your mum in?'

'Mum's out. So's Dad.' Minnie smiled. 'You can come in, Tim, we don't 'ave to go walkin'. We can just do sittin' and cuddlin'.'

157

'That's it, get me locked up. So long, Min – oh, tell your mum thanks for the eggs.'

'Oh, you're rotten,' said Min. 'I'll find a GI, you'll see.'

'Not if your dad finds him first,' I said and hurried away.

''Ello, Tim.' Young Wally Ricketts materialized. 'I just seen yer talkin' to that Minnie. Ain't she an eyeful? I got yer the rabbits, trapped 'em meself, I did.'

'Didn't I tell you I only wanted them when the right kind of bloke was going on leave and could drop 'em in for me?'

'Yes, course yer did, Tim,' he said, 'an' I 'eard yer Bombardier Wilkins is goin' tomorrer. I 'eard as well that 'e lives near Camberwell.'

'I see. All the village dicky birds use your earhole as well, do they?'

'Well, fings do get around, Tim,' said young Wally. ''Ere y'ar, I got the rabbits under me jersey.' He pulled out two rabbits wrapped in brown paper. 'I'll only charge yer one an' six.'

'Hold on, it was a bob last time.'

'Yer, well, they gone up a bit since, yer see.'

'Ninepence,' I said, 'and stop trying to teach me how to suck eggs.'

''Ere, ninepence is only fourpence-'apenny each,' he said indignantly.

'Ninepence and a clip round each ear for coming it, you horrible little Peeping Tom.'

'Well, I was only sayin' like, that Mr Beavers ain't

158

keen on 'is Minnie goin' kissin' and all – 'ere, what yer doin', Tim?'

'Turning you round so that I can boot your backside.'

'I dunno, yer can't do nuffink round 'ere wivout someone givin' yer a wallop. An' what about me ninepence?'

'All right, here you are. Now beat it.'

'Well, ta. I likes it that you're me mate, Tim.'

I gave the rabbits to Bombardier Wilkins. Aunt May had thoroughly enjoyed the others. She'd had a friend round to enjoy them with her. Bombardier Wilkins made a fuss about delivering them. I said all right, one bunny for her, one for you. I had to make a concession to the fact that he was an NCO. He was happy then.

Some of us were beginning to wonder if the War Office had lost us, if we'd fallen out of their files. A lost record and a battery can cease to exist. A whole regiment even. It could mean missing the rest of the war. Outside the UK, the war was going on in the Atlantic, the Pacific, Sicily, Russia, China and Burma. We hadn't seen action for a year and more. No-one complained, of course, except Major Moffat, a man who definitely hadn't joined to sit the conflict out.

Walking along the path to the ablutions one evening, I saw the major and Sergeant-Major Baldwin coming the other way. We had to meet. I had my towel over my shoulder, a cake of soap in my hand and no cap on. As I couldn't salute without a cap on, I came to attention.

'What's this?' asked Major Moffat.

'I appreciate your question, sir,' said Sergeant-Major Baldwin, who had a waxed moustache. 'Answer it, Gunner Hardy.'

'Well, frankly, sergeant-major,' I said, 'I can honestly say I'm a loyal conscript and subject of the Empire.'

'Did you hear that waffle, sergeant-major?' asked the OC.

'Sad case, sir,' said the sergeant-major.

'Has he done any soldiering?' asked Major Moffat. His dog came up and investigated my trousers. 'No never mind. There was something else. Let's see.' He eyed me in a razor-sharp way. 'Gunner Hardy, I understand you've put it about that this battery, during certain actions against German bombers, shot down two Spitfires.'

'Just joking, sir.'

'Spreading false and malicious information detrimental to the war effort is no joke, Gunner Hardy. It's punishable by a dawn execution.'

'Yes, sir,' I said.

'Saddest case I ever come across, sir,' said Sergeant-Major Baldwin.

'Where are you going with that towel, Gunner Hardy?' asked the major.

'For a shower, sir,' I said, doing my best to keep Jupiter from making a bone of my left leg.

'Any chance that you'll drown yourself?'

'Hope not, sir.'

'Well, carry on,' said the major, 'make an attempt.'

I carried on. I had a shower.

Coming out of ablutions a little later, I saw Kit. She

stood in my way. She saw the towel over my shoulder and my still damp hair.

'You've just showered,' she said.

'You wouldn't say that if you'd seen our shower,' I said, 'you'd say I was an optimist in search of a miracle. Still, I managed to get rained on for ten seconds. That's a minor miracle. By the way, I'm going to be executed at dawn for telling you we shot down two Spitfires.'

'Serve you right,' said Kit. 'I'll get you for that, Tim, I'll get you good. You made a Patsy of me. Major Moffat was talking to me about the bombing raids and I naturally said it must have been disastrous news to him when it was reported that his battery had downed two Spitfires. I said you'd mentioned the disaster to me. He said he was going to have you torn apart by elephants. I'll be there watching.'

'Sounds painful,' I said. 'For me, I mean, not you.'

'You know, old buddy,' she said, 'I sometimes wonder if you're not just something I dreamt up.'

'Lucky you,' I said, 'we don't all have pleasant dreams.'

'You're cute,' she said. 'Are you going out later?'

'Only to the pub.'

'Well?' she said.

'Pardon?'

'Wake up,' she said.

'Meet you at the gates in twenty minutes, love?'

'OK, twenty minutes,' said Kit, 'but don't overdo it, soldier.'

We had quite a nice evening together.

*

On three Sundays in succession, I worked on fixing a door to Mary's porch. Kit came with me on each occasion, and took a keen and interfering interest in my labours. Mary's cottage echoed to the sounds of sawing, planing and hammering. I got quite involved with the job and having got involved, I wanted to make a resounding success of closing in Mary's porch. Mary said I was a really nice chap. Kit said I was quite a useful guy, but just a little screwy.

My relationship with her was friendly. At times she was a bit like a sister and at Mary's she was a bit like a foreman. I didn't really need her as either a sister or a foreman. She was a lot too kissable. I couldn't think of any other girl I'd like to have for keeps. There were occasions, of course, when she needed talking to. That was when she was bossy. If I could work myself up to it, I'd do that, I'd give her a talking to.

I was sweating and swearing a bit on the third Sunday. I'd got everything in place, including a deep lintel that filled in the gap above, and I'd bolted on the well-planed doorposts and chiselled out the hinge beds. But I couldn't get the perishing door flush, shave it though I did.

Kit appeared. She watched. And she listened. Then she said, 'If you took the door into the shed and planed it there, you'd be free to throw things about and swear your head off without offending anyone.'

'Listen, gaffer,' I said, 'I'm working here because I have to keep checking the size of this large lump of wood with the size of the large hole and it would be too inconvenient and too harrowing to cart the walloping hunk backwards and forwards from the shed. I'd get injured. And who's throwing things about?'

'You are,' said Kit, 'all Mary's tools, one after the other and sometimes three at a time. It's worrying Mary. She thinks it's all becoming too much for you.'

'Well, bless my soul, fancy that. And who's swearing?'

'You are.'

'Oh, dearie me,' I said. I hefted the door. It slipped, I grabbed at it, and all it did was to drop on my right foot. 'Oh, dear,' I said, 'well, I never, clumsy me.'

'You clown,' said Kit and went away.

I sweated a bit more, planed a bit more and suddenly the door was flush and house-proud. I held it in place against the temporary struts I'd nailed to the posts. I felt weak with triumph, so much so that when the door tilted and leaned on me, I gave in and we hit the ground together. Mary, hearing the noise, rushed to the scene. She gave the anguished cry of a motherly body.

'Oh, lor'! Kit quick, it's Tim, the door's on top of him! Oh, help, he looks struck dead.'

Kit's arrival was calmer than Mary's. She made a professional survey of me and the door. 'I can't see any blood,' she said.

'Kit, he's hurt,' protested Mary.

'Try him,' said Kit, 'give him a prod.'

I lay there not unhappily. I took the weight comfortably enough and the door, which had spent most of the afternoon being mucked about and reviled, seemed as glad as I was of a short break. It pressed fondly on me and we became friends.

'Tim, say you're all right,' pleaded Mary.

'Oh, bless us, Mary, yes, of course I'm all right,' I said. 'Dearie me, it's only a door and I'm only half unconscious.'

'He's showing off,' said Kit.

'Oh, hadn't we better get the door off him?' asked Mary.

'OK, let's humour him,' said Kit.

They lifted the door.

'Don't let go,' I said and got up. I shoved the door into place and they held it while I screwed in the hinges. And there it was. My door, firmly hung. I'd done it. It even opened and closed. I removed the struts. What a work of art. Mary had a closed-in porch and a little entrance lobby where she could hang wet coats.

'Tim, what a treat, what a nice door you've done for me,' she said and gave me a kiss. 'You're a real love, I don't know anyone who could've done it better. I'm ever so grateful.'

'Light the geyser, that's all I ask,' I said.

'It'll have to be painted and a bell fixed,' said Kit.

'Painted?' I went hoarse. I'd removed all the old paint and rubbed it down to the grain. 'A bell?'

'Sure,' said Kit.

'Painted?' I said again. 'It's oak, woman.'

'Excuse me?' said Kit at the word 'woman'.

'You don't paint oak,' I said, 'and whoever painted it in the first place was probably some woman having a female fit.'

'I don't like the way you said that, old buddy, and I think a nice coat of white paint—'

'Nice? Nice?'

'Oh, lor',' said Mary.

'It would look very nice,' said Kit, 'and you could fit one of those bells that chime.'

'Bananas,' I said hysterically, 'piddle, pee and essing bananas.'

'Oh, dear, we've upset him now,' said Mary. 'Couldn't we go and see if Winston Churchill's makin' one of his uplifting speeches on the wireless?'

'Bananas,' I said.

'Control yourself, soldier,' said Kit. 'Really, all this verbal mayhem. Mary and I are only making suggestions.'

'Kindly pay attention,' I said. 'This is my door, my labour of love. All it requires is a little oil from year to year. If I ever see paint on it, I'll fire thunderbolts at it. And it needs no ruddy bell. It's got a handle that opens it and there's a knocker on the inside door. The nancified ping-pong of chiming bells is out. Out. Is that clear, Sergeant Masters?'

'He's shouting now,' said Kit, 'but God knows what he's saying. Do you know what he's saying, Mary?'

'I'll go and do some nice scrambled egg on toast,' said Mary and hurried to the calm of her kitchen.

'Now see what you've done with all your shouting,' said Kit, 'you've upset Mary.'

'How would you like a good hiding?' I asked.

'You and your ambitions,' said Kit and made a crisp getaway through the cottage to the kitchen. I went after her. She hared through the back door into the garden.

Mary said, 'Oh, lor',' as I chased in pursuit.

I caught Kit on the lawn. She whirled inside my arms and we fell. There was a flurry of legs in fully-fashioned Waac stockings and then a kiss as I trapped her mouth. She gurgled and brought her knee up to smartly punish my navel. I let her go. She lay on the grass, skirt rucked, sparks in her blue eyes.

'I could get you for that,' she said.

'Court martial?'

'Can you be court-martialled for assault?' she asked.

'You could ask Major Moffat.'

'I'll ask his dog and set the brute on you.'

Mary came out. 'Are you two fighting?' she asked.

'Not now,' I said, 'I won that one.'

'That's a laugh,' said Kit.

'I don't like to see you two having a quarrel,' said Mary. 'Shall I do the scrambled eggs for supper now?' It was seven-thirty. I'd had a long afternoon.

'I'd like a bath first, Mary,' I said.

'You know you're welcome,' said Mary.

'Cold shower, try that,' said Kit and laughed.

I had a good soak in hot water and thought about her. Lovely girl really, even if she was bossy. I'd heard you had to expect that in most American females. Funny thing about Cecily, though. All that aggression to begin with. She'd looked as if she could see off Top Sergeant Dawson, given the right kind of provocation. Now she went around like a genuinely feminine bird, saying a friendly 'Hi!' to all the personnel. She even liked it at BHQ, she said all the guys there were great. She and Cassidy were popular figures. They mingled with the ATS girls and other ranks in the canteen some evenings.

166

Kit did most of her mingling in the sergeants' mess, as an invited guest.

Mary served scrambled eggs on toast with a salad for supper. 'Kit did the salad,' she said, 'she's been a nice help.'

Having this fondness for the way women can perform in a kitchen, I said, 'I like that piece of news, I like the picture.'

'Can you work out the meaning of most of what he says, Mary?' asked Kit.

'Oh, I think Tim likes us with our aprons on,' said Mary.

'Don't fall for that one, Mary,' said Kit, 'guys like that point girls like us only one way, to the kitchen.'

'Oh, well,' said Mary pacifically, 'that's where our work is mostly, Kit, while they go out and make doors and windows.'

'Good point, Mary,' I said.

'Yuk,' said Kit.

We left immediately after supper, Mary giving me a pat and thanking me again for my joinery work. The double summertime meant the evening was still full of warm light. Everything that was rural was a pleasure to the eye, the hedgerows dappled with colour. Kit was chatty as we pedalled side by side, and made kind remarks about the countryside. Old England wasn't bad to look at, she said. It had trees too. In New England it was mainly pines and maples.

'Well, that's good, lovey,' I said.

'Lovey sounds as if you're trying to strangle Shakespeare's English,' she said.

167

'It's London talk, it's matey.'

'What a guy,' said Kit.

'Shall we stop at the pub? We'll be in time for a quick one.'

'Great idea,' said Kit and pedalled away, humming a song of summer.

When we got to Sheldham, Mrs Lottie Ford popped out of her cottage and called to me. We stopped and wheeled our bikes up to her gate. Lottie Ford, in her early thirties, had her husband away at the war, two children whom she handled indulgently, an evacuee – none other than young Wally Ricketts – whom she had to watch like a hawk, and the same kind of healthy look as most of the women of Sheldham.

'I saw you comin', Tim,' she said, 'so I thought I'd have a word.'

They all had good eyesight, either from their parlours or anywhere else. They could see through curtain, blinds and garden fences and they could see round corners.

'Evening, Lottie,' I said and introduced Kit.

'Pleased to meet you, I'm sure,' said Lottie, 'I were only wonderin' just now if Tim was out with you again.'

'Were you?' asked Kit.

'Hadn't you heard, then, Lottie?' I asked.

'I been that busy today,' said Lottie. 'Tim's a nice obligin' young chap,' she said to Kit and Kit gave me one of her searching looks.

'Shed still standing up, Lottie?' I asked. Hers was the shed that young Wally said accidentally fell to pieces around him and which I'd rebuilt.

'Oh, that shed weren't never standin' up better, Tim.

168

It's my Welsh dresser now, it's comin' away from the wall. It's the screws, they're comin' out.'

'A Welsh dresser screwed to a wall?' I said.

'Oh, it were always old, I expect they did put screws in in them days,' said Lottie, fair-haired and a country-jumper-and-skirt type.

'It won't fall over,' I said, 'it's got a heavy cupboard foundation.'

'Yes, you seen it when you fixed my shed and come into my kitchen for tea and cake,' said Lottie. Kit rolled her eyes. 'It's got them little brass flaps, where the screws are comin' out. I'd be that grateful if you could fix it, Tim, afore young Wally gets at it with his mendin' hammer. Anything goes wrong around the place, he thinks a bang with his hammer will mend it. That boy, he'll knock the house down one day. I know you been busy fixin' little things for Mrs Beavers and your widow woman up at Elsingham, but if you could come in some time and do my dresser, Tim—'

'All right, some fat new rawlplugs will do it,' I said.

'You're such an obligin' help to a woman,' said Lottie. To Kit she said, 'Not many like Tim, that there aren't.'

'Don't I know it,' said Kit and we went on our way. 'Are you a compulsive fixer of women's problems?' she asked.

'Are you kidding? I'm just an odd-job bloke, not the village doctor.'

'Tim! You Tim! Come 'ere!' Minnie was at her gate and not caring who heard her or saw her.

Kit turned and took a look at her. 'I can't believe this,'

she said. 'Young ones as well, you fix their problems too? What about the war?'

'You're looking after that,' I said and told her to go on and I'd join her in a tick. She went on, leaving me to find out if anything new was biting Minnie. In a Sunday dress she was everything a senior Boy Scout could wish for, except that her eyes were flashing storm signals.

'Is there a fire?' I asked.

'Yes, there is,' she said, 'you been out with that tarty Wac again!'

'She's just a soldier mate of mine.'

'You're makin' me ill, you are! You're goin' out with her all the time! And you've never took me out once, not once, not ever!'

'Well, I can't, can I?' I said. 'It's against the King's Regulations. I told you, soldiers can get stoned to death for going out with under-age schoolgirls. Can't you wait a few years? Then, if you're still keen and I'm not doing anything much, we can write to each other.'

'Oh, rats and rotten leavings to you!' cried Minnie. 'You're doin' me down, you are and I'm sixteen now – well, I will be in ten days.'

'Yes, good luck, Min, happy birthday. You'll soon be a growing girl, then you can look around for a really deserving bloke.'

'Don't want a deservin' bloke,' she said, 'want you. Better you don't get soft on that ugly American sergeant.' Her eyes went dark and brooding. 'I'm not well, I'm not.'

'What's wrong with you?'

'Don't know, do I?'

'Well, buck up, Min. So long now, regards to your mum.'

'Oh, I could spit,' breathed Min.

In the pub, Kit had found a place at a table with Cecily, Frisby, Cassidy and Top Sergeant Dawson, whose bulk made Cecily look hemmed in. But she wasn't fraught about it. She was cured. It was Frisby who had worries. He had fashioned a psychoanalyst's couch for her and he had to make up his mind whether he was going to lie on it with her or not.

Kit gave me a smile and asked for a cider. First I had a word with Jim, who was in his usual place at the far end of the bar counter, sucking his pipe and his beer alternately.

''Ello, Tim lad,' he said, 'thought you might foller Kitty Lou in, 'eard you was out with 'er again.'

'Something ought to be done about your ears,' I said. 'Listen, your Minnie. Find her someone who can keep her company.'

'Ain't goin' to find 'er no bleedin' GI,' said Jim.

'Well, how about a young chicken farmer?'

'What's she done to yer?' he asked, grinning. 'Told yer not to get too close, told yer she'd eat yer. Still, it's up to you, lad.'

'I don't know why I bother,' I said. 'First you encourage me to help myself to your Missus, now you're pointing me at your daughter.'

'Don't you damage 'er, Tim. She's a ripenin' girl, but still pure.'

'Oh, you're a nut on purity now, are you?'

'I 'ope you ain't goin' to start shoutin', Tim, not in 'ere.'

Kit came up. 'Excuse me, Mr Beavers,' she said and drew me aside. 'Listen, old buddy, after a woman who's having trouble with her kitchen dresser and a girl young enough for Peter Pan and now that old coot Jim Beavers, I guess I'm not sure if you're sure who you're with. I thought it was me. Is it OK, mentioning it?'

'I'm glad you did, Kit. You should have had your cider by now. Sorry.'

'It's nothing serious,' said Kit, 'just that you're not a bad old buddy.'

'You're a good old sergeant,' I said.

'You're cute,' said Kit.

CHAPTER TWELVE

It couldn't last, of course, this lack of action. No-one was surprised when rumours began to circulate, rumours that the whole regiment was finally going to be posted to Burma, where our Fourteenth Army was locked in jungle warfare with the Japs. Well-travelled people, especially well-travelled writers, who liked the masses to know where they'd been, had always said what a nice polite race the Japanese were, going in for very civilized cultural stuff like flower arranging, honouring their parents, bowing to visitors, taking their shoes off before going indoors and producing soft twittering Geisha girls. It had been a shock to find out from war correspondents that the Japanese could be horrendously nasty. Accordingly, Burma postings were very unpopular.

The rumours put some of us off our food. I thought I'd better ask Jim or his Missus about them. They'd know whether they were true or not. Some evenings I was on fire picquet or guard duties, but I was free most evenings to make myself out a chit and go off to the village.

I put it to Jim, were we going to Burma? Jim said he didn't reckon Burma. Didn't need our kind of artillery in Burma. 'Cutlass, more like,' he said.

'Cutlass?'

'For chopping and sticking Japs,' he said. 'No, don't reckon Burma, lad. Italy, more like.'

'Italy? Are you sure?'

'Well, I ain't the War Office, mind, but I reckon,' he said.

I passed the word around to all my mates at BHQ. Italy? Nothing was happening in Italy, you twit. Just some bombs on Sicily.

'Horse's mouth,' I said.

'Horse's arse, more like,' said Gunner Parkes.

I went to fix Lottie Ford's kitchen dresser one evening. Lottie was grateful to see me, showing me where the old original screws were loose and plaster crumbling. Young Wally Ricketts appeared.

'I got me 'ammer, Tim,' he said, 'I'll 'elp yer.'

'This is a repair job, not a wrecking one,' I said. 'Buzz off.'

'But I can bash the new screws in with me 'ammer,' he said.

'Where'd you get that hammer?'

'Found it, didn't I, Mrs Ford?' said Wally.

'I were thinkin' you'd like to go out and play,' said Lottie. 'Clara's in the garden with Neddy.' Clara and Neddy were her two children.

'Can't I 'elp Tim? 'E's me mate.'

'Hoppit,' I said.

'I dunno,' said Wally gloomily, 'yer can't even 'elp a mate round 'ere, I fink I'll go back 'ome and 'elp me mum.'

'Poor old mum,' I said and Wally took himself and

174

his hammer out into the garden, where he was immediately set upon by sturdy Neddy and ferocious Clara and buried alive. Well, almost.

'Kids,' said Lottie indulgently and watched while I made short work of the little job. I fitted fat new rawlplugs, borrowed from the QM stores and put in new screws.

'There we are, Lottie.'

'You're a nice chap, Tim. Other people, well, you'd never believe. Mrs Roach round in Farm Lane, she has American soldiers goin' in and out every evenin' after dark. Well, not every evenin'. Most, though. What goes on, I hardly dares think. And with her husband in the Navy too, like my Nathaniel is.' Nathaniel Ford was her old man.

'Have you noticed if they're young GIs?' I asked. You had to go along with a chat. They all liked a chat.

'Oh, all sorts, Tim.'

'It's not a question of Mrs Roach learning them, then?'

'Learning them?'

'I just wondered,' I said.

'That were a funny question, Tim, I never heard about learning them,' said Lottie. 'Learning them what?'

'Nothing they don't know, I suppose, if they're all sorts.'

'I heard she's bought herself two new coats for the winter, ever such expensive ones and where could she have got the clothing coupons from, I wonder? Funny, that is. Well, I mean, like. I don't like thinkin' about such things. Oh, you finished already, Tim?'

'Those screws and rawlplugs will hold for years, as

175

long as you don't let young Wally loose on the dresser.'

'Little monkey, that boy is,' said Lottie. 'That Mrs Roach, though, the money as well for them coats, where did she get it all from, I'm sure I don't know.'

'Look under her mattress.'

'Oh, I couldn't do that, Tim, I don't go round there a lot these days. Would you like a glass of something? I were thinkin' a minute ago you might like a drink, there's some nice bottles of beer that's been at the bottom of the larder ages.'

'Thanks, Lottie, but no.' I tidied up. She hovered. 'Well, I tell you what, give us a kiss for the odd job and keep the beer for Nat.'

'Oh, I don't know I should kiss you, Tim,' she said and gave me a warm and generous one on the lips. Her bosom made warm contact. 'A nice soldier, you are, Tim,' she said shyly. I couldn't quite make out where that suddenly came from, the shyness, but it takes a mature and experienced bloke to understand women and I dare say he can still get it wrong.

Actually I was a bit shaken by what was happening to women. I knew GIs were everywhere, they could even be found under beds as well as in them, but all the same I was losing a lot of my admiration for the integrity of the women of old England. I hoped they weren't falling from grace in Scotland and Wales too. I liked to think there was some faithfulness about, I liked to think that my own wife, if I had one, wouldn't be getting GIs in and out of the house and that I wouldn't be going in and out of the house of somebody else's wife. Being a bit of a prude, I did think like that.

176

'Must go, Lottie,' I said, 'they want me for the war.'

'Oh, you can drop in anytime, Tim, that you can,' she said. 'Nathaniel wouldn't mind.'

Holy cows, wouldn't mind what? 'Well, I did do a good job on his shed,' I said jokingly. 'So long, Lottie.'

Young Wally made one of his shifty appearances when I left the cottage. ''Ere, Tim, could yer lend me a tanner?'

'Why should I?'

'I wasn't lookin' on purpose, honest,' he said. 'I only seen yer kissin' Mrs Ford by accident – 'ere, what yer doin'?'

'Twisting your lughole off.'

'Cor, it don't 'arf 'urt and I wouldn't tell on yer, Tim, you're me mate.'

What a funny old lot we all are.

'Gunner Hardy!' Wheeling a bike over the forecourt towards the open gates, I stopped and looked back. One man and his dog had just come out of the house. The dog bounded forward. Major Moffat advanced. I saluted.

'Sir?' I said.

'What's that?' he asked, pointing with his stick at the bike.

'WD bicycle, sir.'

'What's it doing next to you?'

'I'm going to ride it, sir. Down to the station, to get a new railway timetable. The orderly room one's just fallen to pieces. Sir.'

'You've a certain kind of genius in you, Hardy,' he said. 'If it ever gets out, you'll blow the world in half.

Tell me, what's the precise nature of your present objective?'

'Pardon, sir?' It was always wise to encourage him to rephrase a question. It gave a squaddie time to think up an answer and it helped the major to lose interest. Sometimes.

'Getting hard of hearing, are we?' he said. The murmur of work in progress reached the ears from the vehicle yard. An ATS girl crossed the forecourt to enter the mansion. Lucky for her that her stockings were straight. 'Deaf personnel get posted to the Pioneer Corps,' said Major Moffat. 'Just tell me if it's true that you're going regularly out of bounds.'

'Not without a pass, sir.'

'And a chit, I suppose. That won't save you if you're mucking about in school playgrounds. School playgrounds are right out of bounds.'

'You're joking, sir,' I said, but I didn't feel like laughing.

'Is your present objective one of the village schoolgirls? I hear it is.'

I tottered. The bike nearly fell over. The daft dog growled at it. 'You've got to be joking, sir. I do happen to know a girl, but only because she's the daughter of friends of mine.'

Major Moffat looked me in the eye. A brutally vigorous figure, he was admired by Suffolk females. He made me feel my number was up. 'Let me tell you, Gunner Hardy,' he said, 'if you're caught going to work on a schoolgirl, it'll count as rape. Have you got that loud and clear?'

'Yes, sir, I've got it and a headache as well. Who wouldn't have? I'm not the type, sir, and you can take my word for it. You've been misinformed about my present objective.'

'That's man to man, is it?' he said.

'If you like, sir.'

'I'm watching you,' he said. 'Well, don't stand about, get going.'

I got going, after saluting him again. I rode out through the gates, his lunatic hound bounding and barking beside me. I stopped when I'd rounded the first bend and detached the pump. The Dalmatian sniffed it, recognized it, turned tail and went off howling.

I cycled towards the village and the station. Missus must have seen me coming a mile off, or she must have heard I was on my way because she was waiting for me at her gate. I had to stop, after all, I was still getting eggs and some of my mates like Frisby, relied on the occasional fried one. And perhaps it wasn't her fault that she'd inherited unmentionable ideas from her Aunt Flossie. She gave me a creamy smile, her beige jumper hovering over her gate.

'Watcher, Missus. Can't stop, I'm afraid. Got the Major checking up on me.'

Missus laughed. It was like the rich sound of churning butter. 'Tim, pet, what you been gettin' up to with Lottie Ford?'

'Just screwing her dresser to the wall, Missus, you must have heard.'

'Heard a bit more than that, lovey. I don't hardly remember any soldier bein' as 'elpful to ladies as

179

you, what with what you done for me, then your Elsingham widow woman and now my friend Lottie across the street, who don't have her husband around to oblige her. Ain't Lottie a nice woman? But a bit starved like.'

'Is that a fact? What a crying shame. Look, send Jim across. When it's dark. He could be there and back in two shakes of his pipe and I don't suppose Lottie will mind if he doesn't take his hat off.'

'Tim, what a vulgar thing to say, I couldn't ask Jim to do that.' Her jumper quivered in some kind of protest. 'I couldn't lift my head up in church if I let Jim commit adultery with a neighbour. Besides, Nathaniel wouldn't like it. He wouldn't mind you, though, you both bein' soldiers.'

'He's a sailor.'

'Same thing, love.' Missus smiled fondly.

'Bloody earthquakes, Missus, you—'

'Don't swear, ducky. Jim don't like swearing and carrying-on.'

'Well, hard luck on the old goat, he'll have to put up with it. Believe me, Missus, what goes on in the wilds of Suffolk is all too much for me and the sooner I get posted to Margate the better.'

'Won't be Margate, Tim. More like where Hitler's lot is.' Missus acquired a comforting look. The parlour curtain moved and I glimpsed Minnie. She looked fed-up. 'Don't you worry now, Tim, I've been readin' the tea cups, and they don't show anything about Hitler's lot gettin' the better of you, just a surprise marriage.'

'A what?'

180

'You're goin' to have a surprise marriage,' said Missus.

'Well, any marriage is a surprise when it happens in a tea cup.'

'You're a laugh, you are, lovey,' said Missus. 'Min says she likes that, she says much better to die laughin' than cryin'. Pity she's not nearer your age, fancyin' you the way she does. Mind, now she's sixteen, she wouldn't mind waitin' a bit for you to start courtin' her, except Jim says he's not goin' to have none of that till she's eighteen. Still, you did send her a nice birthday card and a little brooch—'

'What's she doing home from school?'

'Feelin' a bit poorly again, poor lamb. Well, think about when you want to come and see me one evening.'

'I've got nothing left to think with, Missus, I'm hollow all over.'

Missus laughed. I had a feeling that the three of them, mother, father and daughter, were all having me on.

Aunt May wrote to say she was quite pleased with my last letter as it told her a lot more about my American lady friend than any of the others. The other letters hadn't made a lot of sense, she said. She thought it was very interesting that I'd got to know an American girl so well. The war is full of surprises, she said. She also said she couldn't think what I meant about Kit being a bit too efficient, she didn't know how anyone could be too efficient. I didn't want to end up with a girl who didn't know how to boil an egg properly, did I? That reminded her to say she was getting used to dried egg, it came out

181

quite good scrambled and was also useful for making cakes.

She said she was already looking forward to my next leave, when I'd be able to talk to her about Kit. She'd never met any girl called Kit before, only Kitty. Still, it sounded quite nice, she said. Yes, she'd really enjoyed the rabbits and had invited another friend in to enjoy the last one with her, as she couldn't eat a whole one all by herself. She wanted to know if I was doing any soldiering, because I seemed to spend such a lot of time doing work for widow Mary Coker, which didn't sound much like soldiering to her.

Poor Edie Hawkins had had her baby, a little girl, and her mother had said it was a lovely mite. It didn't look a bit like it had been born out of wedlock and perhaps when Edie's husband saw it he might not want to give Edie a good hiding. Aunt May wondered just how he would behave to a wife who had fallen from grace. By the way, she wrote, your friend's uncle, Mr Clayton, happened to come round to see me and offered to re-paper the kitchen one weekend, he's got some rolls of nice pre-war wallpaper. She couldn't say no to such a kind generous offer.

I had another word with Gunner Simpson. 'Is your uncle getting ideas about my Aunt May?' I asked.

'Is he? How do I know?' said Simpson.

'Well, find out. I'm particular about whoever might get his feet under her kitchen table.'

'Listen,' said Simpson, 'you can make that your business, if you like, I ain't makin' it mine.'

'Have a gasper,' I said. We both had one, we both lit

182

up. 'The point is, Simmo, I don't want my Aunt May being taken in by some old goat who's lookin' for free board and lodging.'

''Ere, watch it, you're talkin' about me mother's brother, who I can guarantee is a gent.'

'Well, that's good, Simmo, I'll take your word for it.'

I saw a fair amount of Kit. Not when she was out of bounds, of course, as Sergeant-Major Baldwin was always on the prowl up there on the first floor. Sometimes when I had an evening pass, Kit came to the pub with me and sometimes she didn't. Sometimes I think she was out with Major Moffat on what he would probably say was official Allied business. Cassidy, the friendliest girl, offered to stand in. I said that was really nice of her, but if Top Sergeant Dawson found out I'd never live to see next day's breakfast. Cassidy said she'd come to my funeral, she'd be a heel if she didn't.

Frisby continued to be Cecily's guide, doctor, mother, father and grandma. She liked it. It did wonders for her. She shone. So did her fully-fashioned Waac stockings. Her skirt, previously very long in length, had been shortened. I assumed it meant she wanted Frisby to see she had legs. I asked him if it did. Frisby said she hadn't said so to him. He hadn't even noticed, he said. I said that had to be a stand-up lie.

'All right, I'll be frank,' he said, 'I don't talk to Cecily about things like her legs. I don't want her suffering a setback. She's still sensitive, y'know.'

'But she doesn't twitch any more, does she?' I said.

'And you're dating her and making her happy, aren't you?'

'I'm doing my best,' he said.

'You going to pop the question or not?'

'I'm just taking my time. You can't rush a girl like Cecily.'

'Well, watch out, mate, someone else might. In case you haven't noticed on account of being her doctor, Cecily's turned into a Lulu.'

'Think so?' Frisby looked proud of his accomplishment. 'I'll make a note of that.'

The rumours about Burma died a death. Others began to circulate. They were all to do with a Second Front, which John Gordon in the *Sunday Express* thought ought to start sometime next week. Sounded dangerous to us. It was no good anyone saying we'd had it cushy so far. Everyone still wanted to stay alive, especially the gunners out on site. They were having a wonderful summer. Only Major Moffat and Sergeant-Major Baldwin wanted to see blood.

A senior officer from Brigade put in an appearance and gave us a lecture on rocket warfare. It meant the regiment was going to be equipped with rocket-firing machines as well as Bofors. It also meant that various personnel would be on a course soon.

CHAPTER THIRTEEN

In the pub, Kit crowned one of her men to make a king.

'There's a clever old sergeant,' I said. 'By the way, someone's been talking to Major Moffat about me.'

'I have,' said Kit. 'I wanted to take his mind off other things.'

'What other things?'

'Yes, you've got it, old buddy,' she said, watching my move. 'I simply told him that in view of your many talents, I couldn't understand why you hadn't made sergeant at least. I said you could fix anything and he said he knew that and that the last thing he'd do was put you in a position where you could fix him as well.'

'I don't fix things,' I said, 'I just do odd jobs for old ladies.'

'What old ladies?' asked Kit, surveying the board. She moved one of her men, forcing me to take it. 'Zap,' she said, 'and bang bang.' She smiled. 'Old buddy, that's cost you two men and a king.'

'Did it when I wasn't looking,' I said.

A gentle hand touched my shoulder. 'Hi,' said a friendly voice. Cecily. She'd arrived with Frisby. 'How's it going, Tim? Hope you're pitching good.'

'He's not,' said Kit, 'he's throwing weird ones as usual.'

185

'Hi, guys,' said Cassidy, arriving with Top Sergeant Dawson. He looked like a brown bear, Cassidy looked like his honey, Cecily looked 100 per cent cured and Frisby looked tidy. Cecily had taken to knotting his khaki tie for him and prettying him up. It was like taking up ownership. Except that Frisby hadn't officially given in yet.

The latest rumour was that our little bunch of seconded Americans, male and female, were soon to leave us. Jim had said he reckoned that was right, right enough. Cecily refused to believe it. No way did she want to believe she was going to be parted from her doctor. Frisby, now in need of a doctor himself, had confided certain relevant details to me. I didn't feel too qualified and all I could give him was a sympathetic hearing. He said that Cecily wanted to know if they'd still get to see each other. Frisby said he'd do his best. Cecily said that she'd have to fight any new feeling of insecurity.

'That's right, you fight it,' said Frisby, 'you're a fully-grown woman now.'

'Oh, sure,' said Cecily, 'but fully-grown women can still have their bad days when someone important to them isn't in contact.'

Frisby said he'd have to do some heavy thinking about what was best for her. I told him to stop all his thinking and get on with things.

At the moment, however, Cecily had gone back to disbelieving the rumour. In her acquired spirit of camaraderie, she paid for drinks for all. We all sat as wartime mates around the table.

Jim came in, looking a bit dark under his hat and sucking his pipe upside-down. He beckoned me.

'Excuse me a tick,' I said.

'Go ahead,' said Kit. 'It's your mafia godfather.'

Jim took me outside, right outside, which I thought meant trouble. Without preamble, he said, 'Missus reckons our Min's in the fam'ly way.'

'Eh?'

'It's what we both reckon,' said Jim.

'What?'

'I ain't goin' to shout it, son,' said Jim. Son?

'You're kidding me, Jim,' I said. I wasn't going to call him dad.

'Wish I was, but I ain't,' he said. 'Missus is fair certain and I been wonderin' meself about Min gettin' broody at times. I asked 'er straight out this mornin', was she pregnant or wasn't she. Told me to mind me own business. Told Missus that too when Missus asked. Missus reckons she's been 'aving a bit of mornin' sickness and said she'd best take 'er to the doctor's. Min said she wasn't goin' to be taken to no doctor's. Told us to leave 'er alone, said she'd got enough miseries as it was on account of you takin' up with yer American lady sergeant. But I'm tellin' yer, son, Missus and me both reckon Min's in the club all right and Missus wants me to ask you a straight question. Did you get up to it with Min?'

'You asking that for a laugh?' I said.

'Ain't no laugh, Tim lad. Puttin' a bun in Min's oven ain't nothing but serious and nor ain't it good manners, neither. Missus is shocked.'

'So am I.' A picture of Major Moffat getting me for rape leapt into my mind. He would too, if he could. 'I wouldn't do a thing like that to Minnie, Jim. I couldn't.'

'Maybe you wouldn't,' said Jim, gloomily eyeing the village street. Cottage windows winked in the evening light. 'But I ain't sure you couldn't. Manly young bloke like you. And Missus reckons Min would 'ave let you. Gone on you, our Min is. She wouldn't 'ave let no Yank touch 'er, she'd 'ave poked 'is bleedin' mince pies out. She's got too much sense to fall for any Yank's fancy talk, got 'er mind set on bein' some nice chap's wife. Yourn, I reckon, son.' I honestly didn't like the way he kept calling me son.

'Listen, Jim, if Minnie really is pregnant, it wasn't me. Have I ever been out with her or had a date with her? You know I haven't. She's too young.'

Jim peered darkly at me. The crowded pub was a buzz at our backs, the village street quiet. Very quiet. I felt every window was looking, listening and winking.

'Well, I ask yer, Tim, 'ow about risin' summer night? I reckon you got pretty close to Min that night, didn't yer? Mind, I trusted yer. Tim won't do wrong by our Min, I thought. She'll maybe get 'im to kiss 'er, I thought, but Tim won't give 'er more than that.'

'Look, I went in search of some fresh air and Min came with me. Then I fell down and that was that. I prefer falling down to having unlawful relationship with a minor.'

'Don't use them there French words, Tim. Makes it worse, that does.'

'Well, hard luck,' I said, but I was having sudden

188

uneasy feelings about that night, especially as Min had said more than once that I'd been loving to her. 'Listen, if it had been me and Minnie is pregnant, she'd say so, wouldn't she?'

'Won't say nothing,' gloomed Jim, 'only that she'd like to do grievous bodily 'arm to yer American lady sergeant.' He gave me a long look. 'Tim,' he said, 'I'm askin' yer man to man, did you get to Minnie or didn't yer?'

'Didn't. Couldn't. Wouldn't.'

Jim sighed. 'So who bleedin' did, then?' he asked.

'Point is, did anyone? If Minnie's not admitting she's pregnant, it's all in your mind, Jim.'

'Well, son,' he said, 'Missus bein' a woman and sharp-eyed accordin', an' me bein' Minnie's dad, it's a bit more than that. Missus an' me both reckon Minnie's moods and 'er bit of mornin' sickness add up to an 'ighly suspect condition. Missus wants to see yer. She's upset, I tell yer.'

'So am I. I'll come and talk to her.'

'I'd better go first,' said Jim, 'or you might cop the chopper. Missus is given to choppin' first and askin' later when she's as upset as this. I'll put a word in, lad.'

'Yes, tell her I'm feeling ill. I'll be along.' I went back into the public bar and told Kit I had to go, that Jim was having trouble with a young chick.

'You amaze me,' said Kit, 'you can fix sick chickens too?'

'I don't know, this is my first time.'

'I'll come with you,' said Kit, 'I've never seen a baby

189

chicken being treated by an enlisted guy filling in as a vet.'

'No, stay there,' I said. Fortunately, she was too wedged in to spring free and I departed at speed.

Jim let me in and took me into the parlour. The parlour meant serious business. Missus was present. She was on her feet and for once she was looking stiff and starchy.

'So here you are,' she said.

'Yes, good evening, Missus.'

'Nothing good about it,' said Missus.

'Where's Min?' I asked.

'Out. Jim told you she's expectin'?'

'He told me you think she is, but that Minnie won't say.'

'It don't matter that she won't say,' said Missus, 'it's my belief she's expectin' all right.' She sighed and her stiffness eased a little. 'Now you know, Tim, there's no-one Minnie would've give in to except you, she can't look at no-one except you. But I never thought you'd take that kind of advantage, I don't know when I've felt more sorrowful.'

'Well, I feel sorrowful myself,' I said. 'I don't know how you can even begin to believe I'd take that kind of advantage. Look, if Min won't say she's pregnant, there's got to be a reason for it. Perhaps she's having trouble growing up. In any case, if you're thinking about me and Min on rising summer night, I can tell you I was incapable.'

'Incapable of rememberin', perhaps,' said Missus and I gritted my teeth at that.

'Well, Missus,' said Jim, 'I asked our Tim straight

190

out, man to man, and 'e answered me straight out. Said it wasn't 'im. Good enough for me.'

'I dare say,' said Missus, 'but all that cider and all. Like I just said, it's maybe he just don't remember. Now, Tim, I'm not sayin' you had it in mind to do wrong by Minnie, only that when risin' summer got you heated up and you found yourself alone with her, you let it 'appen. And I don't suppose she wasn't willin'. All I'm sayin' is that I hope you'll do right by her now she's in trouble.'

'Pardon?' I said.

'Any decent young chap's that's done a girl wrong ought to do right by her,' said Missus.

'I'll fall over in a minute,' I said. 'You're talking about me marrying Min?'

'What else?' said Missus.

'If you don't mind, I'll wait till Minnie's seen a doctor and I'll wait till she says it was me,' I said.

'Tim can't say fairer,' mused Jim.

'I'll talk to Minnie again,' said Missus.

'I'd like to have a talk with her myself,' I said.

'Got to be careful 'ere,' said Jim. 'Min was under age when it 'appened. The doctor won't like that. 'E might 'ave a duty to tell the coppers. They'll come round. Best keep this quiet, Missus.'

'Well, I've got to make 'er see a doctor,' said Missus. 'I'll take her to one in Sudbury but I won't give our right address or our right names.'

Minnie arrived home then. She came in through the open front door and put her face round the door of the parlour. 'Oh,' she said.

191

'Tim's here,' said Missus unnecessarily.

'That's a change,' said Minnie.

'Listen, Min,' I said, 'your mum and dad have been talking to me.'

'That's nice,' said Minnie, 'but you can talk to me now, we can go for a walk, it's still a nice evenin' and fancy you not bein' out with that ugly American sergeant.'

'Stop actin' up,' said Jim, 'let's get things straight. Yer mum's goin' to take you to a doctor's in Sudbury—'

'Oh!' Minnie was in a paddy then. 'She's not takin' me because I'm not goin'!'

'Now look, Minnie,' I said, 'are you in trouble or not?'

'Who said I was?'

'Your dad and me's not blind,' said Missus, 'so you'd better speak up, my girl.'

'Won't,' said Minnie, 'ain't goin' to.'

I felt then that if she was pregnant, it had to be somebody else, not me.

'I'm lookin' at you, Min and I'm thinkin' things,' said Jim. 'I'm thinkin' some geezer 'elped 'imself to what 'e wasn't entitled to and yer maybe don't even know 'is name.'

'Oh,' gasped Minnie, 'me own dad sayin' a thing like that to me!'

'Now see what you've done,' said Missus to Jim, 'you've been and upset your own flesh an' blood. I never 'eard anything more upsettin', specially when we all know Min wouldn't ever go with no-one but Tim. That's right, isn't it, Minnie love?'

'I'm not sayin', I'm not talkin',' said Minnie. 'I been

192

insulted rotten by me own dad and I'm goin' to bed. So there.' She disappeared. I heard her running up the stairs.

'It's 'er condition, poor lamb,' said Missus, 'it's put her in a terrible upset state. I just hope you'll be a nice understandin' chap, Tim.'

'I still ain't sure we can lay it on Tim,' said Jim.

'Now don't you get more upsettin',' said Missus, 'you've done more than enough of that. Tim knows how Minnie feels about him and that she wouldn't go with any Yank. Oh, lor', I never thought I'd suffer this kind of worry. Still, I hope you can make up your mind and not take too long, Tim. You take too long and Min might be about due. I wouldn't be able to 'old me head up if Min got to be a bride and a mother all on the same day.'

'Get in all the papers, that would,' said Jim gloomily, 'an' maybe on the wireless too.'

'All right,' I said, 'I'll go away and have a good long think about it.'

'There, I thought you'd act decent, Tim,' said Missus and was kind enough to see me out and down to the gate. 'I'm not givin' you hard blame, love, I expect it was bein' tiddly that done it. That risin' summer cider's special, Jim should've told you.'

'Special? Lethal, more like,' I said.

'I'm not one to keep on,' said Missus, 'and not to say you got to marry Min. It's up to you, Tim. Doin' right because you ought to isn't the same as doin' right because you want to. You wantin' Min for a bride is a lot better than bein' sorry for her. She's a handful, but better than you maybe think. She's got loyalty, Min has, love. You marry her and she'll stick to you through thick

193

and thin. Mind, I know she's a mite young, but she's grown up quick. That's 'er trouble.'

My trouble was that I was thinking about what Aunt May and everyone else would say about me walking down the aisle with a pregnant schoolgirl. 'If you'll excuse me, Missus, I've got a headache.'

'I dare say you 'ave, love. So has poor Min.' Missus sighed at events. 'Still, off you go now. I know you're a decent young chap, likin' to do what's right.'

A jeep passed by. In it were Kit, Cecily, Cassidy, Frisby and Top Sergeant Dawson, all getting a lift back to BHQ. Kit gave me a wave. I was too numb to ask for a lift myself. I said good night to Missus and walked back to BHQ in a frail state of mind.

CHAPTER FOURTEEN

I hardly slept that night. I kept thinking of the night in question, racking my memory in a mental search for something that would give me a clue to exactly what had happened. I told myself I'd have known if I'd had Minnie. I've never had any girl, so if I'd gone over the top with Minnie, surely not even the cider would have blanked it out. But might she be prepared to say I had, even if I hadn't? The gnawing uncertainty kept me awake most of the night.

In the orderly room the next morning, I felt haggard. Deborah Watts asked about my health. I said it was feeble. I left most of my midday dinner uneaten and wandered around a bit, thinking about how Aunt May would react if I told her.

'Hi, Tim, old boy.' It was Kit. The sun was shining on her as she came out of the ATS quarters.

'Hello,' I said.

'You're looking sick,' she said.

'Large headache,' I said.

'Oh, jolly bad luck,' said Kit, trying out an English accent.

'Fancy an alcoholic time at the pub this evening?'

'Love to,' said Kit, 'but I'll be busy.'

'Overtime? That's for civilians. Ask anyone. Even ask Major Moffat.'

'It's Major Moffat I'll be busy with.'

'That's against the regulations,' I said, although I was past caring, of course.

'How did the ailing chick make out?' she asked, as we walked a path together.

'It's pregnant,' I said in a mad moment.

'A chick?' Kit laughed. 'Who's responsible?'

'Some old rooster, I suppose.'

'You kill me,' she said. 'Have a ball at the pub, but don't fall about, it'll hold up your promotion.' She disappeared at a brisk pace into the house.

Cassidy and Cecily caught me up. Cecily gave me a smile as she followed Kit. Cassidy stayed for a friendly word. 'Getting nowhere fast, Tim?' she said.

'I think I'm still stuck on the starting line,' I said. It hardly mattered now.

'I guess you picked a tough one,' smiled Cassidy. 'Try being a forceful guy.'

'How forceful?'

'Take a turn at being boss,' said Cassidy, 'answer her back. Have fun, old buddy. See you.' Off she went.

Duty Sergeant Harrison took her place, plonking himself in front of me. He had a roster book in his hand. 'Gunner Hardy, I presume?'

'I think so, sarge, but in several ways I wish I wasn't.'

'I feel the same,' said Sergeant Harrison. 'Right, then, where was I? I know, Gunner Poole's gone sick. You're next on the roster. Guard duty tonight.'

'Gunner Poole, you said? No, look, sarge, that twit is

196

always going sick. It's about time he passed permanently on and saved the rest of us all the inconvenience he causes.'

'I'm not inconvenienced,' said Sergeant Harrison.

'No, well, you're not next on guard duty roster, are you?'

'Tck, tck, cross, are we?' he said. I hardly cared. 'Well, save it for Adolf. Get yourself blancoed for guard duty. All over.'

There were millions of Germans and Russians making mincemeat of each other around some place in Russia called Byelgorod and thousands of Allies and Germans at each other's throats in Sicily and I was on quiet guard duty in rural Suffolk. All done up in full kit, my webbing thick with Khaki Green Blanco No. 3. I supposed I ought to be feeling fortunate. But I didn't feel like that at all. I had Minnie's condition on my mind and also the possibility that I might be definitely responsible.

Guard was mounted at eighteen-hundred. Four of us each had to do a spell of three hours. I drew from twenty-one-hundred to midnight. After that, I might get six hours kip in the guardroom as long as Bombardier Weekes, the guard commander, didn't keep walking about and treading on me.

Nothing much happened for my first two hours, except personnel coming in after an evening out. I was supposed to poke my best friend at them and ask them to declare themselves and show their passes. I didn't bother very much, unless they had stripes. I wasn't in the mood to bother. Then Jim stole up on me. How he knew I was on guard was a mystery, until he told me he'd got the information from Frisby in the pub.

'Thought I'd come an' cheer yer up, son,' he whispered to me outside the gates. 'Missus, of course, is dependin' on yer to do right by Min. Well, Missus 'as got principles, like.'

'Oh, you reckon, do you?'

'Now, now, Tim, it ain't 'er fault she dotes on Min, Min bein' our one and only. Women is made to be dotin', specially if there's a one and only. Me, I'm wonderin' about the real whacker, the geezer that really put Min in the fam'ly way.'

'Wait a bit, is that definite now, that she's pregnant?'

'Well, Min still ain't sayin' and still won't go to no doctor's, but Missus knows all right, 'er bein' a woman, like I said before. Keen to 'ave you in the fam'ly, yer know.'

'Nice of her,' I said, 'but isn't there any good news?'

'Nothing good about this mess, Tim lad, only that you're me friend and a man don't ask 'is friends to be what they ain't. I ain't askin' you to be a husband to Min if you ain't acted like one. That ain't friendship. One thing I will say, though, which is that Suffolk'll suit you, like it's suited us. Come yer do wed Minnie, she won't say no to livin' 'ere.'

'Stop pushing me,' I said.

The dark night sighed. In the Pacific, the high and most honourable Japanese sea lords were engaged in titanic ocean battles with the American fleets, but I still wasn't having a very good time.

'Ain't goin' to push yer, Tim. Goin' to look for some

198

Yank. I'll lay it was some Yank that got to Minnie some'ow. No wonder she ain't 'appy. That's it, yer see. If it 'ud been you, she'd be proud and 'appy. But it wasn't you, so she don't even want to admit it.'

'Poor old Min,' I said.

'You leave the geezer to me, son, I'll find 'im. 'Ere, Missus sent you some eggs.' Jim slipped a cardboard box into my hand. 'Wants you to know she don't blame you all that much. Car's comin', lad, I best be off.'

He vanished and I put the eggs in a safe place. I heard the sound of an approaching car. I could have been caught napping with so much on my mind, but Jim's warning had alerted me. I planted myself in the path of the vehicle as it reached the open gates. Its masked headlights were reduced to narrow wartime slits. But I knew it. It was Major Moffat's Hillman. He'd have me shot if I didn't challenge him.

'Halt!' I ordered loudly. The car stopped with my rifle nosing its radiator. I went round to the driver's window which was open and asked for identification.

'Major Moffat and Sergeant Masters,' said the Major. So her overtime had been conducted in the Hillman, had it? I went prickly.

'Recognize you, sir. Can't recognize your passenger, sir. Can't see her.'

I saw the gleam of his teeth. 'Too bloody dark for your failing eyesight, is it?' he hissed.

'Sorry, sir, but must ask your passenger to present herself.'

'Try going round and taking a look.'

I went round and pointed my rifle at the window

199

of the passenger door. 'Alight and be recognized!' I hollered.

The window wound down and a face appeared beneath an American Wac cap. I switched on my torch. Kit looked up at me.

'Yes, it's me,' she said. Then, in a whisper, 'You big ape, you're showing off.'

I glimpsed movement in the back of the car. 'Sir,' I called, 'there's another passenger.'

'It's Jupiter,' said Kit. 'Don't shout at him or he'll make a late night hamburger of you.'

The great retarded canine lump dribbled and growled.

'Pass, friends and a dog,' I said, getting out of the way and I thought the Major was actually grinning as he drove in. It did nothing for my depression. Life was giving me a hiding at the moment. On top of everything else, the female sergeant I fancied was getting thick with Major Moffat, who was making his own rules. He was ignoring the fact that it was seriously *verboten* for officers to socialize with other ranks, including sergeants. I ought to write an anonymous letter to Brigade Headquarters about him.

But did it matter?

Yes, it did. I'd got to stand up and fight.

It occurred to me then that I needed to talk to young Wally Ricketts.

The following afternoon, one rumour turned into fact with the official news that our American mates were definitely leaving us. On Saturday. At the end of my day's work I went out of bounds by slipping into Kit's office. I didn't knock. Anything like the sound of a knock on an out-of-bounds door could alert all the wrong kind of people.

Only Kit was present. She was standing on a chair and unloading files from shelves. Her legs looked first-class. She glanced down at me.

'You're out of bounds,' she said, 'so at least close the door.'

I closed it. She continued pulling out files and dropping them into a large tea chest. Each time she reached her military stocking seams lengthened.

'I'd offer to help,' I said, 'but I'd just as soon watch.'

'Don't overdo things, honey,' she said.

'Can I help it if I like your Wac stockings?'

More files dropped into the chest. 'Be my guest,' said Kit, 'but don't stand on your head to improve your view, it's not decent, old buddy.'

'You're missing out on being human,' I said.

'Take that,' said Kit and hit me over the head with a file.

'Thanks. Where are Cecily and Cass?'

'Cecily's having a breakdown because we're leaving tomorrow and Cassidy's gone to ask Claud to do something about it. I'm tidying up.'

'Well, you're good at that. Did you enjoy yourself with Major Moffat last night?'

'Yes, I met a Suffolk squire and his wife. We had dinner with them.'

'Cute, was it?' I asked.

'Entertaining,' said Kit and came down from the chair.

'Exactly where are you moving to?'

'To the new base at Chackford,' she said.

'That's not far, about seventeen miles. All the same, it's a blow.'

'I guess it is, Tim.' Kit smiled. 'It's been fun. I'll miss our bike rides to Mary's. Give her my love next time you see her. Tell her I'll write. She's a sweetie.'

'Will I be getting a letter or two?' I asked.

Kit regarded me quite affectionately. 'Tim, you're not trying to say you're getting serious about me, are you?'

'Well, I happen to be human. You don't mind that, do you?'

'I'm flattered,' said Kit. 'It really has been fun knowing you, but don't get serious, honey. I honestly don't think we're made for each other.'

'We could give it a bit of a go,' I said.

'Let's just be good friends, mmm?' said Kit.

'That's death,' I said.

'Buck up, old buddy. You should have taken a shine to Cassidy. She's a real sweetie and she likes you.'

'Oh, well, san fairy, too late now,' I said.

'Look, it has been special to me, the fun we've had, Tim. Don't think I don't appreciate that.'

'Me too,' I said. 'Just good friends, then.'

'See you,' smiled Kit. 'Anytime you're near Chackford. And look me up in Boston when the war's over.'

'I'll come for a weekend,' I said.

Perhaps it was as well she hadn't fallen into my arms. If I'd proposed and she'd said yes, what on earth could I have said to her if we'd found Minnie on the church steps with a baby in her arms?

*

202

There was a farewell party for the three Wacs in the pub that evening. On my way there, I knocked on the door of Mrs Lottie Ford's cottage. She gave me a very nice smile.

'Well, fancy you, Tim, I were just thinkin' about where you might have got to just lately.'

'Yes, nice bit of thinking, Lottie,' I said. Lottie fussed with her hair. 'Is young Wally around?'

A yell from the interior answered my question. A little girl's yell.

'That boy,' said Lottie, shaking her head, 'always treatin' my Clara like she were a football.'

'You could drown him I suppose and get a friend to say it was an accident. I'm a friend. I'll stand by you.' I raised my voice. 'Wally! Come here!'

Out he came, his jersey rumpled, his hair all over the place, a grin on his face. ''Ello, Tim,' he said. 'Tim's me mate,' he said to Lottie.

'Come here, mate,' I said and took him down the street. 'Now listen, monkey, you said you saw me with Minnie Beavers on rising summer night. Right?'

''Ere, I wasn't lookin' on purpose, yer know,' he said. 'I just seen yer, like.'

'Yes, and exactly what did you see?'

'Kissin'. Cor, ain't yer well orf, Tim, kissin' Minnie? Ain't she pretty? I wouldn't mind givin' 'er some smackers meself.'

'I bet you wouldn't. Come on, what else did you see besides kissing? Own up, or I'll slice you in half.'

'Could yer let go me ear, Tim?'

'Not yet. Let's hear everything first.'

'What d'yer mean, everything?' he asked. 'I just seen yer kissin', then yer did a slide, then some Yank give me 'is boot.'

'Gave you what?' I asked.

'Yer, so 'e did, the bleeder booted me up the bum. It didn't 'arf 'urt. Then 'e told me to scoot, so I did. I wish I'd 'ad me 'ammer wiv me, then I'd 'ave 'it 'im back.'

'That's the truth, Wally, is it?'

'Course it is. Tim, d'yer want some more rabbits?'

'Yes, in a week or so.' I was due for leave again soon. On home service, leave came along four times a year. 'All right, Wally, here's a tuppence. I'll let you know about the rabbits. Now scoot again, back home and stop chucking little Clara about.'

''Ere, she bites me ears, yer know,' said Wally.

'Glad to hear it. Buzz off now.'

'Ta for the tuppence, Tim, I dunno I ever 'ad a mate good as you.'

Off he went and I walked on to the pub, still not sure what had happened after I'd slid to the ground that night.

The pub was packed with squaddies and GIs. The squaddies did a strong piece of work in keeping the GIs from making off with our Wacs, for the GIs were masters of social manoeuvres. Any girl was fair game to them, even if she was in the protective custody of her mum and dad. They could whip her away in record time.

However, we all stood our ground around Kit, Cassidy and Cecily, and Bombardier Wilkins had the honour of giving each of them a present we'd all subscribed to. English pottery. They were touched. Cassidy's eyes, always bright with friendliness, turned quite moist. Top

Sergeant Dawson and the two American officers had already departed, so Cassidy was able to hand out kisses of thanks to the nearest squaddies.

Kit was in a smiling mood, but Cecily looked a lot like I felt, as if there was no point in going on. Frisby kept dropping crumbs of comfort, but I thought that what Cecily wanted was the whole loaf. The uncertain twit was still worrying about whether or not he was the right kind of bloke for an American girl. Cecily actually liked England. Well, she liked Suffolk. She wasn't a big-town girl. She was a natural for making Frisby a loving wife, not a bossy one. I thought that deep down she wanted a marriage of love and kindness, the opposite of what her parents had had.

She touched my arm. She had a gin and tonic in her hand, the same one she'd had all the time and she'd only drunk half of it.

'Hello, Ciss.'

'Hi, Tim.' She grimaced. 'I feel sick.'

'What kind of sick?'

'Oh, you know, I guess. Tim, do the guys like me?'

'What a question. Of course they do. Look at them, can't you see we're all going to miss you? You're one of us, you're our mate, except you're better-looking than we are.'

'God, I wish I could stay,' she said. 'The base at Chackford is lousy with concrete and stacked to its roofs with a million uniforms.'

'You'll survive, Ciss, you're a new woman and you're nice as well. And Claud'll come and see you, won't he?'

'God, he'd better,' said Cecily.

'The food will be an improvement, won't it?'

'Who's hungry?'

'You're right, Ciss, the food here can ruin your appetite as well as your stomach. Still, you should get some good coffee and hamburgers at Chackford. That'll lick your appetite back into shape.'

'Sure, cheer me up,' said Cecily. I put an arm around her shoulders and gave her a squeeze.

Cassidy turned up. 'Who's getting all the buckshee hugs?' she asked, so I gave her a comradely squeeze too. Kit was enjoying laughs with Bombardier Wilkins and some ATS girls who had arrived to swell the party. The latter were soon collared by GIs and were lost to view for the rest of the evening.

'Tim's a nice guy,' said Cecily.

'Sure, I'm rooting for him too,' said Cass.

Frisby pushed his way through. 'Anyone seen Cecily?' he asked. 'I've lost her.'

'This is me,' said Cecily.

'Well, d'you know, I was just thinking who's that lovely Wac over here – good on you, Cecily, you'll end up in Hollywood.'

'Over my dead body I will,' said Cecily.

The drink swam about. The squaddies began to sing 'The Long And The Short And The Tall.' The Wacs joined in. Frisby and I were sitting down at this stage, with Cecily perched on his knee and good old friendly Cass on mine. Kit, singing, gave me an encouraging smile.

The GIs came in next with 'She'll Be Coming Round the Mountain.' And so it went on.

It was a good evening. We all had late passes and didn't leave until the pub closed. Kit had an escort of ten squaddies. Cecily walked with Frisby and Cass walked with me, her arm tucked in mine. I think she was trying to make up for Kit being a disappointment to me and I think Kit was letting me see that Cass might be willing to be my American pen pal. I asked myself the same question. Did it matter?

Yes, it did. I was still alive and Minnie's condition might be only a bad dream.

When we got to BHQ, I kissed Cass good night. She was very co-operative.

'Who's a kissing guy, then?' she said. 'I liked that.'

'Mutual,' I said.

'You bet,' said Cass.

'See you off tomorrow,' I said.

'That's my buddy,' said Cass.

Along with several other squaddies and some ATS girls, I was there when the American girls were ready for the off the following morning. Major Moffat was also there, standing at the rear of the forecourt, hands behind his back, his dog squatting beside him. He didn't interfere, nor did he order the gunners back to their work. He simply watched. Cass was handing out more kisses. The three Wacs were to be driven to Chackford in a jeep. Cecily refused to climb aboard. She seemed on the verge of dementia. Frisby was absent.

'Where is he, Tim?' she asked. 'Oh, the lousy loser, he's running out on me.'

'No, I think Sergeant Johnson's got him pinned down,' I said.

'Private Peterson!' Kit was shouting from the jeep. She'd said her friendly goodbye to me. 'Move yourself!'

Proper sergeant she was at this moment. But Cecily was deaf to her. 'Oh, I can't believe my guy could do this to me,' she said.

Frisby, flushed with the shame of a soldier who had meant to duck it, suddenly materialized. Cecily's mood improved dramatically and Kit conceded her a little extra time to say farewell. She pounced. Frisby quivered as she talked to him. She seemed agitated, he seemed to be saying nothing. But his mouth opened eventually and he delivered a few words. Cecily went dumb, stared at him, then flung her arms around him and in full view of various gunners and ATS girls and Major Moffat as well, glued her mouth to her doctor.

When that was over, Frisby said coherently, 'Now don't go off your rocker, scout.'

'Oh, you cream cookie,' said Cecily. 'Can we live here, in Suffolk?'

'No, Reigate,' said Frisby. She didn't argue. She was happy.

'Wrap it up, Private Peterson,' called Kit, 'mount up.'

Cecily mounted the jeep with such reckless abandon that she was a treat to every manly eye. Frisby looked shocked at her leg show, but gave her a forgiving and fatherly nod when she blew him kisses. Without ever realizing what it would do to him, he'd done a first-class job on mixed-up Cecily.

Off they went. They waved. We waved. I felt the end

of a chapter had arrived. Kit had said to drop in anytime I was near enough to the base, but I couldn't see much point in that.

'You popped the question, then, did you?' I asked Frisby, as we made our way back to the orderly room.

'What else could I do?' he said. 'No mum or dad, well, not to speak of, and dying to prove herself normal. I couldn't let her go off and have a relapse. Anyway, she's a lovely piece of machinery, as good as I'll ever get, so it's no sacrifice.'

'Yes, you don't want to marry her simply because she's a patient of yours,' I said. 'Better if you fancy her. She's a good 'un, Cecily is.'

'I suppose you know you sound like a bit of Suffolk folklore at times, do you?' said Frisby.

'I know. It gets you after a while.'

'It's not getting me. I still like Reigate. Hope it'll suit Cecily and I hope I'll live.'

Sometime, I thought, I've got to face up to Missus again. She was leaving me alone at the moment, giving me time to have a good think, but I hadn't been capable of any good thinking for days.

CHAPTER FIFTEEN

Aunt May wrote. Poor Edie Hawkins, the young woman who'd been unfortunate enough to fall from grace on Wimbledon Common, was back in the news. Her mother, Mrs Cossey, had been round to have a cup of tea with Aunt May and to tell her all about the latest developments. It seemed that Edie's husband Ron had arrived home on leave in an unexpected fashion. He hadn't written to say he was coming. Edie didn't even know he was back from overseas. He was all sun-tanned but looked ever so grim and stern. It was an awful shock to Edie when he walked in, especially as she was just putting the baby in its pram. Mrs Cossey was there herself. A widow, she lived with her daughter and son-in-law in Cotham Street. Ron just said hullo, that was all. Just hullo. Then he went upstairs with his kitbag, having ignored the baby. Then he came downstairs again, put the kettle on and made himself a large pot of tea, without saying a word. It put Edie in an awful state and she begged him to say something. Ron said he'd got nothing to say, that he was going down to the pub to get drunk and to ask for advice on the quickest way to get a divorce.

Down to the pub he went and didn't come back till late. Edie was in bed, but couldn't get to sleep, of course.

She heard him come in and waited for him to come up. But he didn't. So she went downstairs and there he was, lying asleep on the parlour sofa, in his shirt and trousers. And he still had his boots on, which made Edie think he was keeping himself ready to walk out on her as soon as morning arrived. But he didn't, he appeared at breakfast. Edie asked couldn't they talk and Ron said no, he was busy thinking about the best way to give her a good hiding before arranging the divorce. Mrs Cossey told him he ought to be a little bit forgiving and wasn't it time he looked at the baby instead of pretending it wasn't there? Ron said he'd give her a good hiding too if she talked to him like that. Mrs Cossey said she'd go and bring the police round if he started handing out good hidings to her. Ron said you bring the coppers round and I'll knock their heads off. It was awful, especially as Edie had made herself up and looked ever so pretty. She said all right, give me a good hiding if that'll make you feel better. Go on, she said, I admit I deserve it. Ron said he'd do it in his own good time.

He went out after breakfast and got back in the afternoon. Then he actually took the baby for a walk, pushing it in its pram, which dumbfounded Edie. He was back an hour later, he came into the house without the baby and pram. Edie asked where the baby was. Ron said he'd sold it. Poor Edie just fainted. Mrs Cossey called him a brute. Ron didn't say anything, he just set about bringing Edie out of her faint. When she came to she begged him to tell her who he'd sold the baby to. Ron said it was outside the house, still in its pram. It was a nice little thing, he said, but they'd have to move,

211

he didn't want to live where neighbours knew the baby wasn't his. He'd been to Peckham that morning and seen a house for rent there. We're moving before my leave's up he said, and don't argue or you will get a good hiding.

Aunt May wrote what a forgiving man he'd turned out, after all. She seemed fascinated by the whole saga of poor Edie and Ron's reaction to her moment of weakness. Then she went on to say that Alf Cook wouldn't go home drunk any more. He'd done it once too often and Mrs Cook had let him have it at last, she'd gone for him with her rolling-pin and he'd had to have ten stitches in his forehead.

Aunt May finished by saying she was looking forward to having me home on leave again at the end of next week.

Days went by and I thought I'd better face up to Missus again. Then I had a re-think. No, I didn't want to put myself in a defensive position again. I'd wait until it was definite that Minnie was pregnant. It had to happen sometime. Sometime she'd have to see a doctor. Wouldn't she? I was fairly ignorant about whether a girl or woman would have to or not. Or could they carry it all off without ever seeing a doctor at all? There'd at least come a time when it would show. I knew that much. And in any case, I was entitled to wait until Minnie admitted her condition, or until Jim nailed someone whom he called the real whacker.

I went down to the village in the evening, thinking to have another word with young Wally Ricketts. I met

Minnie herself. She looked a picture of girlish health in a summer dress, her naturally curling hair lightly dancing in the breeze. But a worried expression arrived as we met, then a tentative smile.

'Come to take me out, Tim?' she said.

'Leave off, Min, I'm having a crisis, you know that.'

'What crisis?' she asked, looking at my army buttons.

'About your condition.'

'Oh, was it something about you 'aving to marry me?'

'Now look, Min—'

'Wouldn't you like to marry me, then?'

'Min, you're a schoolgirl.'

'Oh, you Tim, I don't mind waitin', I'd wait ages for you as long as I can be your best girl in between.' She was still looking anywhere but straight at me. 'Don't want no-one else, honest, only you.'

'Min, you're only just sixteen, you can't know that.'

'Well, I do, so there,' she said.

'Listen, Min, are you or aren't you?'

'Am I or ain't I what?' she asked, sparking a little.

'All right, in plain English, are you going to have a baby or aren't you?'

'What's that got to do with it?' she asked.

'It?'

'Me bein' your best girl.'

'Min, you're giving me terrible headaches,' I said.

'They're not as bad as the ones you're givin' me, goin' out with that fat American sergeant,' said Min angrily. 'I bet you're still seein' 'er, don't you mind that she's fat and ugly?'

'She's not fat and ugly and I'm not still seeing her

213

and if you don't stop acting up, I'll smack your saucy bottom.'

'Now?' said Min and she was hardly believable. She was laughing at me. Not out loud, it was all in her blue eyes. Ruddy terror, she was. 'Mum an' Dad's out, you can come 'ome with me an' do it there. Be bliss, Tim, honest. Then I might tell you about my condition.' A cheeky smile peeped. 'And risin' summer night.'

'You're going to be my death, you are, Min.'

'No, I'm not, just your best girl,' she said, 'and I can leave school now instead of next year.' She was a clever girl right enough, attending the grammar school near Long Meiford, which made Jim and Missus proud of her. 'Then I won't be a schoolgirl any more, will I?'

'I'm ill,' I said and left. I heard her laugh softly. What a monkey at just sixteen. I thought about the Yank who had applied his boot to young Wally because the little devil was watching Minnie and me. What happened after that?

I knocked on Lottie Ford's door. She opened it and presented a shy womanly smile. 'Oh, it's you again, Tim, I just seen you talkin' to Minnie Beavers and I were thinkin' isn't she growin' up quick. Pleasure it is, havin' you call.'

'Mutual, Lottie. Is the demon around?'

'That young Wally?' said Lottie. 'I don't have a minute's peace when he is around, nor when he's missin'. Well, like, I'm always expectin' him to come in and say he's broke someone's window accidental. He's in me garden now, tryin' to mend a branch of the

214

apple tree with that hammer of his. A bit of it fell off, he said. You can go through and talk to him, Tim. Shall I make you a nice cup of tea?'

'Thanks, Lottie, but Frisby's waiting for me in the pub,' I said and went through to the garden.

There was young Wally, up on a step-ladder and hammering nails amid apple tree foliage and fruit. 'That won't do any good,' I said.

'Oh, 'ello, Tim.' Wally came down the step-ladder in a matey rush. Halfway down he fell off. I picked him up. 'Cor, bleedin' ladders,' he said, 'yer just can't trust 'em, can yer? You come for yer rabbits? Only I ain't got 'em yet, you said you'd say when.'

'I'll let you know, don't worry.'

'Right, I gotcher, Tim. I'll only ask two bob.'

'You can ask, you won't get. Listen, sunshine, that Yank who booted you on rising summer night. What did he do after that?'

''Ere, I dunno, I 'ad to 'oppit sharpish or 'e'd 'ave booted me again. Still, I did 'ear 'im talkin' to Minnie as I scooted. I dunno nuffink else. Except 'e was a big dark corporal an' you was lyin' down. Was yer drunk, Tim?'

'I did have some cider in me. All right, Wally, good enough. I'll pay a bob for the pair of rabbits, next Thursday evening, as long as they're not nicked. If they're nicked, I'll make a hole in your loaf of bread with that hammer. Get me?'

'Me? I don't do nickin', Tim.'

'Bet your mum's proud of you.'

*

215

Jim came into the pub as I was buying a round. I went aside with him.

'Ta, son,' he said and took one of the half-pints from me.

'That's Frisby's,' I said.

'All right, I'll drink 'is 'ealth,' said Jim and took a long swig. 'Yer saw Minnie a bit ago, I 'ear.'

'Not much you don't hear, is there?' I said.

'Yer goin' on a course, I 'eard that.'

'You're up a gum tree for once,' I said, 'I'm going on leave. Friday.'

'It's a rockets course, I reckon,' said Jim. 'It's rockets all over now, yer know. Well, Tim lad, I ain't yet copped the whacker that done our Min wrong. I been watchin' 'er and follerin' 'er, hopin' to catch 'er with 'im, but it ain't 'appened, not yet. Still, she'll be on 'er school 'olidays soon, an' she'll be gettin' about more. I'll be on 'er tail. Point is, though, she don't want 'im, even if 'e did put 'er in the club, she wants you. Got a woman's feelin' for you, she 'as.'

'She's not a woman, you daft old goat.'

'Near enough, though, Tim. Ain't got far to go now.'

'Listen, if she doesn't want this Yank, whoever he is, why'd you feel she might be meeting him?'

'Stands to reason,' said Jim. 'If 'e's 'ad 'is pleasure with Min, 'e'll be after more. I don't reckon Min's told 'im he's landed her in the club. What I do reckon is she don't want 'im comin' round. Give the game away, wouldn't it? So she's got to keep 'im out of sight by meetin' 'im.'

I didn't feel he was too right about that, but I did tell

216

him there'd been a Yank around at the time. I told him what Wally had told me. Jim said that had to be the whacker all right. He took a look at the crowd of GIs at the bar. There were no corporals among them.

'But I'll get ''im,' he said, 'you leave it to me, Tim. Anytime you see Missus, just tell ''er you're thinkin' sympathetic, like. Play for time, eh?'

'Look, don't think I'm not sorry for Min,' I said.

'Min's sorry for ''erself, I reckon.' Jim frowned. 'It just don't seem like my girl to let a Yank make a tart of ''er. She's an ''andful, but not that kind of ''andful.'

'She didn't seem sorry for herself when I saw her this evening, Jim, she was as lively as she's ever been.'

'Well, she was moody again when I saw ''er ten minutes ago,' said Jim.

'Oh, hell,' I said.

Sergeant-Major Baldwin entered the orderly room on Monday morning. 'Bombardier Wilkins, Gunner Hardy, Gunner Frisby.' The Sergeant-Major was brisk and gravelly. 'You're proceeding with other personnel to Brigade HQ first thing Wednesday. A week's course. You'll join site personnel there. That's all.'

'Excuse me, Sergeant-Major,' I said, 'but I won't be available.'

'Who's that talking like someone from the Naafi?' asked the sergeant-major.

'I'm starting my seven days leave on Friday,' I said.

'You're not. You're postponed.' And the sergeant-major left.

So I had to write to Aunt May and tell her my leave had been postponed for a week.

The course was all about rocketry and it was all top secret, which everyone knew was a laugh. Rockets were common knowledge. Still, it was an interesting week of lectures and demonstrations and it took my mind off all my troubles and setbacks. Getting nowhere with Kit represented my major setback and Minnie represented my sea of troubles.

And if rocketry represented anything, it had to be active service. The villagers of Sheldham would know when, of course. Their grapevine was always on active service.

After the course I went on leave. Aunt May received me with a kiss and a cuddle. She looked as content with life as ever. She might have let the war irritate her and ruffle her a bit, but since she knew there was nothing she could do about the colossal nature of the worldwide conflict except keep her pecker up for the sake of her country's morale, she did exactly that. At the same time, she carried on as if the war was other people's worry, not hers. It was her opinion that men liked to hear things go off bang, even if the bang blew their heads off, while women liked to get on with living. Women had to put up with the bangs, she said.

I handed over a pair of rabbits, a dozen rashers of bacon, kindly donated by Bombardier Jones from the ration stores and a box of a dozen eggs from Jim. I received another kiss and cuddle. I noticed the kitchen walls had been re-papered and I commented.

'Yes,' said Aunt May, 'I told you in a letter about Mr Clayton offering.'

'Oh, that bloke,' I said, 'the short, fat, bald, bandy-legged uncle of Tosh Simpson's.'

'I'll give you short and fat,' said Aunt May, 'I told you he wasn't like that.'

'So you did,' I said, 'but you know how it is, you get stuck with first impressions.'

'I know what you get stuck with,' said Aunt May, 'all your jokes.'

Over lunch, we had a long chat. I could always chat to Aunt May. We were a couple of gossips together. She first wanted to know all about Kit and how I was getting on with her. I explained how it had all come to a full stop, that Kit was an efficiency expert and would probably only marry a bloke who'd invented something that would do the washing for you, hang it on the line, iron it and put it away. Someone like Henry Ford. Aunt May said that would be like marrying someone's grandfather. And besides, he was in motorcars, not laundry, wasn't he? Good point, I said.

'A pity, though,' said Aunt May. 'I thought you'd found a really promising young lady. Never mind, you'll get over it, Tim, you've never let things get you down in the dumps.'

I said nothing about Minnie Beavers. That horrendous situation had to be kept to myself for the time being.

Aunt May asked if I was ever going to be sent overseas.

'Yes, to Italy, probably,' I said.

'Italy?' said Aunt May. 'But there's no war going on there.'

'Not yet, no,' I said, 'but Jim Beavers—'

'Oh, your friend whose wife gives you eggs? The London family that went to Suffolk?'

'That's them.'

'There's a daughter too, isn't there?' said Aunt May.

I don't suppose any bloke can make women out, but sometimes you can see exactly how their minds are working. Aunt May's mind was fastened on my future.

'Yes, she's at school,' I said.

'Oh, she's as young as that?'

'Most girls are when they're at school.'

'How old is this one?' asked Aunt May.

'About forty,' I said unthinkingly.

'Forty? Forty?'

'Well, fourteen, say.'

'I thought you said forty,' said Aunt May, 'and I thought when you first wrote about them that she was older than fourteen.'

'She probably is,' I said. 'Anyway, her dad reckons the battery will be going to Italy.'

'How does he know?'

'Well, Aunt May, there's a lot of dicky birds flying around Sheldham and he gets all his information from them.'

'You're a real joker, that's what you are, Tim. By the way, Mr Clayton's calling this evening. I told him you were coming home on leave and he'd like to meet you.'

'What, the short fat—'

'I'll hit you,' said Aunt May.

220

I forgot my troubles and concentrated on what might have been happening in the life of the woman who'd been a mother to me nearly all my life. I looked hard at her. She stood up to it with her equable smile.

'Aunt May, I think you've got a boyfriend.'

'A what?'

'You cheeky girl,' I said. 'Still, good on yer, lovey and good luck, I'll be pleased to meet the cove.'

'He's just a friend,' said Aunt May.

'Yes, of course.'

'It's nothing serious.'

'No, of course not.'

'He did the kitchen up very nicely.'

'I can see he did, but not seriously, of course.'

'What d'you mean, how can you do a kitchen up not seriously?'

'Only if there's nothing in it.'

'Nothing what?' asked Aunt May.

'Nothing serious.'

'What's the use?' asked Aunt May and laughed like a girl.

Aunt May, I thought, was not only contented, she was happy about something. Bill Clayton, of course, Simpson's uncle. Well, if she was getting fond of him, he had to be a likeable bloke. Her instincts were sound. I felt glad for her. My Aunt May was a good 'un.

She'd made no mistake about the man she'd let into her life. Bill Clayton, a soldier of the last war, with a limp to his left leg, was very likeable. A Walworth man, he'd bettered himself in several ways and his iron-grey hair and regular features gave him quite a distinguished look. He complemented Aunt May's well-preserved attractiveness. They fitted and they talked and behaved as if they'd known each other all their lives. He had her laughing and Aunt May liked to laugh. So did Minnie Beavers. A laugh was always ready to spring from Minnie.

The three of us had a very talkative evening together. Bill gave me a good account of what the Army had been like in the last war and I gave him my impressions of what it was like in this one.

'No difference,' said Bill.

'Same boots, it seems,' I said.

'Same sergeant-majors?'

'No difference,' I said.

'But you've got ATS girls in your gun crews.'

'Not in our battery. Our major would set his dog on them. As it is, the hound's after chewing every ATS skirt in our BHQ.'

'That's one of your jokes, of course,' said Aunt May.

'It's no joke, Aunt May, that dog's six feet high.'

'How d'you get on for time off?' asked Bill.

'Most evenings and most Sundays,' I said. 'You need a chit, of course, if you want to go out and a late pass if you don't want to be back too soon.'

'Same army,' said Bill.

'Same chits,' I said.

'Same kind of men too, if you ask me,' said Aunt May.

I had a peaceful leave. Well, the whole country was relatively peaceful now that the German *Luftwaffe* was having to concentrate on the Russian front. Bill Clayton dropped in most evenings. He had a good job in the drawing office of an engineering company, which to me meant he was going to be able to keep Aunt May in comfortable style if they decided to marry. I couldn't see Aunt May letting him keep her in any style unless they did marry.

'Is Bill going to?' I asked her one day, when I was peeling potatoes for her. Her gentleman friend was joining us for supper. He lived in lodgings himself.

'Is he going to what?' asked Aunt May.

'Ask you.'

'Ask me what?' She had a smile on her face.

'To be his one and only.'

'How do I know?' she said.

'I'll have a word with him,' I said.

'Don't you dare.'

'It's my duty.'

'Your what?'

'You're right, Aunt May, someone's got to ask him what his intentions are. I'm not saying—'

'That's it, you're not saying anything,' said Aunt May. 'The very idea.'

'Yes, good idea,' I said, 'there's only me, I've got to be the one to ask him. After all, I'm away most of the time, which makes you a helpless little woman all on her own.'

'Don't make me laugh,' said Aunt May and laughed. 'And don't you ask him anything, my lad, I'm not too helpless to go for you with the frying-pan.'

'Well, he's a decent bloke,' I said. 'I can probably leave it to him to make up his mind.'

'Well, thanks,' said Aunt May. 'I hardly know when I've been more grateful.' She gave me a direct look. 'Tim, d'you like him?'

'Yes, of course I do.'

'That's nice,' she said. I knew why she wanted me to like him.

Bill was present on the last evening on my leave. We went for a short visit to the Browning Street pub before Aunt May served supper. At Bill's invitation. We had a half-pint each and a little chat.

'What I wanted to say, Tim, was this.'

'Good,' I said.

'I haven't said it yet.'

'No, right, go ahead, Bill.'

'Thing is,' he said, 'would you mind if I asked your Aunt May to walk up the aisle with me?'

'Ruddy marvellous, good on yer,' I said. 'Bloke after my own heart, you are. Look after her, she's not just one of the best, she's the best. Mud in your eye, old man.'

'You're a case and a half, you are, Tim,' he said, 'easy to see you're her nephew, there's a fam'ly resemblance. So let's have another, we've got time.'

'My shout,' I said.

The burly figure of Alf Cook barged in beside us. 'Shandy,' he said in a hoarse whisper to the publican.

'Eh?' I said.

'Shove off,' said Alf.

'What d'you ask for, Alf?' enquired the publican, gaping.

'You 'eard,' said Alf in a hoarser whisper.

'Gawd strike me beer barrels,' said the publican.

'Lemonade or ginger beer shandy?' I said to Alf.

'Leave orf, will yer?' said Alf. 'Lemonade,' he said to the publican.

'My treat, Alf,' I said, 'I've just come into some good news. Same again for me and the other gent,' I said to the publican.

'I got to drink something,' said Alf, 'I'm goin' bleedin' rusty. 'Owdjerdo, cock,' he said to Bill. 'Seen yer around a bit.' He received his shandy and took a swallow. 'Bloody blimey,' he said, 'it's bleedin' wee-wee.' He eyed our glasses of beer enviously.

'Cheers,' said Bill.

'Don't mind me,' said Alf, 'enjoy yourselves. I'll just kill meself with this stuff.'

Life was hard for Alf at the moment.

After supper, I did my good deed. I washed the dishes while Aunt May and Bill had time together in the parlour. I let them have extended time. Aunt May finally appeared in the kitchen doorway when I was lighting up a fag.

'Well, bless me,' she said, 'you're keeping yourself to yourself a bit this evening, aren't you?'

'Any news?' I asked.

'It'll be the same as it was at six o'clock, I expect,' said Aunt May, 'but you can turn the wireless on now, if you like. Perhaps the war might be over.'

'What a thought,' I said. 'Any news?' I asked again.

225

Aunt May's expression, as equable as usual, was uninformative. 'Is there something on your mind, love?' she asked.

'Nothing serious,' I said.

'That's good,' said Aunt May, 'I thought it might be something really serious keeping you out here on your own. Come and join us in the parlour.'

'Look, what's the news?' I asked.

'Bill asked me to marry him,' said Aunt May, 'and I told him I'd think about it.'

'Think about it? What for?'

'Because I have to.'

'Why?'

'Never mind, I just have to,' said Aunt May and that was all she would say. Somewhere, I'd gone wrong in taking her willingness for granted. All the same, it puzzled me.

CHAPTER SIXTEEN

Back from leave, I exchanged a few words with Frisby.

'How's your fiancée?' I asked,

'Eh?' he said, looking startled.

'Have you seen her?'

'Oh, you mean Cecily. Yes, I cycled over last Sunday. Chackford, what a place. Big as New York, I should think. And where'd they get all that concrete from? Beats me. Cecily said she's going to turn into a boiled cabbage if I don't get her back to BHQ inside a month. I said she'd have to wait until I was friendly with Eisenhower.'

'Apart from that, how was the reunion?'

'Don't get personal,' said Frisby.

The next day I got copped for guard duty. The following evening I met Jim in the *Suffolk Punch*.

'Yer back, then,' he said. ''Eard you was. It relieved me, I tell yer, lad. Thought you might've done summat silly.'

'You only thought? Didn't you know? What happened to your personal dicky bird? Had a day off, did it?'

'I don't like to 'ear you bein' sarky, Tim. I'll 'ave an old 'an mild as it's your turn.'

I got him one.

'Well?' I said, hoping all my troubles were over.

'Missus'll be glad yer back all in one piece,' he said.

'As for our Minnie, well, I dunno she ain't bloomin'. Gets some of 'em like that when they're in the club.'

'Listen, you old goat, don't talk to me about how she's blooming or about anything else that's mucking up my life. Just tell me if you've found that Yank.'

'Don't like to 'ear you bein' ratty, Tim,' he said. There was a dried bird dropping on his mossy hat. 'Missus is waitin' patient for you to call. You got to remember that even if she still thinks it's you that's the whacker, she's still got a lot of lovin' regard for you. Minnie's actin' quiet. Yer know what? I reckon the reason why she still won't say is because bein' under age at the time she's worried the police might cop you.'

'I'll fight that,' I said. I felt irritated for once by the rowdy GIs and their giggling village maidens. 'I didn't do it.'

'I'm believin' yer, ain't I?' said Jim. 'Now, son, I been thinkin' while I been watchin' Minnie. I ain't copped that Yank young Wally told yer about, but I will. I been thinkin' why don't yer take our Min out walkin' one evenin'? She can't go on not sayin' anything, Missus says it's worryin' not seein' a doctor when she's so young, yer know. Missus reckons that if anyone can get Min to admit 'er condition an' go to a doctor, it's you. Maybe yer right, maybe at 'er age she don't really know 'er own mind, that she'll 'ave different feelings in a year or so, but right now she's still gone on yer. So why don't yer take 'er out walkin' one evenin' an' get 'er to talk to you, eh? She won't talk to me or Missus.'

'OK, Jim,' I said.

'Good on yer, son,' said Jim.

I wasn't sure I liked the way he said that.

'Well, Min?' I said the following evening, as we walked down the village street towards the country lanes.

'Fancy you takin' me out,' said Min, shapely in a sweater and skirt. 'Am I your best girl now?'

'I don't know why you're in such a hurry,' I said, 'can't you wait a couple of years till you're eighteen? Then I'll come knocking, how's that?'

'A lot can 'appen in two years,' said Min darkly.

'Yes, the war could be over by then. That'll be the time for me to make plans about the future. The only thing is – well, let's face it, if you're going to be a mother—'

'Oh, yer daft lump,' said Minnie, 'course I'm not, I've got more sense than to let that 'appen to me. There's girls in Sudbury and Long Melford and a girl in our school too that's let it 'appen to them, the silly things, all because they think they'll get taken to Hollywood. What a laugh. Their GIs won't even marry them, let alone take them to Hollywood unless they get permission from their officers.'

'You know that, do you, Min?' I said. I knew it myself.

'Course I do,' she said, as we entered a lane and strolled between the bursting hedgerows of summer.

'Your mum thinks you're pregnant, so does your dad,' I said.

'Well, I'm not and I'm cross with me mum an' dad,' she said. 'It's your fault they thought I was and I been really wild with you. Goin' out with that rotten boss-eyed

American girl like you did, no wonder it's made me act like a sick woman.'

'A sick what?'

'Good as,' said Min.

'Min, you'd better tell your mum and dad and stop them worrying.'

'Not goin' to,' said Min with a hoity-toity toss of her head. 'I can't 'ardly believe me own mum an' dad can believe I'd let 'em down like that. I wouldn't have, not even with—' She stopped. She went on. 'Except – oh, I don't know what I'd 'ave done.'

'What does that mean?'

'Tim, I've got real lovin' feelings for you an' they're never goin' to go away.'

Oh, hell, poor young Min, she'd got a crush that was heavy even for a schoolgirl and she was taking it seriously. I'd had crushes when I was at school, I'd had a crush on a nurse and on a young woman who ran the local Girl Guides and I'd thought them lifelong crushes. I'd taken them seriously too.

'Well, in a couple of years, Min, when you're really grown up, when you're a young woman, let's see how we both feel then.'

'But I—'

'That's fair, Min, you know it is. I'm being fair to you because you're only sixteen, so be fair to yourself and give yourself time.'

'Oh, I hate you!' cried Min and turned on her heel and ran. She ran away from me, back up the lane to the village.

I didn't feel very happy about that, but I did feel enormous relief that she wasn't pregnant.

Two days later, I had the old Austin utility out, taking a late delivery of mail round the sites. Usually it was delivered by the rations lorry, but the lorry had left before it arrived. Driving through the village, I saw Missus at her gate. I stopped. Up she came.

'Just thinkin' about you, Tim, I was,' she said. 'There's some spare eggs.'

Irresistible, her fresh eggs were. I got out. Missus, overflowing with country health and natural goodness, took me round to the back of her cottage and into the chicken shed. Chickens squawked and fled. On the table where Jim sorted his eggs was a box containing six. She gave me the box.

'There, Tim love,' she said. 'Jim says you're thinkin' very sympathetic about our Min.'

'Hasn't Min told you?'

'Told me what?'

'That she's not pregnant.'

'Oh, me gawd,' said Missus and put a fluttery hand to her bosom. 'She went walkin' with you, but when she come back she wasn't very talkative. Jim said 'e'd ask you what she said to you.'

'She told me quite definitely she's not pregnant.'

'Bless me upset heart, what a relief,' said Missus. 'But why hasn't she told me an' Jim?'

'Well, Missus, the fact is she's cross with you for believing she could do a silly thing like getting herself in the family way.'

'But she acted like she was, she kept not bein' very

231

well and I just know I 'eard her bein' sick once or twice in the mornings. Jim said he never saw her more broody.'

'Well, she's been cross with me too, Missus,' I said. 'She complained I made her sick because of Kit, the American sergeant. And she's ratty with me now. Well, I told her to wait a couple of years and to see what her feelings were then.'

'Oh, me poor Min,' sighed Missus. 'I never did know any girl more gone on a young man. I'll 'ave to talk to her, or get her Aunt Flossie to.'

'Leave off, Missus, don't let that naughty old bird get near Minnie.'

'I 'ope you're not speakin' ill of Aunt Flossie,' said Missus.

'Just tie her up and put her in your attic with the rocking-horse,' I said.

'We don't have no rockin'-horse,' said Missus, a trifle indignant.

'Well, stuff her up the chimney, then,' I said. 'Still, ta for the eggs, you're a lovely chicken, Missus. Got to push off now.'

I went on my way, I motored out of the village and dropped mail in at three sites. I motored on. I slowed approaching a crossroads. Two American military personnel were thumbing, one male, one female. Giving lifts to civilians was forbidden and giving lifts to the military was discouraged. They might be disguised German parachutists. But camaraderie counted for more than piffle typed in triplicate. And besides, I knew the female. So I stopped and put my head out.

'Watcher, Cass,' I said.

Cass, the blonde Wac, was with a lanky GI. She gave a happy little yelp at seeing me. 'Oh, you dog,' she said, 'long time no see, but see good now. Number one Limey guy. You go all alongee Uncle Sammy's base?'

'I'm not that kind of Chinaman,' I said. 'Your base is ten miles from here.'

'Ten miles is right,' said Cass, 'so it's great to see you and your old mousetrap. Legs – this is Legs – was driving me to Ipswich to pick up a Wac there, but our jeep caught a cold or something. Anyway, it coughed itself sick and died.'

'OK, love,' I said, 'hop in, you and Johnny.'

'Pardon me, bud,' said the GI. 'How do I get myself in without a can opener?'

'Through the back curtains,' I said, 'and would you mind chucking yourself in sharpish? I'm supposed to be delivering mail and I'll get shot out of a cannon if I'm late back.'

'OK,' he said.

'Don't read the mail,' I said. 'It's private.'

He got himself aboard and Cass tucked herself in beside me. I drove at a lick for Chackford. I didn't want any more trouble than I already had. If I got back late to BHQ, Staff-Sergeant Dix was going to ask questions about time, distance and petrol. The Austin utility rattled along gamely through the winding roads.

'All right, Cass?' I asked.

'You bet,' she said. 'The lift I mean and seeing you. I guess I got to like your homely base. Ours is a concrete dump. No rating. When it's all over I'll settle for homeliness if I can't catch me a millionaire.'

233

'Try for a millionaire, Cass, you'll both get a bargain.'

'Well, thanks,' said Cass, 'but I guess it's Cecily who's really suffering. She's crying her eyes out for a one-way ticket back to your coconut palms.'

'Not really, is she?' I said.

We were making good time. A great spread of American bombers appeared in the sky ahead of us. Up they came from the west, flying east towards occupied Europe and the thunder of their engines drowned us for long minutes.

'Cecily's hooked,' said Cass when she could make herself heard.

'On Claud?'

'On the buttercups and daisies as well.' Cass laughed.

'Still, no more mental turmoil?'

'Claud did a great job. Say, would you ever think a guy by the name of Claud could have done that for Cecily?'

'There's a first time for everything, I suppose.'

'I guess so,' said Cass and chatted on in her chummy way, while her GI friend made what he could of the mousetrap. I did a very fast ten miles without anything falling off and the American Army base outside Chackford came up at us out of the cloudy summer day. It was new and vast. I turned in at the gate on Cass's instructions. Two Snowdrops pushed me back to a white line. The Austin quivered.

'Hold it, bud,' said one, 'what's your hurry?'

'Is this a can?' asked the other, eyeing the Austin in disbelief.

'Can?' I said.

'Yeah, d'you make water in it?'

'Better not,' I said, 'you'll swamp the mail. And the passenger. I'm delivering.'

'Papers, bud,' said the first Snowdrop, extending an enormous mitt.

'Give over, I'm delivering American personnel, one male, one female.'

'OK, you guys,' said Cass, putting her head out, 'move over. He's doing us a favour. Straight on, Tim honey.'

'Well, it's your say-so,' said the Snowdrop, 'but I ain't sure it'll make it.'

'Make room,' said Cass, 'it's an old and dear friend of mine.'

They grinned at her. Cass was a character. I hoped she'd catch herself a millionaire. I drove along a clean concrete road that seemed endless with intersections and with camp buildings erected in square complexes on either side. Horrible, it was. It made me feel sentimental about the bits and pieces that made up BHQ.

'Big,' I said.

'Painful,' said Cass. 'Turn left, lover.'

I turned left, entering another long stretch. They must have had fifty thousand Yanks packaged in this place. Hitler wouldn't have liked it, since it was only one of many similar American bases in the country. Cass told me to pull up outside a long admin block, so that she could go in and report the demise of a jeep. The long GI unfolded himself and climbed out.

Cass gave my knee a pat. 'Many thanks, Tim, you're every girl's best friend,' she said.

'You're welcome, Cass, shan't forget you.'

'Me too.' She planted a kiss on my cheek. 'Take care, old buddy, the war's coming.' She got out.

The GI showed his face. 'Yeah, well, thanks, Limey,' he said.

They went off and Cass disappeared into the admin block. I was in a hurry, but I stayed a moment for another look around. Barrack blocks. Clusters of GIs and Wacs. Stars and stripes. Colossal, it was. Had to be, with Uncle Sam behind it all. It was Kit's place. She was welcome to it. I started up and began a three-point turn. I heard quick footsteps on the concrete and then a voice.

'Stop!' It was Kit.

'Hello, lovey,' I said, 'can't stop, must dash, only came to drop Cass off.'

'So she's just told me.' Kit's hair was rippling in the breeze and her face looked slightly flushed. There were sparks about. 'Were you going without seeing me?'

'I'm short of time and what difference would it have made?'

She disappeared. The next thing I knew the passenger door was open and she was climbing to sit beside me. Angrily, she reached and switched off the engine. 'You stinker,' she said.

'Oh, is that a fact?' I was fed up with fate and fortune. 'Well, let me tell you, mister, I've just come a hundred miles out of my way to bring Cass back to you.'

'Mister? Mister?' Kit looked furious. 'You cheap comic, is that supposed to be funny? Are you trying to prove something petty by coming here to drop Cass off without looking me up?'

The concrete complexes must have done something to her head. 'What's your problem?' I asked.

'Listen, you earthworm,' said Kit, 'you dropped Cassidy off right outside admin. You must know I work in there. Why didn't you come in and see me?'

'I didn't have time. I haven't got time now. Honest. I'm late enough already.'

She gave me a look full of rage. She got out. She slammed the door. The Austin shuddered. She walked away. I put my head out and called to her. She turned.

'First sergeant I ever loved, you were,' I said, then started up again and drove off. She watched me go, but she didn't wave.

When I finally got back to BHQ and returned the Austin to the vehicle stand, Staff-Sergeant Dix checked the petrol gauge and the spare can. And the mileage. And the condition of the vehicle.

'I make you a bit up on mileage,' he said.

'Thought you would, Staff,' I said. 'I hit a diversion outside Long Melford.'

'You would,' he said. 'All right,' he said. He wasn't a bad old lump.

In the orderly room, Sergeant Johnson, checking the time I'd taken, asked me whose war it was, Churchill's or mine.

'Well, we're both in it together, sarge. Actually, I hit a diversion—'

'Don't give me a load of rockcakes,' he said, 'you've been gone long enough to organize your own second front.'

'I've kept a place for you, sarge. First landing party.'

Bombardier Wilkins grinned. Deborah and Deirdre giggled. Frisby winked.

'And where will you be?' asked Sergeant Johnson.

'Right behind you, sarge.'

'What a comfort,' said Bombardier Wilkins.

'Yes, not everyone's like me,' I said.

'Hoo-bloody-ray,' said Sergeant Johnson.

I called on Jim and Missus. Minnie was out with a girlfriend, but Missus said she'd come out with it at last. She'd admitted she wasn't in the family way. Not that she seemed pleased she wasn't. She was still having upset moods.

'Like you said, Tim, she's ratty with you all right. Hates you, she said, but she don't, of course.' Missus looked a little sad. 'Shame she's too young for you, love.'

'Maybe Tim's right, though,' said Jim, puffing on his pipe. 'Girls of our Min's age don't get lastin' feelings, Missus. Little Turk she was, though, lettin' us think she was in the club.'

'She didn't know where she was with Tim, that's why,' said Missus. 'A girl's emotions an' feelings can make her do funny things. Be different if she'd been old enough for Tim and they'd been 'itting it off, she'd 'ave been singing all day.'

'Yes, well, when she's eighteen, Missus, I'll pop in if I'm around,' I said.

'Now don't say things like that, Tim,' said Missus, 'you know it don't make sense. Still, I'll make a pot of tea, there's always sense in that.'

So she made a pot of tea and we all chatted, mostly about Suffolk. Cockneys born and bred though they were, Jim and Missus had long decided this was where they were going to spend the rest of their lives. And Minnie liked it too. Minnie didn't want to go back to the smoke.

Dusk was just about giving way to dark night when I left. I stood at the gate to let my eyes adjust. Minnie, I thought, should have been home by now. She emerged from the dusk then. A little way behind her was a man. I made him out after a moment as a GI. Her head was turned and she was speaking in a vexed way, over her shoulder.

'Go away, stop followin' me, d'you hear?'

I heard him say, 'Honey, you sure are being difficult.'

'Hello, Min,' I said.

She jumped. She stopped. 'Oh, you Tim, I didn't know you were there,' she said.

'Hi,' said the GI and came to a halt a little distance away.

'Looking for someone?' I asked.

'Yeah, well,' he said uncertainly. 'Guess it's kinda crowded now. See you, maybe,' he said to Min.

'Not if I see you first,' said Min and off he went. 'Tim, you made me jump, but crikey, nice you bein' here, 'e was tryin' it on with me.'

'I'm not surprised. Young girls out in the dark are asking for it in this kind of war.'

'I'll hit you,' said Minnie.

'Now, Minnie—'

'Don't you now Minnie me. I've been out with Jane

Goodwin, me best friend, to the pictures in Sudbury and I've just walked 'ome from the bus stop. That Yank started comin' after me when I passed the pub, so don't you try an' make out I've been walkin' around askin' for it.'

'Sorry, Min.'

'So you should be,' said Min. 'You know I don't go with any of them GIs. They all look the same to me, they all never stop chewin' gum – ugh, fancy bein' kissed by someone with a rotten wad of gum in 'is mouth. Tim, you do like me a bit, don't you?'

'You've got me licked, Min, I'd like you even if you fired a rocket up me waistcoat.'

Her laughter burst. 'Oh, ain't you something, Tim? You never say soppy things like the Yanks do, like hiya, baby, you're the cream in my coffee. I never 'eard anything soppier. And Hollywood, what a laugh, I bet most of them come off chicken farms in Kentucky and we've got our own chickens and I bet Suffolk's nicer than Kentucky. Tim, I don't mind about the two years, then, I don't mind waitin' till I'm eighteen if it means—' She stopped.

'If it means what, Min?' I asked, feeling I'd set a trap for myself.

'If—' The darkness came and wrapped itself around us. 'If it means you could fall in love with me.' She was still serious. It amazed me that any girl still at school could think like this. They were all over the place, girls of sixteen. Walworth was thick with them. Too young to be called up, they were either at school or working in their first jobs and they were all gigglers and they all had crushes on people like Clark Gable or Gary Cooper. Yet here was Minnie Beavers talking about waiting until she was eighteen for me to fall in love with her. And compared to Clark Gable, I knew I wasn't just nobody, I was almost invisible.

'Well, I'll come knocking, Min.'

'Honest?'

'I'm banking on the war being over, of course.'

'Kiss?' she said.

'All right, for old times sake, Min.' I gave her a kiss. She didn't go mad, she actually gulped a bit. 'Good night, Min.'

'I don't mind waitin',' she said again and ran up the front path and home.

CHAPTER SEVENTEEN

It was announced next day that all leave was stopped. I was lucky, I'd recently had mine, but it put anticipation right up the spout for other men here and on site. And it had to mean something uncomfortable was about to arrive.

On Sunday, Frisby took out a chit, a pass and a bike and rode over to see Cecily. In possession of identical items, I cycled to see Mary and to get away from it all.

Mary was an uncomplicated woman. Whereas Missus thought sex should be thoroughly gone into, Mary said it was something that was all right when you were in the mood, but in a sixteen-hour day it would never take up more than a few minutes of your time. The other eight hours you were asleep. So what was all the fuss about? Two people had to think seriously about what they had in common for sixteen hours less a few minutes a day, or they'd end up boring each other.

'Why did you want to know?' she asked, having answered my enquiry. I'd made it after saying hullo and so on.

'Well, I'm naturally interested in what it's all about,' I said. 'I might get married one day.'

'Oh, you loon,' said Mary, 'it all happens natural, like.

If it doesn't, you'd better get unmarried. Let's have a nice cup of tea.'

Over a very nice cup of tea, she said she'd do a cold chicken salad for proper tea later. Had she cooked one of her chickens, then? Mary said no, she jolly well hadn't, she couldn't ever eat one of her own chickens, she'd feel like a cannibal eating a family friend. The chicken she'd cooked was one of Fred Plummer's. She didn't mind eating one of his and he and Mrs Plummer likewise didn't mind eating one of hers. I said the chickens in question probably appreciated that kind of thoughtfulness.

The August afternoon was warm, her garden inviting, so I offered to trim the edges of her lawns, front and back. Mary said that as it was hot I could take my army things off if I liked and she'd find me one of her late husband's cricket shirts, which would be cooler for me. Also a belt.

'Just a shirt and belt, Mary? I'll look a bit undressed, won't I?'

'You great lummox,' said Mary. 'I don't mean take your trousers off as well. I've got neighbours, I'll have you know.'

'Everyone's got neighbours. It's a problem for some people.'

In the open-necked cricket shirt and belted khaki trousers, I began work on the front lawns.

I nearly trimmed my left foot off when a jeep pulled up outside the cottage and Kit emerged legs first. She unloaded a bike from the jeep and spoke to the driver, a corporal. He nodded and charged off. Kit came down the path, wheeling the bike.

Mary appeared, smiling in welcome. 'What a nice surprise,' she said.

'You don't mind?' said Kit, who was taking no notice of me.

'Mind? Of course not, it's lovely to see you,' said Mary. 'Tim's come too.'

'Yes, I heard he was here,' said Kit. 'Is that him, the guy in the white shirt?'

'I let him borrow it,' said Mary. 'Tim, hold Kit's bike for her, I expect she'd like to tidy up.'

'She looks tidy enough to me,' I said, 'and I'm already holding these trimmers.'

'Just put it somewhere for me, thank you,' said Kit, getting rid of the bike by leaning it against me, then disappearing with Mary through my porch door. Typical. And why had she come? The bike, I noticed, was one of ours. I put it with mine at the side of the cottage and resumed my pleasant labours. Kit reappeared after a while, her jacket and cap off, her military shirt in clean crisp contact with her disciplined bosom.

'That shirt's too big for you,' she said.

'Oh, the shirt's all right,' I said, 'it's my flat chest that doesn't fit. What's brought you here?'

'A jeep took me to your BHQ,' she said. 'Deirdre told me you were here. She helped me to help myself to one of your bikes. I thought you and I could ride back together. The jeep's picking me up at BHQ at eight this evening. Is that explanation good enough for you?'

'Sounds all right,' I said. 'Sounds as if we're friends again.'

'What a cosy little war you're having,' she said.

'I'm hoping it stays that way. I'm sold on a peaceful post-war future. There ought to be more people like me, then there wouldn't be all these muck-ups every so often.'

'Don't give me hysterics,' said Kit.

Elsingham was sunny, quiet and sleepy. The sky was quiet too. Flying Fortresses seemed to be having a rest day.

'What are you doing with those things?' Kit asked.

'Trimming the edges of Mary's grass.'

'Let's make a fresh start,' she said.

'On the edges?'

'No, you idiot, let's you and I make a fresh start. Did you bring Mary anything?'

'Oh, a bit of tea and a bit of sugar that were going spare in the ration stores,' I said, wondering exactly what was on her mind.

'You crook,' said Kit. 'I've brought her a few things from our PX stores.'

'What a kind sergeant you are,' I said.

'I hope your conversation can improve,' she said. 'Well, I guess I'll go and talk to Mary now and leave you to your good deed. See you when she serves tea.' She disappeared again. She was a Chinese puzzle to me.

I did the trimming, back and front and got rid of some weeds. The chickens clucked as I dumped the weeds on the compost heap. Mary called that tea was ready. We took it inside. She said there were too many wasps about to have it in the garden.

It was a first-class Sunday tea, a chicken salad on a day when summer had risen to a peak, plus a cake that

245

was a masterpiece considering the wartime shortages. Mary and Kit gassed, of course. Kit said angel cake was an American favourite. Mary asked what the recipe was. Oh, you don't need a recipe, said Kit, the mixture comes in a carton that you buy at a store. Mary asked was that a dried fruit mixture and Kit said no, a cake mixture.

'Fancy buying a cake mixture', said Mary. 'I like to mix my own.'

Kit said ready-made cake mixtures were labour-saving.

'It's all to do with efficiency, Mary,' I said.

'Yes, fancy that,' said Mary and asked Kit if there was food rationing in America. Kit said oh, sure, but nothing like there was in England. According to the letters she received from her parents, they were still living quite well and her father was overweight.

'Too much cake mixture, I suppose,' I said.

Mary laughed. Kit looked sorry for me. But there it was, the conversation was all like that, she and Mary gassing and me throwing in bits and pieces.

We left at six-thirty, at Kit's insistence. Mary said how nice it had been and to come again. We cycled fairly companionably. Kit stopped when we reached the spot where the little wood was visible, the wood that reminded her of a Constable painting.

'That'll do,' she said.

'Do for what?' I asked.

'I don't want to rub noses here, in the road,' she said, 'we'll get run down by a truck.'

'Pardon?'

246

'Wake up, old buddy, we're making a fresh start, aren't we?'

'Is this serious?' I asked, as we wheeled our bikes over the verge and began to descend the gentle slope.

'Well, I thought you were,' she said. 'OK, I'll make myself clear. On the day you dropped Cassidy off, I was in the office and one of the girls said the door handle had come loose. I said, "Oh, get Tim to fix it." "Who's Tim?" she asked. I came to then, in a worried way. I asked myself why the worry should be about you. Then Cassidy came in with some story about a jeep that had run out of engine power and how you and your good old mousetrap appeared and gave her a lift. I asked where you were and if you were coming in and she said she thought you were already on your way back. I couldn't believe it. After giving you the best months of my life, you weren't even bothering about me. That was hard to take.'

'Was it?' I asked. 'Why?'

'I wish you'd wake up,' said Kit. We reached the little wood and the stream that ran through it. Kit led the way, trundling her bike along the path that skirted the trees. Finding a gap, she entered. I followed. I had a feeling something very unexpected was going to happen.

She stopped and we propped the bikes against a tree. She turned to me. 'Will this help?' she said and she wound her arms around my neck, lifted her face and kissed me warmly on the lips. Giddy, it was. I kissed her back. Her lips were very receptive, her body warm and firm against mine. Her eyes were closed. She sighed as I released her lips to draw breath.

247

'Is this happening?' I asked.

'It's not happening yet,' she murmured, 'but you want to, don't you, if I'm the only sergeant you've ever loved?'

'Pardon?' I said.

'Be my lover,' said Kit.

I couldn't believe my ears. 'Here and now?' I said. I wasn't even sure about the exact procedures.

'Honey, I'm sorry I gave you a rough deal,' she said. 'I was a supercilious bitch to you and the roof fell in on me when you didn't bother to come in and see me the other day. Serve me right. But I'm glad that you love me, so be my lover.' She pressed herself close again. It charged me with adrenalin, but I wanted the whole thing to be right.

'I can wait, Kit,' I said. 'I can wait for a church wedding with you in virgin white.'

She stared at me. 'That's a serious proposition?' she said.

'It's a proposal, Kit,' I said.

'That's awkward,' she said.

'Why?'

'Well, honey, for one thing, I'm not a virgin.'

That shook me and it shook all my old-fashioned ideas as well. 'How did that happen?' I asked.

Kit wrinkled her nose. 'A sergeant instructor at my enlistment camp. A guy, not a Wac. I thought him everything a girl could ask for. It was my first affair and over before I was posted. He wasn't everything, after all.'

'Sounds like a hooligan to me,' I said, feeling deflated.

'I don't know, what a war this is, it's mucking up everything that's decent.'

'Don't go over the top, honey,' said Kit and wound her arms around my neck again. 'We don't have to talk about marrying, in any case, do we?'

It all fell apart then, the picture I'd had of her as my little woman cooking for me and doing the ironing. It had struggled valiantly to stay in its frame. It gave up now.

'Oh, well,' I said, 'it was worth a try. Shall we go?'

'Go? Now?' Kit looked mystified. 'But we haven't got anywhere yet.'

'Well, there's not much point, is there?'

'That's another serious comment?' she said.

I felt then that the whole thing wasn't very important to her. It was just going to be sex. I was only going to rate as her second affair. I wasn't going to like that. 'Let's get going,' I said.

Abruptly, she disengaged, her mouth compressed. We wheeled our bikes in silence up to the road and resumed our ride to BHQ, where she was to pick up her transport back to base.

After a while she said, 'What went wrong?'

'I'm old-fashioned, like my Aunt May,' I said. She knew about my Aunt May.

'Oh, shoot,' she said, riding beside me in the light of the dipping sun. The fields and farms were radiant with colour. 'I know what's wrong, I know what's bugging you. Every man thinks every woman should only make love with him alone. It's the male ego. You've all got it. You're sore because the sergeant instructor beat you to it.'

249

'Don't talk like that,' I said, 'you sound like a tart.'

'I think you'd better take that back,' said Kit.

'I didn't say—'

'You called me a floosie.'

'I didn't. I only said you sounded like one. I'm sure you're not, but I just don't get it, I don't understand someone like you having a casual affair. I'd have thought you'd have been dead against it unless the two of you had marriage in mind.'

'Oh, you'd like to write the rules for me, would you?' she said.

'I'm just telling you what I think.'

'You're a prig, Hardy, a prig first-class, with a very tiny mind. Goodbye.' And she cycled away fast.

I let her go, knowing there was no point in trying to catch her up. I felt her store in Boston was her first love, that it was always going to be her main interest and that in other fields she'd make do with an affair from time to time. I wondered if there had been anyone else after the sergeant instructor. She'd said he'd been her first affair. I wondered if Major Moffat had taken a turn.

I didn't go back to BHQ. I rode on to the village, feeling like a drink at the pub. Minnie was outside her front door, cutting gladioli blooms from the border running parallel with the path. She straightened up when she saw me. A quick smile flowered. I stopped.

'Hello, Min.'

'Tim? Oh, you comin' in?'

'Yes, why not? Your mum might come up with a pot of tea.'

'Oh, I'll make it,' she said happily.

'Atta girl, honey, you're the cream in my coffee.'

'Oh, yer cuckoo,' said Min and she laughed.

It was a prize pot of tea and Missus heated up some sausage rolls to have with it. I didn't ask how she got the ingredients that had enabled her to wrap the sausage meat in flaky pastry. Min poured the tea and Missus handed round the sausage rolls.

Jim said, 'Yer goin' up to foreign parts, I 'ear, Tim.'

'All right, I give in,' I said, 'what foreign parts? The North Pole?'

'Oh, no, course not the North Pole, Tim,' said Minnie.

'Exmoor, I 'eard,' said Jim.

'Exmoor's not up to foreign parts,' I said.

'Foreign to Suffolk, Tim lovey,' said Missus.

'It's not up, anyway, it's west,' I said.

'Tim goin' west?' Minnie looked alarmed. 'Mum, I don't like the sound of that, not when the rotten old war's still on. Oh, can yer read your tea leaves, just in case?'

'Here, I thought you told me you had sense, Minnie,' I said.

'Well, it's good sense, it is, for Mum to read teacups,' declared Minnie.

'Yes, soon as I've finished this cup, I'll do some readin',' said Missus. 'Minnie's right, Tim, goin' west has sometimes got unfortunate meanings.'

'Barmy,' I said.

'What's that you said?' asked Missus.

'I was talking to Jim,' I said. Jim winked.

Missus finished her cup of tea, carefully drained the residue into the slop basin, placed the cup back in its saucer and studied the pattern of the tea leaves.

'Oh, you're goin' west all right, Tim,' she said.

'Isn't it my tea leaves you should be reading?' I asked.

'No, I've got it all in me own cup, lovey. It's only the west country, Minnie. Well, look at that, you're goin' to distinctive yourself, Tim.'

'Distinguish?' I suggested.

'That's it,' said Missus. 'It don't say how, but it looks like a medal all right.'

'I'll win a medal on Exmoor? Missus, those tea leaves of yours are upside-down. Anyway so we're off to Exmoor. So that's why leave's been stopped. Ruddy hell—'

'Language, Tim,' said Missus in soft reproof. 'Jim don't like language at fam'ly gatherings, not since we come up from Camberwell.'

'Well, dear oh dear,' I said. Minnie giggled. 'All I'm asking is how the ruddy hell do you lot get to know these things?'

'Don't get in a temper, love,' said Missus.

Minnie flashed a laughing look. 'Would you like the last sausage roll, Tim?' she asked.

'I'd like an answer,' I said.

'Well, I do a bit of business with yer adjutant,' said Jim.

'Captain Barclay?'

'Just a bit 'ere an' there,' said Jim. He lit his pipe and the aroma of fresh tobacco drifted around the parlour. Colourful gladioli blooms stood in a bright vase on a table by the window. 'Well, yer adjutant's got a large fam'ly down up to Epsom, yer know.'

'Down up to Epsom?' I said. 'You daft old coot, what's that mean?'

'Well, I never did,' said Missus. 'That's not 'ardly nice, Tim.'

'Down up to Epsom my foot,' I said.

'Five kids yer adjutant's got,' said Jim, 'so I get 'im a few things 'ere an' there, round and about, like. Then there's yer sergeant-major.'

'All right, I see it all now,' I said. 'So we're going on manoeuvres up to Exmoor and I'm going to distinguish myself. Do any of you know if I'll break a leg?'

Minnie yelled with laughter. 'Dad, ain't our Tim funny?' she said.

CHAPTER EIGHTEEN

The following day we were given twenty-four hours' notice to prepare ourselves for field exercises. It was going to be a short twenty-four hours considering reveille tomorrow would be at five in the morning.

That night, Frisby sat on his bed writing a long letter of farewell to Cecily. He was convinced we were going straight from field exercises to some fatal battlefield. Italy, no doubt. The Allies had landed there. He said something about leaving his Post Office savings to Cecily so that she could buy some helpful books written by qualified mind doctors.

'Waste of money, you twit,' I said. 'Cecily doesn't need mind doctors, just an armistice.'

'Can I help it if I worry about her?'

'Glad you do. Cecily's a love.'

I thought of Kit just before I dropped off. I could have had the ultimate experience with her. What a chump. I'd passed it by. On the other hand, Mary was right. People worry about it too much, that was what she felt. There was a lot of living to do outside of something that hardly took up any time at all, she said. Good old Mary.

The weather turned grey and sour over Exmoor. There were moors, certainly, but there were also dark little hills, knobbly peaks and boggy lowlands. We were instructed not to muck the place about and spoil it for citizens who liked to ramble over it at weekends. We couldn't think who'd want to ramble over it at the moment, it looked damp, soggy and uninviting. Chuck in a rainforest said Frisby and it would be easy to imagine it was Burma waiting for a monsoon to happen.

We spent a month there, a month of being toughened. That meant escaping death and broken bones only by certain acts of cowardice. We all went in for some of that. Major Moffat was an exception, of course. He enjoyed it all.

The climax came at the end of the month when he and the battery, in competition with the other two batteries of the regiment, were required to storm a granite peak held by the enemy, the enemy being regimental headquarters personnel under the command of Colonel Carpenter. There was a marshy bog in the way. A number of us had to scout around, looking for a way through. Major Moffat refused the temptation of going up the obvious way, from firm ground. God was kind to me that day. I found a way through and reported back to Major Moffat. He took us up not at dawn but at dusk and we caught the regimental lads eating hot stew.

Major Moffat sent for me afterwards. 'Gunner Hardy, did you fluke that?'

'The bog, sir? I suppose you could say so.' Still, I was fairly pleased with myself, I'd led the way through.

'Some fluke,' said Major Moffat. It was a triumph for him. We'd left the other two batteries floundering. And the whole thing had been an infantry not an artillery exercise. 'Are you turning over a new leaf?'

'Pardon, sir?'

'Are you doing more soldiering than fiddling?'

'Well, I'd like to help get the war over with as soon as possible, sir.'

'Dismiss,' said Major Moffat.

Frisby came out of it all in a condition of perfect health. He could hardly wait to show himself off to Cecily. I had an idea Cecily would love the new sinewy look of his muscles. I liked Cecily. I felt there'd always been a real young woman inside her, trying to get out. She was out now and she'd got herself a guy. Frisby wasn't a bad bloke at all. He and Cecily actually added up to a good old-fashioned romance. Ruddy good, I thought.

Some personnel were a bit gaunt when we got back to Suffolk, but most of us were as fit as fiddles. Gunner Dunwoodie no longer looked like a sack of potatoes trying to stand upright and Bombardier Wilkins had lost the best part of his portliness. It had taken a hiding.

Two letters from Aunt May awaited me. She never failed to write regularly. Both letters were full of homely gossip about friends and neighbours. If the chapter on Edie Hawkins was closed – she and her mother having gone to live in Peckham, as ordered by Ron – there were other happenings that made Aunt May declare people's behaviour in wartime left an awful lot to be desired. She really did have a thing about civilized behaviour. She often said most of our mistakes in life were the result of silly, reckless or headstrong behaviour. She would never have believed, she said in one of the letters, that respectable Walworth mums and dads could have such a trying time keeping an eye on young daughters who were going up West every night in the hope of being picked up by American soldiers. And even some house-wives were doing it, young housewives whose husbands were overseas. She was sad about that and about silly girls. If only young girls would give themselves time to think, she said, they wouldn't do the things they are doing.

She mentioned Bill in each letter, in a kind but casual way, which didn't make sense to me. Obviously she hadn't given him an answer yet and it didn't seem as if she was in any hurry either. I hoped it wasn't because of me. It would be like her to tell herself she couldn't get married until I was married too. I might have to do a bit of arguing with her. Bill seemed a bit of all right to me, just the kind of husband to care for her, look after her and even spoil her a bit.

I wrote in reply, telling her I'd survived a crippling four weeks and that I was expecting her to make up her mind about Bill before she was ninety. I told her to put herself first for a change and while she was still young and pretty. If you wait till you're ninety, I said, you'll be old then and so will Bill. I also said yes, it was shocking about people's behaviour, that I favoured old-fashioned values myself and what was going on up and down the country was a headache to me.

I also wrote to Kit. I felt I owed her an apology. I felt I really had been a prig. So I wrote saying I was sorry, that her past life was her own affair. I said I realized she wasn't the marrying type and that she probably had more to offer the world than rolling dough and ironing Monday's washing. I wished her luck with her store after the war and hoped that my apology would make her understand I liked her and respected her preference for being independent.

The following evening, Frisby cycled all the way to Chackford with a chit and a late pass, in the hope of seeing Cecily and letting Cecily see him. I went down to the *Suffolk Punch* with Simpson and Parkes.

Jim was at his gate, waiting for me, I suppose. He'd heard I was on the way. His pipe waved and beckoned. 'Join you blokes in a few minutes,' I said. Simpson and Parkes went on and I walked across to Jim.

''Eard you was back,' he said.

'Turn-up for the book if you hadn't heard,' I said. 'How's Min?'

'Fairish,' he said. 'She's out this evenin'.'

'With a feller? A boyfriend?'

'Now don't talk daft, Tim lad. Min ain't interested in boys. Growed out of boys before she was thirteen. Boys ain't grown up, she always says. They're kids, she says.'

'Don't tell me she's found a six-foot Yank with a moustache.'

'You all right, Tim?' Jim looked concerned. 'Ain't like you to talk like you don't know the alphabet. Min won't stand for any Yank gettin' too near 'er, you know that. She knows too much about 'em. Didn't she tell yer there's a fifteen-year-old girl at 'er school been put in the fam'ly way by a Yank that's disappeared like a bleedin' puff of smoke? That ain't goin' to 'appen in Min's life. I dunno why I ever come to think it 'ad, except there she was, growin' up fast an' ready to eat you about risin' summer night. I remember givin' yer one or two warnings. Still, I ought to 'ave 'ad more faith in me own flesh an' blood.'

'You old haybag,' I said. 'One minute you're offering to let your Missus teach me things I ought to find out for myself and the next you're congratulating yourself on your daughter's purity. Anyway, as long as she's all right—'

'Fairish, Tim, fairish. She's round at the Goodwins 'ouse, with 'er friend Jane.'

'Well, give her my love,' I said.

'Now I ain't goin' to go that, Tim lad,' said Jim, wagging his pipe at me. 'She'll think you mean it, she'll take it serious. That sort of thing you got to say to 'er yerself, only I know she ain't the right age for you, specially seein' I also know you got certain feelings for that there Wac sergeant that's more your age, like. Mind, not that I'd tell Minnie that, or she'd be up to Chackford with a chopper.'

'Give her my regards, then,' I said. 'I'm fond of her.'

'Fond of Missus too, ain't yer, lad?' said Jim and he chuckled.

I went on to the pub.

CHAPTER NINETEEN

I actually received a reply from Kit. She said my apology
was a happy surprise and a welcome one, as she hadn't
wanted to be left with only unpleasant memories of me.
She was willing to meet me at Mary's next Sunday
afternoon, when we could talk things through.

Talk things through, yes, I'd got to know that American females had a thing about talking things through. I
wasn't sure if that would get me anywhere, but the
temptation of seeing Kit again made me reply by return,
saying yes to the meeting.

Sergeant-Major Baldwin entered the orderly room. 'On
your feet, Gunner Hardy,' he barked. 'Cap on. Right,
this way.'

He marched me up to Major Moffat's office. He
presented me to the Major, who had his own cap on. So
I came to attention and saluted.

'Is this him, Sergeant-Major?' he asked.

'Gunner Hardy present and correct, sir,' said the
sergeant-major.

'I see. Very well. Gunner Hardy, from tomorrow you
will accept promotion to the rank of lance-bombardier.
That's all. Dismiss.'

The sergeant-major marched me out of the office and

down the stairs, telling me to draw stripes from the stores and to get them sewn on by tomorrow. Were there any questions?

'Well, yes, Sergeant-Major. Are you sure there hasn't been a mistake?'

'No, I'm not sure,' he said, 'but it's done now. We'll have to live with it.'

Promotion. What for? Distinguished service in getting the battery through the bog on Exmoor? Ruddy hell, Missus and her tea leaves. If that wasn't second sight, what was?

Life was suddenly being kind to me. I no longer had to worry about Minnie and Kit was going to meet me again. And wait a tick, hadn't Missus seen a surprise marriage for me in a previous teacup?

I felt I ought to knock my head against a wall and bring myself down to earth. All that might happen on Sunday was the possibility of Kit psychoanalysing me to find out what my real problems were and then buying me the kind of helpful book that Frisby had had in mind for Cecily. Well, I'd have to take what she dished out.

My first day as an NCO landed me with my first responsible duty, as guard commander. Major Moffat, accompanied by Sergeant-Major Baldwin, came out to inspect the guard himself, sharp on the dot at eighteen-hundred hours. I brought my four men smartly to attention and saluted as the major came up. He made his inspection. He didn't say a word, not until he'd given every man a good look. Then he said, 'Carry on, Lance-Bombardier Hardy.' I was almost certain he had a little grin on his face as he departed. I think it meant,

'Try that for starters, you bugger.' I saw it all then. He was going to wear me out with responsibilities.

Later on, just after dark, the man on duty called me from the guard hut, where I was wondering if the night was going to be peaceful enough for me to risk taking my boots off.

'Bloke in a hat wants to see you, Tim.'

'You're supposed to call me lance-bombardier.'

'Laugh a minute, that is.'

Outside the gates, Jim was darkly hovering. His ancient van was parked adjacent the workshop. 'Watcher, Tim lad. Just passin', I was, thought I'd stop. I 'eard you was in charge of the guard tonight.'

'Well, you help write out the day's orders, I suppose,' I said. 'Which reminds me, you forgot to tell me I was getting promotion.'

'Now, Tim, Missus told yer, didn't she? Told yer before you went up to Exmoor. An' we're all pleased for yer. You'll be a sergeant soon, Missus reckons an' she's got some eggs goin' spare. You can step in for 'em tomorrow evenin', eh? She's sorry yer goin'.'

'Going? Going where?'

'Italy, lad. Well, bound to be, ain't it, now the Yanks and our lads 'ave got Mussolini by 'is tail. We'll miss yer, but as Missus says, you've got to start winnin' medals sometime.'

'Look, you old dicky bird, don't come round here twittering about things that give me headaches.'

'No good lettin' yer lid rattle, Tim, that won't 'elp,' said Jim. 'The country needs yer and you've got to go.'

'The country needs you too,' I said, 'but you're not going.'

'Not at my age I ain't,' he said. 'Besides, I got me chickens, me small 'olding and me bits of business.'

'You sure we're off to Italy?' I asked.

'Well, it's just something I 'eard, Tim. Still, won't be for a week, or so, and it might only be a rumour.'

'Tell Missus to do a teacup job and find out for sure.'

'If yer want, Tim. Minnie ain't too 'appy about it.'

'Nor am I, it's ruddy dangerous in Italy.'

'Hello, Tim love,' said Missus the following evening. 'My, don't you look manly? And with a stripe as well. Did you good, goin' on them moors. Told you it would.'

'Yes, your teacup did a good job, Missus,' I said, as we went into the living-room. 'You look a bit of all right yourself, is that a new jumper you're wearing?'

'Yes, it is, love. Aunt Flossie just finished knitting it for me,' said Missus, her proud bosom softly enclosed by the knitwear, her chocolate-brown eyes melting with pleasure because I'd noticed. 'It fits nice, don't you think? Jim's special fond of it.'

'So he should be. After all, what's yours is his, seeing you're married to him.'

'Oh, saucy today, are we?' Missus laughed softly. 'Mind, women like a bit of sauciness in some men, men they're fond of. Pity you never let me learn—'

'We'll keep quiet about that, Missus. Best thing. Minnie enjoyed her school holidays, did she?'

'She's upset, Tim, knowin' you're goin'.'

'Well, I don't know and no-one else does either. Those ruddy dicky birds of yours ought to be fed castor oil, then they wouldn't fly about so much.'

'Now, Tim, no good bein' like that. You've got to put up with it, like we have. Everyone's sorrowful—'

'Oh, the whole village has heard, of course?'

'Well, yes, love, course they have. Jim reckons Italy.'

'What does your teacup reckon?' I asked.

'Oh, yes, Jim said you wanted me to do some consultin', so I did. It come out like the Pope blessin' the multitude and Jim said that's it, it's Italy where the Pope lives.'

'First time I've ever heard of the Pope blessing the multitude in a teacup,' I said. 'Missus, you're having me on.'

'A body can't do that, Tim love, not with what's in a teacup. It's the guidin' 'and of fate in a teacup. Minnie's gone out, by the way, she said she'd better when she knew you were comin'. She said when you've gone we won't ever see you again and the best thing she could do was try and get over you. She said something about you wouldn't come knockin' in two years time, that you'd have forgot us by then. Well, you see, love, she asked her dad about that American girl of yours and if you were still keen on her and her dad wouldn't say, so Minnie got upset about still bein' only a schoolgirl. Blamed us for it, sayin' it was our fault she was only sixteen and that you wanted that American girl instead of her.'

'Hell, don't we all have problems, Missus, when we're only sixteen?' I said, feeling rotten.

'Can't be helped, Tim,' said Missus gently. 'Did you tell her something about knockin' on our door in two years?'

'I thought that was one way of giving her time to get over it. I mean, she is only sixteen, Missus and no-one's the same at eighteen as they are at sixteen. She's just got a young girl's crush at the moment, hasn't she?'

'Well, love, I'm not sure that some girls of sixteen aren't already grown up as much as they ever will be. Well, in some ways, I mean. Still, like I said, it can't be helped.' Missus looked a bit sad, all the same. 'There, I'll put the kettle on. Jim'll be in in a minute and I'll make a pot of tea for all of us. And I've got some eggs for you.'

When Jim came in from doing a bit of business, the kettle was boiling and Missus made the pot. We sat and had a long chat. Minnie was conspicuous by her absence. Nor had she come in by the time I left at nine-thirty. Missus gave me six new-laid eggs and I shared them out at breakfast the next morning, giving one to the sergeant-cook, who let us fry the rest.

On Sunday I had my reunion with Kit. She arrived in a jeep, driving it herself. She was warm and friendly, showing no hard feelings at all. She even kissed me. Mary smiled at that.

Noticing my stripe, Kit said, 'Is that promotion?'

'A small step upwards,' I said.

'Yes, fancy Tim a corporal now,' said Mary, pleased for me.

'Lance-bombardier,' I said.

'That sounds like a guy who drops bombs from Flying Fortresses,' said Kit, looking like my idea of an all-American girl.

'Oh, we don't want Tim goin' up in one of them things,' said Mary.

'Sure, let's keep him on the ground, Mary,' said Kit. 'We can see what he's up to then.'

Mary laughed.

Kit and I wandered around the garden a little later. It was a nice autumn afternoon, the sun warm. Mary kept out of the way. I think she thought Kit and I had reached a lovey-dovey stage. But all we were doing in the garden was trying to work out exactly what kind of a relationship we had at the moment. At least, I was. Kit was talking things through, so that she could chuck out everything that wasn't satisfactory. Well, I supposed she was. She said that when she left BHQ for the Chackford base she thought that was the end of a close personal friendship with me. She had to go her way and I had to go my way and that was that. But she kept thinking of me, she said, and it was a shock to her when I didn't bother to call in and see her after I'd dropped Cassidy off. She also said that after the fiasco of our last meeting she thought she could just make me a turned page in her life. But the page wouldn't turn, with the result that when she received my letter of apology she knew she was sunk.

'Sunk?' I said. And she went on in her American fashion about how a crisis in one's emotions could make a woman feel she'd fallen out of the lifeboat. That sounded to me as if she was trying to complicate the issue. To me it was just a question of did she like me or didn't she? I was in love myself, she fascinated me, even if I was a bit miffed that she'd never be a virgin bride.

'Well, you're back in the lifeboat,' I said. 'You must be, or you'd have sunk without trace.'

'Yes, but do you want me?' she asked.

'As what, Kit?'

'OK,' she said, 'we won't talk about being lovers. You're a sweet old buddy and you've got principles. Fine. Look, I'm sorry, real sorry that I threw that instructor guy at you the way I did. I didn't like myself very much for that and you were right to give me a poke in the eye.'

'No, my mistake,' I said. 'I think I showed I was a bit out of date. Point is, I used to believe you only made love to a girl if you were going to marry her. No, correction: I used to believe you didn't make love to a girl unless you were married to her. I've got to face it, I'm all behind, that stuff's all gone overboard.'

'That's not being out of date, that's having principles,' said Kit, doing her best to find excuses for my old-fashioned outlook. We stopped to look at the pecking chickens, which immediately cocked suspicious eyes at us. 'No-one's made those kind of principles a crime yet. In the States magazine surveys have shown that most girls still don't make love until they're married. So what made me step out of line? Infatuation and a totally new environment, I guess.'

She talked on. I'd heard that American females could talk and liked to. Kit indulged in lots of American self-examination, while I did what I could not to sound as if I expected her to be on a par with the Virgin Mary. She said she and I must really get to know each other, to meet as often as possible, to get good and compatible until we could decide if we had a future together. She didn't mention any need to make love. I think she thought it had nearly ruined a beautiful friendship.

'I've already decided,' I said.

'Decided what?' asked Kit.

'That I'd like to marry you.'

'Well, that's sweet,' said Kit, 'that really is. You don't mind that I'd like to have more time to think about it?'

'I can wait till the war's over,' I said. 'Next year, I should think.'

'That's my old buddy,' said Kit. 'How about a kiss to seal the agreement?'

I kissed her. She had a lovely mouth. But I guessed, from all she had said, that she wasn't sure if she was in love with me or not.

Mary called us in to have tea then. Good old Mary. She knew how to serve up a welcome Sunday tea. She knew, in fact, all there was to know about the simple pleasures of life. She was a simple soul all round, whereas Missus was a bit subtle. When we asked her if we could meet here again next Sunday she said she'd love to have us. She did add that the putty wanted replacing around her kitchen windows, that Fred Plummer had said he'd do it, but still hadn't.

'Tim will fix it,' said Kit, then looked at me and wrinkled her nose. 'I mean, we could ask him.'

'Pleasure,' I said. 'I'll bring some putty from

the stores, some that's lying around and not doing anything.'

'He's a first-class fixer, Mary,' said Kit.

'I don't know anyone more helpful than Tim,' said Mary.

'Well, I don't know anyone who puts on better Sunday teas,' I said.

'All the same, I guess Tim rates, Mary,' said Kit and gave me a smile.

We said goodbye to Mary at seven-thirty. Kit told me to heave my bike into the jeep and she'd drive me to BHQ. I did so and got up beside her. Off she went, Mary waving to us. We hadn't gone more than a mile before I came to a startling conclusion. My efficient American sergeant couldn't rate as a driver. Well, at least she couldn't handle a jeep with its four-wheel drive. She was all over the place on bends and corners and on the tightest corners she was inclined to end up on the wrong side of the road. There was little traffic, but she was a danger to life and limb all the same. How she'd arrived at Mary's all in one piece I'd never know.

'I think you'd better pull up, Kit,' I said.

'What's the idea?' she asked, careering round a bend.

'Let me drive,' I said.

She pulled up, but not to hand over the wheel. 'Come again?' she said.

'Yes, I'd like to drive,' I said. 'I've only handled a jeep once and then only for five minutes. I'd like another go. Don't mind, Kit, do you?'

'Hold your horses,' said Kit, 'is there something wrong with my driving, then?'

'It's the road, Kit, there's not enough of it. Well, except for people used to it.'

'Listen, you male big shot, are you one of those guys with a prejudice against women drivers?'

'No, I'm just an ordinary bloke who wants to get where he's supposed to be going,' I said. From under the peak of her cap her blue eyes were threatening. 'You're a lovely sergeant, Kit,' I said, 'but the jeep's running away from you.' Actually, I quite liked the fact that there was one thing she wasn't too good at. It made her more lovable.

'I can handle it,' she said.

'So can I. Come on, be a sport, give us a go.'

'You kook,' she said and she laughed. 'OK, take over.'

I liked that too. She'd made her protest, but wasn't going to turn it into an argument or a fight. I took over and drove her all the way to her base to make sure she got there. When we arrived at the base, I stopped at the gates. The Snowdrops came out of their cubby-hole to give us the once-over. Kit said this was crazy, now she'd got to drive me to BHQ. I said I'd use the bike. I unloaded it. The evening dusk made me switch the lamp on.

'I can do with the exercise,' I said.

'You can do with a poke in the eye,' said Kit.

'See you,' I said.

'Do I get a kiss?' she asked. I gave her a smacker, much to the amusement of the Snowdrops.

'Next Sunday,' I said. 'So long for now, lovey.'

'So long, sweetie,' said Kit and I left, hoping she'd manage to drive the jeep back to where it belonged without running anyone over. She called after me. 'Pick you up at BHQ, Tim!'

'Drive at ten miles an hour!' I called back and I heard her laugh.

CHAPTER TWENTY

The following day, Sergeant Johnson, returning to the orderly room after twenty minutes of absence, stood to attention to make an announcement. 'Right, lend your ears,' he said. 'Embarkation leave. Ten days. Starts Thursday.'

'Who's going?' asked everyone.

'The regiment, all three batteries.'

'ATS as well?' asked Corporal Deirdre Allsop.

'Not this time,' said Sergeant Johnson.

'That's it, leave us out,' said Corporal Deborah Watts, 'we're only the backbone of BHQ, don't take us to exciting foreign places.'

'Safer not to,' said Frisby, 'you'll only end up in a harem. Here, half a tick,' he said, as the news sunk sharply in, 'I don't like the sound of this, sarge.'

'Thought you wouldn't,' said Sergeant Johnson, 'but make a note, all of you, to read standing orders to make sure you know you've got to finish up in Liverpool next Sunday week. It'll probably mean a sea cruise to the Pacific.'

Bombardier Wilkins said he'd only go if he had to, Frisby said he wouldn't go under any circumstances and I said I couldn't go.

'Dear oh lor',' said Sergeant Johnson, 'you sure you couldn't?'

'Positive,' I said. 'It's my private life, I'm expecting developments. I don't mind the Isle of Wight, but anywhere farther than that would muck things up considerably.

'No problem,' said Sergeant Johnson, 'just get your developments sorted out and the rest of us will wait for you.'

'They can wait for me too,' said Frisby. 'I've got certain medical responsibilities.'

'Yes and we know who your patient is,' said Sergeant Johnson. 'Take her on leave with you and give her an operation.'

'I've got to go down to the village,' I said.

'Don't come it,' said Sergeant Johnson.

'It's all right, I'll make out a chit,' I said.

He let me go, it was that kind of a day. I cycled down to the village to use the public phone box and got the operator to ring the American base at Chackford. I put my tuppence in and asked for Extension 151, which was Kit's office. She answered and I gave her the news. She asked if I understood what I was saying and was it true. I said yes. She said it wasn't the best joke she'd ever heard. I said it was no joke. Don't make it worse, she said, go sick, fall ill. That wasn't like her at all, she'd always been inclined to think I was having too easy a war. She asked where the battery was going to. I told her that Jim Beavers had said it would be Italy.

'Don't quote that old ratbag,' she said, 'I'm sick enough as it is.'

273

'I suppose you couldn't get ten days off and share my embarkation leave with me, could you?' I asked.

'Now I'm really hurting,' said Kit, 'I had a week's leave in London while you were living it up without me in BHQ and I'm beginning an officers' training course in a few days. From next Monday.'

'I don't like the sound of that, I'll have to salute you next time we meet, which looks like being when the war's over.'

'Tim, that's not funny.'

'Well, how about if we arranged a wartime wedding for tomorrow, with a one-night honeymoon?'

'That's even less funny,' said Kit.

'After the war, then?'

'Yes,' she said.

'Is that yes to the proposal?' I asked.

'Yes, love you,' said Kit.

'You mean you're going to be my little woman?'

'I'm going to marry you,' she said, 'not be your little woman. I—' She stopped. I heard a voice in the background. Kit rushed a few words, 'Write to me. Take care. Write to me.'

'I'll write. All the best, love.'

When I came out of the phone box I hardly knew where my feet were. When I got back on the bike I hardly knew where the road was. Twice I mounted the verge and once I rode into the hedge.

I had a post-war future with an all-American girl.

As soon as my work was finished for the day I went to the village, giving army tea a miss. Frisby had already

274

disappeared to cycle to Chackford, where Cecily was dwelling in blissful ignorance of his imminent departure to war, unless Kit had given her the news.

I posted a letter to Aunt May, then called on Jim. Minnie answered my knock.

'Hello, Min,' I said. She was still growing up in a ripe and creamy way, but looked as if she'd lost some of her exuberance. It was understandable.

'No-one's in,' she said.

'You're in and you're not no-one,' I said.

'Are you here to see me?' she asked.

'All of you.'

'Well, there's only me,' she said, 'and I'm goin' out, I've got a date.'

'Have you? Well, that's good, Min, but does your dad know?'

'Yes,' she said and there wasn't even the ghost of a smile around.

My stomach rumbled. 'Sorry,' I said, 'I missed out on tea.'

'Fancy that,' said Min, unimpressed. Having some of her own back, Min was. 'Well, you'd better come in, I suppose.'

'Not if you're going out, Min.'

'You can come in, can't you?' she said. 'Not goin' to jump all over you, am I? All right, I'll give you a bit of tea.'

'I didn't come for that, Min. I came to let your mum and dad know we're definitely going overseas.'

She bit her lip. 'Yes, we thought you'd be goin' soon,' she said. 'Oh, don't keep standin' there, just come in.'

'All right, Min, I'll come in and wait,' I said, 'it's my last chance of seeing your mum and dad. From tomorrow we're confined to barracks until they let us out on embarkation leave on Thursday.'

I stepped in. Minnie closed the door and went through to the kitchen. I followed.

'What d'you want to eat?' she asked with her back to me.

'Min, don't worry about that,' I said, 'go and get yourself ready for your date.'

'Just sit down, will you?' Minnie was huffy. For the sake of peace and quiet, I sat down at the kitchen table. 'I'll do you scrambled eggs on toast and a pot of tea. I don't want Mum sayin' I wasn't 'ospitable. She an' Dad are in Sudbury, doin' shoppin'. They went in his van.'

'Well, I hope they'll be back before you chop me in half, I'd like to see them.'

'Best if you don't talk, you don't make me laugh any more,' said Min and got on with scrambling two eggs.

'Min, you told your Mum that after I'd gone I'd forget all of you.'

'So you will,' she said.

'Of course I won't.'

'You won't ever come an' see us again, I bet you won't.' She was keeping her back to me all the time. 'You're goin' with that Wac sergeant again, we 'eard you was seen out with her on Sunday, in a jeep.'

In the jeep, Kit and I had been an obvious target for eyes that were always wide-awake in this part of Suffolk, where everyone seemed to know every BHQ soldier.

'Well, Min—'

'Don't bother,' said Min. 'I already got the message. I suppose you thought you were bein' nice to me in tellin' me you'd come and see me when the war was over, but I don't think you were bein' honest. Never mind, it don't matter now, I've met someone.'

'Then I'm pleased for you, Min.'

'That's a laugh,' said Min. She rustled up the welcome snack in no time, a fluffy golden mound on two slices of toast. Then she plonked a pot of tea on the table. 'There's the milk, there's the sugar and there's a cup an' saucer.'

'Thanks, Min, it looks a treat,' I said, wondering if Kit could perform as quickly and as well.

'I'm goin' to get ready for me date now,' she said and whisked out. The little meal was first-class, although I'd have enjoyed it more if she'd served it up with a smile. Her missing sparkle made me grieve a bit for her.

I was on my second cup of tea when Jim and Missus arrived home, laden with two full shopping bags. Most people these days were lucky to come home with one shopping bag half-full. Jim and Missus, of course, had their own sources of supply. Missus beamed at seeing me.

'My, it's nice to see you makin' yourself at home, Tim,' she said. 'Has our Minnie been givin' you some tea?'

'Scrambled eggs on toast,' I said. 'I dropped in to let you know the battery's moving out on Thursday – embarkation leave. You probably know already, of course.'

'I didn't know we knew that, did we, Jim?' said Missus.

'Sort of,' said Jim.

'Well, perhaps you also sort of know how much longer the war's going to last and if I'm going to come out of it alive.'

'Blessed if our Tim's not teasin' us, Jim,' said Missus, taking her hat and coat off.

'You'll be all right, lad,' said Jim, seating himself and testing the pot for contents. He poured himself a cup.

'Shame you got to go, though,' said Missus, 'specially as we heard you're goin' round courtin' your American lady sergeant in one of them jeeps.'

'Yes, we did 'ear, Tim, an' good luck to yer,' said Jim. 'She looks a good 'un to me. Where's our Min? Gone out, 'as she?'

'She's upstairs getting ready,' I said.

'Yes, she's met a nice young chap in the RAF,' said Missus.

'Well, that's good,' I said.

'Maybe,' said Jim. ''E ain't like you, Tim, nor us. More of a foreigner, like. Comes from Yorkshire.'

'Still, he's a kind boy,' said Missus, 'only eighteen an' just joined up. Mind, we're goin' to miss you, love.'

'Well, you've been good friends, you and Jim, Missus,' I said. 'Your place has been home from home to me.'

'Stay for the evenin' and have a bite of supper with us,' said Missus, 'there's a nice sausage and onion puddin' simmering away in that saucepan. I'll just go up and show Minnie the new dress we bought for her

278

in Sudbury, Jim 'appened to find some spare clothin' coupons.' She took a parcel from one of the shopping bags and went upstairs with it.

Jim sat drinking his tea, his mossy hat nodding pensively. 'Buy yer a pint at the pub after supper, Tim,' he said.

'Well, good on yer, mate,' I said. I heard voices upstairs, then the sound of descending footsteps, followed by the opening of the front door. Minnie called.

'See you later, Dad.'

'Not too much later, Minnie girl,' called Jim.

'No, all right,' called Minnie and the front door closed.

Missus reappeared. 'Well, she liked the look of the dress, Jim,' she said, 'but didn't 'ave no time to try it on. Said she was already late meetin' her young man. She's still a bit low.'

'Nothing you said to 'er, was it, Tim?' asked Jim. 'You wasn't unkind to our Min?'

'Give you my word,' I said. 'She did me proud with the scrambled eggs, told me she'd got a date and went upstairs to get ready.'

'Funny she didn't say goodbye to you,' said Jim.

'Not funny at all,' said Missus.

'This ain't yer last evenin' before you go, Tim, is it?' said Jim.

''Fraid so,' I said. 'We're confined to barracks tomorrow and Wednesday. We've got to clean the whole place up and leave it looking tidy. Didn't you know?'

'We don't 'ear everything,' said Jim.

'Yes, dicky birds don't fly in all the time,' said Missus.

'Anyway,' said Jim, 'we'll go to the pub after supper,

279

Tim, an' you can stand me that jug of ale you mentioned.'

'I thought you said you were treating.'

'Did I?' Jim's old green titfer looked as puzzled as his face. 'I thought goin' off to a place like Italy made it your turn, lad.'

Yes, bound to be Italy, I thought. Mussolini had done a bunk, the Italian government had surrendered and its navy was in the hands of the British. But the German armies in Italy were giving the Allied troops a hard fight. Well, the battery had had it cushy so far, we couldn't complain about being sent to join the fighting forces in Italy.

Missus served a luscious sausage and onion pudding for supper. I had no problem in tucking in, although I'd had my army dinner at midday and the teatime snack of scrambled eggs. Missus said she was pleased to give me that kind of treat for my farewell. Afterwards, Jim and I went to the pub. It was a lively hour or so, with some of my battery mates there as well and several Suffolk natives. They all knew about us going, the locals. They always seemed to know everything. It was no good the government warning everyone to keep whatever information they had under their hats. It all escaped and flew into the ears of the inhabitants of Sheldham.

I went back with Jim to his cottage to say a final goodbye to Missus. Young Wally Ricketts appeared out of the night.

''Ello, Tim, yer goin', then,' he said.

'Seems like it,' I said.

'I might as well fink about goin' meself, back to me

mum an' dad in 'Oxton,' he said gloomily. 'I mean, you're me only mate round 'ere. Well, except for Mr Beavers – 'ello, Mr Beavers. I only get fick ears from everyone else. Honest, Tim, if any of the kids fall in the pond, I get the blame. D'yer want any rabbits when yer go?'

'I won't be able to collect them,' I said.

'I'll bring 'em, don't you worry, I'll bring yer a pair, like before. Only times bein' 'ard, I've 'ad to put the price up. Say a couple of bob for the pair, Tim?'

'That lad's got the makin's,' said Jim, grinning.

'Young war profiteer,' I said. 'Still, all right, Wally, bring 'em along on Wednesday and I'll find you a couple of bob. But I want fresh bunnies.'

'You betcher, Tim mate,' said young Wally.

A few minutes later I was saying goodbye to Missus. She gave me a kiss and wiped a tear away. 'We're goin' to miss you something chronic, Tim love,' she said.

'I'm going to miss you too, Missus, all of you. So long, you old Suffolk cockney,' I said to Jim, shaking his hand.

'I ain't as old as that,' said Jim. 'Me an' Missus, well, it's been a pleasure knowin' yer, Tim. You watch out for yerself now.'

No-one had mentioned Minnie.

'Sorry Minnie's not here,' I said, 'I'd have liked to say goodbye to her.'

'Ah, well,' said Jim carefully.

'Best thing she's not here in a way,' said Missus.

'Well, give her my love,' I said, 'and wish her the best of luck for me.'

281

'Goodbye, Tim,' said Missus and gave me another kiss.

'I'll come knocking one day,' I said and I left.

As I reached the gate, Minnie appeared on clicking heels. 'Oh,' she said.

'Hello, Min.'

'I thought you'd be gone by now,' she said.

'I'm just off,' I said.

The village street was dark. I'd known it bright, sunny, rainy, misty and icy and I'd known it as neighbourly as any Walworth street. I'd known smiles, looks, country greetings, soft voices, rich voices, friendly eyes, curious eyes and knowing eyes. I felt as much a part of this village street as I did of my home street in Walworth. And I felt that Jim, Missus and Minnie were family. I also felt, at this moment, that Minnie meant as much to me as a lovable, teasing sister and that I had a lot to make up for in the way I'd treated her.

'Had a nice evening, Minnie?'

'Yes, thanks.'

'He's a Yorkshire boy, your dad said.'

'He's not a boy, he's in the RAF,' said Minnie.

'Well, the very best of luck, Min—'

'Yes, all right, goodbye,' she said and came through the gate, her elbow brushing me. There she was, still a schoolgirl, the apple of her dad's eye and a treasure to her mum. A young girl with her own way of being saucy and teasing.

'So long, then, Min, and I shan't forget you.'

'Yes, goodbye,' she said again and I realized that at last she was going off me.

'Bless you, Min,' I said and left.

She called me back. 'Oh, blow, I'm sorry,' she said. 'I can't not wish you good luck, you been nice to me mum an' dad. I – well, look after yourself.'

'I'll drop your mum and dad a line,' I said and bent my head to kiss her on the cheek. She avoided it, turned away and walked up the path and into the cottage. The door closed behind her.

I felt a bit sad then.

Young Wally brought the rabbits on Wednesday afternoon, handing them over to me at the gates. I gave him half a crown as a parting gesture and his eyes rolled about in rapture.

'Cor, good on yer, Tim,' he said, 'I 'opes yer win the Victoria Cross.'

'Leave off,' I said, 'I'm not going in for any charge of the Light Brigade. Off you go, Wally, and don't smash up Mrs Ford's apple tree.'

'Course I won't, yer me 'ero, Tim,' he said and went happily back to the village.

Carrying the rabbits to my quarters, I came face to face with Major Moffat. And his dog. 'What's that you've got there?' he asked, pointing with his cane at the wrapped rabbits.

'Present from one of the evacuees, sir,' I said. His daft dog, sniffing the parcel, dribbled with excitement and made a mad attempt to get its teeth into it. The major asked what kind of a present it was. 'Couple of rabbits, sir, and could you call your dog off?'

'It's your problem, lance-bombardier,' said the major

and went on his way, his fiendish grin undisguised. I had a running fight with the hungry Dalmatian all the way to my sleeping hut, where Frisby got me out of trouble by chucking a spare boot at it. It had its own back by running off with the boot.

'Get after it,' I said, 'it'll chew that boot to pieces.'

'It's your boot, not mine,' said Frisby.

I had the devil's own job rescuing one half of my spare footwear. I couldn't get a replacement from the stores. The stores had closed down and everything had been packed up. I cornered the animal on the first floor of the mansion and tickled it with a bicycle pump I'd picked up on the way. It howled and dropped the boot. Major Moffat came out of his office.

'What's going on?' he asked.

'Have to inform you, sir, that Jupiter pinched one of my spare boots and this bicycle pump. Thought I'd better pinch 'em back, sir.'

'I heard it yell for help,' said the major.

'Not Jupiter, sir. He's always been able to stand up for himself. Good dog, Jupiter, good boy. Sit now.'

'What a specimen,' said the major.

'Yes, dog and a half, sir.'

'Not him, you,' said the major.

CHAPTER TWENTY-ONE

On my way home to begin my embarkation leave, I thought I'd call on Charlie Chipper and his fish stall again. I hadn't bothered him on my last leave. I'd got the rabbits, but no perks from the ration stores. All surplus rations had been returned to the main Naafi depot at Earls Colne. I thought some prime fillets of smoked haddock or a couple of fresh haddock might be welcome to Aunt May.

The East Street market was a jostle and bustle and stallholders who knew me let me know they'd seen me. Charlie had customers at his stall. I waited.

''Ello, 'ello,' he said, when he'd finished serving them, 'is that you there, Tim old cock?'

'Still surviving,' I said.

'Glad for yer,' said Charlie. 'Mind, I ain't got nothing for yer in the way of kippers.'

'All right, I'll do you a favour,' I said, 'I won't ask for kippers, I'll take some fillets of smoked haddock.'

'Ain't got none of them, neither,' said Charlie, straw boater on the back of his head. 'Bleedin' shame, I grant yer, but I ain't.'

'All right, I'll just have two and a couple of fresh ones to make up.'

''Ere, yer comin' it a bit, ain't yer, me old cocka-lorum?'

'Wrap 'em up before there's a crowd, Charlie.'

'That's it, break me arm,' said Charlie.

'I'm on embarkation leave,' I said.

'Gawd blimey an' now yer pullin' on me 'eart-strings,' said Charlie.

'You've always had a warm heart along with your cockles, old mate.'

Charlie grinned, shook his head in defeat and came up with two fresh haddock. 'No smoked, cross me warm 'eart,' he said.

'OK,' I said and he wrapped the fish up and charged me a packet. On account of the war, he said.

Aunt May wasn't around when I arrived home. I wondered if she'd got my letter. Everything looked in apple pie order, as usual, everything tidily in place, except for her veneered box of little personal items. Normally, she kept it in her bedroom. There were old photographs in it, family photographs of herself, her parents and my parents. Also letters and other little things. The curved lid was open. I took some of the photographs out and saw her as a small girl, a growing girl and a young woman. They'd turned sepia with age. I'd seen them before, on the occasions when she'd sit with the open box on her lap and reminisce. I wondered if there were any snaps of the man she'd lost, I'd never seen any. No, I couldn't rummage, not sporting.

I saw her birth certificate. I'd not seen that before. May Elizabeth Hardy, born in New Cross of Arthur Henry Hardy and wife Margaret Lilian, 19 March, 1904.

Funny. That made her thirty-nine, not forty-one. She'd always given her age as if she'd been born in 1902. I took a look at her National Identity card, issued to the population at the beginning of the war. That showed her born in 1904 as well. I'd thought she was twenty-one when she took on the responsibility, with her parents, of looking after me when I lost my own parents. Perhaps the little deception was something to do with legalities, perhaps the law would not have allowed her to have me unless she'd come of age. But then I suppose the law would have required to see her birth certificate. Or perhaps it was her parents who took formal charge of me. Whatever the reason for saying she was two years older than she was, I'd have thought that after a while she needn't have bothered.

Should I ask her questions about it? No. She had had her reasons and they were her own business. All the same, it was very unusual for a woman to keep up the pretence of saying she was older than she was.

I put the items back in her box and left it as it was, with the lid open. I put the haddock in the larder, on a plate. I stowed the rabbits in too, then took myself, my kitbag and my rifle up to my bedroom. I'd left Suffolk for good and on Sunday week would rendezvous with the rest of the regimental personnel at Liverpool's main railway station.

I heard Aunt May come in. I called down to her. 'I'm home, Aunt May.'

'Oh, that's good,' she called up, 'sorry I had to go out, love. Come on down, let me take a look at you.'

287

I went down. We met in the passage and she gave me the customary kiss and cuddle.

'How's tricks?' I asked.

'I can't grumble,' she said, looking very personable in her hat and coat. We went into the kitchen. I showed her the fish and the rabbits. 'Well, you don't ever come home empty-handed, do you?' she smiled. 'I didn't want to be out when you arrived, but I had to go to the doctor's.'

'Nothing serious, I hope.'

'No, of course not, just some twinges from eating something that disagreed with me.'

'What kind of twinges?'

'Just the twinges you get when your stomach's not well,' said Aunt May. She took her medical card and a bottle of medicine out of her handbag. She put the medicine on the mantelpiece and the card back where it belonged, in her veneered box. She closed the lid. 'Now why did I leave that box there? I hope I'm not getting absent-minded, that's a sure sign of old age.'

'You're a youngster,' I said. 'Were the twinges painful?'

'They caught me a bit sharp,' confessed Aunt May, 'so I thought I'd better go to the doctor's and get some medicine. But I'm all right now.'

'You sure?'

'I'm fine. The twinges have just been catching me now and again. No need to fuss.'

'Still, would you like to put your feet up while I get some lunch? Or are you off food?'

'I'm not off food, not now I'm not and I'm not putting

288

my feet up,' said Aunt May. 'I'll get the lunch, but before I do, I want to know something. Are you in trouble, Tim?'

'I could have been. The major's dog could have had those rabbits and my right arm as well yesterday.' Aunt May knew all about the ravenous and scatty Dalmatian. 'But I won that one.'

'What I mean is why are you on leave again, love?' Aunt May was gently enquiring. 'You had your usual leave only a little while ago. You haven't gone absent, have you? You just said in your letter you were getting more leave and I thought that's funny.'

I wondered if I should tell her the reason. I thought I'd better. 'It's ten days embarkation leave,' I said.

'Oh, I see.' Aunt May took that with a wry little smile. 'I see, you're going overseas.'

'I've been lucky so far, I'm not complaining.'

'Yes, we've both been lucky, Tim, so I won't complain, either,' she said, and gave my arm a squeeze. Then she got on with preparing lunch. Aunt May never went over the top. Although she never hid her likings and her affections, she never became emotional.

I kept glancing at her over lunch, seeing her now as a woman who was under forty, not over. Perhaps there wasn't much difference between thirty-nine and forty-one, but it was one reason why I'd thought she never looked her age. Another reason was her equability. It kept away frowns, lines and creases.

I asked how Bill Clayton was. Aunt May said he was in the pink the last time she saw him. I wanted to know why she still hadn't made her mind up about him. She said it was something she needed to think long and hard about.

'You don't usually shilly-shally,' I said, 'you usually make your mind up fairly quickly. Bill would be good for you.'

'I don't have to have anyone just because he'd be good for me,' she said.

'But you're fond of Bill,' I said.

'I'm fond of the vicar and some of the market stallholders,' said Aunt May, 'but I don't have to marry them.'

'Be a sensation if you did. But I thought Bill was a bit special.'

'I'll make up my own mind, Tim.'

'Well, it's your life, Aunt May,' I said, 'but it strikes me you're playing hard to get.'

'The very idea, as if I'd do that,' she said. She was hedging. It was most unlike her. 'You haven't mentioned that American girl,' she said, changing the subject. 'Is it really all over? From your letters, I thought you were keen on her.'

'I am,' I said, 'and I've got news for you. It's on again. Well, more than that. She's said yes and if the war's kind to us we'll marry as soon as it's over. Next year, I hope.'

Aunt May beamed. 'Well, I'm glad for you, Tim,' she said, 'but when am I going to have the pleasure of meeting her?'

'I'll give her your address when I write to her, I'll suggest she pays you a visit. How's that?'

'Well, I would like to meet her,' said Aunt May and

asked me to tell her more about Kit. So I did and Aunt May said she sounded as if she'd make a nice efficient wife.

'I shan't worry if she turns out slightly inefficient,' I said.

'Now then, Tim, you don't want a wife like that.'

'Why don't I? I'm a bit inefficient myself. Two of a kind's best, Aunt May.'

'Go on with you,' said Aunt May and she laughed.

The days went fast. I looked up old friends and neighbours and heard that Meg Fowler had become engaged to a PT instructor in the Marines. That would suit exuberant Meg. She liked a wrestle and a PT instructor in the Marines would be just her kind of playmate. I spent a couple of evenings in the Browning Street pub with some of the locals and joined in a cockney singsong. And I took Aunt May on a day trip by train to Brighton, one of her favourite places, although the pier was closed and there were certain wartime restrictions to be observed. But we had fun.

I noticed she had thoughtful moods, as if there was something on her mind and I wondered if that something was the reason why she wouldn't give Bill an answer. He called one evening. Aunt May treated him like an old friend, which was nice enough, but not quite like treating him as a lover. He and I repaired to the pub for half an hour, Bill saying he'd like the pleasure of buying me a jug of ale, seeing I was due to go overseas. In the pub, I asked him what he was doing about Aunt May's indecision.

'Nothing,' he said, 'it wouldn't be too clever to start pushing her.'

'I wonder what's holding her back? You haven't got a wooden leg and a glass eye, have you?'

'I've got a bit of a limp,' said Bill, 'but no glass eye and all my own teeth. All the same, I don't fancy pushin' her. She's been a long time unmarried and she's looked after you nearly all your life. That could mean she wants to stick to what she's used to.'

'Well, she knows that's going to change after the war, when I get married.'

'Hullo, are you givin' me news?' asked Bill.

'Yes, I'm fixed up to get spliced as soon as the war's over, Bill,' I said. 'An American girl.'

'Ruddy fireworks, that's good goin',' said Bill.

'A Wac sergeant,' I said.

'You've pinched one of theirs?'

'Their GIs have pinched most of ours,' I said.

'That calls for another jug,' said Bill, 'a quick one. Drink up, Tim, I like a celebration.'

'All ready to go, love?' said Aunt May, as I came down the stairs on the morning of my departure.

'I'll keep the letters coming,' I said.

'You'd better,' she said, her smile a bit unsteady.

'I'll get the war over as soon as I can.'

'Well, now you're a bombardier, I'll expect you to,' she said. 'Only don't try doing all of it by yourself.'

'Your tummy all right now?' I asked.

'Oh, that's nothing,' she said, 'the medicine soon cured it.'

292

'Be good,' I said. I felt a bit mournful. I loved my Aunt May and I'd no idea how long it was going to be before I saw her again. She wasn't a woman to fret about being alone. She'd been alone a lot since I went into the Army. Now she was going to be alone all the time. Bill had said he'd keep an eye on her. All the same, it was a bit mournful leaving her.

'Off you go now,' she said and I thought her eyes a little overbright.

I gave her a kiss and a cuddle. 'Love you, Aunt May,' I said. I didn't think I could go without telling her that.

'Bless you, Tim, you've been good for me all your life,' she said.

'Mutual,' I said and hefted my kitbag and picked up my rifle. She came out to the gate with me and stood there watching me go on my way to Browning Street, kitbag over my shoulder, rifle slung. At the corner, I turned and waved to her. She returned the wave.

It really hurt, leaving her on this occasion.

CHAPTER TWENTY-TWO

It was Italy, of course, where the signoras and signorinas had quickly discovered the GIs had unlimited stocks of candy bars and fully-fashioned stockings, in return for which the GIs asked only for the use of a bed.

'Ah, whose bed, Johnny?' The Italians called all the Americans Johnny.

'Yours, honey.' The GIs called all females honey.

Italy was where the Allies were trying to get the better of General Kesselring and his German armies. If we were initially relieved to find ourselves here and not in the jungles of Burma, that relief didn't last long. Kesselring was a demon and a tenacious one. His Germans were just as tenacious as well as grim, mean and moody. They didn't like the way the war was going now and they showed it.

I wrote home. I wrote to Jim and Missus. I told them that their grapevine had been right. I wasn't allowed to mention the regiment was in Italy, I merely referred to the grapevine. And I sent my regards to Minnie. I wrote a chatty letter to Aunt May to give her the idea that where I was was almost like home from home, except there was no toad-in-the-hole or kippers. I wrote a lengthy letter to Kit, telling her what my idea of post-war bliss was. I suspected she'd find it old-fashioned, and if

I knew Kit she wouldn't hold back from letting me know how she saw our future. Fair enough. I'd have to work out a compromise.

Mail was erratic, but not hopeless. I heard from Aunt May, a long long letter about home, friends and neighbours, with frequent mentions of Bill. He was turning into a fusspot, she said, but I read between the lines and guessed he was turning up two or three times a week to keep an eye on her. I liked him for that, he was a sound bloke with sense.

Kit wrote, putting together a whole heap of affectionate words, plus some humorous quips about my idea of post-war bliss. But she didn't mention she had a different idea, only that I was basically a comic. But she liked me like that she said and told me to take good care of my assets.

Frisby heard from Cecily and Cecily, apparently, was now a level-headed old scout easily able to cope with propositions from all the GIs who fancied her. She was saving herself for her one and only Limey guy, she said. I told Frisby that that was really nice. Can't believe it, can you, said Frisby, a lovely girl like her sitting at home waiting for me.

But would he get there? Would any of us? After months of shot and shell, the regiment knew at last that there was a war on. Major Moffat, all vigour and adrenalin, turned 424 Battery into a kind of heavy ack-ack commando unit, refusing to occupy static positions whenever it was obvious he could profitably rush us elsewhere. But his idea of profitability wasn't always the same as ours. Elsewhere was often close to suicidal, for Kesselring had command of experienced *Luftwaffe* squadrons that were as mean and moody as German panzers and there were too many occasions when our guns and rocketry were raked and blasted by cannon-fire from planes that screamed in low.

We took casualties. Frisby and I had gone back to being true gunners, serving with the crews. Italy's winter was diabolical. Talk about the country of sunshine and ice cream, what a joke. It rained, it snowed and did everything else that was miserable. It was a cold and treacherous winter for all units, with German resistance always formidable. I didn't envy the infantry.

But at least the Italians in liberated towns and villages caused no trouble. Having taken themselves out of the war, they welcomed the Allies. Their short portly leader, poor old Mussolini, had had to run for his life to Hitler. They clustered in their streets to cheer advancing Allied units and all they asked for in return for their hospitality was food. Well-shaped ladies enquired about chocolate and stockings as well. For chocolate and stockings, feminine gratitude knew no bounds. Italian virginity was non-existent, never mind the Pope. I despaired. I hoped Cecily and Kit weren't giving in.

In action, the regiment supported the RAF against the *Luftwaffe*, usually operating in defence of makeshift RAF landing strips. The German pilots liked nothing better as targets than ack-ack ground units. That kind of lethal threat was responsible for a certain amount of blind response. Colonel Carpenter, the regiment's commanding officer, was violently blasphemous on the occasion when a message was received from a fighting wing of the RAF: *You missed. Try again on our way back.* The culprits were 423 Battery. Lucky for us. Major Moffat would have flayed us alive. He was in the war now and wouldn't suffer muck-ups lightly.

Mail arrived sporadically. Aunt May kept writing. And Kit answered all my letters. She gave me news of her life as it was at the moment. By the spring of 1944, she was a lieutenant. She didn't make a big thing of it, she made much more of a suggestion that she knew would buck me up no end. She suggested, in fact, that if I managed to get home on leave our marriage could take place. In my reply I told her that that suggestion was as good as a Christmas present. I thought about her often, not so much while we were in action, but during the mucky boring slogs.

I thought about Aunt May too and kept wondering why she couldn't or wouldn't make up her mind about Bill. I was sure her feelings for him were special.

Frisby said that Italy and Hitler and the Jerries were all making a mess of his nerves. He had Cecily on his mind and why not? Cecily was lovable. He suggested in a mad moment to the sergeant-major that if only General Montgomery would push all ack-ack units forward to within touching distance of the Jerries, we could go in and surrender. The sergeant-major did a Queen Victoria act, but in more ferocious terms.

I got no reply from Jim or Missus to my letter. I fancied neither was much of a letter-writer. I wondered if Minnie was still going steady with her RAF bloke. I hoped she'd got her sparkle back.

The Allies slogged on into spring and then into

summer. I was prodded awake one morning. My head came out from under a blanket on the floor of a bomb-damaged house on the outskirts of a village. Major Moffat, his ruggedness a bit leaner, took the toe of his brown boot from out of my ribs.

'Who's this inert lump, Sergeant-Major?' he asked.

Sergeant-Major Baldwin said smartly, 'Can't tell, sir. Not under all that hair. Might be Lance-Bombardier Hardy.'

'What a sight,' said Major Moffat, 'the bugger's not even shaved. Why's that?'

'Answer up,' said the sergeant-major.

'It's not reveille yet, sir,' I said.

'Has this NCO been present and correct ever since we embarked?' asked the major.

'God knows,' said the sergeant-major, 'but he's here now.'

'Yes, present and correct, sir,' I said, coming to my feet.

A German shell struck then, about two hundred yards away, pre-empting reveille. It got men out of their pits at lightning speed. The major didn't turn a hair. I think he liked war. I think he thought everyone should.

'Don't stand about gawping, Bombardier Hardy, move yourself,' he said and that was how he advised me of my further promotion. Another shell landed. It blew up an already damaged house and the house collapsed in a riotous welter of disintegrating bricks. Clouds of smoke and dusk spewed upwards. I moved myself and later I sewed on my second stripe. And Frisby was given his first stripe.

Italy continued to be a hell of a grind, but Rome was eventually taken and the GIs swarmed all over the Eternal City, asking why the Colosseum hadn't been repaired. Shortly afterwards the invasion of Normandy took place and in July the regiment was transferred to France.

Just before that came about, I received a letter from Bill. He'd got my army address from Aunt May, having told her he'd like to drop me a line sometime. His letter was all about the fact that she was ill with some kind of stomach complaint that kept recurring and was obviously causing her pain. He had had to bully her into admitting it had been going on for some months, that the doctor had finally made her go to King's College Hospital for an examination and that the hospital, after the examination, had made a date for her to have an operation. She was going in tomorrow wrote Bill and he was getting time off from work to take her himself. She didn't want me to know but Bill said he thought I ought to know. In your place, he said, I'd want to. He said he'd let me know how the operation went, then gave me his regards and signed off.

It left me worrying myself sick about what she was suffering from exactly.

I spoke to Sergeant-Major Baldwin about being allowed compassionate leave. He grimaced.

'Not now, Bombardier Hardy, not now,' he said.

'Have a word with Major Moffat, Sergeant-Major.'

'Sorry, not a chance and he wouldn't wear it, anyway, you know that. It's only an operation and only your aunt.'

'She's as good as a mother to me.'

'Sorry,' said the sergeant-major gruffly, 'it's no go.'

So I was left with nothing but worry.

Two days later, when we were lining up on the quayside of an Italian port and about to embark, further mail was distributed to the regiment. There were three letters for me. I recognized the handwriting on two of them. Aunt May's and Kit's. The third I didn't recognize, but the postmark was Sudbury, Suffolk. There was too much going on for me to read any of the letters in peace, so I waited until we were established aboard a troopship. I opened Aunt May's first.

'Dear Tim,

I thought I'd better write and tell you the news. I wasn't going to, I didn't want you to worry, but I decided I'd better. First, it's this silly tummy of mine, it's been playing me up, so I'm going into King's College Hospital tomorrow, they gave me an examination and X-ray last week.

'I'll be all right, I'm sure, but I've been thinking a lot lately. There's things I ought to tell you now you're a grown man and know a lot about life. I don't know I'm doing the right thing, though, they say it's best to let sleeping dogs lie, don't they? But I don't think I should keep secrets for ever, I think you ought to know just who you are, though I don't want to hurt you.'

I read on, mesmerized by the words that came to my eyes from several sheets of writing paper. At the end, I was far from hurt, I just felt a great wave of deep affection for her and my whole being was concentrated on a desperate wish for her to come out of that hospital alive and recovered, because I knew exactly why she had written this letter. She felt, or she'd been told, that at the most the operation was only going to give her a fifty-fifty chance. So she'd decided to tell me who she was and who I was.

It was all there, the story. In 1917, when she was thirteen and her brother Leonard twenty-one, she was a bridesmaid at his wedding to a lovely young lady, Edith Palmer. He was home on leave from Flanders. Afterwards he went back to the trenches, but was invalided out early in 1918 because of the results of serious wounds. He recovered, he pushed himself like a Trojan and his wife Edith was a loving help to him. He managed to get a decent job. Aunt May, still at school, went to see them often, being very attached to her brother and liking her sister-in-law Edith very much.

But early in 1920, just before she was sixteen, an awful thing happened. She developed an intense girlish crush on a young man, a lodger with neighbours next door to her home in New Cross. It was her first crush and a fateful one and she fell headlong into the trap set by emotions and the devil-may-care charm of the young man. The consequences were a dreadful shock to her family and appalling to herself. She nearly died when she realized she was going to have a baby.

At a family conference, a solution was offered by her brother Leonard and his wife. Because of the original nature of Leonard's wounds, it wasn't possible for him to father children, so willingly they would take the unwanted baby immediately it was born, register it as their own and bring it up as their own. Its real father had disappeared. Aunt May, now sixteen, begged her parents to agree. They did more, they helped to arrange it all with Leonard and his wife. Three months before the baby was due, Aunt May and her sister-in-law went to stay in a rented flat in a house in Brighton, where Leonard visited them on Sundays. Mr and Mrs Hardy senior visited once a month, getting a friend to look after their shop on those occasions. A careful eye was kept on Aunt May and her condition, her mother giving her all kinds of helpful advice and Edith a great deal of companionship and affection. Aunt May endured her nine months in remarkably healthy fashion and when the critical time arrived, her mother was there, as well as Edith. Her mother took her to the hospital in a taxi at just about the right time. She was wearing a wedding ring. Her mother asked for her to be admitted to the maternity wing, giving her name as Edith Margaret Hardy, her daughter-in-law, eighteen years old. She was ready to field questions, but the hospital made no fuss. Aunt May was already in pain and she was admitted immediately. A nurse, writing down details given by Aunt May's mother, including the patient's address which was Lewisham, asked who her doctor was. Mrs Hardy senior said you'll never believe this, but the poor girl never ever realized she was pregnant, she simply complained she was getting fat. The nurse smiled and said that wasn't the first case of that kind.

The baby arrived several hours later, the hospital recorded the birth, and the certificate was subsequently issued by the registrar in Brighton to Leonard and Edith Hardy. The baby was a boy and was registered as Timothy Edward. They all returned to London a week after the birth. Edith and Leonard happily took the infant to their home in Lewisham, for Edith had told friends and neighbours months ago that she was expecting. Aunt May stayed a week with them, saw the delight her brother and sister-in-law had in the baby, and then went home to her parents in New Cross, relinquishing all claim on the child. After all, it was still in the family.

She and her parents visited and she watched it grow into a healthy three-year-old boy. He was with her parents one Saturday afternoon when Leonard and Edith were braving the Christmas crowds in London's West End, buying presents. The train carrying them to New Cross, where they were to pick up the boy, hurtled into collision with another and they were among the tragic casualties.

'The rest you know, Tim, except for the fact that I always stuck to being eighteen at the time of your birth. I felt, she said, that if you ever did find out you were my son, I just didn't want you to know I was a silly silly schoolgirl at the time and to think of me as young and tarty. I wanted you to think more of me than that, so I invented that soldier and a romance with him to make you think he was your father if you did find out I was your mother. Have I hurt you by telling you all this? I hope not because of all you've meant to me during our years together. Take care. All my love, Aunt May.'

But she wasn't my Aunt May. She was Mum. I'd have been tickled pink if I hadn't had the operation on my mind. The date on the letter meant it had taken place three weeks ago. I wouldn't know whether she had come safely out of it or not until we got to France and then any letter from her or Bill would be delayed because of our move from Italy. I was sick at the thought of carrying my worry about with me for an indefinite time, sick to my eyebrows.

I should have found Kit's letter a consolation, because it was so warm and affectionate. Absence can loosen ties and change feelings, but there was no change in Kit's. The Allies were going to win the war, she said, there was no way they couldn't and it will all be over by Christmas. She was making the best kind of plans for the wedding and for our future. She was due for some well-earned leave, she'd had none for months prior to D-Day and for weeks since. She was going to write to my Aunt May and arrange to call and meet her. Keep the mail coming, she said, I worry if there's too much of a gap.

That was a bit heart-breaking, her intention to call on Aunt May – my newly-confessed mother – at this moment in our lives. She might, in any case, receive no answer to her letter. She might never receive one. The realization made it difficult to feel consolation in all that Kit wrote.

I opened the third letter. The troopship, crammed with men and their equipment, was under way. Minnie had written, young Minnie, the girl who had gone off me because I hadn't been any real help to her when she'd

304

wanted to be my girl. She wrote hoping I was well, that her mum and dad wanted to thank me for my letter and had meant to write back, but they weren't much good at writing letters. She said they were still going strong, that some nosy person from the Ministry of Food had been round to see her dad about him registering as an egg producer, would you believe. Her dad had talked to him until the nosy parker didn't know if he was coming or going, but he still left her dad a form to fill in. Then Mr Ford had come home on leave and Mrs Ford was going about looking very pleased with life, especially as Mr Ford had put his foot down with young Wally Ricketts and given him a thick ear. Minnie gave me other bits of news about the village, just in case I was interested, she said, although she didn't suppose I was. Still, her mum and dad wanted to be remembered to me. She signed herself, 'Yours truly, M. Beavers.'

M. Beavers? She really had gone off me. I felt a twinge, but it was hardly important now. Aunt May. No wonder her one mistake had taught her to rate behaviour.

We were on the move south of Falaise and in the heat of August. We halted to await further orders. The Germans were in retreat, the skies relatively clear, the fading *Luftwaffe* looking for new landing grounds. I'd had a letter from Kit. She hadn't had her expected leave, she'd been transferred to American Headquarters in London and was working round the clock. But she'd written to my Aunt May she said and was waiting for a reply.

I was waiting myself for a letter from home. None had come.

A supply truck from Brigade arrived in the middle of the afternoon, when we were brewing up by the roadside in Eighth Army fashion. Among other things, the truck brought delayed mail. In that mail was a letter from Bill, weeks old.

'Dear Tim,

I'm glad to write to you, old son. What a turn-up for the book as we used to say in my outfit and your Aunt May's just beginning to see the funny side of it herself. It's a strain on her stitches. She's had her appendix out. That was the cause of it all, her appendix, nagging, niggling and giving her gip, but I don't know how the devil the doctor and the hospital didn't cotton on to it. What a lot of blind old Aunt Sallies, they need things being chucked at them.

When I received your reply, just before your aunt went into hospital, I guessed you were thinking the same as me about what was wrong with her. I asked some questions after the operation and it seems it wasn't until the surgeon opened her up that they found the trouble. Her appendix was a mess, to put it bluntly. What luck they took her in when they did, another week would really have been serious. It was a close-run thing, Tim, believe me. But she's sitting up now, well, near enough she is and by tomorrow I think she'll be as lively as a cricket. But they won't discharge her until they've taken the stitches out, which will be in a few days.

I let her know I'd written to you, spilling the beans about her operation and she said she'd written to tell you herself, after all. Then she said she shouldn't have told you anything and looked upset. I said not to worry, that it was right for you to know, that you wouldn't have liked it if you'd been kept in the dark. But she had a quiet five minutes about it and then visiting time was up.

Well, Tim, I know the news will cheer you up, it's cheered me up a hell of a lot. Good on you, old son, keep after the Jerries, you've got them on the run now.

Sincerely, Bill.'

I felt Aunt May – she still came to my mind as Aunt May – hadn't meant she shouldn't have told me about hospitalization. She meant, I was sure, that she shouldn't have told me her life story. But with the operation to face and suspecting the worst, she'd gone over the top for once in her adult life. She'd be fretting now because she'd told me I was the son of an unwed mother, a schoolgirl at the time. God, Minnie as a schoolgirl had frightened me.

One thing I could tell this mother of mine, one thing that was quite true, that I wasn't in the least upset about how conventional society would see me. She was alive, she'd only had her appendix out and I had an extraordinary giddy feeling at knowing she was my mother. Who wouldn't?

'Bombardier Hardy!' Captain Marsh was shouting at me. 'What the hell are you doing?'

'No idea, sir. What am I doing?' I was dancing on top of a Bren carrier.

Major Moffat broke through ranks of grinning, dusty men and looked up at me. 'Gone off your clever head at last, have you, Bombardier Hardy?'

'Only for the moment, sir. News from home. A very close relative of mine had a baby.'

'Get down, you clot,' he said. I climbed down. 'You pancake,' he said, 'I'll chop your legs off next time you behave like that.'

'Yes, sir. Still, it was good news.'

Life was worth living again. The war wasn't over yet, not by a long shot, but Kit was right, there was no way we could lose it now.

In France, Frisby felt much nearer to Cecily than in Italy and Cecily was still faithful. Moreover, she felt she belonged really to our tight little island. Remembering her paternal grandmother's maiden name was Martin and that she had been born in Somerset, she had been to Midsomer Norton, the birthplace, and actually discovered the graves of her grandmother's parents, and her aunt and uncle. She was tickled to death and she told Frisby in one of her many letters that she felt this gave her a rightful stake in the buttercups and daisies of England.

'How about that?' asked Frisby, having related the news.

'You realize what it means, don't you?' I said.

'Don't get funny,' said Frisby.

'It means Cecily's a romantic, a genuine woman and you're a lucky old sweatbag.'

308

*

A letter from Aunt May herself, at last, which I received at the beginning of September. I'd written to her after receiving the glad tidings from Bill and I'd told her at length that the only thing that mattered to me was the happy fact of knowing she was me mum. That's it, I said, nothing else is important, nothing is a worry to me. But I suggested we should keep it to ourselves. After all these years, what was the point of turning her background upside-down? You know and I know, I said, nobody else has to know. It's our secret and it's one secret that's in the happy file. I asked was it that and the suspected nature of her illness that kept her from giving Bill his answer? If so, do some more thinking.

In her reply, Aunt May poured forth her regrets for telling me her story. She felt it couldn't possibly have made me happy. It was a selfish thing to do. Yes, she had thought her illness was going to kill her and she didn't want to go to her death without giving herself the natural pleasure of letting me know she was my mother. So many times she'd wanted me to know that, especially as our life together had been of a kind to make her proud of me and in the end she had given in to selfishness and told me. She hoped I'd forgive her and yes, she agreed it would be our own secret. But she asked if I thought she could marry Bill with a clear conscience.

I wrote her another long letter and put her mind at rest. I might have said I knew now why she had been sympathetic about poor Edie Hawkins, but I didn't.

CHAPTER TWENTY-THREE

Colonel Carpenter was promoted in September, when we were moving up with 30 Corps and he disappeared into Brigade HQ. Major Moffat was given command of the regiment and elevated to the rank of colonel. Sergeant-Major Baldwin became the Regimental Sergeant-Major.

Colonel Moffat immediately reorganized RHQ. He arrived at our battery bivouac one morning and was out of the Bren carrier almost before it stopped.

'You, that man there!' he shouted.

That was me, in my shirt sleeves. 'Sir?' I said, arriving in his presence and saluting him.

'Get your kit,' he said. 'And where's God's gift to mixed-up American females?' Frisby's caring attachment to Cecily and her problems had never been a secret.

'He's writing a letter to one of them, sir. It's the first chance he's had for a week. I'll fetch him.'

'Stay where you are. Just fetch your kit. You're moving to RHQ, where I can keep an eye on you before you start flogging the regiment's rocket launchers to Stalin. That goes for Romeo Whatsisname as well, your hitman. You're both promoted to sergeant, God help me.'

So Frisby and I moved to RHQ, where things should

have been more comfortable, but weren't. Colonel Moffat didn't like anyone looking comfortable, not when there was still a war to fight. He was quite prepared to win it on his own, never mind that Monty had the same idea. Frisby and I, grateful for our promotion, went along with the necessity of being mucked about. In any case, we didn't have to suffer the hazards of the infantry and the tank crews.

Mail deliveries became fairly regular and letters from home kept coming through. Aunt May was going to marry Bill. Was it possible I could get leave so that I could give her away? If so, she and Bill would arrange a date to coincide. Oh, and she'd finally met my American love, Kit. An officer, for goodness sake, but a lovely young lady and so friendly and talkative. You didn't tell me she was an officer, Tim, you said sergeant. Still, I could see what you mean about her being efficient, you can tell she is. And so on.

In one letter, Kit asked if I still had a good supply of chits. If so, she hoped I was using them to help the Allies win the war. But I wasn't, she said, to use them to ingratiate myself with Frenchwomen. Some hopes.

When 30 Corps advanced in Belgium, the welcome was rapturous. Subsequently, Monty's advance took us over the border into Holland. In Eindhoven, the people showered us with flowers. Colonel Moffat, every inch a conqueror, received more than flowers. Trapped by a score of delighted Dutch ladies, he was smothered with kisses and bosoms. He was rescued by a charming Dutch war widow with smooth blonde hair. When we halted for the night just outside the town, he was prevailed upon by the lady to billet himself in her house. He put a smart military face on the arrangement by making the house his temporary headquarters. At ten o'clock that night, he disappeared from sight. He reappeared at eight in the morning. By arrangement, I was outside the house, having arrived in a Bren carrier to pick him up. I watched the widow saying goodbye to him, her smooth hair a morning-gold, her smile soft. She really was charming.

Colonel Moffat heaved himself in beside me. 'Get going,' he said.

'Had a good night, sir?' I enquired. The widow was looking on, her smile a little wistful now.

'Is that your imagination getting to work, sergeant? Just get going.'

Still, he did salute her as we moved off.

I'd written to Aunt May to tell her to go ahead and get married. There was no home leave coming up. I received her reply, saying she and Bill would wait. Another few months wouldn't matter and they both wanted me to be there.

The winter held up the Allied advance. So did the Germans. In December, the Ardennes offensive by the Nazi hordes took the Americans by surprise and their touchy generals had cross words to say when Eisenhower put cocky Monty in charge of the battle. But Monty did his stuff and the line was straightened out eventually. Our feet were freezing. After Ardennes, 30 Corps broke through, liberating Holland completely and went for the Rhine. By this time, Hitler was aiming flying bombs at

312

England, but Churchill had the bit between his teeth now and so did the UK.

The advance went on, 30 Corps crossed the Rhine, the Ems and the Weser to complete the longest sustained advance in military history when Bremen was reached.

VE Day arrived. Our regiment's officers celebrated in a commandeered mansion. During the evening, Colonel Moffat, pickled but still upright, met me on the stairs when I had four bottles of wine clasped to my chest. I had just acquired them from the wine stocks reserved for the officers.

'Got you at last, Hardy, you pilfering haybag,' he said.

'It's fair cop, sir, but it's VE Day as well and the NCOs are running a bit short.'

'Damned inefficient organization, then. Not like you, is it, to under-equip the sergeants' mess with perks? Losing your touch, are you, Sergeant Hardy?'

'I've always been a loyal—'

'Don't make me fall about,' said Colonel Moffat. 'Tomorrow you'll get a chit making you responsible for the cost of that grape juice you've just nicked. By the way, next stop Tokyo.' We were spared a voyage to the Pacific, however. The Japs were atom-bombed out of the war in August and Frisby looked forward to carrying himself back to Cecily all in one piece and with nothing injured.

Demobilization came up for some of us in October and I'd been able to advise Kit and Aunt May of my approximate day of arrival. With Frisby and several others, I packed for the journey home. I said goodbye to Colonel Moffat.

'I'm off now, sir.'

'Best piece of news I've had in years,' he said, looking up at me from his desk. 'By the way, stop off when the truck reaches Eindhoven and deliver that parcel for me.' I looked at it, a large, square, well-wrapped parcel on the floor beside his desk. It was addressed to Mrs Marta van Hoyk. I guessed what was in it. A consignment of goodies. Things were tough for the people of the Low Countries and just as much for a charming Dutch war widow as anyone else.

'I'll do that, sir. I know the address.'

'I know you know.'

'I'll buy her a large bunch of Dutch gladioli to go with it. On your behalf, sir.'

He eyed me with the faintest glimmer of a smile. 'Kind of you, Sergeant Hardy,' he said. 'I wonder, before you go would you mind telling me if it was your skullduggery that shot to pieces my inquiry into flogged WD juice two years ago?'

'I don't think I'll answer that, sir, not while I'm still in uniform.'

'All right, push off,' he said.

'Goodbye, sir, good luck.' I saluted him for the last time.

He came to his feet. He smiled. 'Good luck, Tim,' he said and shook my hand.

I didn't mind the errand. The war was over and I was on my way home on a fine autumnal day. Aunt May – I knew I'd always call her that – was going to get married and Kit was waiting for me to marry her.

314

Europe was war-torn and ugly, but its people were already pulling themselves together after years of being under the Nazi jackboot. The widow lady of Eindhoven was so overwhelmed to receive the parcel and the flowers that moisture turned her eyes a liquid brown. I thought she might as well have Colonel Moffat's telephone number in Bremen and the address of his billet. He was a bachelor and as the war was over for him, too, he ought to have something else to think about. Besides, it was obviously love at first sight as far as the lady was concerned. A good idea, I thought, to give her first crack at him. The Dutch had been good to the British Paras at the time of Arnheim.

'Ah, so kind you are,' she said, accepting the phone number and address. 'Now I can thank your colonel, yes?'

Seeing she spoke good English, I said, 'Do you have children?'

'Little ones? No. Married I was only for a month.'

'Well, you can have some chits instead,' I said.

'Cheets?'

'That's right, chits. I'll make them out and sign them. I've got some blank ones with the Regimental stamp on them. They'll entitle you to travel up to Bremen and claim back the expenses.'

'Excuse me?' There was a little smile in her eyes.

'Just present the chits to Colonel Moffat when you arrive. Let him know you've come to thank him in person. Pack some clothes, of course. Enough for a long weekend.'

'Sergeant, you are pulling my leg, you are joking with me?' She looked as if she hoped I wasn't.

'That large parcel isn't a joke,' I said, 'it means something.'

'Ah? Yes? What does it mean?'

'That Colonel Moffat will be delighted to see you. When will you go?'

'Tomorrow?' she said with perceptible delight.

'Give my regards to Colonel Moffat when you arrive.'

'Yes. Yes. Thank you. Such a sweet man.'

'Colonel Moffat?'

'You,' she said, so I gave her a kiss when I left.

It wasn't until the first reunion of the regiment in September 1946 that I was introduced to Colonel Moffat's wife. It was her, of course. He managed to stand on my foot when I shook hands with her. It told me that in her innocence she had given him a full account of my conversation with her at her house in Eindhoven and I limped a bit for the rest of the evening.

From Eindhoven we drove to the Hook of Holland and Frisby and I were ferried across the North Sea with a boatload of other demob squaddies right on schedule. Frisby had advised Cecily of the date our arrival was expected at Harwich and told her he'd phone her from there.

The crossing was rough, but we disembarked with our stomachs intact and the whole detachment of soldiers was ushered through Customs without fuss, much to the relief of those whose kitbags or valises were bulging with stuff that had fallen off the back of every kind of military truck. A special London train was waiting for

316

us. From London we were to proceed to a demob centre in Guildford.

A few military personnel were on the platform. A long-legged girl in an olive-green uniform, with three upside-down stripes on each sleeve, detached herself and came running. She threaded her way through troops and headed for Frisby. It was Cecily, now a Wac sergeant. She had obviously wangled her way to Harwich in the hope that Frisby would arrive. She flung herself at him. Frisby, laden, didn't know what to do with his two bulging valises, one of which was lumpily between him and Cecily's bosom. Coming to, he dropped them. Cecily wound herself around him and kissed him with healthy abandon. Troops whistled.

'Claud, don't you look great? Oh, you honey.' She kissed him again.

'Steady, not here,' said Frisby. 'Oh, OK, here, then.' And he gave her a smacker.

'Help, Tim too,' she said, 'don't you both look great?' She treated me to a kiss too. 'Hey, isn't that great as well, that we all made sergeant? What's next, Claud?'

'A cosy compartment,' said Frisby.

'Bliss,' said Cecily, high on adrenalin and seized one of his valises in the spirit of her forthcoming role as his little woman. There was plenty of room on the train and we found a compartment just for the three of us. It wasn't until the train pulled out that I realized I was probably in the way. Cecily and Frisby were eating each other and Cecily was showing her legs. They uncoupled for short bursts of talk now and again and she told him she had received notice of her discharge. She was entitled to a free trip back to America, but did Claud think that was necessary? There was no-one she wanted to go back to. What she wanted was to see another English spring-time, to see it with him and to be here when the first primroses appeared. Cecily had turned into an incurable romantic and Frisby didn't need to doctor her for that.

'You're not getting shipped back to America,' he said, 'you might fall overboard. We'll get married tomorrow, or next week, or next month. Meanwhile, get yourself permission to billet with me and my family in Reigate.'

'Could I do that, sweetie?' said Cecily. 'I know where Reigate is, remember, I've been there to show myself to your family. Claud, it's lovely there. Say, did you know there used to be a castle, that your town hall was built on the site of an old chapel dedicated to Thomas Becket and that Lord Howard, who commanded the English fleet against the Spanish Armada, is buried in your parish church?'

'Not my parish church, ours,' said Frisby, 'we'll be getting married there.'

'Great,' said Cecily, 'but isn't it all historical? We don't have anything like that in the States.'

'Still, you've got blueberries,' I said.

They took no notice, they snuggled up again. But Cecily did say, after a minute or so, 'Claud, my legs, we're embarrassing Tim.'

'I'm not embarrassed,' I said, 'I like the picture.'

'Tim's nobody,' said Frisby. 'Tell you what, lover, you can share my room when we get home.'

'Claud, we can't do that,' said Cecily faintly.

'Sure we can. For an hour, say.'

318

'Claud, we can't, not with your family there.'

'They've got their own rooms,' said Frisby, giving her a pat, 'they don't live in mine.'

Cecily laughed and hugged him. I got up, left the compartment and idled around in the corridor. I watched the green fields rolling by. I thought about Aunt May and Kit. I was in advance of the date I'd given them. I wanted to see them both, but it suddenly occurred to me how close I was to Suffolk. Jim and Missus. Jim was probably already up to some post-war larks.

The train stopped at Colchester, then went on to Marks Tey, the station with a connection to Sheldham. Might be nice to drop in on Jim and Missus and go on to London and Guildford afterwards. The time was just after one. We'd left the Hook of Holland twelve hours ago.

Approaching Marks Tey, I told Cecily and Frisby I had somewhere to go. They asked no questions, but Frisby did say I might as well come to the wedding. Cecily said it wouldn't be the same if I didn't. I said I'd come, but that the rest of it was just between her and Claud. Cecily laughed, and the sparkle in her eyes reminded me of Minnie the saucy schoolgirl.

I left the train at Marks Tey. I must phone Kit, I thought.

CHAPTER TWENTY-FOUR

I caught the right local train quite soon. It was early afternoon when I walked past the *Suffolk Punch* on my way to Jim's cottage, having left my kit in the care of old Shuttleberry at the station. Left luggage it was he said and he'd have to charge me a bob.

The village looked russet with autumn, the day bright but cold, the thatched roofs guardians of the inner warmth of cottage dwellings. I knocked on Jim's door. A very good-looking young lady in a Waaf uniform opened it.

'What's happened?' I asked. 'I thought the war was over.'

She stared. A healthy Waaf she was, with a country look. 'Oh,' she said and swallowed.

'Told you I'd come knocking,' I said. 'That is you, isn't it, Min, under all that Waaf blue?'

It was all of Min, a young and shapely edition of her mum. Peaches and cream and no longer a schoolgirl. And an inch or more taller. Well, of course, she was now in her nineteenth year. Her blue eyes stared uncertainly at me.

'What have you come for?' she asked.

'To see your mum and dad and you, to see how you

all are,' I said. 'I'm on my way to London and thought I'd break the journey to pay a call, Min.'

Her mouth compressed at that. 'D'you want to come in, then?' she asked.

'What a question. Of course I want to come in. I almost used to live here. I bought my eggs from you.'

'No, you didn't, you got them for free,' she said. But she stepped aside and I went in. She closed the door and led the way into the living-room, where a fire was crackling. It looked good, it made a warm and homely place of the room. The hearth basket was full of logs and an iron kettle, on its stand over the fire, was beginning to steam.

'You've grown up, Min,' I said.

'I suppose you have too,' she said, 'I suppose you must have, seein' you've got three stripes.'

'Am I interrupting something?' I asked. I'd hoped for a cheerful welcome. 'Shall I go away and come back wearing a different face?'

'I don't know if that would matter, would it?' said Min, edgy and distant and I thought well, here's a disappointment, she's still cross with me.

'Look,' I said, 'I just thought—'

'I'll tell Mum you're here. Dad's out, on one of his jobs.' She gave a little shrug. No-one had ever seemed to know exactly what any of Jim's jobs entailed. He was probably doing some post-war spivving right now.

Minnie went into the kitchen. I heard the murmur of voices, which went on for quite a few minutes before Missus appeared. She looked as country-ripe as ever, like a healthily mature dairymaid who had never been able to resist helping herself to the cream. Country life suited Missus and Jim too.

'Why, Tim love, look at you, here you are and all, back safe and sound. I'm that pleasured to see you,' she said and kissed me. Minnie, reappearing, sat down beside the fire and gazed at the steaming kettle.

'No need to ask how you are, Missus,' I said, 'you're blooming.'

'Yes, bloomin' glad the war's over,' said Missus, chocolate-brown eyes pensive. She glanced at her silent daughter. 'What d'you think of our Min, don't she look nice in her uniform?'

'You bet she does, Missus,' I said.

'My, and don't you look a real manly soldier now, Tim and a sergeant and all. Don't he, Min?'

'He doesn't look like Humphrey Bogart, that's for sure,' said Min.

'No, well, that Humphrey Bogart's not a soldier, is he, only one of them Hollywood gangsters,' said Missus.

'Film stars,' said Min.

'Not much difference, love,' said Missus. 'You can sit down, Tim. Min, didn't you ask Tim to sit down even?'

'No, I didn't,' said Min disinterestedly, 'I didn't know he was stayin'.' Something really was bugging her.

I sat down. So did Missus. She began to chat away at a fair old lick, asking questions and answering all of them herself. Minnie said nothing. The iron kettle was beginning to sing.

Getting a word in, I said, 'I'd no idea Min had joined the Waafs.'

'Sorry I didn't ask you first,' said Min, 'but I didn't know I had to.'

Missus gave her an old-fashioned look. 'No need for that, Min,' she said. 'You on your way home, Tim?'

'Well, I was on my way to the Guildford demob centre via London,' I said, 'but I thought I'd look you up first, to see how you all were. I can go to Guildford tomorrow, after I've been home.'

'Well, stay for a nice high tea,' said Missus. She caught the look of disgust Minnie gave her. 'We couldn't let you go without a nice high tea, Tim. Min's on a week's leave, aren't you, Min?'

'Kettle's boilin',' said Min, whose bouncy vivaciousness seemed to have gone for ever.

'I'll make a pot,' said Missus, 'your dad'll be in in a minute.'

Jim arrived home just as the pot was made. His old hat had acquired another coating of moss. He exploded into loud chuckles at seeing me. He wrung my hand, said I looked a real good 'un as a sergeant and that I'd done a handsome job by winning the war. He told Missus to start pouring. Missus did. The large steaming cups were handed out. She and Jim talked to me, often together and at the same time. I answered Jim's questions, while Missus continued to answer her own. Minnie just sipped her tea beside the fireside and said nothing. Jim asked how the nice American sergeant was and I said I was going to phone her and find out.

'How about you, Min, how's your boyfriend?' I asked.

'Which one?' Min was casual and indifferent.

'The RAF bloke,' I said.

'Oh, him,' she said, 'that didn't last, they all come an' go.'

'Yes, always goin' out with different soldiers, she is,' said Missus disapprovingly.

'Well, I can't stop them lining up for me,' said Minnie.

'Now, my girl,' said Jim, 'that ain't nice talk, nor sensible, neither.'

'You're never goin' to settle down if you carry on like that,' said Missus. 'You won't grow real affection for no-one, Min.'

'I ain't 'aving it,' said Jim, 'I ain't 'aving no daughter of mine turnin' into a restless little nanny goat with nothing on 'er tail except randy old billy goats.'

'I don't want any of that vulgar talk,' said Missus, 'you don't hear our Tim sayin' things like that. Still, I've got to say the war's done bad things to girls, Tim, it's made them think havin' a good time's more important than havin' a good husband and nice fam'ly.'

'I wish you two wouldn't talk about me like that in front of strangers,' said Minnie, suddenly furious.

'Strangers?' said Jim, his hat seeming to wear a frown. 'What's she on about, Missus? Tim ain't no stranger.'

'Never mind,' said Missus placatingly.

'I think while I'm here I'll cycle to Elsingham and see Mary Coker,' I said.

'What, that widder woman?' said Jim.

'Bit of a foreigner, she is,' said Missus. 'Still, you was always a good friend to people, Tim, foreigners as well. I'll get that nice high tea soon as you come back.'

Jim had a bike and said I could borrow it. He went off, back to his country spivving no doubt and I got his

324

bike out of the shed. There was another bike there, a female machine. I returned to the cottage and looked in on Minnie. She was still sitting beside the fire, a book on her lap, but was watching the burning logs. Missus was in the kitchen.

'Min?' I said.

She jumped. The book slid to the hearthrug and she made a little gesture of irritation. 'Oh, it's you again,' she said.

'Fancy a bike ride to Elsingham with me?' I suggested. 'Be nice to have your company.'

She retrieved her book. 'No,' she said.

'OK. Just thought I'd ask. You're probably better off toasting yourself, it's a cold day.'

'Just go away,' she said.

'The war's over, Min. Still, never mind—'

'Oh, all right, I'll come. I don't want to be nagged all day,' she said.

'That's a sport. I like company. Come on, then.'

Missus was pleased that Min had stirred herself. Wearing her cap and Waaf overcoat, she rode her own bike. Her coat skirts frisked back and her blue-clad knees peeped. Her peaked cap gave her a smart military look and her face began to glow in the keen country air. We took the route Kit and I had used, along the winding lanes, where quietness hung about. I wondered what on earth I was doing. I had Aunt May – my mother – to go home to and there was Kit to see. So what was I doing, spending time cycling to Mary's with Minnie, who wasn't exactly bright company?

'D'you like it in the Waafs, Min?' I asked.

'D'you like it in the Army?' she countered.

'I haven't liked it all the time.'

'Well, hard luck,' said Min shortly.

'Yes, it wasn't my idea of bliss. Damn old inconvenience, more like. Better off, I was, hiding under the bed.'

'Why'd you talk like that?' Minnie sounded scornful. 'It's silly.'

'Picked it up in Suffolk.'

'It's not Suffolk talk, it's daft talk. But you like showin' off, you do. Anyway, I never thought the war bothered you. Easy come, easy go, that's you.'

'Only for the sake of peace and quiet, Min,' I said. The hedgerows glinted with autumn tints. 'I like peace and quiet.'

'Can't always have what you like, can you?' she said.

'No, I suppose not.'

'Still like that Waac sergeant, do you?' she said. We were both cycling at a good pace in the tingling wind. 'Goin' to ask her, are you, now you're back?'

'Ask her what?'

'To marry you, of course.'

'The date needs to be fixed. I'll have to phone her about meeting her. I'd like to get married and settle down in a humdrum way, wouldn't you, Min?'

'No, I wouldn't, not for the sake of it,' she said. 'I just like havin' a good time.'

'You don't sound as if you're having one.'

'Do me a favour,' said Min, 'mind your own business.'

'OK, fair enough, Min.'

When we arrived in Elsingham, Mary's welcome was

demonstrative. But she was a bit flummoxed that I'd turned up with a Waaf. I think she thought it should have been Kit. However, when I introduced Minnie as the daughter of Jim Beavers of Sheldham, Mary received her in her warm friendly way.

Minnie, who seemed to have acquired some kind of anti-social outlook, thawed a bit and said, 'Nice to meet you, I'm sure.' Then she was more like her old self, liking the look of Mary's cottage and saying so and liking too, the view of the garden from the living-room. Mary, always more willing to give people the benefit of the doubt than to form prejudices, showed a smiling appreciation of Minnie's interest in her home. They began to chat about Elsingham and about life in the country. They had both come to Suffolk from London. While they chatted, I went down to the village phone box and called Kit at the American Headquarters in London.

'Captain Masters, please,' I said to the switchboard operator. Kit had been made up to captain on moving to London.

'Who's calling?' asked the girl on the switchboard.

'General Hardy.'

'Oh, hold the line, sir.'

Kit came through after a moment or two. 'Hello? Who's this?'

'Me.'

'Tim! Oh, you screwball, I was told some general was on the line.'

'I pride myself I could have made general if Colonel Moffat hadn't been in my way.'

327

'General idiot, you mean,' said Kit and I heard her laugh. 'You're back, you're actually here in the good old UK?'

'I'm in Suffolk, I dropped in to see Mary on my way home. I'll be in London tomorrow, then on to Guildford to get kitted up for civvy street. Could I see you lunchtime, say?'

'You'd better, or I'll get you peppered with rockets,' said Kit. 'Meet me outside the American Embassy at twelve-thirty. Will that do, lover?'

'That'll do. Can't wait to see you.'

'Yes, you can, you creep, or you'd be here now instead of in Suffolk. Give Mary my love and be good to me when we meet, because I'm going to be very good to you.'

'How good?'

'You'll find out,' she said. 'Do you know how long it is since we last saw each other?'

'Yes, I know. Two years. Do I have to salute you when we meet?'

'I'm not in your outfit,' said Kit, 'but if you want to, you can. Just don't be late, not after two years. I must hang up now. Kiss, kiss.'

Minnie gave me a look when I returned to Mary's. 'Spoke to her, did you?' she said.

'Yes, I'm meeting her in London tomorrow,' I said.

'Oh, you mean Kit?' asked Mary, bringing in a pot of tea on a tray.

'Yes,' I said.

'That's nice,' said Mary.

'Rapture,' said Minnie, 'if you like funerals.'

328

'Funerals?' said Mary, pouring the tea.

'Good as,' said Minnie, face as straight as Jim's when he was being cryptic.

'I don't think I understand,' said Mary, serving cups of tea. Minnie and I had both had some from Missus, but I could always accept an encore from a fresh pot.

'It's only what Harvey told me,' said Minnie and thanked Mary as she took the cup and saucer.

'Who's Harvey?' I asked. Minnie was worrying me. I couldn't help having a soft spot for her and I felt her don't-care attitude meant she was keeping the wrong kind of company.

'A GI friend of mine,' she said. 'He knows why American soldiers are fallin' over themselves to marry English girls. He says you're a dead duck if you marry an American girl, he says you're bossed for the rest of your life.'

'Oh, that's just talk, I'm sure,' said Mary.

'Well, I've heard that American society is pretty matriarchal,' I said.

'What's that mean?' asked Mary. 'You sound all French sometimes, Tim.'

'Oh, he's always spoke peculiar,' said Minnie.

'A bit of a laugh, really,' smiled Mary and went on to say she was going to sell the cottage and move to Ipswich, where her daughter and son-in-law lived. They'd bought a very roomy house just recently and the top floor was a self-contained flat. That was for her. And there were two young grandchildren to enjoy. Besides which, Mary said she was going to get lonely if she stayed in Elsingham to grow old.

329

'It's right, livin' near your fam'ly,' said Minnie, 'and you shouldn't have trouble sellin' a nice cottage like this.'

'No-one's offered for it yet,' said Mary.

'I bet a young couple will,' said Minnie, 'a young couple that likes livin' in the country.'

'Not many young couples like a life as quiet as this, though,' said Mary, 'and nor would they get very rich, either.'

'Why would they have to get rich?' asked Minnie, who seemed more comfortable talking to Mary than to me. 'A cottage like this and enough to live on, why should anyone want more, I'd like to know. In the country you just need enough, you can grow all the flowers and vegetables you want, like my dad does. He makes a livin', but I've never heard him and my mum talk about wantin' to get rich.'

'You can't always make people see that,' said Mary.

'Some people can't see anything,' said Minnie. 'Still, I'll tell my dad you want to sell, he'll find someone who'll buy it and he won't charge you much for his goodwill. I never knew a room more warm and cosy than this.'

'That's because Tim fixed a door to my porch,' said Mary. 'It keeps the draughts out.'

'Yes, he fixed things for a lot of people,' said Minnie. 'Not everyone, but a lot.'

'Oh, Tim's always been good to people,' said Mary.

Minnie didn't look very impressed. Abruptly, she said, 'I've got to get back.'

We left a few minutes later. Mary asked me to give

330

her love to Kit, who'd kept in regular contact with her and had been up to see her three or four times. I wondered if Kit would like to live in the country, if she'd favour us taking out a mortgage on Mary's cottage and if I could get a job in Ipswich.

I cycled back to Sheldham with Minnie. The day was losing its best light and the air was nippy. Minnie discouraged conversation and went up to her room when we reached her home.

Missus put on a high tea of ham and eggs, with crusty bread and a bowl of butter. With food rationing still on, that was food for kings and queens. Good old Jim still had his sources.

Over tea, Minnie said very little, Jim was chatty and Missus wore her creamy smile. She said she couldn't hardly believe I was back, it didn't seem no time at all. Jim said I'd come back looking a fine full-grown bloke. Minnie made no comment. Missus said you're not having much to say, Min.

'I don't go in for small talk,' said Minnie, 'it's borin'.'

'Well, I'm blowed,' said Jim, 'got yer nose up in the air a bit, 'ave yer?'

'It's all right, Jim, leave her be,' said Missus.

Jim asked me about Kit again. Well, he asked about the female American sergeant with the good pedallers. I said she was a female American captain now and that I was having a reunion with her in London tomorrow.

'Ah,' said Jim and winked.

Missus cast me a knowing smile. 'Be a sweet pleasure to her, you will, Tim,' she said, 'now you're all of a man.'

What did she mean by that? That she thought Italy and France had introduced me to the rites? That she knew it just by looking at me? Well, she was wrong.

After tea, Jim said goodbye to me. 'I'd 'ave liked yer livin' up 'ere, Tim lad,' he said, 'but I don't reckon that there American Kitty fancies it quiet, like. Still, come up an' see us when yer can, me an' Missus is fond of yer and I ain't tellin' no lie. I wish yer luck.' He disappeared again.

I told Missus I'd help to wash up before I left and Missus said what a nice chap I was, that I could give Minnie a hand.

In the kitchen, with Missus leaving us to it, I said, 'I'll wash, you dry.'

'Bloody cheek,' said Minnie, jacket off and apron on, 'don't tell me what to do.'

'Ruddy fireworks,' I said, 'leave off, Min.'

'I'll wash, you dry,' she said.

'OK. When d'you come out of the Waafs?'

'How do I know? I've only been in five months. Of all the potty things, VE Day comin' not long after I'd joined. I felt stupid. Still, I've always been like that. Stupid.'

'Never thought it would come to this,' I said.

'Come to what?' she asked, using a washing-up mop ferociously.

'That you'd turn into a hard luck story.'

'Bloody cheek,' she said again, furiously. 'Why don't you go home?'

'I am going, soon as I've finished the drying,' I said

and wondered again what I was doing, why I'd come here when Aunt May was beckoning.

The moment the chore was over, Minnie said, 'Well, that's it. I'll say goodbye now.'

'Well, at least we had a good bike ride, Min.'

'Oh, grow up,' said Min and left the kitchen to go up to her room again. I went and started my goodbyes to Missus.

'Where's Min?' she asked.

'Up in her room. She's a bit fed-up.'

Missus looked at me a little sadly. 'You surprised?' she said. 'Well, you're not usin' your sense, are you? You've got a bit of manly sense by now, haven't you? You think a proud girl like Min is goin' to let you see what she really feels about you goin' off to marry that American Wac?'

'All right, let me have it,' I said.

'I'm not sayin' it wasn't a pleasure that you dropped in, Tim. But the way you did it, out of the blue, like, well, it all started up again for Min. Still gone on you, she is. Always has been, always was from the day she met you. Won't look at no-one else. Can't grow out of you, that's what's up with her. She might have stood a chance if you'd kept away, if you hadn't turned up like this. She said to me after comin' back from the bike ride, she said, "I can't stand it, Mum, send him away." That's what she said, Tim.'

'Oh, Lord,' I said and Missus looked sadder.

'Of course, I couldn't send you away,' she said, 'not after I'd said stay for high tea. Wouldn't have been right. Can't be helped, it's not your fault the way a girl gets

333

a fixation and you've got your own life to live. But Minnie's not goin' to come down and give you a smile and wish you luck, that would be askin' too much of her. Min's my love and it's her who can do with some luck.'

'I know, Missus.' I felt sad myself. 'I hope she gets all she wants. She's had a rough ride. Oh, hell. Give her my love, anyway. See you again sometime.'

Missus bussed me with warm arms and warm bosom. 'Off you go, Tim. Don't think Jim and me don't appreciate you remembered us. Go on, off you go now to your Aunt May.'

'Blessings, Missus,' I said and went.

CHAPTER TWENTY-FIVE

I let myself in. The light was on in the passage. I put my valises on the floor and closed the door. Aunt May, hearing the sounds, came out of the kitchen into the passage. We looked at each other and she drew a little breath. She had told me her story and I knew she wished she hadn't. But who couldn't have understood her natural wish, under the circumstances, to let me know what our relationship truly was? And perhaps she had felt I'd be resilient enough to accept the fact of being the son of an unwed mother. That aspect hadn't bothered me at all. What difference did it make to me that some young and promiscuous idiot hadn't married her? It didn't make any difference, even if I was a puritan in some respects. I'd been brought up by a woman who, having made a sad mistake as a girl, had impressed on me that decent behaviour was more civilized than the antics of randy intellectuals. All in all I felt privileged that the woman I'd always known as Aunt May was my mother.

'Hullo, Mum old love,' I said, 'I'm home.'

She swallowed. I thought what an attractive woman she was and that Bill Clayton was going to get a gem.

'Tim—' She swallowed again. Then, with a smile, she said, 'You're a day or so earlier than I expected.'

'Better earlier than later,' I said.

'Bless you, lovey,' she said and gave me a kiss and a cuddle in her affectionate and customary way. 'Tim, I have to be sorry about—'

'Don't be,' I said, 'that's all over, that's just between you and me and it's something I'm very happy about. So bless you too. And you're still my lovely old Aunt May, just for the record. Right?'

'Just look here, I'm not old,' she said, game to play the moment lightly.

'You don't look it, either,' I said. There was one certain thing that would guarantee we could get together in our former way. A pot of tea, even if I was going to drown in it before the day was over. 'How about some tea?'

'Oh, I'll make a pot,' she said, looking glad at the suggestion.

'Come on, then.' I took one valise into the kitchen and while she put the kettle on I extracted presents for her. French perfume, a white lace tablecloth from Belgium, two large tins of American blueberries, a cameo brooch from Italy and six pairs of fully-fashioned stockings. The stockings and blueberries were from American buddies I'd met around Falaise. Aunt May gazed at the array of gifts with eyes quite dizzy.

'Oh, Tim,' she said and she looked misty-eyed then.

'Just something in recognition of you know what, Aunt May.'

'You don't feel hurt?' she said.

'No talking, not about that, I like our little secret. Make the tea, love, and let's have an old-fashioned chat. It's only nine o'clock and we've got time for a long talk.'

'Tim, all these lovely presents—'

'For your bottom drawer, but not the blueberries, they're for making pies.'

She was in a bit of a tizzy, but in a glad way and she made the tea and it helped us to chat away without constraint. She told me that her wedding to Bill was arranged for Saturday fortnight. They'd felt I'd be definitely home by then. I was to give her away.

'I wasn't going to get married unless you were there,' she said.

'You're happy about Bill?'

'Yes, I am, love, and I'm happy about you too,' she said.

I told her I was seeing Kit tomorrow, when I hoped to fix our own date. She said what a handsome young lady Kit was and very brainy. I'd have a lot to live up to in America.

'America?' I said. 'I'm not going to America.'

'Oh, I felt from the way she talked that you were going to set up home there,' said Aunt May.

'That's not my scene,' I said, 'she'll get me fixing things in her store.'

A little laugh escaped Aunt May.

'You look like yesterday, I'm happy to say,' remarked Kit.

'Yesterday's dog's dinner?' I said. We were in an Oxford Street restaurant, where you could get a fairly eatable three-course lunch for the limit of five bob that had been imposed by the Ministry of Food and where you could mix with officers without the risk of military Redcaps butting in and putting you on a charge. Redcaps could be very interfering.

'You simply look as if you only left yesterday,' said Kit. 'Oh, sure, you're a good advertisement for the popular war hero look, but you're still the same old lanky lump of British beef.'

'You're lovely too,' I said. She looked a picture in her tailored olive-green, a perfect example of how to reach the rank of captain without getting worry lines on the way. Stunning, she was, with her American smile and her visible air of excitement.

'I like you, honey, you know that?' she said.

'That must mean something,' I said.

'Well, love is surely necessary to a marriage, of course, but if you have loving and liking both, that's a guarantee of a really great relationship.'

'It rates?'

'Top billing, Tim. I know it sounds corny, but did you miss me?'

'All the time and Sunday afternoons especially. Sunday afternoons always reminded me of the way you took Suffolk to your bosom.'

She laughed. She wasn't eating much. We'd plumped for the day's speciality. Country omelette, made with powdered egg, of course, mixed with parsley and chopped bacon rind. It wasn't bad, but we were more interested in each other than in food.

'You haven't seen it yet,' said Kit.

'Haven't seen what?'

'My bosom,' she said.

338

'Well, don't show me now,' I said, 'not here and not when you're in uniform. It's against Uncle Sam's regulations, isn't it? Wait till we're on a train or bus. Anyway, can we talk about when you'd like us to start life together?'

'I wrote telling you I was going to be good to you,' she said. 'First off, lover, I can apply for a discharge whenever I like. I thought a New Year wedding would be just fine. In Boston. We'll do that, shall we? I've been in touch with my parents about it and they can't wait to meet you. I've also told my father how good you are at fixing things and he's going to give you a position that will suit you perfectly. Could your Aunt May come over for the wedding? We'd love her to, she could travel with us a week before Christmas. My father will arrange first-class tickets on the *Queen Mary* for us—'

'Hold on.' I felt that while her vision of the future was clear and uncluttered, mine had become slightly blurred. 'What position?'

'My father's in packaging,' she said, enthusiastic in her ambition for me. 'He owns the Masters Packaging Company Incorporated.'

'What's packaging?'

'Merchandise wrapping,' said Kit. 'Cartons, boxes, wrappers, anything you can put around any kind of consumer goods to make them look more attractive on a store shelf. There's a job waiting for you in the design department. And there's something else. My father has his eye on a house for us, just outside Boston and not far from our family home. We only need to say and we'll be able to move in as soon as we're married. My father

339

will arrange the loan through his bank, which likes dealing with real estate business.'

'We're going to live in America?' I said.

Kit smiled. 'You weren't thinking of China, were you?'

'No, I was thinking of a cosy little cottage in Suffolk.'

'Not seriously, were you?' she said. 'Tim, England is so run-down. You know it is. It's exhausted, the war has worn it out, it can't offer any real opportunities to guys like you. You'll do so well in the States.'

'What's a design department in a packaging company?' I asked.

'It's where you'll work on ideas for new packaging, honey, while Effie and I pour new ideas into our store. We've been exchanging thoughts and suggestions by mail for months.'

'Aren't we going to have a family?'

'Oh, I guess we can discuss and analyse our feelings about that later on,' said Kit.

'How long is later on? When we're both past wanting to bother about being a mum and dad?'

Kit regarded me with the mystified air of a woman who knew she had worked everything out with maximum advantage to both of us, so why was I trying to pick holes in it? 'You want to make alternative suggestions, Tim?' she asked.

'Yes,' I said, giving up my half-eaten omelette. 'Let's stay here. The old UK may be a bit worn out, but it's earned a try from some of us. I'm willing to give it a go. Let's live in Suffolk. I know of a cottage going cheap. Mary's. We only need enough to keep us in food, drink and socks. I can earn that much by starting a joinery and house repairs business with my gratuity.'

'Joinery? House repairs?' Kit looked astonished.

'Fixing doors and things,' I said. 'I don't think much maintenance has been done to too many properties during the war, what with the shortage of materials and labour. I've a feeling there's going to be a large demand for maintenance work. I like carpentry and nails and hammers and jobs like putting in new window frames and redecorating. And look, this store of yours. You don't need that. That's not what wives are for. Wives are for building homes and families not stores and if you change all that you'll change family life. My suggestion is that we buy Mary's cottage and that you stay home, have some babies and do the cooking.'

'Tim, you're goofing,' said Kit and I had to admit that as a Wac captain she didn't quite look as if she'd fit the role of a village mum. She did have the right shape, but would probably lack application. Still, I had to try.

'You could have a go once you got out of that uniform,' I said. 'Have you thought that if you run a store you'll come home each night whacked out? You'll get headaches. You can cook and bake, can't you?'

Kit laughed. Cooking and baking obviously didn't rate with her. 'Do you want a wife or a kitchen slave?' she asked.

'Well, I'll be a joinery and redecorating slave, so what's wrong with you being a kitchen slave?'

'It doesn't appeal to me,' she said. 'You're asking me to channel my creative energy down a kitchen sink.'

'Selling ankle socks to kids is creative?' I said.

The blur had gone. I knew what I wanted and what I didn't want. I wanted an old-fashioned life and someone warm and cuddly to come home to. I wanted to come home to the aroma of baking cakes, I didn't want to be dragged off to America and organized. I knew now why it hadn't felt right, leaving Jim and Missus and Minnie to come to London and meet Kit. Jim and Missus and Minnie were my kind, I'd lived among that kind all my life. Kit was an all-American beauty, a goer, a professional. She'd leave me behind. I'd been in love with a hope and with what I wanted her to be, not with what she was. My instincts had warned me right at the start, but I'd let infatuation take over. What I wanted, what suited me, was up in Suffolk.

'You don't want to be a conventional housewife, Kit?' I asked.

'Tim, if you only knew how unexciting that sounds.'

'OK, you and Effie get fixed up, then. I think that's top billing for you. I don't think you really need me. Let's call it a day, with no hard feelings.'

Kit actually flushed. 'Listen, you kook, I want a lover as well as the store,' she said angrily. 'I want you as my lover. Legal lover. And you want me, don't you?'

'No, I want a homely wife who'll iron my shirts for me.'

'You've got to be joking,' said Kit. 'There aren't many women who are going to fall for that iron age stuff, not after a war like this one, when millions of us have come out of the kitchens.' She looked at her watch. 'Oh, shoot, I've got to go.'

'Yes, I've a feeling you'll always be saying that, Kit.

You were right two years ago when you said let's just be friends.'

'Oh, shoot,' she said again, angrier than ever.

When we left the restaurant she told me to call her. She said we had to talk this through. I said it would be better if we parted now, while we still liked each other.

'No, call me,' she said, 'we've got to meet again, we've got to talk.'

I didn't say I would, because I knew I wouldn't. I just said I'd think about it. She hailed a taxi. She was still angry.

'So long, Kit, it's been—'

'Call me!' she said.

I watched the taxi as it took her out of my life, then I walked to a bus stop. Oxford Street was crowded, but it had lost its pre-war look and taken on an atmosphere of austerity. Shoppers were looking for what wasn't there. London didn't look as if we'd won the war. But in Suffolk it was peaceful at least and the scars of war didn't show up there. I had to get to Waterloo Station and from there to the Guildford demob centre. Tomorrow, I had to go back to Suffolk. This evening, I had to tell Aunt May I'd changed my ideas and my plans. I had a feeling she'd just smile and tell me to do what I thought best.

'Tim, you again?' said Missus, big-eyed with surprise and not too certain that my arrival was the best event of the day.

'Is Minnie around?' I asked, hoping I was going to be able to cope with the situation.

'She's upstairs,' said Missus, leading me into the living-room. 'But she's goin' out soon, to meet her GI. I won't say he's not a nice chap and I won't say he's not genuine keen on her. Makes a change, considerin' what most of them have got up to durin' the war. He's goin' back to America in two weeks and it wouldn't surprise me if he doesn't ask our Min to go with him.'

'Then I'd better see her, Missus, before he beats me to her and carries her off.'

'What's that you're sayin'?' asked Missus.

'I'll say it to Min.'

Missus eyed me shrewdly. Then her smile showed up, soft and creamy. 'I'll call her,' she said. She patted my shoulder with motherly affection and sat me down in a fireside armchair. 'Best if I don't say it's you, though. She might not come down if she knows it's you again.'

She disappeared. I heard her call up to Minnie, telling her she was wanted in the living-room. Minnie came down, walked in and stopped dead. She was in her Waaf shirt, tie and skirt. Her dressed hair was full of harvest gold. Seeing me, colour swept her face.

'Oh, no, not you again!'

'A bit sickening, I suppose,' I said, getting to my feet. 'Still, as I'm here, I'd like to—'

'What d'you want, free eggs?'

'Not today, Min. It's you I'm after.'

'Oh, don't talk daft. What've you come for, to invite me to the weddin'?'

'There's no wedding, Min. We met, we talked, we said goodbye and that was all.'

Minnie stared at me. 'She didn't want you?' she said.

344

'Not really.'

'I don't believe you.'

'It was mutual, Min. We both had the wrong ideas about each other. She wanted her dad to look after me while she ran a store in Boston and I wanted someone who'd stay home and make the beds.'

Minnie looked as if she couldn't make me out. 'That's some kind of a joke, I suppose,' she said. 'No-one ever gets any sense out of you, you don't know what serious life is all about, nor what people feel. You've just come back again to send us all daft. I'm goin' out.'

'To meet Harvey?'

'I said I would.'

'Well, don't go yet, Min, I want to talk to you.'

'Oh, really? Well, hard luck, I'm goin'.'

'I'll tan you if you keep on like this,' I said. 'Do you good, it will, stop you from giving me all this sauce.'

'Stop talkin' like that!' Minnie showed agitation. 'Just go away, just push off.'

'I'll chuck you in the pond in a minute,' I said.

'Like to see you try,' she said, 'you'd get a broken leg.'

'Now look, Min, you'll be coming out of the Waafs soon. It'll be time then for you to settle down and behave yourself—'

'Oh, you cheeky devil!'

'Listen, I've just come to after years of being unconscious. How about if we settle down together? Legally, I mean. Holy wedlock, like your mum and dad. How about it, love? You're a Camberwell girl who's turned herself into a lovely country girl and I'm a Walworth bloke willing to turn myself into a country

345

bloke. And it hit me yesterday, the fact that I'm gone on you.'

Minnie's face flooded with colour. 'Oh, it's not fair,' she breathed, 'you're havin' me on, it's a joke.'

'No, it's true, Min. Love you, I do. Can't we give it a go? I like it here. My Aunt May's getting married, which makes things right for me to get married myself. But only to you. We could take over Mary Coker's cottage. I've got a bit of money saved and there's my war gratuity. I'd like to have a wife, I'd like you, Min, if you'd have me.'

'Have you?' she asked, more agitated.

'Would you, lovey?'

She rushed at me then. 'Oh, you Tim, I'd have you anytime!' She jumped me. I fell over, landing on the hearthrug and Minnie piled herself on top of me. Her Waaf skirt was any old how, her legs all over the place.

'Get off, Min, you're showing your militaries.'

'Don't care,' she said, excited little breaths escaping.

I kissed, she kissed, we kissed. I ate her, she ate me, we ate each other. Lovely meal, it was. But there was something wrong about her being on top.

'Min, get off.'

'Won't,' she said. 'Got you, I have, and goin' to hit you, bite you and twist your arms off for givin' me all the miseries.' She sounded like the old Min. But she wasn't the old Min, she wasn't a schoolgirl any more, she was a young woman and she already had me where she seemed to want me. I'd got to fight this, or she'd always be on top. 'Goin' to have my own back on you,' she said, 'goin' to kiss and bite you all over.'

346

'What, now?'

'Every Saturday night,' she said and she laughed, her face above mine, her eyes sparkling with light.

'Get off,' I said. 'If your mum comes in—'

'Don't care,' she said, 'and Mum won't, either, when she knows I'm your best girl and goin' to be your best wife.'

'Best? I'm only goin' to have one.'

'Yes, me.'

I shifted her and we lay on our sides in front of the fire. 'Listen, Min, you don't mind cooking and baking and making the beds?'

'Oh, you daft thing, what a silly question.'

'And ironing my shirts?'

She gurgled with laughter. 'Oh, you're funny, you are, Tim, and don't I know it. Always made me laugh, you did. Oh, I thought you'd never want me. Months after you'd gone I woke up, I thought no wonder you only saw me as a silly schoolgirl, because that's what I was, wasn't I, when I played you up, and Mum an' Dad too, over that business about if I was in the family way or not. You always said I wasn't grown up, and I wasn't, was I, actin' like that, givin' Mum an' Dad all that worry and makin' them think you'd seduced me on risin' summer night. Before that, I was only teasin' those times when I told you you'd been lovin' to me that night.

'Then you started making eyes at that Waac, and it nearly made me ill. Yes, it did and it did make me sick up once or twice, so when Mum started to think I was pregnant, I acted up, I wanted you to come round and be nice to me. Oh, poor Mum, what she really wanted was

347

a proper engagement and you marryin' me when I was older, she didn't like it a bit that you might have to marry me because of doin' right by me. She was so relieved when I stopped actin' up, but she told me I'd been the silliest girl ever. She told me I'd lost any chance I ever had with you. On risin' summer night I'd have let you love me if you'd wanted to, I was so gone on you, but you just slid to the ground and some GI came up and said he'd give me what I wanted. He tried it on too, and I kicked him so hard he could hardly walk.'

'Good for you, Min.'

'I won't ever be silly again, really I won't. Tim, you're not cuddlin' me proper.'

'I thought I was doing quite well.'

'Yes, nice, but cuddle me here.'

'Here?'

'Oh, yer daft thing,' said the old Min, 'that's me Waaf tie. Here, you silly.'

'Feels all right. Well, you're grown up now, Min and that's a fact. Min, are you still—' I hesitated.

'Am I still what?'

'Never mind,' I said, but there it was again, my old-fashioned self hoping Min was old-fashioned too.

'Well, I do mind. I know what you mean. I could have, lots of times, specially since I've been in the Waafs. But I always thought about Mum an' Dad and besides I only ever wanted you, Tim, no-one else and I kept hopin'. I kept thinkin' suppose he does come back. Then when you did, I just felt it wasn't really because of me—'

'Enough said, Min.'

348

'What about you, anyway?' she asked. 'I bet you've been with Italian and French girls.'

'Well, I haven't. I've been brought up not to do things with girls.'

Min looked wide-eyed at me then. 'Tim, are you sayin' you've never had a girl? I don't believe you.'

'You're really still a virgin, lovey?' I asked.

'Yes, I am,' she said firmly.

'So am I.'

She sat up. 'Oh, you Tim, I'm goin' to be your very first girl? Lovely, that is, the best thing I've ever heard. You haven't and I haven't. Oh, bless yer, Tim, isn't that magical? All that bliss, learning each other how to make love?'

'I hope we don't fumble it,' I said, at which point the front door shook to a peremptory rat-tat.

'Oh, help,' gasped Min, 'me skirt.'

'Could that be Harvey?' I asked.

'No, Aunt Flossie,' said Min, scrambling to her feet. 'That's her knock, she always makes the door shake.'

I got up. Missus put her head in. She looked at Min's flushed face, then at me. 'No-one answering the door to Aunt Flossie?' she said and went herself.

A few moments later I had my first look at Aunt Flossie. A sweet-looking old lady of about sixty. She was apple-cheeked, button-eyed and alert. She wore a grey coat and a black hat, the hat sitting neatly on her silvery hair. She gave everything and everyone a quick, inquisitive glance.

'My, my, what's going on?' she asked in a pretty piping voice. 'Who's this young soldier chap?'

'That's Tim,' said Missus, who was eyeing Minnie shrewdly.

'Ah,' said Aunt Flossie and her bright button eyes quizzed me. All over. I hoped I hadn't picked up any of the hearthrug. 'So you're our Tim,' she said.

'And you're our Aunt Flossie,' I said.

'Oh, saucy chap, are we?' she said and quizzed Minnie. Minnie turned pink. 'What's our Tim been doing with our Minnie?' she asked Missus.

'It wouldn't be nothing disrespectful,' said Missus, 'our Tim's a well-behaved young man.'

'What's our Minnie blushing for, then?' demanded Aunt Flossie.

'I'm all giddy, Aunt Flossie,' said Minnie. 'I don't know what day it is, Sunday or Monday or what.'

'It's not what, it's Friday,' said Aunt Flossie.

'Friday's special, then,' said Minnie, 'Tim and me are goin' to be married.'

Aunt Flossie lifted her gloved hands. 'The Lord be praised,' she said, 'our Minnie's ship has come home. Not before time, though.' And she embraced Minnie and gave her a pat. And she gave me a wink. The racy old darling.

Missus smiled. Her teacup had been right and she knew it.

THE END

THE LODGER
by Mary Jane Staples

Life in the teeming streets of Walworth in 1908 was not easy – especially if you were a young widow with four small daughters. For Maggie Wilson it was a hand-to-mouth existence, and without the lodger she wouldn't have managed at all.

Constable Harry Bradshaw thought the Wilsons a gutsy little family – from cheeky young Daisy to the elegant thirteen-year-old Trary. But most of all, he admired Maggie and the way she battled against poverty.

But a murderer was loose in South London – a sinister strangler who knew the area. A full-scale investigation was put in hand and Harry was told to enquire into any new lodgers in his district. And there was something very peculiar indeed about Maggie Wilson's lodger.

0 552 13730 8

A SELECTED LIST OF FINE TITLES
AVAILABLE FROM CORGI BOOKS